The Scorpion
Book 6 in the Dan Stone Series

A Novel

David Nees

Copyright © 2022 David E. Nees

All rights reserved

This book may not be reproduced in whole or in part, by electronic, mechanical or any other means, without the express permission of the author.

The Scorpion, Book 6 in the Dan Stone series is a work of fiction and should be construed as nothing but. All characters, locales, and incidents portrayed in the novel are products of the author's imagination or have been used fictitiously. Any resemblance to any person, living or dead, is entirely coincidental.

To keep up with my new releases, please visit my website at www.davidnees.com. Scroll down to the bottom of the landing page to the section titled, "Follow the Adventure".

You can visit my author page and click the "Follow" button under my picture on the Amazon book page to get notices about any new releases.
.

Manufactured in the United States
ISBN 9798819477991

For Carla

You inspire me to be my best.

Many thanks to Eric who not only encourages me but gives me critical feedback that makes a rough text shine. Your generous gift of your time and attention is very much appreciated.

Thanks go to my narrator and now editor, Jonathan. You are the best with insights to the larger themes that need to be played out in Dan's life.

The Scorpion

*"So do the dark in soul expire,
Or live like scorpion girt by fire;
So writhes the mind remorse hath riven,
Unfit for earth, undoom'd for heaven,
Darkness above, despair beneath,
Around it flame, within it death."*--Lord Byron

"The world is a dangerous place to live; not because of the people who are evil, but because of the people who don't do anything about it."—Albert Einstein

"O, full of scorpions is my mind!"—Wm. Shakespeare

Chapter 1

The morning sun slid over the horizon in the gap between two mountains, illuminating the haze on the desert floor. Rashid stood in front of his tent and took in the panorama. He was camped at an ancient oasis whose surface water had long ago dried up. It was deep in the interior of the Saudi desert. His encampment consisted of multiple tents in the Bedouin style. They were made in the traditional manner from goat and camel hides. The joining was loose, allowing the breeze to penetrate the enclosure and, when it rained, something rare in the Arabian desert, the joints swelled to make the tent water tight.

Rashid's tents, while an homage to tradition, were not humble, but large structures, some of them subdivided into multiple rooms. Lavish carpets provided a floor and low cushions made for comfortable seating, although not to the Western mind. He sipped his sweetened tea and enjoyed the vista spread out in front of him.

He had a claim to the land through his ancestors and had dug a deep well to tap into the water that was still underground even though it no longer percolated to the surface. The well provided a reliable source of water, so he could establish this retreat. Few knew about it and it was far away from Riyadh where he and his brother ran their empire.

Rashid felt a kinship with his ancestors here in the dry, empty land northeast of Tayma. The camp was located on the edge of a massive expanse of dunes, a full two-day drive from the small town. The dunes were like a sand sea, with static waves thrown up by the wind. To the west, was a canyon of sand leading into the distant ramparts with towering monoliths of stone sculpted by the wind until they resembled a giant child's set of rounded discs stacked up into huge pyramidal shapes.

The views were dramatic, and a person began to feel one's insignificance in the face of this landscape. Allah had found his prophet in such a landscape and his prophet had established a religion that would conquer the world. Rashid felt it was his duty to help fulfill that destiny. He came from royal Saudi blood but his mother had distant connections to the Bedouins which left him tainted to the higher-placed members of Saudi royal society. Still, it hadn't kept him from amassing a multi-billion-dollar fortune from his many businesses. If he harbored any resentment, he kept it hidden. He knew that he would be ultimately recognized as a vital figure in the destruction of the west, something he had dedicated much of his life to.

As he was ruminating on the desert and its effect on humans, an aide came up and whispered something to him. Rashid dismissed him with a nod and a wave. *So much for contemplation.* This was, after all, partly a business trip. His family would join him in a few days, but for the next twenty-four hours he had business to conduct. And that business involved a particularly odd and dangerous person, the Scorpion. He was not someone Rashid could be seen with; not someone he could have visit him in his offices. *One must deal with unsavory characters in war.* Scorpion was distasteful to Rashid, but necessary. Even though a true believer, he was a dangerous and unpleasant tool, albeit a useful one. He sighed and finished his tea, then stepped back into his tent.

† † †

Dan sat in the living room of Jane's townhouse in Arlington, Virginia, located near Key Bridge. It was a short drive up the George Washington Parkway to the CIA headquarters and an easy hop into DC either by car or metro. She rarely used public transportation, however. Her old instincts as a field operator never having gone away completely, she tended to avoid underground structures with limited exits. Now in charge of a deep, black-ops operation, she had less enthusiasm for public exposure. Dan had refused to go to headquarters. His early experiences in the field had left him with a distrust of the bureaucracy there. Jane hadn't tried to argue him out of the sentiment. In the current climate, with a political appointee at the helm, the CIA seemed compromised to her. Henry Mason, her boss, had advised her to keep her head down for the time being. He made it clear he was including Dan in that directive.

It had been almost six years since Jane had recruited Dan. Her actions had helped him escape the trap that the FBI had been laying for him during his vendetta against the mafia boss that ordered the torching of his restaurant and the killing of his pregnant wife. Almost immediately there arose a chemistry between them that both worked to keep suppressed. Over the years it had only grown as Jane watched Dan navigate the world of an assassin. He had become quite effective and deadly, yet fought to keep his new profession from corrupting him. The intensity of his work which spilled over into hers as his handler, created moments where their developing attraction to one another nearly emerged into a full-blown affair. Both realized when being honest that they would someday consummate their feelings. But neither could predict what the results of that would be.

For Jane, Dan filled an emptiness in her life. Her work for the CIA, both in the field and then running agents, allowed her little time for personal relationships. She had to keep her work secret from her family and the few friends she was able to maintain. She had sacrificed much personally to pursue this fight against jihadists who looked for any opportunity to attack the U.S.

As Henry said, they were the silent soldiers keeping the wolves from the door so regular people could carry on with their lives. There was a price to pay, however; the price of an emptiness that she had felt for so many years...until Dan.

After giving him some time to recuperate in Montana with his sister and brother-in-law from the injuries he had incurred in Africa, Jane had called Dan back to Washington. Now he was sitting around, frustrated, ready for action, but held back. He decided he'd have it out with Jane when she came home that day.

In the meantime, he would cook her a good meal. He had learned his way around a kitchen in Brooklyn when he and his now-deceased wife had started a restaurant. The skills came in handy, and he managed to not eat as haphazardly as most bachelors. Cooking had its rewards in impressing the ladies, although that was not Dan's primary intent.

Right now, he wanted an assignment. Sitting on the sidelines made him feel like the jihadists were gaining the upper ground, advancing while he was being idle. The feeling gnawed at him.

When Jane came home, Dan had a dinner of shrimp scampi Florentine ready to go in a saucepan. He handed her a chilled glass of Vernaccia di San Gimignano, a jewel of a white wine from the Tuscany region.

"I could get used to this," she said as she sat down on the couch and kicked off her shoes.

"Don't. I'd get bored and surly. In fact, that's already happening," Dan said.

"Cooking me dinner is how you express your surliness? I'll take it."

She saluted him with her glass and took a long sip.

"This is quite good. What is it?"

Dan told her.

"So, are you buttering me up for something?"

"In a way, but let's enjoy the wine and dinner first," Dan said with a wink. Jane always was able to make him smile, even when he was feeling combative. He had to admit he liked her effect on him. It made their attraction to one another awkward at times since she was his boss.

After finishing his glass, he poured Jane a refill and went into the kitchen to finish the meal. Jane followed to watch, sitting on a stool. The meal consisted of pesto, garlic, and plum tomatoes, seeded, and diced. They were cooked in a skillet with butter and olive oil until the tomatoes started to soften. Then the shrimp was put in to cook until pink, followed by spinach until it wilted. The result was laid on a bed of farfalle or butterfly pasta.

Conversation lagged as the two of them dug into the dinner.

"That was wonderful," Jane said when they had finished.

After putting the dinner dishes in the sink, they took the bottle of wine and went back into the living room to sit and talk.

"How are things at headquarters," Dan asked.

"Still keeping our heads down. Henry's adamant that we must wait out this initial flurry of witch-hunting. The new administration wants some heads to roll to showcase how they're reforming the CIA. Henry figures they'll get tired at some point and we'll be able to operate again."

"But not like you used to do."

Jane shrugged her shoulders. "It was never easy. We were always a very deep operation. Thankfully, our budget is still hidden, but no one wants to meet with us for now."

"Tainted merchandise, I get it. But where does that leave me? I'm going to go nuts around here. I'm better off either in Montana or back in Venice."

"Montana's out if you want your sister kept out of things. There's the off-chance, you could leave some breadcrumb trail to her. that wouldn't be a good thing."

"And Venice?"

"Maybe. I think it's actually safer to keep you stashed right under everyone's nose. No one knows about you, so the less you move about, the less you leave a trail."

Dan started to object, but Jane stopped him.

"Something has come up," she said. "It may be nothing, but it could be something very serious. It also may be a way to relieve your boredom."

Chapter 2

Dan studied her face, which evidenced the worry he heard in her voice. "Tell me what's got you so worried."

"You know Warren, our tech geek, is in love with Evangeline—"

"He's still carrying a torch for her?"

Jane nodded. "Anyway, he keeps an eye out on her security. He set up quite a system at her estate. Since that time, he's been monitoring it and tweaking where he sees a need. It's a very impressive setup by now."

Evangeline was a young woman Dan had rescued from being a captive in the pornography industry. She had been an unwilling rescue, and Dan had killed the pornographer in the process of freeing her. That act had set the two of them on an odyssey through Europe culminating in the capture of Evangeline's father, Jan Luis Aebischer, the man she had run away from.

Aebischer had been a millionaire banker who handled money for terrorist and criminal financiers. He lived in a mansion just outside of Embrach, Switzerland. It was a large estate on thirty acres of land in an exclusive hilltop area. After his capture, he was convinced to turn over his fortune to his estranged daughter in exchange for his life. Evangeline had come to terms with now being a young woman with a sizable fortune.

She had turned the estate into a retreat for abused women. There they found a place of refuge as well as a place of learning, so they could put their lives back together.

Evangeline's mission was to create more refuges in other parts of Europe.

"And you're worried about...?" Dan said.

Jane took a sip of her wine and continued. "Warren says he's uncovered evidence of surveillance on Evangeline's mansion in Embrach. He thinks someone is spying on the place."

"It's not just inquisitive journalists or fortune hunters?"

"Warren doesn't think so. Apparently, it's pretty sophisticated."

"What exactly is it?"

"There's been some electronic intrusion attempts. Attempts to get into the security system. Warren's software foiled the attempts, but he couldn't track back to the source. It appears the software had attempted to implant a virus. It would have allowed someone to get into the system undetected and roam around, checking out the security, the scheduling of reports, controlling the cameras, anything to do with the building security. There seems to have been no interest in other files, which Warren had sequestered into different silos of information."

"You're talking about Evangeline's operations, separate from the building and ground security."

"Right. Whoever made the attack only wanted to get access to the security. That in itself is an ominous sign even without factoring in the sophistication of the attempt."

Dan thought about what Jane had just said. "I get that Warren has an interest in Evangeline. I get that you indulge him in this by letting him manage her security. That's a good thing. But are you suggesting some greater danger? Something to do with our operations?"

Jane smiled. "Maybe lying low as we are, gives me too much time to think. I may be connecting dots that don't exist."

"Explain yourself, lady."

Jane turned to Dan, still smiling. "We know Jan Luis was the connection to the jihadists. It was from him we learned of the Frankfurt attack and thwarted it. Now Evangeline has physically stepped into that nexus."

"I still don't see the connection. She isn't involved in that world. All anyone knows is Jan Luis retired and turned his wealth over to his daughter."

"And disappeared. And since then, more jihadists have been uncovered and killed, thanks to you. This must have registered on those directing and funding them. You know that there's a figure out there, somewhere, looking for who's responsible for the increase in the jihadist mortality rate."

"We always knew this would be the result. It's not a bad thing to have them not sleeping well at night, worrying when they might get struck down."

"True. That's why you're kept so undercover. No one above Henry, really knows who you are. Not even Roger."

Roger Abrams was Henry's immediate boss and was kept blind to the details of the black ops Henry ran with Jane. Roger set Henry up but didn't want to know any details of what Henry did, or who he hired. He was happy to have the deniability. Such blindness offered some security, even though he suspected that if the operation was uncovered, his head would roll along with Henry's and the others. At least a forced retirement would be in his future. Still, like Henry, Roger was an old-school fighter who wanted to take the undercover fight to the terrorists that threatened the U.S.

"Here's the potential problem," Jane said as she continued. "It's not hard to connect Aebischer to you even if no one knows who you are, or whether you're one person, or a team. And now Evangeline is sitting in

Aebischer's old offices." She paused to let that sink in for a moment. "If someone was looking for the assassin or team of assassins bringing death to the terrorists, one might want to start there…it's as good a place as any to start looking for breadcrumbs."

Dan sat quiet. He thought he had made sure Evangeline was kept clean from his activities so she could rebuild her life and deal with her fortune as well as her personal issues without the complicating facts of Dan's assassin activities. Now, it seemed, the enemy might have intruded on the young woman's life. And that intrusion was his fault in a way.

"There's another thing," Jane said, breaking the silence.

Dan looked up at her.

"We've picked up some chatter about someone seeking information about the Jabbar killing."

Jabbar was the jihadist that had led the failed attack at the Frankfurt airport. Dan had tracked him down in Marseille and assassinated him in a rather messy operation.

"Someone could be trying to pick up your trail, even if they don't know who you are. Both of these signs, the cyber-attack on Evangeline's security and the questions about Jabbar make me nervous."

Dan didn't answer. Had he rescued Evangeline, only to have her become a target for terrorists? The thought made his stomach turn.

Chapter 3

A month earlier

Rashid heard the helicopter approaching. The sound traveled far in the desert with no other noises to mask it. Rashid stood in front of his main tent to watch the approaching chopper. It was one of his own, part of his private air fleet, which included two helicopters and three private jets. The helicopter arriving was a Eurocopter 120, also known as the French Hummingbird. It was a quiet, five-seat, single engine machine that had a range of 440 miles and a top speed of 135 mile per hour. Rashid's other copter was an Augusta Westland AW139, a ten-passenger, twin-engine machine with a range of 775 miles and a cruising speed of 190 mile per hour. His family used this machine when flying out to the desert retreat. The smaller Eurocopter was bringing, not family, but business; necessary, but distasteful business involving the Scorpion.

The machine landed on the pad, scattering sand with its downwash. When the blades had cycled down, the door opened and a small, wiry man emerged. He went down the steps quickly. He wore dark pants and jacket with a lighter shirt under. His face was thin, with a long nose. He had dark hair, slick, and combed straight back. He walked towards the encampment with sharp, agile steps while one of Rashid's servants collected the bags he brought.

Rashid waited and watched his approach.

"As-Salam-u-Alaikum," Peace be unto you, the man said as he approached Rashid.

"Wa Alaikumussalam wa Rahmatullah," May peace, mercy, and blessings of Allah be upon you, Rashid replied.

They shook hands and went into the tent. Coffee, water, and an assortment of fresh fruits and pastries were laid on a low table. The two men relaxed on the cushions and waited for the servants to leave the room set up in the massive tent.

The Scorpion's real name was unknown, even to Rashid, who admired the man's skill in covering his identity and past. Up close one couldn't help but notice his eyes. They were black, to the point of seeming to not have a discernable iris. Their intensity unnerved most who received a direct stare from the small man. His strength, even with his smaller stature, could be seen up close. He was a figure who could easily blend in, but also, when seen up close, cause one to fear for one's safety.

"Your trip was comfortable?" Rashid asked.

"Yes, *Sayyid*. That is a comfortable and quiet machine."

Rashid smiled. He didn't need to be told, but he appreciated the man's compliment on his choice of helicopter.

"You have information? Something important enough to meet and talk about directly? You may go to your tent and freshen up. We will spend the day going over what you have. Tonight, we will dine and then you can retire to your own tent for the night. I have brought something for your entertainment this evening. Tomorrow morning you can return to Riyadh to continue your business."

Rashid laid out the agenda quickly and clearly. His business with the Scorpion was necessary, as was his duty to hospitality, but he wanted no anticipation by his guest of any extended time in his retreat.

The Scorpion nodded in understanding. He knew his position. He was the assassin, a tool for Rashid. He was comfortable with that fact. They held a common goal, the destruction of the west, and he knew his role in pursuit of that goal. Scorpion harbored no illusions about himself or his status.

All afternoon, the two men sat together in conversation.

"You be sure it's the same group?"

"One can't be sure, but we know something happened in Mexico. All the men my agent smuggled into Mexico were killed before they could infiltrate the U.S. And there was a massacre of cartel leaders, the very one's helping us smuggle our men into the country.

"And you think that is connected to other issues? In Europe and Russia?"

Rashid shook his head. "I don't know. What I do know, what you know, is that the mission in Frankfort was a disaster. What should have been a massacre, both on the ground and in the air, turned out to be neither."

"And Jabbar was killed after he fled to Marseille," Scorpion said, completing Rashid's thought.

"As you say. And the anthrax cannisters were taken with one winding up at the bottom of the Caspian."

Rashid looked across the tent which expressed a casual luxury, honoring tradition with the addition of modern comforts.

"It is a puzzle," he continued. "But it looks to me like some group getting information about my plans and then destroying them."

"You think they are all the work of one group?"

"I don't draw any conclusions." Rashid leaned forward. "I want you to find out who is causing these disruptions and eliminate them. If it's more than one group, eliminate all of them."

He looked Scorpion in the eye. "You think you can find the trail of those interfering with our plans?"

Scorpion nodded. "There are many rumors. Your man from the Frankfurt raid, Jabbar, was tracked down and assassinated in Marseille. From my investigation, it was the work of one man who seemed to disappear when some of the faithful had him trapped."

"One man? You think one man is responsible for all the killings?"

"The disruption of the Frankfurt raid involved more than one man. That is clear, but the other killings could be done by a single assassin."

"Also, in Mexico?" Rashid was not convinced.

Scorpion nodded. "You said your man, Tariq, did not know who had struck. But the trucks were blown up. One man could have done that." He paused for a moment. "And there were the assassinations of the drug leaders at the same time. Including the man Tariq was working with."

"That also the work of one man?"

Scorpion shrugged. "One can't be sure. It is possible. "But not probable."

"But the Marseille killing was one man. Others since then have the markings of one assassin, individual killings, both from a distance and up close."

"One assassin or a team of assassins," Rashid said. He took a sip of the strong coffee he favored. "And we have no trail to follow? How do you find a ghost? Where do you start?" He took another sip as he thought about how to proceed. "Do you start in Marseille? We have contacts there and they may be able to help you."

Scorpion smiled. Rashid noted it did not make his severe face any friendlier.

"I will do as you wish, but as I said, I may have a different point to start from."

Chapter 4

Rashid looked at him with some anticipation.

"Your banker," Scorpion said, "Aebischer I think you said his name was. This man suddenly disappeared. It was just before the Frankfurt operation, was it not?"

Rashid nodded.

"No one knows what happened to him. But I think he never completed the money transfers for you. Is that correct?"

Again, Rashid nodded.

"And he financed all the failed operations, correct?"

Rashid nodded.

"Now I find that he has a daughter. She is living in his mansion in Switzerland and seems to have inherited his fortune."

"I'm not sure what you think she has to do with this. She's not involved in Aebischer's world."

"I understand. But she is a nexus, a connection. What if Aebischer was kidnapped by the Americans or Israelis? He disappeared and we don't know where he's gone."

"He also could have decided that it was getting too hot for him, either due to pressure from me or some authorities. He has enough money to hide away on his own. If he did, it would make sense to put most of his assets in his daughter's hands."

Scorpion looked across the tent, thinking. "But what if he didn't go voluntarily? What if he was taken by the authorities? That could explain how all your agents have been killed."

Before Rashid could interject, Scorpion continued.

"If he was taken by some authorities, the girl may know something about it. She may have some idea of who was involved."

"That sounds pretty thin," Rashid said after a moment.

"It is. But it's the only start I have, to see if there's a trail, a clue to find a ghost."

They talked late into the afternoon.

Finally, Rashid asked, "What do you need from me?"

"Sayyid, I want your permission to capture the girl. I can get from her any information she may hold. It might give me a trail to follow."

Rashid knew why Scorpion asked for permission. The Scorpion would extract anything the girl knew, but she might not survive the ordeal. She might not even want to survive it. It would be messy if she were found, since she had become wealthy. By giving his assent, he was condemning the girl to a horror of pain and probably death. Still, if she knew anything…they were grasping at straws to pick up a trail. At this point, they couldn't even determine if it was a single individual or team disrupting his schemes. The source of the disruption had to be found. If the girl was the answer, so be it. It was unfortunate, but necessary. He was in a war.

Later, after a sumptuous dinner, Rashid dismissed the servants and sent them to their quarters at the far corner of the compound. They were to stay inside and not go wandering about. Even with such orders, some would hear and know his visitor had tastes beyond what civilized people considered acceptable. They would say nothing, however. Rashid was a fair, if stern, employer, and also very powerful. They knew he had to deal with unpleasant characters sometimes in his business. The servants consoled themselves that it was God's will and didn't concern them.

"You have permission to seek information from the woman in the estate, but first, go to Marseille to see what you can learn." Rashid said over coffee. "If you take the girl, you must not make a scene. If she suffers, she must disappear. We don't want to upset our Swiss hosts. I'm still working on securing another agent to handle my funds. Your actions cannot bring problems to that effort."

"It will be done efficiently, effectively, and with discretion. I will remove her from Switzerland before interrogation. There will be no connection to you or the Swiss."

"And after?"

"She will disappear. It will not be a problem."

Rashid nodded his approval.

"It is getting late. You will return tomorrow morning in the helicopter." Rashid stood, as did Scorpion. "Your tent is at the edge of the compound, near the helipad." He walked the man to the tent entrance. "There is a gift waiting for you. Use it as you wish."

Scorpion bowed and departed across the sand.

Rashid went back inside his tent to contemplate what the next moves might be. First, he had to find who was attacking his agents. And he had to find out how they were identifying them. Once he did that, he would have more freedom to act. Sporadic attacks on European targets were one thing, but the goal was to bring terror to the U.S. To disrupt their society with attacks while the Muslim lobbying groups kept up a cry of discrimination. The leaders would be paralyzed, not knowing how to react, as would the press. They would be reluctant to be painted as anti-Muslim, so their reactions would consist of mostly sound and fury. The press, long since co-opted to an accommodating position, would also support inaction while crying for greater control over guns. They would bend the public's attention to domestic terror groups, which would obscure the real threat he was mounting. Rashid smiled. Patience. *Find the assassin or assassins. Then carry on.*

Later that night his sleep was interrupted with the partially muffled screams of a female. It came from the far tent where Scorpion was staying. They were repeated, interspersed with sobbing and an occasional sound of short relief filled with words he couldn't understand but which Rashid assumed were entreatments for mercy.

Rashid tried to tune out the sounds. The girl would not be permanently harmed, Scorpion understood that limitation on the hospitality offered him. Her family would be richly compensated for her night's ordeal, and she knew her place. She would not make a public fuss. It would backfire on her and she would be branded a harlot and face either imprisonment or execution. Still, he wondered how many years she would be haunted by this night? He turned on his bed and tried to find sleep. She was also a victim in this war.

Chapter 5

"I should go there," Dan said. "I don't want to just hole up in your townhouse. I can talk with Evangeline and assess her security. Warren is good with equipment, but I need to see the situation on the ground. Afterwards, I can stay in Venice."

"I don't think it's a good idea to fly, your face will be recorded too many times."

"You have a nice private jet. Can you come up with an excuse to send it to Europe? I can just hitch hike along with it."

"I'll give it some thought. Maybe Henry can help. Checking out a jet can be just as noticeable as flying commercial. In the meantime, you should talk with Warren. I'll bring him by tomorrow."

Jane sat on the couch, her face showing concern. She stared off into space, her usually sharp glance now seemed unfocused.

"Is something wrong?" Dan asked.

Jane shook her head as if waking herself up.

"Sometimes I just wonder where it's all going to end. Where it's all going."

"I'm not sure I follow you."

She turned to Dan who was sitting at the other end of the couch.

"I guess I wonder about…us…our relationship."

Dan watched her carefully. He didn't know where her thought came from, or where it was going.

"Don't you wonder? I mean, we can't ignore our feelings. I have them, you have them. Yet we've kept them hidden. We don't talk about them. It's like we've pushed the topic under the rug without even agreeing to do so."

"Well." Dan started to speak—cautiously. He didn't know where this would lead and could see Jane seemed unusually fragile. Something quite unlike her. "I think we both understood, without saying anything, that some things were better left unsaid. We are attracted to one another. I don't deny that. But you were the one to pull back. I don't think either of us know how things would work out if we went forward."

"The Watcher, the one in St. Mark's Square, she said our lives were entangled, intertwined was the word I think she used." Jane looked up, directly into Dan's eyes. Her strong gaze had now returned. "I hold on to that when things get dark." She paused for a moment. "And things get dark a lot around me lately."

"The fight never ends."

"There's that, too." She shrugged and stood up. "We have one another. We live in the same world and have that affection. Even if we're not ready to be open about it. It's a comfort, when things are crappy to know it exists. Not only for me, but you as well."

Dan stood up and pulled Jane into his embrace. "You are a tough cookie. You have more courage and boldness than most of the people I know. I love that about you. If you have to let yourself be vulnerable, you can do it with me. I won't tell and I know that it's just a moment for you. We're in this fight together."

The next day Dan sat down with Warren who went over in detail what he had uncovered about the intrusion attempt on the security system. Jane was working on an excuse to fly to Italy. She told Henry to tell Roger Abrams that she needed to have a face-to-face conversation with a contact of his in the AISE, the *Agenzia Informazioni e Sicurezza Esterna,* or external security agency.

Henry was able to set up the trip with two days' notice. Dan would be an unregistered passenger on the Gulfstream G280. It had a range of 3,400 miles, so they had to route from DC to London, England with 200 miles to spare. With an expected tailwind from the prevailing westerlies, their range would extend a, more comfortable, extra 400 miles.

"Now don't get into trouble," Jane said.

Dan had finished packing a small bag. In an additional bag he carried a Sig Sauer M11-A1, a fifteen round compact 9mm semi-automatic pistol. It was a good pistol, but Dan couldn't wait to get back to his house outside of Venice and pick some other weapons from his extensive collection.

The jet left at night with everyone aboard stretching out to sleep on the fold down seats. Morning brought a landing at London's Heathrow Airport where the plane was refueled. During the stop, everyone stayed on board, away from video cameras and officials. It was just another diplomatic jet on its way to the continent.

Late that afternoon, they landed at the Leonardo da Vinci Airport outside of Rome. An SUV from the embassy was there to pick them up. Their bags, under diplomatic protection, were loaded into the car with no inspections and the passengers, Jane, Dan, and Warren who had managed to talk Jane into letting him go along, were passed through customs with minimal inspection.

Dan was dropped off at the train station while Jane and Warren went on to the embassy. From there, Warren left immediately to travel to Switzerland. Dan headed to his home near Venice and would drive to Evangeline's mansion in the next day or two. After meeting with the Italian security agency, Jane flew back to DC, completing her announced trip and successfully ferrying Dan to Europe.

Arriving in Venice, Dan took a taxi to Maghera and walked to the bar where Marco Favero, a street hustler who he had hired to be his lookout, usually hung out. After a few inquiries, Dan was directed to another bar. Inside, he stopped to watch Marco working on a tourist, acting as the man's fixer who could hook him up to the nightlife in Venice or the surrounding area. Dan listened as Marco painted a picture of young Italian girls interested in wealthy Americans and who would be happy to spend the evening with one in exchange for favors, especially help in getting a visa.

Marco was weaving an enticing picture, when he looked up and saw Dan smiling at him across the room. Marco quickly wrapped up his pitch, eliciting a promise from the American to meet him at 9 pm at the same bar, where he would show him around.

With the mark dismissed, he walked over to Dan and shook his hand.

"You have been gone a long time. I thought maybe you weren't coming back, that something happened to you."

"You got paid regularly, didn't you?"

Marco nodded. "The money was deposited each week, on time."

"That's always a sign I'm still alive and kicking."

Marco reported no unusual activity at the house, which relieved Dan. Whoever was searching for him didn't know where he lived, and Dan could conclude he didn't know who he was.

"You're some kind of spy, aren't you?" Marco asked.

They were sitting down in a booth. Dan ordered a Cortigiana, a golden ale with a medium body, intense aroma, and strong taste, while Marco ordered a Birra Moretti.

"Marco, you know better than to try to quiz me on who I am and what I do. Just leave it as I'm someone who likes their privacy and goes to some effort to maintain it."

"Yes, but your interest in privacy goes beyond the normal. That suggests you are more than you seem to be."

"How are your scams going?" Dan asked, trying to divert Marco from his line of questioning.

"Va bene. I make enough to keep a small crew going." He shrugged. "It's a living."

"Pick pocketing?"

Marco shook his head. "The gypsies do that. Too much competition and the *polizia* are always looking out for it." He flashed a smile at Dan. "We are doing tours now. We show the *turisti* the more interesting sides to Venice." He gave him a wink.

"I guess that doesn't include museums."

Marco laughed. "If they want that, we give it to them. But we find a niche with the...how shall I say it...adventurous tourists? We make it easy to access some of the more risqué aspects of life here."

Dan smiled back. He couldn't help but admire Marco's creativity as well as his irrepressible good humor. Marco was a street hustler, but also a friendly guy. One who might steal from you, but pat you on the back while doing so.

"Don't laugh. It's *molto redditizio*, very profitable."

They carried on in Italian while finishing their drinks. Dan's Italian, while not good enough to pass for a native, was quite fluent. His accent did not betray his American roots. He could manage the same in German, but his French was somewhat lacking.

They finished their drinks, and Dan listened to Marco's report and stories of his exploits. He seemed to be trying to impress Dan. He figured the hustler was looking for more opportunities to make money from their connection. After some time listening to Marco, he finally said goodbye and started for his home.

Chapter 6

Dan lived in a mansion built in the fifties. It was designed after classical Italian houses of the late nineteenth and early twentieth century, generally called Italianate-style in the U.S. The exterior was stucco with brick accents on the corners. There was a recessed front door accentuated with two pillars on a front entranceway that was raised up five steps from the walk. The first-floor windows were tall with elaborate, arched tops. The upper floor windows were plain rectangles so as not to compete with the more elaborate lower-story windows. The roof was done in red tile and was pitched low with generous overhangs. The house was located in an industrial section of Maghera. The area had steadily transformed from residential to industrial as the canals improved and brought in ocean freighters with their cargo to unload and process. The owners had refused to sell and had tried to hold on after they left by renting it out. The location made it a hard sell, and when Dan offered them a large amount of money—too much, actually—to change their minds, they took the opportunity to get out. Dan liked the anonymity of it; no neighbors and an area that shut down at night. The location made it easy to spot any surveillance attempts.

After keying in the security code, Dan entered the mansion and proceeded to check out his old-school markers for signs of intrusion. He had strung thin, hair-like fibers across doors and ground-floor windows. Even if his security system had been compromised, these strings would leave a telltale sign of anyone entering the house. After going through the house and finding no signs of disturbance, he went to the bar and poured himself a whiskey. He took it and sat down in the living room.

There was a grandeur in the fourteen-foot ceilings, although they made the rooms a bit hard to heat on the worst of winter days. The mansion featured elegant crown molding, elaborate chandeliers, and an ornate staircase that opened gracefully at the bottom, like a woman's formal gown, with a banister rail that curved like liquid in a spiral at the bottom of the steps. Jane had helped him furnish the house with almost period furniture. The choices only being modified by Dan's insistence that chairs and couches be comfortable as well as fitting into the style and period.

He felt as though he rattled around in too large of a space. It was too much house for one person, and Rita, his wife, killed years ago by the mob, always came to his mind when he was here. Still, it had begun to feel like home to him; a place where he could let his guard down. Something he had not felt since Rita's death. His thoughts turned to Jane. She would make a nice addition to the place—a nice addition to his rather spartan life.

Their relationship had continued to deepen, and Henry had come to accept the fact of their growing connection. Someday it would come to a head. Dan was beginning to feel that the time was past for keeping themselves at arm's length from one another. Jane's frustrations had spilled out, indicating she felt the same. Still, becoming lovers, carried its own risks. What they had, was working so far. But each mission always seemed to have them starting all over again after it was completed.

Now he faced another mission. Some vague threat to Evangeline, plus his desire to get a lead on the Scorpion. He needed to hunt down the assassin so he wouldn't have to keep looking over his shoulder.

The Monseigneur in France, who turned out to be a Watcher, had warned him about an assassin named Scorpion. He could tell him little except that the man was dark and deadly. And Dan would have to confront him at some time in the future. Was this the threat he faced?

Two missions, it seems. Things were never simple. If a mission did have a simple goal, Dan usually expanded it and created something larger and more disruptive. Henry railed against some of his escalations, but never criticized his results.

He sighed. *First Evangeline. I need to protect her. Then the Scorpion.* Warren could only do so much, which was why Jane wanted Dan involved. And the threat could be connected to the Scorpion figure. Dan thought it was a stretch, but it didn't hurt to be cautious. His life...and Evangeline's, might depend on it.

Dan resisted the urge to call Jane. *No time for romance or nostalgia. Get your gear ready and get going tomorrow for Switzerland.*

Dan's car was a Peugeot 607 that he had modified. It had a supercharger on the rebuilt V-6 engine, upgraded suspension, wheels, and brakes. It sat in his garage next to his Range Rover. The car blended in on the highway, an anonymous executive sedan, which could run with the fastest super sedans on the highway. The only clue to its capabilities lay in its more aggressive stance and wider tires, something only someone very knowledgeable in cars would notice.

He set out first thing the next morning. His route took him on the A4 to Milano, passing just to the south of Lake Garda. From Milan, he drove north towards Como and then on to Lake Lugano, which he crossed on the bridge. He followed the A4 as it snaked through the mountain valleys. Dan was frustrated as he drove; the Swiss made massive use of speed cameras and they were not clearly painted as they were in the UK. To drive at a pace that he found enjoyable, would result in a serious amount of money having to be paid to each canton he passed through. He didn't want the publicity, let alone the blowback from Jane or Henry. He'd have to save the fun for Germany or sections of France and Italy.

Five hours later, he was making his way around the north side of Zurich and on the last leg to Embrach. He phoned the mansion to let them know he was coming. A half hour later, he stopped at the main gate and announced himself to the camera. Dan was pleased to see the gate was substantial. It would take a large truck to breach it.

After being let through the gate, Dan drove up to the mansion and parked on the gravel circle that went past the front door. He had barely gotten out of the car, when a blond figure shot out of the door, bounded down the stone steps, and flung herself into his arms.

"You've come back, *mein Liebe*," Evangeline said as she hugged him tightly.

Dan held her up in his arms as she nuzzled her face against his neck. Finally, she let herself be lowered to the ground and stood looking up at him, her face radiating with affection and joy.

"You look wonderful," Dan said.

Her smile brightened. "I'm better now you are here. I have missed you so much. I have so much to tell you. She pointed to his car, "Grab your bags and come in."

They walked up the stone staircase and into the large mansion.

Later, the two of them were sitting in a sunroom facing south. The warm sun of late spring bathed the room in a strong light, diffused by the many plants that were growing in what essentially seemed like a greenhouse.

"I know why you are here," Evangeline said. "I would like to think that you are here because you have realized you should be with me, or you discovered you missed me." She paused for a moment and looked at the floor. "But it is for business, *ja*?"

Dan thought for a moment. "There is the situation that Warren brought to our attention, but I *am* glad to see you."

"I am not the confused girl you rescued. The one who didn't want any part of Aebischer's money. I'm a mature woman now." She looked him in the eye. "And I still haven't changed how I feel about you."

"Evangeline, you know I have a great affection for you. It would be easy to just allow ourselves to indulge our attraction for one another—"

"But you don't think that's right, do you?"

Dan shook his head. "It's not that—"

"You think you're too old for me? I'm too young? I've grown up a great deal these past years. Look at what I'm doing." She swept her hand around the room. "I can run this household with all the assistants and servants. I am creating a chain of refuges for abused women and girls. Starting here.

"I'm housing fifty victims on this estate. I provide shelter, drug rehabilitation, counseling, and learning. I want these women, some young girls, some older than me, to recover from what they have gone through, rebuild their strength and courage, and help them go out from here to be successful in life. I want them to be armed against any further abuse."

She gave him a serious look. "An immature girl could not do these things."

"You have done amazingly well. Believe it or not, even if I haven't always been in communication with you, I've kept abreast of your progress. It makes me happy to see you succeed."

"But it doesn't entice you? I am a wealthy woman. We could share a wonderful life together."

"Evangeline, please…"

"I know. You would get bored, feel like a kept man. That would violate some macho code of yours."

"I have a mission. One I took on years ago. One I'm very good at, and one I feel is important. I'm not going to leave that field of battle." He paused. "And that's what it is. A battle with those who would like to kill us and destroy our civilization."

She smiled and looked out the window. "You could do that, while I do my work…my mission, as you say. But we could share our lives outside of those missions."

Dan knew his face showed his pain. "My dear girl, that is very tempting. But that would create a vulnerability that my enemies could and would exploit. They could come at me by coming at you. I couldn't put you in that situation, as much as I might be tempted to do so."

Evangeline's face fell in sadness, then brightened. "So, I tempt you?"

Dan smiled. "Indeed, you do, *fraulein*."

She gave him a look of almost triumph. "Then I will hold on to that little victory. Maybe, as you get used to the idea of us being together, and Warren makes this place even more secure, you'll change your mind."

She got up and leaned over to him, her face close to his. Dan took in her scent, all fresh, all feminine, all enticing. She kissed his cheek and then his lips before he could react.

"*Ein Mädchen muss es versuchen*," a girl must try, she whispered in his ear.

Dan felt a shiver of arousal flow through his body. *Careful, boy.* Evangeline sat back with a smile on her face, all aglow, gazing at Dan. He knew she understood her effect on men, even him. And she was even more adept at using her wiles on him than when he had first encountered her.

Just then a maid came in to announce lunch was ready to serve.

"We'll take it in here, Marie," Evangeline said.

They ate the luncheon spread of sausages, cheeses, fresh fruits along with a champagne punch Evangeline had made just for Dan's visit. Afterwards, she took Dan on a tour of the mansion. It was castle-like in the French fashion. Built of stone blocks, weathered to a soft, creamy color, it had ten-foot-high windows with elaborate tops on both floors. There were seven chimneys sprouting from the sloped roof along with various vents. The drive from the road flowed into a circle in front of a grand, granite staircase that spread open at its base in a welcoming fashion. In the circle was a formal garden with a fountain. The grounds spreading out to the right and left were immaculately manicured.

Dan noted from his arrival that the staff were all professional with everything carefully maintained to the highest level of Swiss attention to detail. Inside,

Evangeline showed Dan the workrooms where her staff worked on various projects.

"In here, we're determining where new retreats can be located. As you know, I want to go beyond this place. This is just a start."

He could sense the pride she took in her mission. One whole wing of the mansion was dedicated to teaching various skills to the rescued women and girls. It varied depending on their age and needs.

"This wing is our education area. It's ironic, isn't it? I never thought much about education, especially after I ran away. And now here I am teaching girls and women, some who are older than me."

"You've done a lot. I'm amazed that you could put this all together so well."

Evangeline smiled at him. "Not bad for an empty-headed runaway, *ja*?"

"Aber ja, mein Liebchen."

As they walked, He tried to steer their conversation back to Evangeline's security.

"You know," Dan said. "Warren is in love with you."

Evangeline looked serious. "I recognize that. He is wonderfully attentive and I owe him a great deal for setting up such a good security system." She looked up from her plate. "But I'm not in love with him. You know that." She pointed her fork at Dan. "You, *mein Schatz*, have ruined me for other men."

Dan laughed. "Now don't try to make me feel guilty. Remember, my rescuing you was a job I took on. I was to turn you over and collect my fee."

Evangeline looked down with a serious face. "That was a bad time." She looked back at Dan. "But you didn't. That's when I began to fall in love with you. Not as a tactic

The Scorpion

to keep you from returning me to that monster, but in response to who I began to see you were."

"Let me get back to Warren, please."

Evangeline put her hands in her lap and stared at Dan. "Yes sir. I am listening."

"I'm serious. You need to be careful with him, with his feelings. I would not like to see him crushed."

"I don't want to hurt Warren, but I'm not in love with him. What great words of wisdom do you have for me to not cause him pain?"

Dan shook his head. "I don't know, dear girl. I'm not so good at this myself, as you can tell. I do know that you are a beautiful woman with a strong effect on men. You wield more power in that manner—as a woman—than you may realize."

"I am aware of my womanly powers, and I am careful with Warren. Perhaps you can talk to him. You or your boss, Jane. She's the one you really love, isn't she?"

"Evangeline, don't go there. Please give it a rest. Let's enjoy one another's company. Jane lives in my world. As a result, there's much we share. I'd like to have things to share with you as well, even if we must live different lives.

With lunch over, Evangeline reluctantly turned Dan over to Warren. The two of them went down to the basement, which housed the servers and monitors.

"I've got some interesting footage to show you," Warren said as they descended the steps.

Chapter 7

In the basement was a room with multiple monitors spread out across a large table and servers humming away against the wall. There was a wall-mounted air conditioning system and the room had a chill to it.

"Servers make a lot of heat," Warren said as he noticed Dan shiver. "It's easier to control the heat down here in the basement, so it's a good spot for them."

"Also, more secure," Dan said. "What do you want me to see?"

"Here," Warren said, pointing to a stack of VHS tapes. "Aebischer had a legacy system that the idiots helping Evangeline didn't tell me about when I put in her new system. It also shows the main gate, but there are a few cameras that are aimed across and down the road."

"Did they think pointing down the road was useful?"

"Maybe." Warren sat down and motioned for Dan to sit next to him. "Since we're here, and I discovered the tapes, I thought I'd take a look at them. Let me show you."

He plugged a tape into an old VCR player and both men watched. Nothing it showed only the road leading up to the gate with a view up to a quarter of a mile away. Dan looked at Warren who fast forwarded the tape.

"I'll get to the interesting part."

He stopped and backed up the tape and then hit the play button. Both men watched as a white van stopped on the side of the road. A man got out and quickly headed into the woods on the opposite side of the road from the main gate. The van then proceeded to drive past the gate and down the road. Warren stopped the tape and put in another one that was recorded from a different camera. After fast-forwarding to the appropriate time point, it showed the van disappearing down the road. Warren stopped the tape and looked over at Dan.

"What do you think?"

"Don't know what to think at the moment. Can you get me an enlargement of the man going into the woods? And how about the license plate number?"

Warren reached into a drawer and produced a file folder.

"I figured you might want that." He opened the folder and laid out some printouts from the tape. "They're not very good, especially of the man. But you can read the license plate."

Dan studied the still shots. The man looked slightly built, not very large. His face was shrouded and indistinct from the enlargement. Still, the shot of the man with his head turned sideways revealed a large, prominent nose.

"He looks Semitic…Arab maybe," Dan said.

Warren showed him more pictures, none of which improved on getting a clear image of the man's face.

"Here's the thing. The camera shows him being picked up by the same van after five hours. And this is significant…it goes on for a week."

"A week. This is definitely a stake out. I'll bet the guy hikes the half mile to the main gate and watches from the woods. He's compiling a log of the comings and goings, looking for a routine."

Dan got up. "This is good work, Warren. You'll make a counter intelligence agent yet."

"Fancy word for a spy? I'll stick with the cyber security, thanks. I don't want to live in the world you inhabit."

"Just hang around the edges?" Dan smiled at the man.

"And help out where I can."

Dan went back up the stairs with Warren's folder in his hands. He found Evangeline in her office. She was busy working on the planning for her other retreat centers. The first two were to be located in Berlin and Marseille, and when those were up and running smoothly, she would expand to more cities.

Carrie was a young woman who worked as Evangeline's personal assistant. She oversaw the handling of Evangeline's calendar as well as coordinating the attorneys' work on permitting. Carrie also helped with the corporate outreach. Evangeline wisely understood the need to spread out the financial burden. Her pitch to corporate interests was that support of the retreat centers was a good way to burnish their public image as good corporate citizens.

One of the way's Evangeline showed her growing skills as a mature woman of means on a mission, was in her presentations to corporate interests. She understood her beauty as well as her sex appeal and knew how to use those to her advantage. She coupled her magnetism with a savvy pitch about helping support women's interests. The combination was hard to resist.

"Did you find anything? Or is Warren just making up scare stories to stay close to me?" Evangeline asked as Dan walked into her office.

"Don't be mean to Warren," Dan said. "He's serious."

Dan laid the file folder on her desk.

"Here's the proof that someone is surveilling your place."

Evangeline studied the still shots as Carrie came over to look at them.

"Do you know who this is?" Evangeline asked.

Dan shook his head. "Can't tell, but they're serious. They've been out there for a week."

"When was this?"

"Last week. It ended the day Warren arrived."

"What will you do? What *can* you do? Should I alert the police?"

"The police have to be handled carefully. Warren and I should not be involved. The less they are aware of us, the better. I'm a non-entity." Dan nodded towards Carrie. "I don't know how much you've told her about me, but the less, the better. Much must remain between just the two of us."

He turned to Evangeline's assistant. "I'm sorry to leave you out of the loop, but you should not know about myself and my relationship with Evangeline."

"I think I understand," Carrie said.

She stared back at Dan with a questioning expression on her face. She was attractive, but with a serious demeanor. Dan sensed she had no flirtatious instincts about her, but was all straightforward in her relationships.

"It only deepens the mystery, but you can relax. As far as I know, Evangeline has not compromised your secrets, whatever they are. I work with her as she is currently, not how she came to this position."

Dan smiled at her thoughtful declaration. She seemed to have a well-organized mind.

"Back to the issue at hand," Evangeline said. "What should I do?"

"First thing is not to go outside the grounds for a while. If you need to run errands, let someone else do it."

"I can do that," Carrie said.

"I'm to be a prisoner in my own house?" Evangeline asked. "For how long?"

"For a while. At least until I can figure out how dangerous this threat is. We have a cyber-attack on your security system, then someone staking out your entrance...for a week. I have to assume these are related events."

Dan gave her a serious look.

"This is not the time to be rebellious. Please take my advice and lie low for a while. I'm going to snoop around and then I have to go to Marseille to see someone. They may be able to help me identify this potential threat."

"Marseille? Who could that be?"

Dan only looked at her.

Evangeline sighed. "I know. It's something you can't talk about, like much of your life."

Dan smiled at her. "You're finally getting the idea."

Now she smiled back and wadded up a sheet of paper to throw at him. Carrie remained standing close by with a serious look on her face.

"I'll do any runs outside of the compound until you get back. Evangeline does not have any trips planned for the next two weeks, so there's no conflict there."

"Thank you, Carrie. That's a big help."

Dan gave the two women a bright smile. "Walk me out to the front," he said to Evangeline.

"Do you trust Carrie?" Dan asked when they were alone.

"Yes, completely. She is very dedicated to this work and we've developed a special bond. She's got the orderly mind that I lack."

Dan nodded.

"Is something wrong?"

"It's just that the more people know about me...about our relationship, the easier it is for our connection to be uncovered. That could be very dangerous for you. That is why I've gone to great lengths to keep certain things from you."

Evangeline started to protest. Dan held up his hand to stop her.

"If even our relationship were clearly known, the basis for it, that is enough to endanger you."

"Please don't fret. I haven't revealed the connection between you and Aebischer. And Carrie is a believer in what we're doing. She has such a heart for this work. I've never met anyone who has felt as deeply as I about the plight of abused girls."

"Did she suffer abuse herself?"

Evangeline shook her head. "No, but she knew someone who suffered. The problem really struck a chord with her. When she heard about my plans through a newspaper article, she contacted me and lobbied for an interview. She was very convincing and has proven to be my best decision to date. I'm lucky to have her."

"So, you see this as a long-term relationship?"

"Definitely. We have a great affection for one another. She's one of the few people I can trust fully. But I leave our past, you and me, out of it. I don't want to muddy things up between her and I. You heard her say she's interested in what we're doing now, not my past."

Dan thought as they strolled down the gravel drive. "Just remember, the more she knows, the less safe you are."

Evangeline reached up and stroked his cheek. "I'll be careful, *mein liebe*."

Chapter 8

Scorpion made his way through Turkey, Bulgaria, the Balkans, and northern Italy on his way to Marseille. He drove a panel van purchased in Turkey under an alias. He had two men with him. They had worked with him before, and he trusted them. They didn't know anything about him, his real name, or where he came from, which was important if they were ever captured. He had chosen them for their willingness to not know things as well as their ruthlessness.

Once in the city, Scorpion connected with the local jihadist cell in the *Font Vert Cité* housing complex; a place that held a large number of Muslim immigrants. After two days of inquiry, he met one of the men who had been at the townhouse where Jabbar was killed and sat down with him.

"You say it was the work of one man. How can you be sure?" Scorpion asked.

The jihadist shifted uneasily in his chair. They were sitting at an outside table drinking tea. He had heard of the Scorpion. The man was a legend in jihadist circles. He had assassinated many enemies of Islam. He worked not only for the Saudis, but others who wanted to attack the West. The Taliban and ISIS had been clients of his. It was said that he could become nearly invisible and then strike without warning, like a cobra. Stories were told of how his victims would be cut up before being dispatched. It was even rumored that he had blades inserted into his hands. He was not large, like the scorpion for which he was named, but he was even more deadly. The man was nervous. Scorpion could radiate a strong aura of danger when it suited him; a sense which only increased the closer one got to him.

"Yes, *zaeim*." He used the word for leader or boss as a show of respect for Scorpion's dangerous presence. "I was in the hallway upstairs when he shot two men. It was one man. We chased him down onto the railroad tracks where he seemed to disappear. He was like a ghost, a *jinn* who takes one's life without warning."

"We do not fear the *jinn* with Allah on our side." Scorpion scolded the man.

"If you say, *zaeim*." The man nodded his head with little conviction.

"You don't know how this assassin found Jabbar?"

The man shook his head. "There are many sources of information here in Marseille. We cannot hide completely. Someone from outside of our community might know of Jabbar's arrival in the city."

"Someone from the criminal class, no doubt."

The man nodded.

"You will inquire around to see what you can find. Who might have talked with a westerner and given him information about Jabbar." Scorpion took out a slip of paper and wrote an email address on it. "You will send an email to this address with what you find out. You will use it only once and then destroy this paper."

The man nodded.

"If you use the email more than once, I will come for you, *fahem* ?" Understand?

He nodded again, now even more agitated by this ominous stranger. He was a man of obvious power, so the jihadist would do as he commanded.

Later that day, Scorpion and his two companions left for Switzerland. He hadn't expected much from his contact in Marseille. He doubted the Muslim community gave up Jabbar and anyone chasing him would come to a dead end outside that community. The western criminal gangs who neither liked nor respected the intrusion by Muslim groups and the operations they ran, would not be helpful. His community's activities siphoned money from their sources of income.

That evening, the three men checked into a house that had been rented for them under a fictitious corporation. If researched, the registration information trail would run into a dead end, which would be incriminating, but that would be the end of it.

After settling in, Scorpion laid out a map on the kitchen table.

"You will drop me off near the main gate. I will watch from the woods across the road. I want to log who comes and goes and at what times. You will continue around the loop on the hill and look for any back way onto the grounds. I want to know how good the fences are and if there's camera surveillance on them."

The men nodded without speaking.

"We will spend some days learning about the routines of the mansion. If we can take someone when they are outside, it is better. If not, we will have to go inside. There will probably be guards to deal with, which will make the job messier."

"We follow your orders," one of the men said. "You are the master."

Scorpion smiled, making his face look more wicked. "I am responsible, so that is appropriate."

Scorpion followed his daily prayer routine as best he could even while on his missions. He assumed Allah wouldn't mind since he was doing Allah's work as a warrior for the faith.

"We will eat as close to halal as we can. But we do not want to draw attention to ourselves, so shop carefully."

They would make one food shopping trip and then hole up. The less they were seen in this small town, the better. Even dressing in western clothes, Scorpion knew they stood out with their Semitic looks and swarthy complexions. The Swiss were very white and western-looking. It was different from operating in a large city like Frankfurt or Paris.

The next day, the two men dropped Scorpion off a quarter of a mile from the main gate. He walked the rest of the way through the woods and settled down just opposite the entrance to watch. He was patient. A hunter had to be so; had to sit quietly for hours waiting for the quarry to appear. Scouting was not to be hurried. The more he knew about his prey, the easier it would be for him to capture the victim.

Throughout the afternoon, there was little traffic. A few people went in, some were contractors, others more business-like in style. One vehicle, a Mercedes SUV with tinted windows, came out. Scorpion assumed it might include the girl, the benefactor of this operation, since the vehicle had not entered the grounds earlier. It was impossible to see inside.

The Scorpion

Two hours later, the same vehicle returned without giving up any more information. Scorpion noted the times and the license plate number. After five hours, he got up and started back to where his assistants had dropped him off. They were waiting by the side of the road as Scorpion emerged from the woods and climbed into the van.

"What did you find?" he asked.

"The fence is solid all around the property, but scalable. No razor wire or anything like that."

"It does not seem to be electrified," the other man said.

Scorpion sat back in the rear seat with his eyes closed. The two men turned back to the front. They remained silent.

"How long did you wait for me to come from the woods?

The men looked at each other.

The passenger said, "Five or six minutes."

"Less than ten," the driver said.

Scorpion kept his eyes closed. "Is an unmarked van sitting on the side of the road a suspicious sight?"

Neither man spoke.

"Well, is it?"

"Yes, *zaeim*," the passenger finally said.

"Indeed."

Scorpion reached out his right hand and wrapped it tightly around the passenger's neck. His hand and fingers had great strength, and the man gasped as Scorpion's claw-like fingers dug into his neck.

"Then why would you risk our operation and do such a thing?"

The driver glanced at his unfortunate partner; his eyes wide in fright.

"We didn't want to make you wait," he said.

Scorpion turned to look at the driver, his black eyes radiated his growing anger.

"Have I ever asked you to treat me special at the risk of an operation?"

The driver shook his head as he turned back to the road. "No, *zaeim*."

Scorpion released the other man's neck and sat back. "And we do not start now. If you are going to be careless, I will replace you."

The phrase "replace you" carried with it much dread since neither man knew exactly what it might mean.

Chapter 9

Scorpion watched as a car drove up to the gate. A man got out. He was about six feet tall, skinny and slightly built. He spoke into the speaker and looked up into the camera. The gate was opened, and he got back into the car and drove inside.

He's known. Could this be the man he was searching for? Scorpion doubted it. The man didn't look like an assassin or warrior, more like a clerk. *But they know who he is. He's connected to the woman inside.* He watched the rest of the day, but no one came out.

Better suspend surveillance for a while. Wait some days before starting again. After getting picked up, the men went back to their house.

"You will not drop me off tomorrow," Scorpion said. "We'll drive by to see if there is any activity, but that is all."

"Is there a problem?" one of the men asked.

"Maybe. There is a visitor, he's someone known to the woman. She gets no visitors other than delivery people, so this is significant. I want to make sure it's not something we have triggered."

"How would we have triggered something? We were discreet."

"We tried to infiltrate the security system and were locked out after some success. She has a very sophisticated defense, and it may show our attack was also very sophisticated. This man may be a response to that."

"But we had to try, did we not?" the man asked.

"If we had been successful, our physical surveillance would not have been necessary. We could have overridden the system and entered to capture the woman. The advantage would have been all ours." Scorpion paused. "Now, I'm not so sure."

† † †

After talking with Evangeline, Dan found Warren and told him to make sure Evangeline stayed on the grounds. Then he headed south to Marseille. His route took him around Zurich and slightly west before heading south again towards Berne. He stayed on the A1 and restrained himself from speeding, holding the Peugeot in check. Skirting Berne, Dan passed south of Lake Neuchâtel and aimed for Lausanne. He passed the city to the west and then followed the north shore of Lake Geneva down to Genève. After a slow passage through the city, he was glad to finally exit into France. Driving could now become more interesting.

Dan drove the M1 south through Chambéry and down the river valley to Grenoble. Grenoble was on the confluence of two rivers, the Isère and the Drac. The city itself was built on the flat river-bed plain, with the mountains rising up around it. Even though the whole metropolitan area has a population of only 650,000 people, the city promotes itself as the "capital of the alps." Even being in the mountains, it has a surprisingly mild climate with an average winter temperature of thirty-eight to forty-four degrees down in the town. A short distance to the south, the temperatures are noticeably warmer and hot summers prevail.

The M1 ended at Grenoble and Dan took local roads across the Isère River to the Rue Ampere and the restaurant known as Le Véritable, or The True. The name intrigued Dan who expected he could get a true French meal there during his break from the road. He grinned to himself as he parked and entered the restaurant. *I'm learning how to travel in a more civilized style. No hammering down the road without any breaks for relaxing and dining.*

Dan ordered a Blanquette de Veau, or veal ragout. It was in the form of a stew consisting of veal, carrots, and onions. The dish was made by first "stewing" the meat with the vegetables, the mix is then drained and pearl onions, already cooked, are added along with a creamy sauce made with butter, flour, veal cooking stock, mushrooms, heavy cream, and egg yolks. Needless to say, it was a substantial lunch, and Dan treated himself to a large coffee and pastry to jazz up his system. He still had four hours to drive.

From Grenoble, Dan headed south. Now he could exercise his modified Peugeot through the mountains as the road coursed up and down the slopes in switchbacks. He thought briefly of Christina. She lived not too far from his route, but he had vowed he would stay out of her life. She was the only woman he had fallen in love with since Rita. But that relationship was doomed. They lived in different worlds and he had let her go a few years earlier when that difference became deadly apparent. Still, the thought of her brought a sad smile to his face. She had named him Rosignol, nightingale. He had come to her in the night, injured, with no memory of who he was. He smiled as he thought about the six idyllic months they had spent together. Him learning about her music, the two of them falling in love. He wondered whether he would have remained happy if he had never recovered. But he did and the outside world had crashed in on them bring it all to an end.

His route brought him to the picturesque town of Aix-en-Provence and from there to Marseille. Once in the city, Dan found an anonymous hotel in the *quartiers nords*. It was a low income; seedy part of the city, and Dan knew it was the place to start in his search for Gaspard.

Gaspard was a local gangster from Corsica. He had helped Dan years ago after manipulating Dan into doing a favor for him. Since then, Gaspard, without having any firm evidence, had correctly guessed that Dan worked for an undercover agency, probably the CIA. He appeared to enjoy being a peripheral part of such operations, especially since they seemed to be directed towards middle-eastern terrorists. He had enough trouble with that group trying to muscle in on his operations, setting up their own drug-dealing networks in his territory. He enjoyed doing anything to disrupt their activities. Helping Dan seemed to be an adventure for him, but was also useful in keeping his competitors off balance.

Dan lay back on his bed after checking it for cockroaches. He relaxed. A little rest, and then he'd troll the bars until he connected with someone who could take him to Gaspard. The man was always in a different high-rise apartment each time he visited him.

After an hour, Dan sighed and got up. He slipped his 9mm Sig P226 into his underarm holster, pulled on his jacket, and stepped out into the night.

He was in his third bar, asking the bartenders where he could find Gaspard. They had all feigned ignorance, but Dan knew the word was getting passed around. Sure enough, while nursing his beer at the counter, two men approached him and sat down on either side. They were both large, with thick muscles. They would be formidable opponents in a hand-to-hand fight. In addition, Dan assumed they were fully armed.

"What is your name?" one of the men asked.

"Victor James," Dan replied. "He might remember me as Abdullah."

The two men looked at each other across Dan. The smaller of the two nodded.

"We will take you to him," the first man said, "but if he does not know you, you will be in trouble."

"He'll know who I am."

Without another word, the two men got up and headed for the door with Dan behind.

They followed a labyrinth of streets and alleys filled with rundown shops and apartments no more than five stories tall, until they came to one of the area's large high-rises. These were oversized structures that packed families in without any consideration of ambience or quality of living. The goal seemed to be to get a roof over as many heads with the smallest footprint and expenditure of money.

At the entrance, the men frisked Dan and removed his Sig 9mm. They led him through the lobby, with an unused concierge counter, to a small bank of noisy, slow elevators. The three rode up ten flights with no one speaking. After getting out, they walked down to the end of the hallway. Along the way, men were sitting in chairs, like sentries, which is exactly what they were. One of the men knocked on the door and then opened it. They went inside.

Inside Dan could smell the pungent aroma of Corsican cooking, more like Italian than French. Gaspard looked up from his easy chair.

"Ah, welcome my friend. When I heard an Abdullah was looking for me, I told my men to bring him here and treat him politely."

Gaspard heaved his bulk out of his chair and offered his hand to Dan.

"So, you are going by Victor now? Given up on the Arabic disguise? That's a good idea. It didn't work well."

Dan shook the man's hand and smiled.

"What brings you to visit me? I assume you didn't just look me up to see how I'm doing?"

He motioned for Dan to sit down. With his other hand, he motioned to one of the women who peeked around the corner from the kitchen to bring some wine. A moment later the young woman came out with a tray, a bottle, and two glasses. It was a red porto vecchio from Corsica.

"One of our most popular wines from the island. You might think it a travesty to bring Corsican wine to France proper, but it reminds me of my home."

He poured two glasses and offered one to Dan.

"To your health, to the health of both of us. We work in a dangerous business."

The two men took a long drink from their glasses. Dan nodded to Gaspard, acknowledging the quality of the wine.

"You only show up when you need information." Gaspard gave Dan a serious look, but let a wry smile spread across his face. "It would be nice to just check in on your friend, Gaspard, occasionally without an agenda. Anyway, what is it you want to know?"

Dan put down his glass. "I suspect this shadow character, the one you told me about, called Scorpion, is out there looking for me. I need to find him."

Gaspard smiled. "So, you think your friend, Gaspard, can help you with your sleuthing? Are you asking me to become a spy in your organization?"

Dan gave him a smile in return. "You know I can't talk about such things. But I know you have been helpful, and you know what is going on in your city."

"I do, I do. I know someone who may be able to help. He's in debt to me. We can go talk to him if you like."

"Let's do that," Dan said.

Gaspard stood up. "Then we go now. Later I'll think of a way for you to repay me for all my help."

They stood up. Dan opened his jacket and showed Gaspard his empty holster. "Do you mind me getting my pistol back?"

Gaspard smiled. "Of course not, my friend. We trust each other. But one can't be too careful."

He motioned to the men who had brought Dan to the apartment. One of them produced Dan's 9mm and handed it to him, butt first. Dan slipped the weapon in his holster.

"Thanks. It feels better having it on me."

The two men went down to the lobby with Gaspard's guards. They waited as the guards brought his car around, a large Mercedes S550. One of the men opened the rear door for Gaspard, and Dan went around to the other side and climbed in.

"Where are we going? Dan asked.

"I have an informant, someone in the Islamic community who lets me know what's going on. He'll have information."

"You got someone to inform for you? That could get him killed.

Gaspard smiled. "It could, but it could save his wife and kids."

"I don't understand. They'd be in as much risk as him."

"No, my friend. You see I'm quite the rogue. One must be to survive and get ahead in this business. I learned it from my uncle in Corsica. He's a very deadly man, but well-respected. I'm a deadly man here in Marseille but the local Islamic community doesn't respect me. So, I must take measures to make sure they do."

Dan looked at the gangster but didn't say anything.

"I have evidence that will mean his wife and daughters are deported if I take it to the authorities. If I don't, he gets to live here, the family gets to live here, but he has to do my bidding. If he doesn't cooperate, they go back to Iraq…or, with a call to my uncle, they disappear. He understands that I would do that only if he gives me reason."

Dan shook his head. "Sounds pretty brutal to me."

"When you don't get respect, you have to be brutal sometimes."

"Are you ever going to let them go?"

"Maybe…sometime. When Omar is not useful anymore…maybe." He sighed. "Right now, it's a useful arrangement."

The car wound through the labyrinth of back streets until it stopped on a particularly dark block. It consisted of more rundown apartments with small storefronts on the street level. The businesses all had a middle eastern focus indicating the nature of the surrounding community. Gaspard took out his phone and made a call.

"Omar. Meet me on the block. Five minutes."

He was silent for a moment.

"It doesn't matter. Make up an excuse and leave. Don't make me wait."

Gaspard hung up the phone.

"He says he's visiting relatives and can't get away. Can you believe that? He must tell them his leader called and he has to meet with him. They will understand. Omar is part of a gang and must obey."

He looked at his watch.

"Now we wait."

Chapter 10

Scorpion waited until he felt those at the mansion had let their guard down. He wanted to be patient, but he also didn't want to stay too long. Switzerland was not an easy place to remain anonymous.

"I don't think the woman who runs this place will be coming out. There is another woman coming and going to run errands for her. Perhaps this woman knows something. She may be close to the one who is in charge. We will have to take her."

"Do we interrogate her here?" one of the men asked.

Scorpion shook his head. "We take her to Bulgaria. To the safe house in Dimitrovgrad."

The next day Carrie went out in the SUV. She, at Evangeline's insistence, took two of the bodyguards with her. They pulled out of the gate and headed down the road to Embrach. Going around a turn, they found a white van blocking the road. The van had a sign in German indicating it was a painting contractor business. The hood was up and a man was bent over, looking into the engine compartment. He was slightly built and dressed in a painter's overalls. The ditches on the side of the road were too deep to drive around the vehicle.

Evangeline's SUV stopped fifty feet away.

"Wait here," the guard said to the one driving. I'll go see what's up."

He got out of the vehicle and called to the man, "What is wrong?"

The man pulled his head out of the engine bay. He had a thin face and a prominent nose. He spoke German with an accent that the guard couldn't place.

"The steering stopped working and I almost ran into the ditch. Then the motor shut off. Maybe the steering broke and the computer shut the engine down?"

He looked back into the engine. "I can't see anything from here? Do you know about these things?"

"No. But you're blocking the road. You have to move your van."

"It won't move. Maybe you can pull it back? Then you can go around. I'll call a tow truck."

He started walking to the rear of the vehicle. "I have a tow strap in the back. It's part of the safety kit."

He smiled, but it was a smile that didn't light up his face. The guard didn't notice and waved the driver forward. The thin man went to the back of the van and took out a strap. He walked to the SUV, but left the van's back door open. The guard headed to the driver's side of the SUV and the driver rolled down the window.

"What's going on?"

"We'll tow this van back a bit and then can be on our way."

As he said this, the thin man came up to them and pulled out his silenced 9mm. He shot the driver in the head splitting it open. Blood and brains spattered out to the side and back. The report was no more than a sharp "thump" that carried only a hundred yards of so. The guard standing outside, turned and started to pull his weapon out. Before he could bring it to bear on the assailant, the man in the painter's overalls shot him in the face, splattering the side of the car with his blood and brains.

Carrie screamed. The man pushed the unlock button and his two assistants came up and dragged her out of the back seat. She writhed in their grasp, trying to break free and run. One of them cuffed her across the head, stunning her. They dragged her to the van and threw her into the back. The two assistants jumped inside with her. The thin man put the hood down and got in the driver's seat and drove off down the road.

They left the SUV in the road with the two dead guards.

† † †

Omar came down the dark block. He walked without any hesitation towards the Mercedes waiting at the curb.

"Here, put this on," Gaspard said as he offered Dan a ski mask. "I assume you don't want to be recognized."

Dan took the mask and put it over his head. Only his eyes and mouth were exposed.

When Omar reached the car, Gaspard heaved himself out of the back seat. "Omar, I'm glad you could come." His voice was cheerful and carried no hint of irony that he had ordered the man to show up. "Get in. I have to talk to you." He motioned for the man to get in the back and then pushed his bulk in after him.

"What's this? What's going on?" Omar asked nervously when he saw Dan in the back seat with his face covered.

"An anonymous friend. Don't worry. He won't hurt you.

"What is it you want to know that it couldn't wait until tomorrow?"

"Omar, in our business, many things can't wait until tomorrow. But I'll get to the point. We need to know about a man who goes by the name, Scorpion. Who is he? Has he visited Marseille?"

"I don't know of such a man."

Omar was squeezed between Gaspard and a masked stranger. One of the two men in the front was looking at him, the other watching the street. Gaspard sighed and reached into his jacket and took out a long switchblade. He clicked it and the bright blade flashed open. Gaspard turned it so the dim light from the street bounced off the polished steel.

"That is unfortunate. Unfortunate that I don't believe you. I know for a fact someone by this name visited our city. I want to know who he talked to. You should not try to deceive me. It will go badly for you…and your family."

"I don't know anything about this man. I didn't meet with him," Omar replied. His shaky voice revealed his growing anxiety.

"I need to know who he met with," Gaspard said as he rotated the blade in the dim light.

"You ask too much," Omar said. "It's dangerous for me to talk about such a man."

"It is dangerous for you not to. Just a name, Omar. Then you can go back to your relatives and enjoy the rest of your meal," Gaspard said.

Omar's head sank to his chest. He sighed. "You will get me killed, yet." He paused and in a quiet voice, continued, "Hakim Alawi."

Gaspard folded his knife and patted Omar on his leg. He opened the door and stepped out. "Go home. If you have told me correctly, nothing more will happen. If you have misled me, much will happen."

Omar scrambled out of the Merc and walked away quickly down the street. Gaspard got back in the car and they drove off into the night.

"You believe him?" Dan asked.

Gaspard nodded. "He knows better than to lie to me. I also have heard this name. He's the leader of a gang. I don't know if they're jihadists, but their local activities encroach on my business, so I wouldn't be upset if you eliminated him for me."

"I'm not so much interested in eliminating him as getting some information from him."

Gaspard turned to Dan and smiled. "Bien sûr, of course. Then you eliminate him."

Chapter 11

Dan ended the call with a distressed look on his face. He slammed his phone down on the bed in the hotel room and started pacing. He had just learned from a panicked Evangeline that Carrie had been abducted and her two guards killed. Dan had to calm her down to get a coherent account of what had happened, but there was little anyone knew, even the authorities, which Evangeline had called. From Warren's statement, they were looking for an unmarked white Toyota van. That description included a lot of vehicles in the area.

After a moment, Dan picked up his phone and called Gaspard.

"Something's come up. I have to move fast. Can you help me find and capture this Alawi guy? Tonight?"

"You *are* in a hurry. I must find him first."

"Find him, and I'll do you a favor after I interrogate him. The situation has changed."

"Things escalated?"

Dan didn't answer.

"Can't talk about that?" Gaspard paused for a moment. "Okay. Give me an hour, I'll call you back."

"Just locate him, maybe provide a diversion, I'll do the rest."

"One hour."

Dan paced the room for the next hour after checking his 9mm and putting his Walther P22 with its suppressor in his jacket pocket. He put his CRKT Tactical knife in his pocket. It was a folding, slim handle knife that locked open to function like a fixed blade weapon.

Dan was ready when the call came in.

"Drive to the apartment building. There's a place outside for you to park. I'll meet you inside the front door."

Gaspard's tone of voice was all business. There was no more banter, but a seriousness that properly accompanied an experienced gangster who had the muscle to manage his territory. Dan guessed he had learned much from his uncle in Corsica before winding up in Marseille.

Ten minutes later, Dan pulled to the curb in the spot open for him and headed in a brisk walk to the front door. He had no more entered the lobby when Gaspard rose from a chair and met him at the door.

"Let's go. We've got a location for our friend, but we must act quickly before he moves to where we can't reach him."

The men climbed into Gaspard's Merc and took off. An SUV filled with Gaspard's men followed close behind.

"He's been seen in an open-air market near Rond-Point Pierre Paaraf. It's located in a parking lot of an empty building. He's got a very large bodyguard with him at all times, so it won't be easy to take him."

"I know the area," Dan said.

Gaspard looked at him, but didn't ask any questions.

"I need you to point him out, drop me off. Can you create a diversion? Maybe a small fire? Then be ready to pick both of us up."

"What about the bodyguard?"

"I'll take care of him." Dan's face was grim as was his voice.

Gaspard eyed him closely.

"Something bad has happened. I see the look of a killer in your face. Someone you know?"

Dan shook his head. "Just help me get this Alawi. He has information I need, and time is very precious now."

"Someone close to you is at risk."

Dan turned to Gaspard. "Don't ask questions. Just help me and you won't have a problem with Hakim anymore."

"Gloves off." Gaspard shrugged. "Suits me."

They drove in silence with Dan mentally willing the car to go faster. Gaspard briefed Dan on what Hakim looked like. He wore a tan jacket with black pants and was wearing a checkered keffiyeh scarf. That last would help Dan locate the man. When they got to the open market, Gaspard instructed the driver to cruise past the shops just outside the pedestrian area. Near the end of their first pass, Dan spotted the man. His scarf and large bodyguard, walking a few paces behind him, identified him as the target.

"Him?" Dan asked pointing to the man.

"That's him," Gaspard answered.

"Let me out behind him, it looks like he's going to walk the length of the market. Set up a diversion down at the far end, where he's headed. He'll be focused on that as will everyone else. You have room in the SUV when I grab him?"

"*Oui*. But not for the bodyguard."

Dan nodded and got out of the Mercedes.

"I'll wait for your diversion."

He headed into the stream of pedestrians. His eyes found the bodyguard with Hakim just ahead. Like a predator, Dan never took his eyes off his target. He didn't need to watch Gaspard, nor the SUV. They would either do their jobs, or not. Dan couldn't concern himself with that. He just needed to be ready.

He carefully closed the gap on the two men. He stopped to check out goods and produce when they stopped. Keeping a half-dozen people between himself and his target made it easy to stay concealed. Additionally, this was Hakim's territory, a place where he was comfortable. The bodyguard was probably more relaxed as well. Dan knew the price of a lapse in vigilance, and now it would work to his benefit.

About the time he expected Gaspard to be ready to start a fire or other diversion, Dan closed to within a few paces, keeping at least two people between him and the bodyguard.

Hakim was looking at some clothing laid out on a table when a commotion arose ahead. He looked up, as did his bodyguard. Dan quickly closed on the two men. His right hand gripped his Walther P22 in his pocket. He stepped up behind the bodyguard and pulled out the pistol. He placed it just behind the man's neck at the base of his brain and pulled the trigger. With the crowd noise growing, no one could hear the shot, but the guard crumpled to the ground.

Hakim started to turn around when Dan pushed the Walther into his back. With his left hand he grabbed Hakim's arm and whispered in his ear, "Walk forward or you'll be dead or crippled for life."

A few people backed away from the two men and the one lying on the ground. Dan quickly maneuvered Hakim to the edge of the crowd, which was now surging forward towards the growing fire at the end of the market.

The SUV pulled up. One of Gaspard's men jumped out and helped Dan shove Hakim into the SUV. At this point, some young men in the market started shouting at what they now saw as a kidnapping, but it was too late. As they came running towards them, the SUV sped off following the Mercedes. Both vehicles drove around the circle and headed at high speed down the Avenue Arnavon. Behind them they could hear sirens heading to the market.

Chapter 12

While Dan and one of Gaspard's men held the struggling Hakim down, Gaspard's man in the front shoved a hood over his head. Then he thrust a needle into his neck and Hakim sagged back as the sedative took effect.

"Where are we going?" Dan asked in French.

"We follow Gaspard," the driver answered.

The two vehicles sped through the city toward the massive Gare du Canet freight rail yard. Just east of the rail yard they turned down a dead-end street and into a dirt field filled with weeds and bits of concrete and steel. At the far end were two empty warehouse buildings along a, now unused, rail siding. The Mercedes pulled up to the warehouse with the SUV right behind it. Everyone got out and Gaspard's guards dragged the semi-conscious Hakim into the empty warehouse.

They walked across the concrete floor littered with broken glass, pieces of wood from packing crates, empty cans and bottles into an interior room that had tarps hung over the windows. There was a chair in the middle. The men tied Hakim to the chair while Gaspard turned on a dim overhead light.

"He is all yours now," Gaspard said. "If you want, I can have my men prepare him, how you say? Soften him up?"

"Not necessary. You've done plenty," Dan said. "I'll take it from here."

"We will wait outside. It is best he doesn't know exactly who abducted him...and you may not want him to be able to recognize your face either."

Gaspard turned and motioned to his men to follow. They left and closed the door, leaving Dan alone with Hakim slowly coming out of his stupor. Dan paced the room, watching Hakim. There was a table to one side with some pieces of steel and a propane torch. *This is Gaspard's torture room*. He hoped he would not have to resort to such methods, but he was impatient. Time was not on his side. When Hakim regained his alertness, there would be no sparring with him, taking time to break him down, trap him with what Dan already knew. Dan had to get information quickly...brutally, if it was called for. While he was waiting, Gaspard opened the door and handed Dan two bottles of water and left without a word.

Hakim began to stir and groan. "Do you know who I am?" he finally said in a slightly slurred voice.

Dan didn't answer, but opened one of the water bottles and splashed water into Hakim's face under the hood. He snapped his head back, gasping and coughing.

"I am an important leader in the Islamic community. If you don't want serious trouble you can let me go now. Later, it will not go well for you."

Dan still said nothing.

"What do you want? Why have you kidnapped me?"

The right questions.

"I need some information that you have," Dan said, speaking in French. Hakim was still hooded. "I'm in a hurry, so it will be best for you to tell me quickly what I want to know. Things will get very brutal and painful if you delay."

"What is it you want to know?"

"I want to know about a man called Scorpion. He visited recently and you talked with him."

"I don't know this man."

Dan stepped closer to Hakim. The man's arms were tied to the chair where he sat bound. Dan grabbed his right hand. He took his tactical knife out and touched Hakim's hand with the blade. Hakim closed his hand in a fist. Dan scratched along the back of his hand, drawing blood.

"I'm going to cut off one of your fingers each time you don't answer my questions, or if I think you're lying to me."

"You are an infidel dog. My people will slaughter you and your family for taking me, for harming me."

Dan didn't answer, but inserted his blade between Hakim's ring and little fingers, slicing the skin along the inside. Hakim jerked his hand, but that only caused the blade to cut into more flesh.

"I have nothing to tell you. If you don't want war with me, you'll let me go while you have the chance."

"Last chance to talk to me."

Hakim's breath was coming in tight gasps, but he said nothing. Dan turned the knife ninety degrees and sliced into Hakim's little finger. The man screamed as Dan pressed down through the skin and into the bone. He pushed down hard and pulled the blade across the finger. The razor-sharp blade cut through the bone as Hakim's screams rose. Then he was through. The finger dropped to the floor and blood spurted from the joint.

Dan went over to the bench and grabbed a piece of metal. He lit the torch and heated the metal. When it was glowing red, he came back to the now-groaning Hakim and placed the red-hot steel against Hakim's finger stub, cauterizing the wound. Hakim began screaming again as the steel seared the stump of his finger.

"That will stop the bleeding. We can keep going like this until all ten of your fingers are gone and you have only palms. You will be a beggar with just pads for hands, like a leper, no way to hold anything. Do you think your people will let such a cripple lead them? You will be dependent on everyone around you."

"I don't know how much I can tell you," he said. His voice was hoarse and shaky, mixed with grunts of pain.

"Don't play games. I don't have time for that. Tell me who he is, where he comes from, what he wanted."

"I am not playing games. I do not know who he is. I am telling the truth."

Hakim was now breathing hard. There was a desperation in his voice.

"I can't tell you what I don't know. I don't think anyone knows, other than he is Scorpion, a dangerous man, an assassin."

"Who does he work for?"

Hakim shook his head. "Please, I don't know. It must be someone with much money and power to hire him. Such people do not let their identities be known."

"What does the community think? Who do they think is behind Scorpion?"

"A wealthy Saudi. That is all anyone knows."

"There are many wealthy Saudis."

"Indeed. That is the point. It gives away no useful information. The Scorpion is like that as well. A ghost. If you cross him, you die, sometimes unpleasantly. Believe me. I'm telling you the truth."

"What did he want, this Scorpion? What did you talk about?"

Hakim took a deep breath, as if to gather his thoughts. "He wanted to know about the killing of Jabbar."

"What did you tell him?"

"I told him I was there. It was one man. He fled down onto the railroad tracks and disappeared, like a jinn."

"Why did he want to know about killing Jabbar?"

"He is chasing an assassin. Someone he thinks is disrupting our operations."

"Your terror operations."

"You say. But it is our struggle. We will take over Europe. It is soft and cannot withstand the purging wind of jihad."

Hakim's attitude had begun to return.

"You are just another infidel who thinks he can stop us. We are inevitable. Our women are more fertile than yours. They give birth to more babies. Your women are empty, they do not breed. We will overcome by jihad and by overwhelming you in numbers. Islam will rule Europe. Your time is over. It is time for the reign of the faithful."

"Nice speech. What else did Scorpion ask?"

"That was all he wanted to know. He didn't believe in the jinn."

"And you?"

"It was a man, but a spirit can disguise itself as a man. He disappeared after killing Jabbar and others. One man, all by himself. That I know."

"Did he say anything else?"

Dan put his blade between the next two fingers.

"No, please!" Hakim yelled. "I will tell you. It won't do you any good anyway."

"I'm waiting."

Dan pressed the blade against the inside web of the fingers, opening a small cut.

Hakim's head jerked and his arm pulled back against the ropes that bound him to the chair.

"I asked how he would find this man or ghost. He said there was a connection in Switzerland. He would find that connection and it would lead him to the man he sought."

"Where is this man from?"

"He came through Turkey. I know that. He had a white van with Turkish plates on it."

"Where is he from?"

Dan pressed the blade harder against the webbing.

"No! No! I will tell you what I know. He is from somewhere deep in the Middle east. No one knows where. It is part of how he remains hidden."

"Hakim, I need more."

"Please, I don't have any more."

"Think hard…"

"I told him Switzerland is not a good place to abduct someone. Too many authorities and cameras. He said he was going to Bulgaria. I know there are safe houses, safe communities for us in Bulgaria."

"He would take a captive there?"

Hakim nodded his head under the hood. "Yes."

"Then where?"

"Turkey, then back somewhere deeper in the Middle east. I don't know where. I'm telling you the truth."

"Where in Bulgaria?"

Hakim hesitated. Dan pressed the blade further into the web of his hand.

"Dimitrovgrad. That is all I know."

"Where in Dimitrovgrad?"

"I live here. I have never been to Dimitrovgrad. I am not told such details."

Dan pressed the blade into his hand again.

"Please!" Hakim screamed. "That is all I know. I'm not an assassin. I live here. I've never been there. I only know about the safe house from others talking."

Dan pulled his knife back. There was no more information to get. He looked at Hakim. A terrorist and a gangster. He dealt drugs to weaken the infidels and to make money to finance terror activities in and around Marseille and the rest of France. He was a cog in the jihadist network. A small cog, but a useful one nonetheless. This jihadist community was important enough that Jabbar went here to hide out after Frankfurt. How many more jihadists would they harbor? How many more did they already harbor?

Dan pulled his Walther P22 out of his pocket. He flicked the manual safety off. Hakim shuddered at the sound. Dan stepped behind him and fired into the base of his skull. Hakim slumped forward.

Gaspard opened the door at the sound of the gun. He looked at Hakim, now dead in the chair. "You get what you needed?"

Dan nodded.

"I see you did me the favor I wanted. Let's go. My men will dispose of the body. He was abducted and disappeared. It could have been by a rival gang of Islamist or other gangsters. No one will know exactly who was responsible. One less zealot to kill civilians. I know you don't like civilians getting killed."

The two men walked out into the dark night and climbed into the Mercedes.

"What now?" Gaspard asked.

Dan sighed. "I have many miles to travel and not much time."

"So, no sleep for you?"

Dan shook his head.

Chapter 13

Inside the van, Scorpion's men put a mask over Carrie's head and one of them injected her with a tranquilizer. As she fell back unconscious, they opened the lid of a bench built in along the wall of the van. Inside was a padded compartment. They tied Carries hands and arms behind her and bound her legs. When she was immobilized, they lifted her into the box and closed the lid. She was gagged and the padding meant she could not bang on the side and be heard, even if she could move. The box had a vent that allowed air in. There was a small fan that circulated fresh air. Someone could be kept for a long time in the box with no ill effects except for claustrophobia.

"She's secure," one of the men said to the driver.

Scorpion nodded. "We head straight to Bulgaria," he said.

They had packed their gear that morning and left the rental house. Before leaving, they had spent the night and early morning cleaning the rooms. There would be no evidence to find if the authorities even wound up investigating the rental house and its occupants' unusual departure. There was nothing to connect them to the kidnapping. Scorpion expected that this event would trigger the Swiss police and a manhunt would be on for the girl. They would be looking for a white Toyota van. But when the kidnappers found a safe place to park, the van's vinyl covering would be stripped off and a dark blue van would proceed to the border.

They would travel through Austria, Slovenia, Croatia, Serbia and into Bulgaria. A faster route could take them through Germany by way of the autobahn. But Scorpion wanted nothing to do with Germany. He preferred the back roads of Austria. The trip would take nearly twenty hours; they would drive in shifts.

† † †

Dan got back to his Peugeot and left Marseille, heading east towards Italy. He was more than a day behind Scorpion. He knew now who had been surveilling the grounds and who had kidnapped Carrie. If he hurried, maybe he could close the gap and find her in time. He had no illusion as to the horror that was awaiting the young woman. Hakim as well as Gaspard had made it clear how the man worked. He was ruthless, brutal, efficient, and, ultimately, deadly.

He raced across Italy to Venice, stopping at his villa to rearm. He grabbed his M4 and his prized Sako sniper rifle, some clothes, and a lot of ammunition, threw them into the Peugeot and headed off, around the top of the Adriatic to Slovenia and on to Croatia. When he could stay awake no more, he pulled over near the Croatian border and slept for a few hours. On awaking, he drove to a restaurant, got coffee and a sausage, and drove on.

That morning, while on the road, he called Jane on the secure phone.

"You always call so early," Jane said, skipping the greeting. "It's 3 am here in DC."

Dan ignored the jibe. "I'm on my way to Bulgaria. Carrie, Evangeline's assistant has been kidnapped. They're taking her to a town called Dimitrovgrad."

"Who took her?"

"Someone called Scorpion. He exists and the jihadist network has a safe house there. Probably more than one in the country, but that's my best clue at this point."

"How...? I thought you and Warren had the place locked down."

"Can't totally lock it down. We kept Evangeline at the mansion, but Carrie volunteered to run the errands. She had two bodyguards with her. They were killed."

There was silence on the other end.

"How can I help?"

"Find out what you can about jihadist activities in Bulgaria, specifically around Dimitrovgrad. Once I get there, I need to find that house. They're in a white Toyota van with Turkish plates, but it may not be white by now."

"Meaning?"

"A vinyl wrap. It's the easiest way to change the color. The authorities will be looking for a white van, so I'm betting they have a way to change its color."

"And you're sure he's headed to Bulgaria?"

Dan paused for a moment.

"Jane, I'm not sure about anything except that Carrie's been taken and it appears to be someone who goes by the name Scorpion. An assassin who's quite brutal with his captives. An assassin who is looking for me, it seems. What I gave you is all I have to go on. If I'm wrong, Carrie dies. If I'm right, I may have a chance to save her."

"When do you think they'll get there?"

Dan thought about that for a moment. The time of the kidnapping had been estimated from the time of death of the bodyguards. That was an estimate, but all they had to go on. He guessed a twenty-hour drive and some time needed to change the van's color.

"They could arrive in the next twelve to twenty hours. I'm sorry I can't be more specific than that."

"It isn't much to work with but I'll get on it."

She hung up and Dan drove on into the graying dawn.

† † †

Scorpion finally had to pull over and let himself and his men rest. It would do no good to crash due to the driver falling asleep. He could also tend to the girl; water, a short walk, and a chance to relieve her bladder before she was put back into the box. Being nice at first, might prove helpful in getting information from her. After taking her out of the box, he untied her legs and took out her gag.

"If you try to scream, I'll gag you and put you back in the box with no relief and no water."

She nodded in understanding. "What do you want from me?"

Scorpion didn't answer as he put a water bottle to her lips. She drank deeply.

"Come," he said and opened the back of the van.

He had to help her down, since her arms were still tied behind her back. They were parked well off the road in a wooded area. There was a deep silence to the night. They were in the countryside, far from any city. Carrie shivered in the damp night chill. Scorpion led her to the edge of the woods.

"I'm going to pull your pants down. I won't touch you and I'll turn away. If I hear you try to run off, I'll catch you and you will regret it."

"You won't hurt me?"

Scorpion shook his head. After pulling her pants down, he turned his back and waited. Finally, he heard her release her bladder. When she was done, he turned back and, while looking away, pulled her pants up.

"I have to put you back in the box," Scorpion told her after they had gotten back in the van.

Carrie's eyes went wide in fright. She shook her head. "Please don't. I'll sit quietly. I won't make trouble."

Scorpion looked at her with his dark, dead eyes. She seemed business-like, dressed conservatively, something he approved of. But her fragility was showing underneath the efficient façade she presented to the world.

"It is how it must be. I can't take the chance. It's for your benefit. If something goes wrong you might get hurt."

That was a lie, but it was easily told. She was, after all, a non-believer, someone in the way of his objectives.

Chapter 14

Dimitrovgrad was located on the Maritsa River. It was a planned city built after World War II as a socialist model for the new age of communism. The economy consisted of manufacturing chemicals, cement, and asbestos mined from the surrounding natural resources. Blocks of identical housing filled parts of the city along with the requisite wide avenues and imposing government buildings. It had only a short history and was not generally on any tourist's itinerary. The safe house was a commercial building, now unused, located south of the dense part of the city and hidden in a large, wooded lot across the road from a row of abandoned warehouses.

The van pulled up, and the two men pulled Carrie from the box and led her into the house. There was an inner room, dark and insulated, containing a few chairs, a table, and a dirty mattress on the floor. Carrie was placed in a hard chair with her legs and arms tied tight. The most she could do was to wriggle a bit, but the chair, strong and heavy, did not move. The light was turned off, leaving her in the dark. The men left and locked the door.

The two assistants went to find some beds and get some sleep. Scorpion would handle what was to come. Scorpion allowed himself two hours of rest. The two hours would increase his captive's fright and make her more ready to give him what he needed.

† † †

Dan hammered down the road on his way to Bulgaria. He knew he was in a race against the clock. Scorpion would not spare Carrie whether or not she gave him any information. There was not much she could tell the assassin about Dan, which would not help her situation.

Jane was the key now. If she could get Dan a location, he had a chance. If not, he'd spend his time in a futile search of the town while Scorpion did his worst. The thought grated on him. This woman was innocent of all the issues swirling around Dan and Evangeline. He felt like a leper who infected everyone with whom he came in contact. Did he need to live the life of a monk, sequestered from everyone in normal society until he was unleashed on the enemy? It was beginning to look that way. Jane's relationship with Dan was fueled by the fact that they inhabited the same world, so he couldn't bring increased danger to her. She was already signed up and in the fight.

† † †

Scorpion entered the room after resting two hours. Carrie jerked her head upright, on high alert, at the sound of his entry. He noted how her body tensed at his purposely loud approach.

He stood in front of her, not making any noise. The woman's head turned from one side to the other, as if trying to locate his presence by sound.

"Wha...what...do you want?" Her voice was timorous, tentative.

Scorpion smiled. She evidenced a high level of anxiety. He would use it. He began to feel his blood surge, the arousal that accompanied his control over the victim before beginning a session.

"Information."

One word. Simple.

"If you promise to let me go, I'll tell you whatever I can about what you want to know. I can find my way back from wherever we are."

Scorpion's smile spread. It made his face more dangerous looking. She was totally powerless and yet trying to bargain. She had no idea of what was to come.

"What is your name?"

"Carrie."

"Who do you work for?"

"You know who. You're the one who's been watching the mansion. The one who tried to hack into our security system, aren't you?"

"Tell me her name."

"Evangeline. Evangeline Aebischer. You can find that out anywhere. We run a shelter for abused women."

"There is a man, an assassin. He has some connection to your employer, this Evangeline. I want to know who he is."

"There is a man, but I don't know anything about him. He is careful to keep himself a secret."

Scorpion took out a knife and began to cut away Carrie's top.

"What are you doing? Please don't do that. I said I'll tell you what I know."

Scorpion did answer but kept cutting away until she sat naked from the waist up with no way to cover herself. Carrie shuddered at her exposure and the sudden chill that swept over her. He picked up a glove from the table and put it on.

At the end of each finger was a razor-sharp blade a quarter of an inch long. He stepped back to Carrie who was beginning to breathe harder as her fear grew. Scorpion grabbed her upper arm with his gloved hand. Carrie screamed as the blades sank into her flesh. He held still for a moment and then pulled down, only an inch before releasing his hold. Carrie's screams increased.

Scorpion took off the glove and reached for a cauterizing powder. He sprinkled this on the wounds to staunch the blood flowing down her arm.

"This is just a taste of what you will experience if you don't cooperate.

Carrie shook her hooded head violently as she sobbed.

"Please...no. I'll tell you whatever I know. But I don't know that much."

Scorpion put on his left glove and repeated what he did to her other arm. After cauterizing her wounds, he waited for her to calm down.

"My blades may caress your face next. Would you like that?"

Carrie shook her head, not trying to speak.

"I ask again. Tell me what you know about this man."

"He visited the mansion. He and Evangeline would not speak about his identity or how they came to know each other." Her words came tumbling out in a hoarse voice as if she were trying to forestall further pain.

"What is their relationship?"

"I told you. They know each other. Well, it seems. But I don't know how it began, but I think they were close at one time."

"But you have a guess, do you not?"

His gloved hand traced across her breasts, only scratching the skin. Carrie shrieked in surprise and shock.

"I'm telling you what I know, please don't hurt me."

"Tell me more, then."

"I think the man saved her life. She's in love with him, from what I can tell. He keeps her at a distance from himself. I don't think he wants to involve her in his world."

"And what world is that?"

Carrie shook her head. "I'm sorry. I don't know. I get a sense it's a violent world."

Carrie's words only convinced Scorpion of what he suspected. The man was responsible for much of the failures of Rashid's plans.

"Is he looking for someone? An assassin perhaps? A terrorist?"

"I don't know." She paused, then said. "I think so. But he never said anything like that. Neither did Evangeline."

"So, you have no hard information for me, only guesses I can make myself. What use are you?"

"I'm trying to be useful. You don't have to hurt me. I said I'd tell you what I know. It's just that this man, Victor is what others called him, but I don't think that's his real name. He made sure I had no hard information to give anyone. Maybe he thought it would keep me safe."

"Do you think it keeps you safe?"

Scorpion smiled. Carrie hung her head and began to sob.

"Don't cry. There is nothing to cry about."

"You...you're going to kill me, aren't you?" The question came out through choking sobs.

"That depends on how I feel and what you can do to make yourself more helpful."

In a tentative voice, Carrie asked, "What do you want me to do?"

"You will call your employer, Evangeline. You will get me the name of this man who saved her life. You will find out where he is and what he is after. Then you will be useful to me."

Carrie shuddered.

Chapter 15

Dan's phone rang as he hammered through Serbia, heading towards the Bulgaria border. The A4 in Serbia changed to the E80 in Bulgaria, on its way to Sophia, the capital. It skirted to the south of the mountain range that crossed the middle of the country from east to west and contained the Central Balkan National Park.

Dan pushed the Peugeot. The risks of getting stopped were outweighed by the need to get Carrie out of Scorpion's hands. Along the way, he stopped to hide his weapons in a compartment under the false bottom in his trunk. The hiding place would not withstand a thorough search, but would get him through the border. Bulgaria was part of the EU, but not yet signed on to the visa-less Shengen agreement. But with an Italian passport, he could be passed into the country under the Shengen rules, which meant no visa required and minimum inspection, he hoped.

"What do you have?" he asked as he answered the incoming call.

"You're in luck," Jane said. "I got the addresses for two probable safe houses in Dimitrovgrad. One in the city proper, the other just south of it."

"Send them to me. I'll check the one outside the city first. That may be more promising."

"Will do." There was a pause. "Dan be careful. We don't have many assets in the country to get you out if you get into trouble."

"Understood. Don't worry about me. I can take care of myself."

He punched the off button. He was in no mood for talk about being careful.

† † †

Carrie punched the speed dial for Evangeline's number with a shaky hand. When the phone was ringing, Scorpion took it from her, put it on speaker, and held it in front of the frightened woman.

"Carrie, where are you?" Evangeline's voice evidenced her concern. "Were you kidnapped? The guards are dead. Are you alright?"

Carrie looked up at Scorpion. The thin man's face registered no hint of his thinking. He just stared back at her with his cold, dark eyes. Then he nodded slightly.

"Yes…I've been kidnapped."

"Oh my God! Where are you?"

"I…I…don't know."

"Are you safe? Did you escape?"

"No. I'm still a prisoner."

"Is someone there? Are they telling you to call me?"

"Yes." Carrie started to sob.

"I know you can hear me," Evangeline said. "It sounds like Carrie's on speaker phone. If you hurt her, you'll be sorry. I can pay you a lot of money, but you have to let her go."

Scorpion shook his head.

"I don't think he wants money," Carrie said.

"What does he want?"

"Information, I think."

"Tell me." Evangeline paused for a moment. "The police aren't here. You can speak to me. Tell me what you want. If you promise to let Carrie go, I'll cooperate."

Scorpion leaned close to Carrie. She cringed from him, but he pressed close and whispered into her ear.

"He wants to know who Victor is...his real identity."

Scorpion whispered again.

"He wants to know who he works for, what his mission is."

Again, he whispered into her ear.

"Is he coming after me? Is Victor coming to rescue me?" Carrie asked.

There was a pause on the phone. Scorpion waited.

"He will come for you, whoever you are. And when he does, he will kill you. Your only chance to survive is to release Carrie and disappear. I wouldn't wait if I were you."

Scorpion's face cracked a thin smile. He looked at Carrie and nodded for her to continue.

"Evie, I don't think he is worried. Can you tell him who Victor is?"

There was a pause. Evangeline groaned out loud. Dan had rescued her, saved her life. Now she was asked to give him up. Trade knowledge about him for Carrie's life. Why wouldn't he take her money? Her mind raced in a panic. He was looking for Dan, just as Dan was chasing him. This man, whoever he was, wanted to kill Dan. Her stomach churned with the terrible choice facing her. She took a breath. Maybe a little information would allow her to thread this terrible dilemma.

"I only know his first name. He's right, it's not Victor, it's Dan. He keeps secrets from me so he can remain safe."

Carrie looked up at Scorpion. He shook his head.

"Evie, he doesn't believe that. Please tell him what you know. He said he would release me if you cooperated."

"Did he promise you that? Did you hear him say that?"

Carrie started to cry. "Please. I don't know." Her sobs choked out her words. After a moment, she seemed to gather her composure and spoke more clearly. "He said I needed to be useful to him. I think that means he won't kill me."

"Carrie, has he hurt you?"

Between sobs, Carrie mumbled a "yes."

"Listen, you must promise to not hurt her anymore. I'll tell you everything I know if you tell me you'll release her."

Scorpion only looked impassively at Carrie without answering. Finally, he spoke. "You do not bargain. You have only to answer the questions. Then I will decide if you have helped enough for me to show mercy."

"You bastard!" Evangeline shouted over the phone. "Dan will find you and kill you. He has powerful friends. I can't tell you more."

"Can't or won't?"

Silence on the phone. Evangeline's mind raced. What else could she offer without being traitorous to Dan?

"Enough," Scorpion said. He stepped forward to end the call.

"No!" shouted Carrie.

"Don't hang up," Evangeline yelled. "I don't have any more information. You must be able to put these pieces together. You can figure the rest out from what I've told you."

"You have told me nothing."

Her words rushed out from her without her ability to stop them. They were full of the bitterness of betrayal.

"He's an assassin. He works for the U.S. government. They hunt jihadists. That's all I know!"

Scorpion ended the call and put the phone back on the table.

"You have what you need. Please let me go."

Carrie's voice was soft and pleading, as if hoping to ignite a spark of compassion.

Scorpion looked at her. She was his prize. A booty of his war with the west. Useful to a point, then not anymore. Compassion did not play a part in his calculations; only his mission and his dark desires, always lurking in the background.

He turned and left the room as Carrie sobbed, bound to the chair. In the outer room, Scorpion woke the two men.

"She is yours to do with as you wish. It is allowed. She is a bounty in our war."

The two men got up; their eyes lit with an eager lust.

The room contained an old, stained mattress on the floor. Carrie was freed from the chair only to be tied with her arms behind her and laid on the floor. Her screams and pleadings could be heard outside the room. Scorpion listened for some moments, imagining the scene being played out inside the room. Then he went outside and smoked a cigarette. He would finish his work when his men were done with their captive.

Scorpion's next steps were more calculated. The assassin, Dan, was probably employed by the CIA or some other U.S. agency. He would be coming soon. It would be best to not meet him here. Scorpion would leave a clue, a trail for him to follow. From Bulgaria, Scorpion would go across the Black Sea to Turkey and then deeper into the Middle east. Along the way, he would leave his breadcrumbs, enticing the assassin to follow. Then, when he had him on his own turf, he'd ambush him and kill him. Scorpion felt the man could not move unnoticed in the middle east. He would not be hard to find and eliminate. The hunter would turn into the hunted. The pursuer would find he'd fallen into a trap.

But first the dragon that lay deep inside of him had begun to stir. It was a familiar feeling; one he could not resist. He had long ago come to expect it and enjoy it. The excitement built, spreading from his loins throughout his body. It always startled him with its intensity. He knew he would satisfy the dragon and it would sleep for a while, only to return again and again.

The men came out to smoke their cigarettes and Scorpion stepped back into the warehouse and the room where Carrie now lay on the soiled mattress.

Chapter 16

Dan arrived in Dimitrovgrad three hours later. He parked his car just off the road at the approach to the suspected building. After retrieving his 9mm Sig and M4 from the hidden compartment, he set off through the scrub woods towards his target. He wanted to race towards the building. If Carrie were still alive, he needed her. But it wouldn't help to get shot trying to rush in and save Carrie. His body fairly trembled with pent up energy, like an attack dog straining to be unleashed, as he made himself go through the woods.

At the edge of the clearing around the building, Dan crouched behind the last of the cover and scanned the building. It was rectangular brick building with a double door and windows in the front. It looked like it could have been a general store or industrial supply shop. He could see no sign of activity. The damp ground in front of the building showed tire tracks indicating a vehicle had arrived and then departed. Were they fresh? Dan's heart sank. Was he too late?

He took a breath and ran across the open field in a crouch. He flattened himself against the wall and peeked through the window. There was no movement inside. With his M4 at ready, he gently tried the door. To his surprise, it opened. He entered in a crouch and swept the room with his carbine. Nothing. He went through the room and into another to his right. Again, it was empty, except for a table, some chairs, and cots. Cigarette butts littered the floor.

He backed out and turned to the room on his left. Opening the door, he saw her. His breath caught in his throat. Bile surged up from his stomach. He backed out and lurched through the front door to retch on the ground outside. In his days of fighting, both in the army and as an assassin, Dan had come across many scenes of death. He had become hardened to them over time. This was different. It touched him somewhere deep down in his psyche. It spoke of a depravity that he could not fathom.

After spitting out the remains of the foul taste, he turned to go back in, forcing himself against an almost overpowering reluctance. He needed to find any clues to where the murderers had gone. And he could not leave Carrie there in the state he had found her.

He slowly approached the dead girl. She was strapped to a chair. A packing crate had been placed behind the chair, projecting up over the chair back. Her head was tied upright, against the crate. The rope went through her mouth giving her a rictus grin as her lifeless eyes stared out at him. Dan felt the accusation.

"Where were you? Why couldn't you save me?"

Her body was flayed with hundreds of cuts. Blood drenched her, now disfigured, body. A pool of blood collected between her thighs. Dan fought down a new onslaught from his stomach. He gently cut her bonds, laid her on the mattress, and closed her eyes. Then he went to find a cloth to cover her. Returning, he spread a dirty tablecloth over her desecrated form and stood back.

"I'm sorry, Carrie. You were never meant to be a part of this darkness. You only wanted to help others. You found someone to latch onto, someone who had a passion you shared. Someone you believed in. Then I showed up and ruined everything."

He paused to choke back growing sobs.

"And I couldn't save you."

He turned to go back outside. He ran through the woods to his car and brought it to the building. He took a can of gasoline, which he always carried with him, from the trunk, and went back inside.

Evangeline can never see this. She can never know how Carrie suffered and was abused. Dan knew Evangeline would blame herself for Carrie's death. It would be bad enough without knowing how she died.

Inside, he picked up her body, covered with the cloth, and took her into the other room. He laid her on the table.

"I'll find them, Carrie. I'll avenge your death. I pursue them to the ends of the earth and I'll not stop until the man who did this is dead with birds picking at his flesh."

He splashed the gasoline around the table, over Carrie's body and around the room. With a last look he lit a match and threw it under the table. The flames quickly arose, covering the table and the body. When the walls caught fire, Dan turned to go. Out in the main room he spotted a leaflet on the floor. He picked it up. It was for a ferry service that departed from the port of Burgas to Istanbul and Ereğli, further along the Turkish coast of the Black Sea.

The destination of Ereğli was marked in pencil.

This is too easy. Does he want me to follow him?

Dan suspected he was probably being led into a trap. But that gave him the trail to follow. He smiled a thin, cruel smile. *So be it. I'll follow, but you will find more than you expect when we come face to face.*

The blaze was now growing. Soon the authorities would be coming. It was time to go. Dan got back into his Peugeot and started down the dirt drive. He headed to the port. He would be at least one ferry trip behind his quarry, but it seemed as though they would leave him clues to follow. He was happy to oblige them in their arrogance.

Chapter 17

The ferry was due to depart in two hours. The earlier one had left just after noon. This one would arrive in the night after a six-hour ferry trip. They would stop in Istanbul, but being already on board, he would have no interaction with Turkish authorities.

They have a good head start, but I'm betting they'll leave me clues. Even if they don't, I'll track them down. Dan's thoughts were bold, but in the back of his mind, he knew he was at a severe disadvantage. He was not a Middle east expert. Help might be needed along the way.

Once on the ferry, Dan placed a call to Jane before they were out of cell range.

"It's the Scorpion. We can be sure of that. They probably wanted to find out about me," he said after Jane answered.

"Were you in time to rescue her?"

Dan muttered, "I was too late."

"Oh no." Jane said. Her voice evidenced her fear. This killing could derail all that Aebischer's daughter had worked to create. "What will you tell Evangeline?"

"He never meant to let her live. You know that. He couldn't. No matter how much information she gave him."

"Could she tell them much about you?"

"No. I kept her completely out of the loop. And Evangeline most likely didn't tell her anything. She did the right thing. But even if Carrie knew a lot, he still would have killed her." He paused and then continued in a choking voice. "It's because of me. The fact that I'm involved with Evangeline, Carrie was involved with Evangeline so she became the target."

"Dan, it's not your fault."

"So, you say. But he's after me. He has killed someone close to Evangeline because of me."

"You can't think like that."

"I don't know how else to think about it." He paused for a moment. "But I'll avenge her death."

"Can you find him? Where did he go?"

"He's headed into Turkey. Probably from there farther into the Middle east. I can follow. I think he's leaving clues. He wants me to follow him."

"Why would he want that?"

"To lure me into a trap. He's out to kill me, right?"

"And you're going to walk into his trap?"

"That's the only way to find him."

"That doesn't sound like a good idea to me."

"Jane, there's no other way. If he's arrogant enough to lead me to him, I'll take advantage of that and use it to my benefit."

"At least let me help."

"How can you do that?"

"I have some connections with Israeli intelligence. You are not an expert in that part of the world. I want to connect you with someone who can help."

"I'm banking on the clues the Scorpion is leaving behind."

"That may be, but let me get someone to help you navigate along the way. It will increase your chances of turning the tables on this Scorpion."

Dan sighed. "Okay. That makes sense. Will you tell Evangeline for me? I don't think I can do that. Tell her the kidnapper would never have let her live, no matter how much or how little she told him. Tell her I'm going after him and will avenge Carrie's death."

"What about her body?"

"That's the hard part. She was so disfigured, I cremated her. I burned down the building where I found her."

"Oh my God."

"Yeah. It was not pretty."

"What do I tell Evangeline?"

"Tell her I found Carrie. She seemed to have died quickly, but the building she was in was torched and I barely got out alive...or something like that. Hell, I don't know. I've got to hang up now."

"I'll tell her. I'll get back to you after I contact the Israelis."

Dan ended the call and stared out over the rail of the ferry. What kind of life he was living? He was a danger to those around him. All but Jane it seemed. The feeling of being like a leper came over him and his stomach heaved. He swallowed the bile, not giving in to throwing up out in public.

Still, I helped Evangeline in the end. A part of him was trying to put things in perspective. If he lost perspective, he feared he might go crazy.

He would chafe against inaction for the next five hours while waiting to dock at Ereğli.

Please leave me a clue, you arrogant son of a bitch.

† † †

Jane made arrangements with her boss, Henry, for a flight to Israel via Switzerland. She didn't want to give Evangeline the sad news over the phone, but in person. When she got to the mansion, Evangeline met her at the door. She looked anxious and disheveled as if from lack of sleep and worry.

"I don't think you are here to bring me good news," she said after greeting Jane.

Evangeline led her through the large house and into her private office. She dealt with the niceties that hospitality required, getting something for Jane to drink, inquiring as to whether she was hungry, then sat down with a serious look on her face.

"You must be here to tell me about Carrie. Let me hear it. If she were safe, I assume she would be with you…but she's not. Should I expect to hear the worst?"

Jane nodded slightly.

Evangeline stifled a cry and waited.

"Dan found her. It was this figure called Scorpion who took her. He wanted information on you, and on Dan."

"I know. He made her call me." Evangeline's voice expressed her bitterness. She looked down at her desk. "She couldn't tell him anything and I couldn't add much to help her." She looked up at Jane with tears in her eyes. "At that moment, I realized Carrie might die."

Jane looked at Evangeline. Her years of running agents had given her a keen sense of reading people and when they were hiding something or not telling the truth. Evangeline was devastated, clearly, but there was something off in her inflection when she talked about the phone conversation.

"He killed her. Before Dan arrived," Jane said.

"Is he bringing her back here?" Evangeline could not use the word "body". It seemed too cold.

Jane shook her head. "When Dan arrived, a fire had been started, probably to conceal the man's murder of Carrie. Dan found her tied down. She had been shot, once and died quickly. He couldn't get her free before the fire overcame him and he had to retreat."

Evangeline looked at Jane with a mix of horror and anger in her face. "Are you saying that she was burned? There's nothing left of her?"

"It was an intense fire. The building was an old paint factory."

Jane was stunned at how easily the lie she had crafted flowed from her lips. She kept reminding herself this was to protect Evangeline. Carrie, her closest friend, trusted assistant was gone and knowing the full horror of what she had been subjected to would only harm her more deeply. As it was, Jane understood that Evangeline might take her loss, her anger, out on Dan…and her as Dan's proxy.

Evangeline got up and went to a window overlooking the manicured grounds. Jane heard her choking down sobs. Finally, she turned, her face blazing with anger and flooded with tears.

"It's you! And him. Your war on terrorists. It consumes everyone around you. It almost consumed me. Now it's taken the one closest to me. You two are death to everyone who comes close to you." Her voice was now rising.

Jane said nothing. There was nothing to say, even if Evangeline's accusations were unfair. They *were* a danger to everyone around them. People who didn't sign up for the danger but got swept up into it anyway. At that moment, she realized how toxic she must seem to Evangeline.

"I'll go now. I didn't want to let you know over the phone." She paused for a moment. "Out of respect for Carrie, and you."

"Yes. You go now. Go back to your cat and mouse games. But know how much they hurt everyone you touch."

Chapter 18

Scorpion and his men drove off the ferry. Once off the boat, they parked the van and went into a coffee shop near the docks. He was in no hurry. If the assassin was close on his trail, he would have to wait for the later ferry which gave Scorpion at least a three-hour head start, maybe more.

The men sat and drank their dark coffee in silence, each one lost in his own thoughts. For Scorpion it was time to separate from his companions. They were Turkish and, after he paid them, they would head back to their home towns and wait for other opportunities to help in the fight against western interests, of course, always with substantial payment.

He reached into his jacket inner pocket and took out three envelopes of money he had assembled earlier. He handed each man an envelope and thanked them. They did not open them but stuffed them in their pockets. Sensing this was a sign for them to go, the men stood.

"*Allah Ma'ak*" God be with you, one of them said.

"*Walden Ma'ak*" And also with you, Scorpion replied.

The men nodded and left the table. Scorpion continued to sit, trying to figure out how to leave a sign for his pursuer to follow without being too obvious. It wouldn't do to let the assassin know he wanted him to follow. Still, the man might just proceed even if he knew he was being lured along. Scorpion had determined that he should not underestimate a man who could assassinate Jabbar under the protection of a full townhouse of supporters, and then disappear so completely as to leave the superstitious men thinking of jinn.

He finally settled on asking too many questions to too many people. The assassin would be talking to dock hands and others who gathered around the ferry terminal in an attempt to learn where Scorpion might have gone. He would not disappoint him.

He spent the next half hour asking as many people as he could about the best way to get to Yemen by car. Most did not know, but a few directed him to take the road south to Ankara and then pick up O21 which headed towards the Mediterranean and then to Syria and Lebanon. Scorpion knew the route he would take, but wanted his pursuer to know it as well. He made multiple contacts with people who gave him the same advice which he voiced agreement with.

As he was preparing to leave, he sensed someone was looking at him. No, it was more than that. It was as if someone was trying to look *into* him. He cast his black eyes around, examining the faces in the crowd. His gaze stopped on a young man, just a teenaged boy, who locked eyes with him before quickly looking away. That quick gaze was unlike anything Scorpion had felt before. It seemed to penetrate him. When the boy looked away, the feeling stopped.

He felt exposed, found out. It was disquieting. He started for the young man who turned and quickly headed into the more crowded part of the market area. Scorpion increased his pace. He wanted to catch up with this young boy and find out what was going on. He had no reservations about adding him to his casualty list. The young man dashed into an alley and was quickly lost to sight. Scorpion followed him in, but could not see where the boy went. He ventured down the alley and checked the side alleys. Nothing. He tried some of the doors opening into the alley with the same success.

After trying several locked doors, he finally forced himself to give up and return to the market area. *What was that?* He had never felt such a sensation before; the feeling of someone seeing beneath your exterior. Scorpion shook his head. It was uncomfortable, but it didn't matter. He had to go now. His plan was not to let his pursuer catch him before he had set his trap. He needed to be on the road. The assassin walked back to the van and headed south to Ankara.

† † †

When the boat docked in Ereğli, Dan tried to talk to the dock hands. In broken English one of them said that a blue Toyota van with three men departed from the earlier ferry. As Dan had suspected, they had managed to change the color, probably by stripping off a white vinyl wrapping.

He stood by his Peugeot and looked around. With no clue, he had no way to guess which direction the Scorpion would go. There was the coast road that ran west towards Istanbul and east towards Azerbaijan and the Caspian Sea. In addition, there were multiple roads going south, away from the sea, towards Iran, Iraq, and Syria. The assassin would probably head south, but in what country did Scorpion have safe haven?

Dan went over the connections in his mind. Scorpion was most likely funded by the rich Saudi who had used

Aebischer. That is how he managed to establish the connection to Evangeline. With that fact, Dan ruled out Iran, which was mostly Shiite. The rich Saudi would be Sunni and have nothing to do with Shiites if possible. That fact, however, left pretty much all the rest of the Middle-East in play.

Dan continued to ask around the dock area, inquiring about anyone asking directions or whether they saw a blue van heading out of town. He finally got two hits from some men who related that someone, not a Turk, had asked how to get to Yemen by road. Both men said they had advised going to Ankara and then on to the Mediterranean coast, all in a southerly direction. One of the men had seen the same man depart in a blue van.

Dan digested the news. *He's leaving a trail. He didn't have to ask directions*. Still, he was happy to follow. A trap would be laid for him. It was going to be up to Dan to not fall into it but rather turn the Scorpion's trap into his own.

He started back to his car when he caught the gaze of a young boy across the square. The boy had the look; the piercing gaze that grabbed you and looked into you. *A Watcher? So young?* Dan returned his gaze and the boy gave him a nod and turned towards an alley. Dan followed, having long since lost his concern of being led into a trap by these strange people he encountered.

The boy went down the alley, occasionally looking back over his shoulder to make sure Dan was following. He stopped at a small door and with a last glance, went inside. Dan arrived at the door and opened it. He stepped inside and stopped to let his eyes adjust to the dim light after the sun-drenched brightness of the market area.

The boy was standing in the far corner of the room next to an old woman seated at a table. She looked to be quite ancient and frail, but her eyes had the sharp, penetrating gaze Dan had come to recognize. *He inherited his gift from this woman?*

The woman motioned for Dan to approach and sit at the table. Her hands were gnarled and twisted by arthritis. *"Hoşgeldiniz,"* she said in Turkish.

Dan nodded. He didn't speak a word of Turkish and wondered how he was going to learn anything from this old Watcher, if there was anything to learn. He turned to the boy standing next to the woman with an expectant look on his face.

"My *Ananne*, my Grandmother, says 'welcome'. She would like you to sit," the boy said. "My name is Hasim. I will try to translate for her."

Dan sat at the table and the old woman gave him a cracked smile. Another, younger woman, emerged from a back room with a pot and cups. She poured strong Turkish coffee in the small cups and offered one to Dan. Then she departed.

The old woman grasped the boy's arm and began to speak urgently to him. He nodded, looking directly at her with his intense stare. After a moment he spoke and she paused. The boy turned to Dan.

"*Ananne* says she knows who you are and why you are here. She said to tell you that I have her gift, but that I am young still. The man you seek is very dark and dangerous. I almost got caught by him. He noticed me, sensed me. *Ananne* says I was foolish to let myself be discovered."

Dan looked at the boy. He was so young yet caught by his gift in a dangerous game. He sighed. "I know the man I chase is headed to Yemen. He seems to want me to follow him. How can you help?"

The boy looked at him with grave eyes. "I cannot, but *Ananne* can."

Now the grandmother spoke again to the boy. After a few moments he turned back to Dan.

"She understands you know where he is going. But she gives warning to not let your anger—"

Dan gave the boy a sharp look.

"Yes, she can see your anger. She told me so. It can make you careless. The dark man counts on it."

"Still, I have to follow him in order to rid the world of him."

The boy nodded. "*Ananne* says that is so. She says you must accept help that is coming. She sees much danger and that you will be faced with a terrible choice."

"And what is that?"

The boy shook his head. "She will not say. It must be shown to you at the right time. But it will test your spirit."

"Too many riddles." Dan's voice began to rise. He was annoyed at being delayed and although Watchers had helped him over the years, this encounter seemed futile.

The old woman, as if understanding Dan's words, or, more likely, sensing his frustration and dismissiveness, spoke up in a harsh voice. Her eyes penetrated into Dan.

"She says you must rid yourself of *küçümsemek*. The boy paused for a moment. "I don't know the word for it. my English is limited. It is like, not believing…or not taking something seriously."

At that moment the other woman came into the room. "It means contempt. My mother accuses you of having contempt for her, for all Watchers."

Dan looked at her. She must have been listening at the door. He could sense she didn't have the gift. Maybe it had skipped a generation; gone from Grandmother to Grandson.

"I don't have contempt, but I am angry and frustrated. Your mother offers only vague cautions. I already know how dangerous it is to follow a killer into his lair. But you didn't see what he did to a young woman and how he continues to threaten me and those around me."

The mother smiled sadly. "Mother told me. She could see. She can also see your anger endangers you and those who may help you." She paused and gave him a direct look. "And you need help."

With that, the woman strode across the floor and gathered up the cups. She spoke to the old woman quickly in Turkish. The boy helped his grandmother stand. Dan could see the discussion was over. The old woman wagged her finger at him and spoke. Dan just gave her a slight bow and turned to go. He didn't need any translation.

Outside, the bright sun staggered him for a moment. He stood there to adjust to the light. The boy came out and stopped next to him.

"If I can help you before you go, *Ananne* says I must."

Dan looked at the young man. He came up to his shoulder with a slight, but strong build. He would be different from the other Watchers when he grew up. Maybe more of a warrior like Tlayolotl, the shaman he had met in Mexico.

"I need to store my car for some time and to purchase a better vehicle for bad roads."

"I can help with that. I will take you to my uncle."

Chapter 19

Jane was met with a car after landing at the Ben Gurion International Airport. The driver helped her through diplomatic security and, after loaded her overnight bag, drove off, not to Mossad headquarters, but north to a nondescript office building just off Kvish Hahof. The modest building was fully rented out by the Israeli government through a shell company and was where the offices of METSADA were located. This was the darker operational part of Mossad and kept at arm's length from the main agency. It was the department that handled assassinations and sabotage: attacking the enemy in a clandestine manner.

She was led into a simple office on the third floor where her old friend, Eitan Malkah waited. Eitan had worked with Jane when she was a field agent. They had run some operations together and gotten into and out of some serious jams.

"Welcome to Tel Aviv," Eitan said with a board smile as he came around the desk to shake hands with Jane and give her a kiss on the cheek.

He was in his late forties, short at five foot nine inches but with broad shoulders indicating a powerful build.

"You said it was urgent and flew here on short notice. What is so important that it must be hurried? I don't have anything on my radar. Have I missed something?"

Jane smiled and glanced at the chair across from the desk.

"Forgive me, do sit down. Can I get you some tea or coffee? I forget my manners."

"Coffee would be nice. And then you must take me to dinner later. I'm starving."

"But of course. However, I will have to let my wife know I'm entertaining a beautiful spy from the U.S. She will be jealous, but I made a promise to only keep state secrets from her."

"You're married now. Good for you."

He smiled as he poured some coffee from a pot on the side of the room and brought the cup to Jane.

"I do hope this is not at the level of a state secret, or worse, emergency."

Jane sipped her coffee. "No, it's not a state emergency. It is just my small section's emergency."

Eitan sat down at his desk. "I'm listening…all ears as you say."

Jane tried to disguise a frown at the coffee. It was overheated and burned after hours on the hot plate. Still, it was what she needed for the moment. *Better will come with dinner*, she thought.

"I have an operative. He's so far undercover that I can't disclose him to you, or anyone. But he needs help."

She put up her hand before Eitan could ask the obvious question. "I know. How do you help someone who can't be identified? We'll figure that out later. But for now, I must keep him anonymous.

"His mission is to go after terrorists. The ones you like to eliminate, the ones both or our countries want to eliminate, but nobody wants to own up to doing it."

Eitan nodded in understanding. "Tell me what you need."

"My agent is pursuing someone named Scorpion. Have you heard of him?"

Eitan nodded.

"We don't know what he looks like," Jane said. "He's trying to find my agent who's been quite successful in his mission. So much so that he has come on the terrorist's radar. We think his financier is a rich Saudi named Rashid al-Din Said but we're not sure."

"We live in a world of 'not sure.' It is a rare victory to be certain about something and able to act on it with full confidence. But how can I help?"

"This Scorpion has disappeared into the Middle-East. He's leaving clues and we think he wants my agent to follow so he can lay a trap for him." Jane leaned forward; her face alight with intensity. "I need someone to partner with my agent. Someone who knows the region and can help find and take down this man."

Eitan looked thoughtful. He leaned back in his chair. "A joint U.S-Israeli operation can only be done at the highest levels, higher than you or I."

Jane stared at the man. She knew him well, his courage and his willingness to operate on the fringes of what his assignment called for. "Let's not think of it as a joint operation of our two countries. Let's think of it as one undercover department helping another out."

Eitan got up. "You look tired. And you said you were hungry. A tired and hungry woman is to be feared, I think. Let's go somewhere to talk further."

Jane smiled and got up. The two left and got into Eitan's car.

"How are things with you and the department?" Jane asked over coffee after they had finished a very satisfying dinner. Both had refrained from talking about Jane's request. She, to consume a large dinner of beef moussaka with matbucha, a dish of ground beef over chopped bell peppers and tomatoes. It was a comfort dish for Jane. They were sitting in a corner of a cozy restaurant which Eitan had chosen for its privacy.

He shrugged his shoulders. "It's the same as it's always been. We're called upon to do the dirty work, but no one wants to associate with us when it's not necessary."

"For us as well. Maybe the same everywhere."

"Except in Russia. I think they embrace the dark side of espionage more readily than do our two countries."

"I worry about our new administration. Right now, they're on a witch hunt for past sins. Everyone is keeping their heads down. My boss, Henry, is making us stay very quiet."

"But not so quiet as to preclude flying over here to ask for my help."

Jane smiled. "Guilty. Operations don't stop just because the politics of the home office dictate hiding out for a while. The bad guys don't stop while we call a time out." She leaned forward; her eyes now lit with intensity. "Eitan, we go back some ways. We have shared a lot of adventures and misadventures. I really need your help now. My best agent is chasing this assassin into his home territory and he'll be out of reach of any support I can give him." She reached across the table and put her hand on Eitan's arm. "I can't lose him."

Eitan's face betrayed his reluctance. "I just can't put any of my agents on this. My directorate boss would have my head." He continued with a sad expression. "We're all getting older. I'm nearing retirement. I've got to think about my family. They suffered so I could be in this fight." He looked out of the window for a moment. "Many in Israel have suffered to be in this fight...and not of their own choosing."

He turned back to Jane. "But now, I don't want to screw things up in my last years and destroy what I've built up, take away the small security I can give my family as my career closes out."

Jane reflected Eitan's sad expression. "I understand your feelings. But I can't help thinking there's got to be a way. You and I have had to work around the bureaucracy for our entire careers. Can't we figure out how to do it again? For my sake? You've at least got a family. I gave that up to be in this fight."

Eitan gave her a sharp look. "Don't try to make me feel guilty at having a life outside of Mossad. You made a choice."

"I'm not. I didn't mean that to be a rebuke. It's just that this is all I have. So maybe I obsess with it more than most. That's not a bad thing in the end. I like to think it makes me and my agents more effective. I'm just asking you to find a way, outside of normal channels, if that path isn't available, to get me some help for my agent. Isn't killing this Scorpion a worthy goal? If you can make that happen, it could be an additional feather in your cap, a trophy for your career."

Eitan smiled. "We're not allowed to have trophies. Only private recognitions, private moments of victory. You know that. And what if it goes wrong? Who gets sacrificed?"

Jane met his gaze. "That is where your ingenuity comes in. To shield yourself in case of that event."

Eitan ran his hand through his thinning hair as he looked thoughtfully out of the window again.

Jane waited.

"I still have some contacts with some retired operatives. They're a little older, but probably still mission-capable. I could reach out to them. They're out of the system, so it wouldn't involve Mossad or METSADA…"

"I'll take anything you can give me."

"I can't order them to go. It would have to be voluntary, and they may not want to do it." He turned back to Jane. "One gets comfortable when one retires out of the fight. The small comforts and joys of domesticity are insidious in their nature. They creep up on you and work their way inside of you until you are taken by them. The thought of going back out into the field, into the fight, becomes too large a step to take."

"Maybe you can find someone who still chafes under domesticity. This could be the adventure of a lifetime."

"Indeed. It could end one's lifetime."

Chapter 20

Dan drove through the town with the boy guiding them. About a mile outside of the center, they pulled up in front of a workshop with its front open to the street. Up and down the road were several shops that offered repairs on cars, trucks, and motorcycles.

"My uncle owns this shop. He repairs cars and he sells them. Maybe he has something for you."

The boy introduced Dan to his uncle, Çetin. He was a large, thick man with beefy hands, toughened by years of working with engines. Grease was ground into his palms and under his nails. His smile brightened after the boy introduced Dan as a friend of his grandmother, Çetin's mother.

Dan explained to Hasim what he needed and the boy spoke to his uncle. The man's smile broadened at the prospect of doing business with what he assumed was a rich westerner. He showed Dan an older Toyota Land Cruiser that had seen better days. Still, it had the ground clearance Dan needed and the tough, if uncomfortable, suspension that could withstand bad roads.

After a short negotiation of the price and how much it would cost Dan to store his much-modified Peugeot, Dan brought up the delicate subject of storing his arms in a secret compartment. Could Çetin make something for him?

During the discussion, the boy remained calm and expressionless. *Did he already know about the weapons? He certainly knew about my mission.* It didn't matter. The uncle was part of the family and would not report anything to the authorities.

Çetin showed Dan where he could build a compartment. It would be inside of the gas tank. It would not be seen from above or below. The capacity of the gas tank, however, would suffer, but only Dan would be aware of that fact. To load or unload the compartment, the tank would have to be lowered. That was a time-consuming job, but worth the effort to keep his cargo from border inspectors. The discovery of his weapons would land him in prison with a long interrogation process to determine what he was up to.

† † †

The next day Eitan called Jane. "I've rounded up three possible candidates for your mission. They know each other, if only by reputation. They've agreed to meet with us tonight to hear what you have to say."

Jane thanked Eitan and hung up. Then she called Dan.

"Where are you?" She asked when Dan answered.

"Turkey. I've run into a Watcher. She has a grandson who also has the gift. I'm storing my Peugeot and switching to an old Land Cruiser. I think it will be better suited for where I'm going…Yemen."

"Where in Yemen?"

"Don't know. I'm banking on Scorpion leaving me clues along the way."

"Well, I may have some help for you. You might need to come to Israel."

"I don't need help. And, besides, how do I get to Israel by land? I've got to go through either Syria or Iraq."

Jane paused for a moment. "Yeah, that's a problem. I'll know more after tonight. Can you stay put for a while?"

"I'm planning to leave for Ankara, first thing tomorrow."

"Wait for my call."

They met in the nondescript office building that was rented by a front company for Mossad. The room had an attached bathroom. There were no windows and it was sound proofed for secure conversations safe from prying electronics. The men filtered in singly. There were three of them. They all had the look of being hardened by years in conflict. They took seats. One of the men went to the side board and poured himself a glass of whiskey.

Eitan introduced Jane who proceeded to outline the situation she faced. When she was done, one of the men stood up. He was portly; an athletic figure gone soft over time.

"Eitan, you know I'd help you out with any trouble you're in, but this is not your trouble and not our fight." He spoke in Hebrew. "I'm not going to run off on some crazy mission to Yemen with no support, to kill someone who has remained beyond our grasp for so long. I've settled now. I have grandchildren. That is my life now. Tending my garden, enjoying my grandchildren and my sons and daughters. I don't need this anymore."

He paused for a moment.

"If you were in need, you'd get my help. But not to help a friend of yours. This is her problem, not yours and I won't make it mine."

"I understand, Lev. I told Ms. Tanner this was purely voluntary."

Lev gave a quiet snort and turned for the door. "You should not take this on. It will come back to bite you."

"And you, Joel?" Eitan asked after Lev had departed.

The second man, Joel, sat and shook his head. He was dressed in an old suit with its worn jacket. His hair was thinning on top and his hands were gnarled and bent. "I don't have the stamina for it. What you ask is a young man's game. I'm too old, too many wounds suffered along the way. I might be tempted if my body were stronger, but, sadly, it is not."

He looked sadly down at the floor.

"I spend my days drinking coffee and more with old men who only talk about the past. That's not who I want to be, but where I'm stuck. My wife is happy, at least."

"Being retired bores you?" Jane ventured a guess.

Joel looked up at her. "Yes. But what else can I do? Be a clerk in a store? Guide tourists around the holy sites? Hell, they know more about them than I do." He spread his hands out. "But this. This is too much for me, even though it promises to be a great adventure. I would be a liability, not a help."

He stood up as well. "Eitan, why do you bring me out and tempt me? You are being cruel."

"Joel, my friend," Eitan said. "I didn't know you were in bad shape. I never would have bothered you." He walked over and embraced the old warrior.

"Give my best to your wife and let's have dinner together soon. It's been too long."

Joel smiled. "At least our stories wouldn't be so boring."

When he closed the door, Eitan and Jane turned to the last man in the room. He had gotten up and was at the sideboard pouring himself another drink. He was dressed in worn jeans, a tattered coat over an old, worn dress shirt. He looked old and worn, but he still moved with some authority and power. His face was covered with a few day's stubble as if shaving was something he didn't like doing. His hair was full and unkempt but his eyes burned with intensity when Jane looked at him.

"This is Uri Dayan," Eitan said by way of introduction. "Uri, what do you think?" he asked.

"Last man standing," Uri said. He grinned and took a drink from his glass. "Civilian life hasn't worked too well for me, as you can probably see." He brushed his free hand over his clothes.

"Are you in any shape to go on such a mission?" Eitan asked.

Uri shrugged. "Would it make any difference? Looks like you're at the bottom of the barrel."

"But the others knew they'd be liabilities if they went," Jane said. "They understood that fact and deselected themselves."

"Are you deselecting me? I thought you were desperate for help," Uri replied glaring at her.

"I can keep looking," Eitan said. "If we know where Scorpion is going, we don't have to rush...do we?" He turned to Jane as he spoke.

Jane shook her head. "I don't know. My agent said he'd wait until morning, but he's anxious to continue on the trail."

"If what you say is true, the trail will be there and Scorpion will be gladly waiting at the other end of it. Perhaps letting him wait will be to an advantage."

"So, are you deselecting yourself?" Jane asked. "We should take our time and keep looking?"

"*S'Emek!*" Uri swore. "I'm the best you'll find. Better than the new guys that Eitan won't let you use. I've got more experience operating outside of Israel than any of them. It's all about intifada and Hamas, striking inside our country now. We've started to ignore the more distant threat…too many close-up ones."

He took another swig of his whiskey.

"You may be the best, but can you operate in your condition?" Jane asked.

Uri glared at her. "My condition?" He raised his glass and took another long pull. "I can outperform those virgins after a bottle of this." He turned to Eitan. "That's good whiskey. I'm glad to see you still spend money where it is important."

Eitan gave him a weak smile in return but said nothing. Jane looked at him as if to say, "Is this the best you can dredge up?"

"I'm hungry," Uri declared. "Let's get some food. Maybe this CIA agent can afford to buy us dinner, Eitan? That's the least she can do after dragging me out to this meeting and then insulting me."

"No one is insulting you, Uri," Eitan said. "She is properly worried about your age and what she sees as heavy drinking. This mission will be hard and dangerous."

"Have I always been a hard drinker?" Uri asked.

Eitan smile and nodded.

"Good. At least we have established that. Now let's get something to eat. And not sidewalk vendor food."

Eitan threw up his hands and got up. "Jane, you're on for dinner tonight. I hope you can handle the bill."

Uri gave Jane an evil smile. "He knows me too well."

The three headed for the door.

Chapter 21

At dinner, Uri ordered drinks for everyone along with some expensive Israeli wine—two bottles of Gva'ot "Masada", a Bordeaux-style dry red. Dinner was at the appropriately named "A Place For Meat" located a mile outside of the old city in Tel Aviv. It was a European style steakhouse with discrete settings.

Uri immediately took control despite his disheveled appearance. He had the waiter prescribe a multi-course dinner, climaxing with a sectioned T-Bone steak done to perfection. Despite herself, Jane enjoyed the meal even though she knew Uri was making it more expensive than needed. Maybe to make a point to her.

After dinner and a layered cake with cream filling and chocolate icing, which no one but Uri could eat, he ordered a round of brandies and coffee. When served, Uri sat back and finally spoke of Jane's mission.

"I may look old and washed up. And maybe I am, but I'm still the best choice, better, as I said, than the young guns Eitan now shepherds. Unlike Lev and Joel, I'm neither burdened with family nor too broken down. My wife left me years ago and took our two kids with her. Apparently, I am an embarrassment to them. You worry about my drinking? What the hell else can I do? Joel said it correctly.

He sits around with old men who tell boring stories about their past."

Uri took a sip of his brandy.

"I'd rather drink."

"But can you let it go? As far as the mission is concerned?" Jane asked.

Uri snorted. "Give me some action, give me the proper tools, I can let it go and never miss it." He turned to wink at Eitan, "Well, maybe just a little."

"Do you think this will rehabilitate you? With your wife and family?"

Uri glared at her. "I don't do it for that and you, of all people should know, this work doesn't get put on the evening news. There'll be no parades or medals. We don't get that. Just a private thank you and then we're sent out again…or put out to pasture."

"But it's what we choose," Eitan said.

"True," Uri replied. "But some required more convincing than others."

"And some needed this more than others," Eitan said.

Jane leaned back. She had a decision to make and she didn't have many options. Uri seemed to be a loose cannon, maybe unreliable, but with surprising self-confidence and, since the mission loomed before him, renewed energy, from what she had first observed in the office.

Dan needed help. She had no choice.

"Uri Dayan, you're hired," she said to both men at the table.

Uri grinned. Eitan looked concerned.

"Great. Now we start planning. You must tell me about this super-agent who is so secret we cannot speak his name. I think his name would be a good place to start."

"We can go back to the meeting room, "Eitan said. "Details should not be talked about in a public place." He turned to Jane. "I apologize for the expense of the meal. Uri can get carried away sometimes."

"I'm like a high-priced whore. I don't come cheap. You have to be able to afford me to enjoy my services. Speaking of which, how much does this adventure pay?" This last was said as they were getting up from the table.

Back in the meeting room, Jane went over who Dan was and how effective he had been taking out the terrorists.

"The way you describe him, he seems to be an accomplished killer. I like him already. He kills from a distance. Not my skill. I did most of my work up close. But I like the fact that he's loyal and not squeamish about his work.

He turned to Eitan, "We'll need a good sniper rifle. One that fits his skill level. We'll also need tactical weapons as well, the Tavor 7 with the 20" barrel.

"What is Dan's favorite sniper rifle?"

"A Sako TRG 42 in .338 configuration. He said one of the saddest things he experienced after one mission was having to dump that rifle in a lake in Africa."

"Getting sad over a rifle? That's a man after my own heart."

Uri turned to Eitan. "We must figure out where in Yemen this guy's going. It's a rugged country and I don't want to go hiking around it during a civil war asking questions. What can you do?"

Eitan shrugged. "Until now, we really didn't have any idea where this guy was based. Now that we know he comes from Yemen, I can ask Head of Services to do some research on for us."

"Maybe they can help," Uri said. "But maybe they will take a month to come up with something. I said we shouldn't hurry, but a month is too long. Our assassin expects his pursuer to show up within days. A month and he will relocate, if only as a precaution. He may think we're doing exactly what we're going to do. Then we're back to square one and he's still out there."

He turned back to Jane. "I don't think your man will like having to keep looking over his shoulder."

Eitan took out his phone. "I'll call the XO office and start the process."

"Make sure they give it a priority. If we can locate him, it'll give us a major tactical advantage."

Uri was now pacing around the room, like a caged animal. As the plans were discussed, Jane could see his enthusiasm and energy grow. Despite a large dinner and enough alcohol to put a horse to sleep, he was now a man charged up. *The mission is revitalizing him*. Her reservations began to ease somewhat.

"We need to get your man here," Uri said to her.

"He's picked up an old Toyota Land Cruiser," Jane said. "He's planning to drive to Yemen."

"He's crazy. Where are his weapons? How will he get through Syria or Iraq? He has no cover story."

"He has a hidden compartment for the weapons. He just can't abandon them."

Uri turned to Eitan. "Tell her. This guy has to come here first. Then we can set things up properly. He can store the damn Toyota if it means so much to him."

"I think Uri is correct," Eitan said. "Your man should go to Ankara, by bus, and get a flight to Tel Aviv."

"What the hell is his name? I don't want to keep talking about 'this guy' or 'your guy'," Uri said.

"It's Dan Stone. But he'll be using Victor James. He has a full set of documents for that cover."

"We'll get our covers coordinated," Uri said. "I'm going to go as an Arab fixer. You still have those documents?"

Eitan nodded.

"Good. Get them assembled. I'll be escorting this Victor who's now a journalist making a documentary on the situation in Yemen and other hot spots in the Middle-East. If we do wind up driving, that'll get us into and through Iraq."

"You're not planning on driving all the way to Yemen, are you?" Jane asked.

"I'm not planning anything yet. Just trying to set the parameters of the game. How we'll get to Yemen is still to be decided, depending on what the boys in Research can come up with."

"Eitan," he shouted as Eitan was heading to the door to make his call, "can you get a satellite diverted to fly over wherever they come up with?"

Eitan smiled at Uri. "One step at a time." And stepped out of the room to make his call.

Chapter 22

Scorpion drove south, hoping that he had made enough impression in Ereğli that his pursuer, whether a single person or a group, would learn where he was headed. Now he had to just make another fuss at the border with Syria. Something that wouldn't get him thrown in jail, but that would be remembered if another traveler came along asking about anyone headed for Yemen.

With no traffic problems, it would be about four hours from the port to Ankara. He would stop there, refuel, and eat. The city was too large to ensure a clue would be found, so he would just have to rely on those chasing him to keep heading south. He would cross into Syria just below the town of Kilis. At the long border checkpoint that forms what is called Abdullah Gul Boulevard, he would talk loudly and repeatedly about how to go through Syria in order to get to Yemen.

Scorpion knew the route heading east to cross into Iraq to avoid Aleppo was an option neither he nor his pursuers would take, if they knew anything about the region. The roads there led through Mosul which was a no-go area, even for many Middle-Easterners. Certainly not a place for westerners. And there were no roads going south through Iraq and into the empty quarter of Saudi Arabia. No, a traveler had to go through Syria. And a westerner had to avoid Aleppo which meant a detour to the west.

In the end, if those chasing him found his clues at the Syrian border, they would be committed to a prescribed route through Syria and the cities of Hamah, Homs, and Damascus. From there, one would travel through Jordan, go around the capitol of Amman, to continue south, and bear off to the southeast before Aqaba to enter Saudi Arabia. From there, it would be on to Tabuk and further southeast, paralleling the Red Sea about fifty to sixty miles inland, to Medina. That path would eventually reach Yemen and one hundred more miles in, the capitol of Sana'a. Once in Yemen, Scorpion could be more explicit in leaving clues with people to guide any trailing westerners. There were so few on the road, it would not be hard to notice them and let any of them know the path.

In Yemen, he was headed for the Hadhramout region southeast of Sana'a. It was a region of fertile wadis, or river valleys, that supported agriculture and many small towns. The population was clustered in the wadi valleys near an unusual town named Shibram, which holds what many call the first skyscrapers. These were ten to twelve-story buildings built out of mud. It was called the Manhattan of the desert.

Scorpion's retreat was not in the fertile wadis, however, but deep into a dryer one that was uninhabited. It was at a higher elevation where he could find solitude and set up a defensible fortress. He stored water during the short rainy season in an underground cistern and that, accompanied by a deep well, provided him the necessary sustenance for life. The structure was an ancient monastery, abandoned long ago. It resembled a medieval castle with high, earthen, and stone walls. A deep, defensive trench had been dug in front of the walls. At the top was a walk where lookouts could keep watch. The platform also made for good shooting positions up high to pick off advancing enemies.

With his pursuer or pursuers following the route designated by him, he could set up an ambush long before reaching his hideaway. There he would dispatch him. There were plenty of choke points along the minor roads that led to his redoubt. Places where he could disable any vehicle, take out any support team members, and leave him with the assassin that his employer, Rashid, so badly wanted to eliminate. Pictures of the capture and execution, if not the man's head on a platter, would bring him a generous bonus. The thorn in Rashid's side would be gone and he could advance his plans unimpeded.

Scorpion smiled at the thought. And, at the thought of the pain he would inflict before dispatching the assassin.

† † †

"You want me to do what?" Dan voice evidenced his anger, close to exploding over the phone.

"You heard me. You store your Land Cruiser, take a bus to Ankara, and fly to Tel Aviv. Let me know what flight, so I can have Israeli security meet you."

Dan took a deep breath and tried to choke down his rage. "I just purchased this piece of junk and had it modified. I can drive it to Yemen and find this guy. I'm on my way to take him out, not to spend time in Tel Aviv getting lectured by Israelis on how little I know about the Middle-East and how much I need their expertise. I've done pretty well so far without it."

Jane waited out his rant. Better to let him get his frustrations off his chest. He'd see the benefits of the help she had arranged after he got here.

"I don't think that's on the agenda. And, listen carefully, this is not a suggestion. I want you on a flight to Tel Aviv before the day's out."

"Jane, you know this is a waste of time. If our quarry waits too long for me to show up, he'll get spooked and just disappear like he's done in the past and I'll be the one looking over my shoulder, not you, not any Israeli agents or bureaucrats."

"I've worked hard, called in some favors, to get you help. And believe me, everyone here understands speed is important. Our friends will have better ways to get you into Yemen and find the Scorpion. And further, an additional able-bodied fighter is not to be dismissed, you know that."

"I know the value of good fighters. But if our friends can help me find Scorpion, why haven't they taken care of him already?"

"They only found out he's based in Yemen after you called me with the info. Now, don't keep arguing with me. Get the Toyota stored and get on a bus to Ankara."

"This is a mistake. A diversion."

Even as he said it, the words of the Watcher came back to him. He should not reject help. He should not be contemptuous.

"Just do it. The sooner you get here, the sooner you can get back on the trail."

With that, Jane ended the call. There was no more to say. No matter how Dan felt, once he got here, she felt he'd get on board.

† † †

Scorpion slept that night in his van. He started the next morning for Kilis. Once at the border, he started asking

The Scorpion

border agents loudly about his travel plans to Yemen. He mentioned where he wanted to cross over into the country, in between the small towns of Sarat Abidah and Najran, Saudi Arabia. It was one of the few places to cross the border and the mention of the two towns would pinpoint exactly where Scorpion would enter Yemen. He asked how he should get through Syria and if driving through Saudi Arabia was safe. Scorpion knew the answers, of course, but the point was to imprint on the border guards his travel plans. After a suitable time of making his point about his travel plans, he passed through and continued his journey.

Soon, within days, he would be ready to ambush those who pursued him. He smiled as he considered the thought. From the start, it had been more than just another assignment. As he had remarked when Rashid had presented him with his task, it was assassin against assassin. Whether it was a team pursuing him or one man, Scorpion felt energized by this challenge to his deadly skills. His defeat of those pursuing him would only enhance his reputation and make him more valuable to his employer. With no life beyond his work of killing Rashid's enemies, this victory would be a crowning achievement in his career.

Chapter 23

By the time Dan finished dealing with the Toyota to the bemused confusion of Çetin, it was late in the day. When he caught the last bus to Ankara, Hasim, the grandson of the Watcher, seemed to understand. He stayed around until Dan got on the bus.

"Maybe this trip is to get the help my grandmother spoke of."

Dan gave him a slight smile. "Maybe. Tell your grandmother, I appreciate her words and will not neglect to use any help I can get."

He was not so sure of that last part, but he felt he should say it to appease the grandmother.

At the airport, Dan found he had missed the last flight, so he took his pack and settled down for an uncomfortable night on the floor in a corner of the lobby.

The sun was sharp and bright the next morning when Dan stepped off the Airbus 320 after a little over two-hour flight. He shaded his eyes and waited for Jane, accompanied by two Israeli security types to meet him. Without any words, they took him to a side door and through streamlined security and into a waiting car. Ten minutes they were at the office where Jane had first encountered Eitan's irregular volunteers.

"Dan, meet Eitan," Jane said when they were assembled in the room.

Dan shook the man's hand without comment.

"Welcome to Israel," Eitan said. "I know you didn't want to divert from your trail, but Jane thinks we can provide some significant help." He paused. "And so do I."

Dan nodded, again, not saying anything. He looked around the room. His gaze paused at the disreputable figure slouched on the couch. He turned to Jane with a raised eyebrow.

"This is Uri," Jane said. "He's going to be traveling with you. He's got some expertise on external missions and speaks Arabic fluently. He's passed as Arab before in his undercover work."

Dan nodded at the man but didn't go over to the couch. The man remained seated and stared back at him.

After an uneasy moment, Eitan spoke up.

"Let's go over the main parts of the plan. While we're doing so, I have our intelligence team working on pinpointing where this Scorpion's nest is located."

Uri got up and walked over to the bar and poured himself a whiskey.

"What makes you think, you can find where the Scorpion is in Yemen?" Dan asked. "There's a lot of territory to cover."

"What makes you think you can find him by driving there on your own?" Uri said from the corner of the room.

"Because he's leaving me clues."

Uri turned back to Dan with his drink in his hand and started back to the couch.

"So, he's leading you in the direction he wants you to go. How do you know it's where he's staying?"

"It doesn't matter. Somewhere along the way he expects to ambush me. That's when I'll find him."

"You'll bet the mission, bet your life on being able to recognize and avoid his ambush and then kill him?" He took a long swallow of his drink. "Sounds like a long-shot to me. I'd want to stack the odds more in my favor."

"It may be a better shot than sitting around in a room like this, theorizing about where he is holed up and waiting, for who knows how long, for intelligence to tell you they can't find him." He took a chair at the table and sat down. "I don't think there's a realistic alternative."

Jane and Eitan didn't say anything. Jane sat down at the table, while Eitan stood off to one side, as if not to take a position on the matter.

Uri sat back down on the couch and put his drink on the side table. He leaned forward in a hunch, looking at the floor. "First, we have to find the clues. If Scorpion is spreading bread crumbs for you, where is the place to leave them so that he'll be sure they're found? Ankara is too big to risk leaving them in a train or bus station. From what Jane told me, you got your first clues from a marketplace in a small town where the ferry docked." He looked up at Dan. "Right?"

Dan nodded.

"So, where can he be sure you'll show up next? Where's the next convergence point, no matter what route you take? Where do you have to go in your journey so he'll be sure you'll pass through and find his clues?"

"Border crossings," Dan said.

"Give the assassin a gold star," Uri said. "Now he can't leave a note, so he'll probably do what he did in the marketplace in Ereğli. He'll talk about his trip loudly, repeatedly, to make a strong impression. He'll mention where he's going, where he'll get into Yemen. From there, he'll probably leave clues about his route inside the country."

Jane looked at Eitan. "Can you get someone to the Turkish-Syrian border to ask some questions? Our assassin will be traveling in a blue van."

Eitan nodded and went to the corner of the room to make a call on his phone. Uri took a long pull on his drink and leaned back. There was no smile of satisfaction on his face. He seemed to be still thinking hard.

Dan watched the man. He looked like he drank too much, and, although he appeared solid, Dan had doubts about his field endurance. An older operative, probably carrying some injuries, who drank too much and was now pretty much out of shape. He could be a liability in the field, even if his strategic thinking was on the money.

"He'll cross either at Reyhanli or south of Kills," Uri said to Eitan. "He won't go to the west. That takes you into Iraq and through Mosul. He knows his pursuer can't go that route. Get people to check those two points and we'll get the next clue."

Now Uri got up and began to pace, his half-finished whisky abandoned on the side table.

"You have some maps? Surely in this bastion of secret planning there's some maps of the Middle-East."

Eitan pointed to the cabinets under the drink counter while he was on the phone. Uri went over there and pulled multiple sheets out and started sorting through them. When he found the one he wanted, he brought it over to the table.

"There're few choices from Syria on. He can't lead you through Aleppo. It's too dangerous for a westerner. But that doesn't matter. The route must be through Damascus, into Jordan, and south towards Aqaba. From that point there are more choices, but, in the end, they come to only three places to get into Yemen."

He spread the map out on the table and traced the path south on it. Dan, Jane, and Uri were bent over the large sheet. Dan took in the route and committed it to memory.

"The problem is still where in Yemen," he said.

Uri looked up at him.

"True enough. But, as you say, he'll leave us clues. If Eitan can get some people in action quickly, we'll soon have confirmation of that fact. Also, we can assume certain areas where he won't go."

Jane looked at Uri with a questioning expression on her face as Eitan came back to the table. "I called the XO and he's pulling some strings to get locals to ask around at the two crossings. We should have a response later today."

"Later, always later," Uri said half under his breath.

"Always impatient," Eitan replied.

Uri turned back to the map. "Here's the point," he said. "He's probably Sunni, since you think he's working with a wealthy Arab. Yemen's been in a civil war for a decade. The country is divided up between Houthi rebels, who are Shia, and Sunni forces loyal to the government, such as it is. Along with that you have al Qaeda staking out its territory as well."

"Sounds like a nice place," Dan said.

"Maybe. If you're in the right area. This Scorpion will head east. The major areas controlled by groups supporting the government, meaning not Shia and not al Qaeda, are there." He planted a finger on the eastern part of the country, north of the port city of Mukalla. "Somewhere right here."

Chapter 24

Scorpion drove on through Syria and Jordan. He stopped in Tabuk after entering Saudi Arabia. It was a town of over 650,000 people, driven by the largest air force base in the country and hosting numerous tourists visiting the many ancient archeological sites. The prophet is thought to have lived east of the city for some time.

After eating in a local restaurant, he relaxed in a modest locals-only hotel. He didn't want to be around tourists of any type. He preferred the shadows. He would make a noticeable commotion at the Yemen border tomorrow. He wanted to cross with as much fanfare as possible. Only now, he would inquire about the safety of traveling around Sana'a. He would be in Houthi territory, but he was not too worried. His Sunni connections were not so easy to spot. He'd just act like a normal merchant or trader who only wanted to come home safely. He'd decide the route in specific while talking to the guards at the border. With enough repetition and emphasis, he hoped those chasing him would get an accurate account of his routing.

It would take him east of Sana'a, skirting the city and then on the road that ran southeast along the edge of the great sand desert. Scorpion had the perfect ambush spot in mind. He'd driven these roads many times. Where the road turned away from the edge of the desert to enter the dry hills, it climbed up from the desert floor with many tight hairpin turns as the tarmac worked its way up the slope. He'd set up with some of his countrymen in the rocks above one of the switchbacks and stop the vehicles. From there, he could fire down on them and eliminate any of those accompanying the assassin, leaving him for last. And, hopefully, alive for Scorpion to deal with.

† † †

The planning went on for hours until Eitan finally called a halt. "I'm ordering food to be delivered. We can work through dinner and into the evening."

"Suits me," Dan said. "The big issue we face is how we pursue this man. Do we follow him in a car? Something I was doing. We can't fly into Sana'a. We'd have no way to bring any weapons with us."

"And there're no diplomatic ties either," Uri said. "One can't get into Yemen if you have an Israeli passport, or even an Israeli stamp on your own."

"So, we drive. Why are we sitting around then?" Dan asked. "You can feed us any info you come up with." He looked at Eitan. "We don't want to keep Scorpion waiting."

Uri sat and shook his head. Again, looking pensive as if lost in thought.

"If you have something to contribute, speak up," Dan said.

Uri looked over at him. "You set out a fool's path. Is it your arrogance, your pride, or your anger that propels you?"

Dan stiffened. He felt his face harden as he stared at Uri.

"You risk the mission and your life on the proposition that somehow you'll escape any ambush Scorpion sets up and then can kill him." Uri got up and went to the side counter to pour himself another drink. "And you will risk my life in this foolishness." He turned back to the table. "That's something I'm not willing to do."

"You agreed to go on this mission," Jane said.

"But not commit suicide."

"So, you just caged a fancy dinner out of me only to drop out as things got difficult?"

Eitan stepped forward to catch everyone's eye. "Let's not degenerate into bickering. We can argue the proper steps, but let's agree we're all on-board for the mission."

"But not for a suicide mission," Uri said again.

"How else to we find this guy unless we follow him? And if we follow him, we'll inevitably run into an ambush. Have you figured a better way? I don't think he's going to leave his address at the Yemen border and invite us in."

Conversation was interrupted when a junior staffer knocked on the door with several large bags of food in his arms.

A modest feast of street food was laid out on the table. There was a large helping of lamb shawarma, fatty pieces of meat that had been stacked up and slow roasted, then thinly sliced. A large order of burika was included. It was a thin, savory crepe filled with mashed potatoes and egg and then deep fried; eaten with the fingers. There was also sabich, a pita stuffed with fried aubergine slices, hard boiled eggs, and tahini sauce alongside of an Israeli salad of diced cucumbers, tomatoes, onions, and peppers. All this food was accompanied by large plastic cups of limonana. After depositing the food, the staffer left and returned shortly with a carafe of coffee and two bottles of wine.

Eitan explained the choices for Dan as he brought plates and dinner ware from the side cabinets and put them on the table. Jane was familiar with such ubiquitous offerings from her previous work in the country. Without a further word, they began loading their plates. Dan took notice that Uri ignored the limonana and refreshed his whiskey.

After eating, Dan poured himself a cup of strong coffee and sat back. He had been thinking hard while the meal had interrupted, at this point, the contentious planning. "We've been assuming that if we don't arrive at Scorpion's ambush, he'll just disappear."

Uri looked up from his plate where he had been lustily eating enough for two people. "He won't wait around forever."

"Agreed," Dan said. "The question is, where will he go? He's been out for some time, going through Europe, abducting and killing the girl and traveling through the Balkans, across the Black Sea, and now the Middle-East. All to get back to Yemen, which is where he has his headquarters, whatever they are."

"And your point?" Uri asked.

"If we don't show up, he's going to go back to his headquarters, his sanctuary, if you will."

"And disappear."

"Disappear. Maybe. But you said you know about where he'd locate his hideout. It can't be completely anonymous. Somewhere, some locals will have noticed such a place. If only for the security he'd set up. You speak Arabic and you say you can pass for one. With you, we could search him out."

"That could take months...and with possibly no success."

"Maybe. But it wouldn't be a suicide mission, as you so strongly objected to. I'm trying to find another way. I'd rather spend time searching parts of Yemen than go back home and declare defeat." Dan now stood up from the table and pointed a finger at Uri. "I made a vow over the body of the dead woman. A woman who was innocently caught up in the intrigue of assassins. She died a terrible death. One so horrendous, I can't tell her employer and friend how it happened. It's a secret I must take to my grave." He turned to Jane. "Even Jane doesn't know the details. So, I'm not willing to give up. I am going to Yemen to find this bastard and kill him. If I have to run into his ambush to do it, so be it. If I have to tramp around Yemen for months to do it, so be it."

He leaned over and struck the table hard with his fist, sending food and drinks spilling out. "With or without your help."

There was a silence in the room. Dan's eyes locked onto Uri's, who didn't flinch away.

"You'll just get yourself killed. Either way," Uri said.

Dan didn't answer, but kept staring back at Uri.

Uri sighed. "We'll search him out. At least we have a better chance of surviving that operation than the one you proposed."

"Back to getting into Yemen," Jane said.

"Driving has its own set of risks at the border," Eitan said.

Uri nodded.

"And fabricating a hidden compartment will take time," Dan said.

There was a pause as everyone thought about the limited options. Finally, Uri looked around at the others with a sly grin on his face.

"I know another way."

Chapter 25

"You can't just jump out of a plane over Yemen. It's a country enmeshed in civil war," Eitan said.

"And how would you fly over their airspace?" Jane asked.

Uri just smiled back at them.

"I think I know how we do it," Dan said.

Uri turned to him, still smiling. "You know what I'm thinking?"

"HALO jump," Dan said.

"Exactly!" Uri said. His voice now full of triumphant energy. "We drop out of the sky like stones. No one sees us. No one knows we've infiltrated."

"Documents?" Jane asked.

Uri waved his hand. "A trifle issue." He turned to Eitan. My ex-boss will make them up, complete with visa stamps from our 'border crossing'."

"How will you travel around?" Jane asked further.

"We'll get ourselves to Mukalla and rent a car, a four-wheel drive. Of course you will have to pay a large deposit," he said to Eitan. "When we're done with it, it may be in tough shape."

"Why Mukalla?" Dan asked.

Uri pushed the food aside and opened the map of Yemen again. "I said he'd probably locate himself in this area. Mukalla is the nearest large city. A port city with an airport nearby and car rentals."

"Where do we aim?"

"North of Mukalla."

He traced a route from Mukalla, along the coast for about thirty miles and then his finger followed a road leading north.

"This road connects small villages with the port. There'll be trucks driving the road and busses as well. We need to target an area to land where we can't be seen. Then hike to a village," he pointed on the map, "say this one, Aldwas. From there we catch a bus or truck to Mukalla. We can make up a story about being abandoned by a fixer. Left here on our own."

"Why would we be there in the first place?" Dan asked. "We'd need a good story for that."

Uri thought for a moment.

"I've got it," Eitan said. "You're looking for old cultural sites around the area. Shibram is not too far away and it's a UNESCO heritage site. You're the interpreter," he pointed to Uri, "and you're the journalist looking to write a story. Neither of you are political. You just want to publicize the ancient heritage of Yemen. Something the Yemenis should be proud of."

Uri clapped his hands. "That's it! Get documents made up right away." He turned to Dan. "Have you done a HALO jump before?"

Dan nodded. "Once."

"That'll have to do. I assume you haven't forgotten everything."

"How do we get you over that territory?" Jane asked.

"That's where we'll need your help," Eitan said. "You Americans are partnered with the Saudis. While some of this territory is in dispute between al Qaeda and the Hadi government, the Saudis control the skies here. You must come up with a reason to fly over."

"A flight from Djibouti to Dubai?" Jane asked almost to herself. "That might work. I'll have to make some calls."

† † †

Scorpion arrived at the Yemen border checkpoint mid-morning. He went through his routine of making a strong impression. Once he felt he would be remembered by anyone inquiring about a traveler in a blue van, he continued his journey.

It was a long eleven hours from the border to the capital, Sana'a. He had a friendly place to stay just outside of the city, which was a stronghold for the Houthi rebels. Scorpion wanted to limit his time among them.

Sana'a is an ancient city filled with multi-story mud block buildings with elaborately painted facades, especially the arched adornments over the otherwise plain windows. The old city is built up from the lower, outer city as an island protecting it from the seasonal floods that wash down the streets during the monsoon from July through September. When the rains come, the higher old city seems to be surrounded by a moat of water.

The city has been continuously inhabited for over 2,500 years and houses one of the oldest mosques in the world, built around 650 AD. The mosque contains the oldest known copy of the Koran along with many other rare Arabic manuscripts. Scorpion was not unaware of the city's ancient heritage, but cautious of its current political culture.

The next morning, Scorpion met with some men associated with President Hadi, who was trying to regain his power with help from the Saudis. They were essentially spies in Sana'a, a city controlled by the Houthi rebels. He explained his plan and where the ambush would take place. The men agreed to assemble the weaponry, RPGs, AK47s, and hand grenades and meet him at the site. They would hide their vehicles, hike into the hills above the switchback, and wait for their prey to arrive.

After the meeting, Scorpion smiled for the first time in many days. Soon, after a patient wait in the foothills, he would capture or kill this assassin and rid his employer of the interference.

Two days later, Scorpion was settled into the rocks overlooking the ambush point with the two men he had contacted in Sana'a. They were used to being in the dry, rugged hills. Each man had water and food to last two days, or more, if needed. The two men chewed on lumps of kat, the mildly euphoric leaf that was grown in Yemen. Scorpion didn't approve, but said nothing. He preferred a clear mind. They spread cloths over their position, nestled among the rocks, to ward off the sun during the heat of the day. At night they huddled under the same tarps, wrapped in their cloaks, to keep warm.

As they waited, the prospect that his prey might not be able to follow his trail began to loom larger in Scorpion's mind. He was assuming a great deal, leaving clues at each border, with the last one needing to be the most detailed and, therefore, complicated. It was quite possible his pursuer or pursuers would lose the trail or suspect a trap.

"You think the foreigner will come *sayyid*?"

"In sha'allh", he replied.

"What do we do if he doesn't come into the trap we have set?"

Scorpion refrained from giving him a look to shut him up. It was a fair question given the low probability of success. "We will return to our normal routine. You will go back to Sana'a; I will go to my compound. From there I will determine the next steps to take. But my hunt for this man, or men, does not stop."

Scorpion disliked the thought of the cat and mouse game that he had set up not ending here, but he had to admit that it was a distinct possibility. From Carrie's interrogation, Scorpion had concluded that it was one man who had disrupted Rashid's numerous plans. He, however, had an advantage. He was willing to use far more brutal tactics in his quest than his opponent. If the man, were truly in the hire of the U.S., then there would be rules that would constrain him. Yet, he had to wonder how many of those rules applied to those who chased him? The man who had thwarted the attack in Germany and assassinated Jabbar, had acted independent of governing rules. Rules might be ignored or discarded. This man might be less constrained than other government agents. It was going to be a man to man dual to the death. As he had thought initially; assassin versus assassin. He admonished himself to not assume too much.

† † †

Late that night in the nondescript office building in Tel Aviv, Eitan received word that a traveler in a blue Toyota van had made a noticeable fuss at the Turkish-Syrian border checkpoint about best to travel to Yemen. It seemed odd, since the driver was obviously Arab, but he insisted that he wanted to know the route and whether or not it was safe.

"You were correct," Eitan said. "This Scorpion made an impression at the border. Enough to get himself noticed. Anyone trying to escape, would not have acted this way. He is trying to lead you to him, somewhere in Yemen.

"You'll get further confirmation of that at the Yemen border," Uri said. He stood up and stretched. "I've had enough of this office." He turned to Eitan. You must get our weapons together, confirm our target has entered Yemen." Next, he looked over at Jane. "And you must get us an airplane we can jump out of. There's nothing Dan and I can do, so we're going out to relax. I'll show him the Tel Aviv nightlife."

He stepped up to Eitan. "Of course, I'll need some money. You can put it on your expense account. Entertainment of VIPs." He looked over at Dan. "Right?"

"I don't think I'm up for going out," Dan replied.

"Don't be silly. I never pass up an opportunity to have a good time on someone else's bank account." Uri grabbed his coat. "Let's go. If I'm going to put my life in danger for you, I want to get to know you better."

He winked at Jane. "It's kind of like, even if you pay me, I want to get to know you better before you fuck me."

Dan signed and got up from his chair. He was tired, but this seemed to be a ritual he was not going to be able to avoid.

Chapter 26

After cruising through some local nightclubs and bars while sampling drinks in all of them, Uri settled them into a raucous club filled with younger people dancing and drinking. The lights were low, and a prism ball broke spotlights aimed at it into shards of glittering light that swirled around the room, bouncing off the dancers as well as those sitting in the booths.

Uri ordered two shots of Tubi 60, a popular nightlife drink. It was a potent liquor that many felt produced effects similar to ecstasy. Alongside of the shots, Uri ordered a whiskey for himself and Dan ordered a Goldstar beer.

"L'chaim," Uri said as he raised his shot glass. He downed the shot in one gulp, as did Dan.

"What's in this?" Dan asked.

"No one really knows," Uri shouted over the din. "It's all legal, but somehow the ingredients remain a mystery. It's a favorite of the millennials."

"This was always one of my favorite places," Uri said leaning over the table to be heard. "I feed off the youthful energy here." He took a drink of his whiskey. "Of course, the music has changed somewhat, to something I don't care for much, but the energy is still here." He paused for a moment. "Can you feel it?"

Dan smiled. "I'm not sure what I feel except the bass line vibrating in my chest. That along with the overall noise level."

Uri sat back, giving Dan a quizzical look. "You sound like an old man. You sure you're up to this adventure? Maybe you can't keep up with me? An old dog, for sure, but one with still-sharp teeth."

He grinned and took another sip. Then he waved to a passing waiter and ordered another round of Tubi 60 shots.

"Are you married? Got family?" Uri asked.

Dan shook his head. "My wife and unborn son were killed by some mobsters in New York some years ago."

"I'm sorry to hear that. Is that what drove you to the CIA?"

"It's a long story, but the short answer is yes."

"Along the way, I hope you got some revenge for what happened."

"Revenge is not all it's cracked up to be. Necessary sometimes, but, in the end, not so satisfying."

"Yet, you pursue it now?"

"It's called for, so I do it."

Uri shook his head. "I'm not sure it's ever called for, but you can find it in our scriptures. I prefer to think of it as dispensing just desserts. The enemy does something that causes us harm, we deliver to them the consequences of their actions."

"They don't seem to get the point, though."

Uri shook his head. "No. If you've interviewed any jihadists, instead of shooting them, you'd know. They can't be rehabilitated. I asked one of them, one of the few I encountered that lived to spend his time in jail, what he would do when he was freed after serving his sentence. He said, he'd go back to trying to kill Israelis."

Dan shook his head. "That's why I do what I do."

"Your boss, Jane. She seems to understand this."

"She does. She wants the fight taken to the enemy, preferably on their own grounds."

"We're certainly doing that now." Uri finished his whiskey. "Don't start nursing that beer. I don't trust people who can't keep up with me." He smiled at Dan. "At least let me buy you a whiskey to go with that beer. Go ahead, order the house's best. Eitan is paying for it."

The waiter arrived with the shots of Tubi 60. Uri ordered two more of the best whiskeys the nightclub stocked. He raised his glass to Dan. To our adventure into dark places."

They drank and Uri slammed down the shot glass.

Dark places. Dan wondered if Uri had experienced the Watchers. He didn't seem like he was the type to be receptive to their approach, but what did he really know about them?

"Tell me, Uri, do you have a family?"

"Oh yes. But I live alone. As I told Jane, I think I'm an embarrassment to them. My wife couldn't handle the stress of being an operative's wife, especially one that kept a lot of secrets." He looked down at his half-emptied whiskey. "Maybe she's a casualty of the war against terrorists. Our marriage certainly is."

"I'm sorry to hear that. I think that's why Jane never got married. She felt it would be impossible to juggle the fight and a family."

Uri looked up. "She tell you this?"

"In so many words."

"Hmmm. I wonder if the two of you are, what do you say, an item?"

"What makes you think that?"

"A woman doesn't talk about such things with her employee unless there's something else going on."

"So, you're a gossip reporter now? I guess being an undercover operative qualifies you for the position."

Uri smiled at him.

"Do you have kids?" Dan asked.

Uri nodded. "A boy and a girl. I get to see them now and then, but don't get to spend much time with them. As I said, I think I embarrass them."

"Maybe if you drank less and did fun things with them."

"So, you're a family counselor now?" Uri laughed at his timely comeback. "I don't see anything in your resume that would qualify you for that position."

He looked around the room at the people. Most of them were in their twenties and thirties. They were dancing, laughing, flirting with not a care in the world.

"We have good looking women here in Israel, don't you think?"

Dan looked around and nodded. "But they're too young for you."

"But not for you?"

"Definitely not too young for me." Dan smiled.

Uri continued to look the crowd over. "They have no idea how tenuous life is. Sixty kilometers from here you're in Palestine and there are people on every street that would like to kill you."

"Maybe that's why they like to party. One can't live in fear all the time. They're also all trained, aren't they? They're required to spend time in the army."

Uri nodded. "Hopefully these beautiful young ones don't forget their training. We live with the threat to our very existence close by, unlike you Americans, protected by two large oceans. Our future is dependent on these happy souls." He shook his head. "I just hope they're up to it when called upon."

"But we have other things to concentrate on tonight."

"Like getting *shakar*?

Dan looked at him.

"Drunk, piss-faced, intoxicated. Something I do very well." He got up. "Let's find a quieter place. The noise of this merriment is beginning to wear on me."

Uri took Dan to a small, local bar where the bartender and the waitresses all seemed to know him. He ordered more rounds of whiskey and plates of greasy, street food that would absorb the alcohol. In spite of his best efforts, Dan was getting drunk and would have a hangover the next day.

"This girl that was killed. She means a lot to you?"

"I'd rather not talk about it."

"I think I understand, but since I'm putting my life on the line, I'd like to know more."

"I hardly knew her. She was a dear companion to someone I'm close to." Dan paused for a moment. "You know the problem. My life exposes me to danger. That exposes those close to me to danger. It seems to have come home in a terrible way. One that may ruin my relationship with this other person forever."

"Ah well. Just like with my marriage. An even closer arrangement that went bad due to my work."

"But your family? They were never in danger?"

"Not before they left. That was a consolation, actually. As sad as it was to lose them, I knew they'd be safer apart from me."

"So, we're destined to live lonely lives."

Uri raised his whisky to Dan and downed it in one gulp.

Chapter 27

It was the early hours of the morning when Uri and Dan stumbled back to Dan's hotel.

"See you later this morning at the office, such as it is. I expect Eitan will have a breakfast spread for us. He knows me too well."

Dan went into the hotel and up to his room. He set the alarm for 7 am, which would give him four hours of precious sleep and flopped down on the bed. Within minutes he was fast asleep.

When he arrived at the office at 8 am, Jane and Eitan were already there along with Uri. Uri seemed, surprisingly, none the worse for the previous night of drinking.

"You look terrible," Jane said.

"Good morning to you too."

"Looks like Uri sucked you into bar cruising," Jane said.

"More drinking than cruising."

Oh, well. It'll wear off, he thought. Like previous benders had in the past. The problem for him, was that those nights of drinking were some years past.

As Uri predicted, there was a breakfast feast laid out on the table. There was a large pan of shakshouka, baked eggs in tomato sauce, the ever-present chopped cucumber and tomato salad with bowels of labneh, a thick, tangy yogurt nearby, pita bread and humus dip, a chocolate spread to put on some bread and a plate of bourekas, with cheese and potato filling. On the side board, were pitchers of fruit juicers and coffee. Without waiting for anyone else, Uri dug into the food with gusto.

"Nothing like a night out drinking to create a big appetite. My compliments, Eitan. You remembered a good breakfast is what is needed before we do any serious work."

Dan sampled some of the offerings more carefully, while Jane and Eitan filled their plates. Afterward, with coffee in hand, Jane announced that she had procured the loan of a Pilatus PC-12. It was a single engine turbo prop plane made in Switzerland. It could be configured as a passenger or cargo plane. There was a large side door behind the wing that would allow easy egress for the jump. It had a ceiling of 30,000 feet and a range of just over 2,000 miles which enabled the plane to comfortably reach Abu Dhabi, only 1,200 miles from Djibouti.

"Our cover is we are transporting some technical workers to Abu Dhabi to help correct some embassy computer issues. You'll jump at the maximum altitude." She looked at Uri directly. "Can you do this? In your condition and age?"

Uri snorted his derision at the question and just glared back at Jane.

"I'm not kidding. I'm not baiting you. The mission depends on your ability to insert this way. If that can't be done, we have to come up with another plan."

"We went over this yesterday. The driving option carries more risk of being detained, or worse, found out. This way is quicker, cleaner." He waved his fork at Jane,

"And I'm up to it, don't you worry yourself." He turned back to his boureka. "Just make sure you have good documents for Dan here. Get Eitan to make them if you can't."

Jane didn't respond and Eitan spoke up.

"We'll set up the passports as we discussed. Uri will be an Arabic fixer and guide. Dan will be a researcher writing a book on the ancient cities of the Hadhramaut region. He should be American, then we have no issues with accents and background. I've already set our techs on this task for Uri and Jane has documents being prepared at the U.S. embassy."

He turned to the two men.

"Weapons? Jane said you favored the Sako TRG 42."

Dan nodded. "Get it in .338 with a Schmidt and Bender 3-27 x 56 scope. I need a suppressor as well."

"Fairly picky, aren't we?" Uri said with a grin.

"I choose the tools of my trade carefully. I'm sure you would do the same, if you had a trade."

"My trade is mayhem and killing, the same as yours. I'm not so choosy about the tools I use."

"Both of you, just shut up," Jane said. Her voice evidenced her anxiety and growing lack of patience. "I get the banter, but let's just get this planning done and move on. You will need other weapons and ammunition along with supplies to keep you in the field."

"Okay boss," Uri said.

The rest of the meeting went on with less banter and more seriousness as the men traded off ammunition with shelter and food supplies. They would each jump out of the plane with a fifty-pound rucksack strapped between their legs, making walking almost impossible. It came with a lanyard that released the pack before they hit the ground, allow an easier touch down. They would have an oxygen mask and bottle to use as they plummeted through the high atmosphere for almost three minutes before landing.

"We jumping at night or during the day?"

Uri looked at Dan in surprise. "Daytime. You want to kill yourself? Break a leg? We don't get to pick a nice, flat, soft, landing zone. It will be hard enough in daylight to avoid rocks and uneven ground. Impossible at night." He shook his head. "Did you do your jump at night?"

Dan nodded. He wasn't going to say more, but that acknowledgement caused Uri to give him an appraising look. As if to wonder about this assassin he was teaming up with.

"Eitan, I need you to reserve an SUV for us at the Mukalla airport. Remember, we don't care how expensive it is, the Americans are paying for it. It just needs to be rugged and reliable."

Eitan nodded. After a two more hours discussing their supplies, they settled on the trade-offs that would be necessary. Uri insisted on balancing choices in favor of ammunition.

"We can always find food to purchase or steal, if there are any villages nearby. If not, we go hungry. Water is more important, second only to ammunition. If we get into any gun fights, we're dead if we run out of ammunition."

The Tevor 7 shot a 7.62mm round and Uri insisted that most of their supplies be in this caliber. Dan took a smaller amount of the .338 round. His sniper rifle was for a particular purpose and if they were in a firefight, he would most likely use the Tevor 7, a smaller, more agile bullpup style combat rifle.

Uri wanted to leave sidearms behind.

"I can do my killing up close with the Tevor...or with my knife," Uri declared.

Dan, however insisted on his Sig Sauer M11.

Chapter 28

The ride in the Pilatus was quieter than Dan's previous experience in the C130 that took him over the Mexican desert. With the gear he and Uri carried, they could not fit into the normal passenger seats. These had been removed to allow for less comfortable, but more roomy bench seats that were bolted in along the sides of the interior. Neither man spoke much as they climbed to their ceiling at 30,000 feet over the Red Sea.

The drop zone had been carefully plotted with Uri's input and the GPS coordinates logged into the pilot's system. Dan and Uri would be alerted a half hour before their drop and start breathing pure oxygen in order to purge their systems of nitrogen to protect from getting the bends from the rapid increase in pressure as they fell to the earth.

Dan's mind went back to his first HALO. It was his first assignment and he had wondered whether or not he was just a disposable asset, sent out to do a job, and no worries if he was lost on the mission. On that assignment, Dan wreaked more havoc than anyone at Langley anticipated. There had been some blowback and that was when Dan understood that Jane was willing to fight and defend him. Her boss, Henry Mason, had proved himself adept at protecting his dark operation and together they weathered the storm that ensued.

Now, Dan more fully understood the landscape in which he operated. The need to strike, the need to get support from the higher management levels, the need to give certain people plausible deniability, and the need to fend off politicians who would snipe away at them for their own gain or protection, the country be damned. Or so it seemed to Dan.

A wry grin spread across his face as he thought about what they were going to do. What a shit storm this would start if anyone on various oversight committees knew about it. It was one thing to vaporize a terrorist in Yemen with a drone missile, even with innocent collateral damage, but quite another to insert assets to operate in a foreign country without any permission from the local government.

Oh, well. That's just the way we have to do things. Dan wondered how long they could keep their section going. And if it were ever shut down, what would happen to him? *Probably get sent to prison. For defending my country.* He turned his thoughts away from that harsh reality. It didn't help one's attitude when one was about to risk life and limb to strike a serious blow to the enemy. He'd just carry on as long as he could.

"What are you thinking?" Uri said, noticing his smile.

"Just remembering my first and last jump. It was my first mission. It seems like a lifetime ago now."

"Wait until you've done as many miles as I have. But no matter how many missions, I can still remember in detail the dangerous moments. It helps, I think. Makes one better at escaping the next one to come along."

The Jumpmaster came by and ordered them to mask up. They were getting close now. Conversation ended as the two men put on their face masks. In addition to the bulky rucksack strapped between their legs, they had altimeters on their wrists. They would deploy their chutes at 2,500 feet and glide down to, hopefully, an injury-free landing.

Two minutes out the Jumpmaster stuck his face in Dan's and asked him his name, where he was, and where he had departed from, looking for any signs of hypoxia that would cause him to abort the jump. Both men passed their exam and waddled towards the door. The pilot throttled back to 120 knots, not quite enough to maintain altitude, but slow enough to not damage the cargo door when it opened. At one minute, the Jumpmaster opened the door and the wind blasted through the cabin with a loud roar. The plane wobbled from the aero disturbance with the pilot working to stabilize it. They had begun a slight descent due to the decrease in speed. Uri looked back at Dan and shouted.

"Watch where I land. When I'm down, I'll look up for you. We'll be hundreds of meters apart. Try to get close."

Dan gave him a thumbs up and Uri stepped out into the sky. Dan quickly followed and the engine roar was instantly replaced by the wind. He scanned the sky below to find the small dot that was Uri. He concentrated on him and tried to maneuver his fall to close the lateral gap. He checked his altimeter dial which was whirling as he plummeted down. As before, he concentrated on the thousand-foot dial.

Below he saw Uri's chute open and a moment later, Dan pulled his cord. Suddenly his feet were snapped below him and everything became quiet and calm. He could see Uri maneuvering and Dan concentrated on finding his own landing amid the rocky outcroppings. He aimed for a clear spot. It might be hard, but it had no jagged rocks which was what he wanted to avoid. He pulled the release cord on his rucksack and it dropped away behind him.

A hard brake of the chute brought his feet in touch with the ground and he allowed himself to roll onto the hard soil. The chute collapsed and Dan scrambled to gather it in.

Once Dan had retrieved his chute and rucksack, he started towards Uri. The two men had come down on a moderately flat hilltop overlooking a valley. Uri was consulting his GPS when Dan came up.

"I think the road to Mukalla is over that hill." He pointed to the next row of hills across a shallow valley. "First thing is to stash our tactical gear and get a ride to the city where we pick up our vehicle."

Dan nodded and they tramped off down the hill. On the next slope, Uri found a large cleft in a rock face that provided a good hiding place for their rucksacks and parachutes. They changed from their insulated jump suits into civilian garb; hiking pants, shirts and jackets, sturdy boots, and hats. Then they started over the hill. Once at the road, Uri consulted his GPS map again.

"There's a small group of houses maybe five miles down the road. Probably a gas station there along with a place to eat. We got a hike, but we should be able to find a ride when we get there."

A little over an hour later they walked into the building behind the gas pumps. It sold supplies and food. Uri bought each of them a liter-bottle of water. He explained that they had been abandoned by their driver and needed to get to Mukalla to rent a car. Uri said Dan was researching a book about the ancient cities of the area, so they would be driving around the region.

The man seemed to accept the story, apologizing for the bad manners of their supposed driver. An hour later, when a truck pulled in, he talked to the driver and convinced him to take the two men to Mukalla. Uri's offer of payment helped sway the driver. Uri and Dan loaded their hiking backpacks in the back of the truck and the three men crammed themselves into the cab for the four-hour ride.

There were no SUVs available and few cars at the airport. Uri held his temper and went over with the clerk how the rental had been set up days before. The man acknowledged that a phone call had been made, but no promises had been given, and someone else had rented the vehicle. He had some small sedans he could rent if Uri wanted one.

"We'll have to go into the city and try to buy one," Uri said, turning to Dan. "That's more complicated, but we have to find something."

"Can you navigate the issues? Sales paperwork, registration, plates?"

"I'll figure it out. I can use the problem here as an excuse. I'll let whoever we deal with know, I'll sell it back to them cheap when we're done. Getting the chance to make a profit on both sides of the transaction, may help grease the wheels of commerce."

Four hours later the two men were on the road back north in a run-down Land Cruiser. It was old, but Uri had purchased newer tires for it to the delight of the seller. The brakes were uneven and squealed indicating the pads were worn out. The steering was loose and unpredictable over the bumps in the road. Dan guessed it would be a handful off-road. The owner had not sold it to them, but rented it to them for a month. He had extracted a deposit more than able to replace the worn machine if they didn't show up.

Chapter 29

Scorpion and his men were in the second day of waiting. While they still had water and food, the men were getting restless. Scorpion felt the same way, but kept it hidden from the others. His pursuer should have only been hours behind him when he left Ereğli. Those chasing him could fall a full day behind, having to go more slowly and figure out the clues, but Scorpion felt that after two days, the odds of them showing up were going to be seriously diminished.

Doesn't matter, he thought to himself. *If the assassin doesn't show, I'll regroup at my hideout and go back out to search for him. I can always go back to Switzerland.* He didn't relish the thought of going there but felt confident he could do so. Maybe this time without any help. He'd be more covert. If he had to, he would infiltrate the compound and kill the young woman. If he couldn't find the assassin through her assistant, and then, through her, he'd just eliminate them. This assassin seemed to care a great deal for her, so it would cause him distress. And distress, Scorpion knew, led to mistakes. And mistakes would lead to his death. The deadly game would play out over a longer time, but with the same end.

† † †

"Now we look for the needle in the haystack," Uri said over the roar of the motor. The air conditioning didn't work well, so they kept the windows open.

"A needle we have to find," Dan said.

"I didn't want to rain on your mission, back in Tel Aviv, but we don't have much chance of success."

"That's disappointing to hear. I don't want to go back empty-handed."

Uri shrugged as he wrestled with the steering wheel. "How long do you plan to stay?"

"Until we find his hideout."

"Or until we get arrested for asking too many questions and not doing enough ancient city research?"

"I'm banking on you maintaining our cover. Many times, such research trips take months to complete. I thought a month rental was cutting it a bit short."

"Maybe, but I don't think the owner of this *shtik drek* would have agreed to anything longer."

Dan looked at Uri.

"Piece of crap."

"Where do we start?"

"We've started. We'll go to Shibam. It's called the Manhattan of the desert. It has a collection of mud-brick skyscrapers. Buildings one can't imagine standing, but they do. It's a cultural heritage site."

"Our enemy won't be there."

"No, but we may be able to find people who know of an unusual compound in the area."

"We may have better luck in smaller villages."

"True, but we'll start at Shibam and work outward. The country is too large to find him unless he placed himself in a friendly region. That's the only thing we can bank on. Otherwise, we're screwed."

"And in for a long stay."

Uri looked over at Dan but didn't respond.

† † †

Scorpion waited through the third day, even though the men he hired were increasingly restless. Finally, he called a halt to the vigil.

"You go back to Sana'a and see if you can learn anything about a westerner, or group of them who were asking about a traveler such as me, where he went, the route he might take. If you come up with anything report it to me."

The men nodded in assent and Scorpion handed them the promised fee for joining him on the ambush. After they had departed back to the west, Scorpion got in his van and headed east in the direction of his headquarters and hideout. He would plan his next move from there. It now seemed as though his pursuit of this assassin, who was also pursuing him, was going to be a much longer "dance" the two of them would play. If he could inflict pain and suffering on those around this assassin, it would help him in this deadly duel. After a long day's drive, he arrived at his redoubt.

It was an old monastery from the earliest days of Christianity, long abandoned after the rise of Islam in the region. It had been built as a retreat, hidden away from trade routes and villages, and so had remained undiscovered for centuries after its abandonment. While parts of it had fallen into ruin, the mud-brick construction proved surprisingly resilient, surviving centuries with little degradation.

Scorpion had purchased the property and surrounding land years ago, before the civil war. After his purchase, he connived to have the records buried so deep that no one would find them. He, of course, had copies, officially stamped so there would be no doubt as to their authenticity, but no searching of government files would turn up any clues to the existence of the monastery and its ownership.

It had been built part of the way up a deep, narrow wadi. There were no villages in the valley floor. The area was inhospitable, even by Yemeni standards, due to the scarcity of rain and the intense flooding that occurred when it did come. The building was built on top of a precipice that jutted out from the cliff walls into the valley but was protected from the seasonal floods by its elevation. The steep assent from the wadi valley made it nearly impregnable and it could not be readily attacked from the cliffs above due their sheer face which offered no climbing path up or down.

Scorpion had the well re-drilled deeper to find a fresh, year-around, reliable source of water. He had installed gun placements housing surplus Russian PK light machine guns around the walls, some facing the valley approaches and some facing the cliffs behind the monastery.

He had a small staff, loyal to him as well as afraid of him. Scorpion knew all about their families and had made it clear that he would be a generous employer if they were discreet and loyal, but he would be a ruthless destroyer, of them and their families, if they transgressed his orders.

Chapter 30

After three weeks of searching, living out of the Toyota with occasional stays in a local hotel to get a shower, both men were getting weary and dejected. They had worked their way around Shibam in ever-widening circles. As they entered each village, some quite isolated and backward, they held high hopes, which were subsequently dashed.

"We're no closer than when we started," said Dan. He slouched in the passenger seat of the Land Cruiser. "And this old beast is not sounding very healthy."

He had noticed an increasing amount of noise coming from the motor, including an ominous collection of knocks and ticks that didn't bode well for the engine's long-term survivability.

"I'm worried that the motor is soon going to give out. I check the oil regularly and we're using an increasing amount."

"I know. The problem is also that we can't always find more to pour in."

"We need to plan on this giving up on us."

"If we don't get a hit this week, we'll go to Shibam and find a mechanic that can patch the engine together."

"Or sell us a replacement, which might not be much better than the original."

Uri shrugged, as if to say, "What else can we do?"

In the market place of the small village, they talked to an old man selling kat along with some dates and other, unidentifiable vegetables.

Uri spoke with him in Arabic. The man spoke the Hadhrami dialect that challenged Uri, but he struggled along. After an intense conversation in which Dan noticed Uri's sharp interest and excitement, Uri finished his talk with the old man. He thanked him and pressed some money into his hands. Then he turned to walk away with Dan.

"We may have a lead. The old man remembers an ancient monastery located a day's travel away from here. He says people that he thinks are from there come to town sometimes to purchase supplies. He's also seen a helicopter fly over his village towards this monastery. He assumes someone is living there."

"But not monks."

Uri nodded. "Right."

Dan digested the news. They had no hits other than this thin lead. "We have to check it out, even if it takes some time."

"Agreed. We don't have much else to go on."

"Nothing else, really. Did he say how we get to this place?"

"In general. But we don't want to drive or hike up the wadi where it's located. If it is Scorpion's den, we can't walk in the front door."

"He'd certainly like that." Dan thought for a moment as they walked back to the Toyota. "We identify the wadi and find a parallel one to go up. Then we hike over the mountain and locate the monastery. From there we can figure out if it's Scorpion's lair."

The men purchased supplies and, after filling the gas tank, started out of town in their crippled machine.

† † †

Scorpion's van crawled up the narrow, twisting gravel road that climbed the steep hillside to the outcropping where the old monastery stood. A guard at the entrance opened the iron gate to let him in. He parked the van in the courtyard and got out. A man came out of the building with an eager step to greet him.

"Marhaban bieawdatik." Welcome back.

"Jayid 'anak qad eudt." It is good to be back.

The greeter's name was Faquir, which means a poor man. His family *was* very poor and had sold him to a rich war lord as a child. The war lord had him castrated and put him to work taking care of his three wives. When the war lord was killed, Scorpion rescued Faquir from certain death by the victorious tribe and took him into his service. Faquir, grateful that his life had been spared, served Scorpion and his dark desires. Having few desires of his own, he focused on learning the fighting arts and doing what was needed to service Scorpion's. That included procuring females for Scorpion's pleasure, attending to the aftermath of the assassin's brutal pleasures, and taking care of the females Scorpion kept for long term, as concubines.

Once inside, Scorpion went to his private suite of rooms and proceeded to bathe away the dust of days of travel.

"Were you successful on this trip, *majistir*? Faquir always inquired, even though he knew his master said little of his trips. Faquir knew his master was an assassin. He had seen his dark side and the hideout where they lived spoke of an unusual need for anonymity and security befitting one who worked outside the laws of most countries.

"No, not this time. That has caused me some distress and makes a greater challenge for me. Nevertheless, I must rise to it and overcome that which is an obstacle to me."

Scorpion spoke as if his work was normal. He understood Faquir was aware his work was far from that, but he knew Faquir would always present a normal front. And he knew Faquir would always be faithful, owing his life to him.

Scorpion had taught Faquir how to fight and defend himself, or those he was in charge of. Over the years, Faquir's position had grown to encompass being the master of the household staff. He was not only in charge of Scorpion's women, but his cook and the maintenance staff as well as the guards. This latter group had resisted being directed by a eunuch, but after Scorpion's brutal purge of their head officer, they accepted Faquir's overall direction, while leaving the details of monastery defense to their captain. It was an arrangement that met with Scorpion's blessing.

After a long bath and a good dinner, Scorpion got on his sat phone and called Rashid.

"Did you complete your task?" Rashid asked after answering the phone.

"I did not, *Sayyid*."

There was silence on the other end.

Scorpion continued. "I was able to find the connection I guessed existed between this assassin and the young woman in Switzerland. But I could not grab her. I captured her assistant, but she was not able to tell me much. I discovered that most of the disruptions were the work of a single man, with some help occasionally from others. But this assassin, even though he knows Aebischer's daughter, keeps much from her. It protects him, but it didn't protect the woman's assistant."

Rashid didn't comment. He understood that this other woman was probably dead. And that she didn't die an easy death.

"You left no clue? No mess in Switzerland?"

"No *Sayyid*. Switzerland has only a kidnapping to deal with. And no clues." Scorpion left out the two men that would have been found dead at the scene of the kidnapping.

"This is most unfortunate. It leaves us in the same place. This assassin interfering without plans. I am not happy with this lack of success."

"I as well, *Sayyid*. But I have an idea of who it is and I did lure him to follow me, as far as Yemen, it seems."

"You know where he is? In Yemen?"

"I set a trap for him, left clues behind me. Unfortunately, he didn't show up. I have sent men back to the border area to find out if he entered Yemen."

"So, you don't know where he is."

"He's in the Middle-East. I'm working to find out where. I want to finish this here on our territory, not back in Europe."

There was a long pause.

"See that you do," Rashid said at last. With that, he ended the call.

Scorpion put down the phone. He had disappointed his benefactor and needed to correct that. His reputation was now at stake. This westerner had not been found, had followed, but not into his trap, and was somewhere unknown in the Middle-East.

Scorpion picked up his phone again and started making calls. He had his own network of informants and spies, just as Rashid. He would activate his network to find this westerner before he left to go back to Europe. If Scorpion could not catch him here, he would return to Switzerland and deal brutally with Aebischer's daughter. He could bring pain to this assassin by killing all those close to him. It would bring Scorpion satisfaction, but also make his foe act in anger and haste, which led to mistakes.

His black eyes almost glowed with his anger and anticipation. He strode out of his quarters and, after finding Faquir, had him bring an unfortunate girl to his rooms.

Chapter 31

Dan and Uri drove southwest up a wadi. This one ran roughly parallel to the one they had identified from the old man's description. It was late in the day. Part of the way, the road ran out and, after engaging the 4-wheel drive, the Toyota continued, lumbering over the uneven ground. Uri insisted on driving, much to Dan's frustration. Uri was not a very good driver but insisted he could see the soft sand that would bog down their vehicle and trap them. He could "read the desert" as he proudly stated. Dan said nothing about the lengthy time he spent in the Mexican desert, including almost dying of thirst. There he had encountered many of the perils that could trap an off-road vehicle.

They labored farther up the wadi, trying to estimate the distance they guessed the monastery was from how the old man had described its location. The smell of burning, a hot engine, grew stronger in the cab of the SUV. Dan leaned over and checked the engine temperature gauge.

"She's overheating. We need to stop and let the motor cool down. If it seizes up, we're going to be on foot for the rest of the mission."

Uri grunted and forced the Toyota forward until he found a place he thought was acceptable for stopping. By that point, there was a definite smell of overheated coolant flooding the inside of the vehicle.

"Took your damn time about stopping," Dan said. His voice was full of the frustration he felt for Uri's lack of sensitivity to the mechanicals of their worn machine.

"The engine will be fine. You can't imagine how much abuse these motors will take."

"And you want to test those limits, it seems."

Uri turned to him and smiled. "Let's not bicker. We have a long, hot hike ahead of us. With full packs." He got out of the Toyota. "And you get the extra load. Your beloved Sako along with its accessories."

Dan grunted and got out. The two men opened the back of the SUV and began to unload their supplies. Water was on the top of their list along with ammunition. Some MREs were crammed into the nooks of their packs. Both men had their Tavor 7 bullpup carbines strapped to their pack. Dan had an extra pack holding the Sako strapped on as well. The two additions made an uncomfortable load, but he was used to it.

With water bottles ready at hand, the two started up the rocky slope. The ground was a combination of sand, pebbles, broken rock with outcroppings scattered along the way. They detoured around the larger rocky sections jutting from the ground like frozen eruptions. There was dry scrub brush scattered along the hillside. Dan wondered how it found any moisture to grow on the dry hillside. Looking across the valley behind him, he could see small, scrubby trees growing on the top of the slope. The air higher up must have held enough moisture to condense and release its life-giving water to allow larger plants to cling to life.

Life finds a way, even in the least hospitable places, Dan thought to himself. It would be harder for them though, if they were trapped here too long and ran out of water. He had little desire to revisit the near-death he had experienced in Mexico.

Uri was shorter than Dan with a thick body. He showed a softness, probably due to his unhealthy life style, but underneath Dan sensed a strong, solid frame. The climb quickly got Dan into a panting rhythm. His breathing made conversation difficult, but after that adjustment, things became stable. In the mode he had entered, he knew he could go for hours on end. Uri seemed to be struggling more, but didn't slow. Dan was pleasantly surprised at how this older, less conditioned man could keep up with the steady pace.

They reached the top of the wall of the wadi as the sun was setting. As Dan had guessed, this hillside also supported low, scrubby trees. They were festooned with thorns and were unpleasant to brush against. *Everything in the desert wants to sting or poison you.* The thorns he guessed protected the trees from the animals which might have grazed these nearly barren hills, if not now, certainly in the past. Any food, however marginal, would be eaten unless it developed a way to protect itself.

"We should settle down for the night," Uri said. Each man had brought a reflective blanket to wrap himself in for the night chill. While temperatures could be over 100 degrees during the day, the night could bring freezing temperatures. With no humidity to hold the heat, it would radiate into the sky, leaving one shivering after a day of sweating in the heat.

"We'll reconnoiter tomorrow, find an overlook point to search the valley," Dan said.

Uri nodded. "For now, we can enjoy a sumptuous meal courtesy of the U.S. Army and have a nice evening sleeping on the rocks."

"You almost sound as if you enjoy this."

Uri looked off in the distance. "In a way, I do. Working in the cities is always full of tension. You must watch for tails, ambush points. There are so many, you can never relax. Not if you want to survive." He waved his arm around in an arc. "Out here, life is simpler. Right now, we're perfectly safe. No need to even hold a watch. Who knows we're here?" He paused for a moment. "No one. I like that."

Dan smiled. He had to admit, as much as he liked city life, the desert brought a simplicity to it. If you were prepared for its challenges, you could appreciate the sparseness and the clarity that came with it.

After eating an MRE and drinking some of their precious water, both men hunkered down under their reflective blankets to get as comfortable as they could for the night on the hard ground. Dan put his backpack under his head and curled up in his jacket. The temperature plummeted as the sun dropped over the mountains. The sky was sharp and clear. With no city lights and little humidity, the stars stood out with stunning brilliance, floating in the sky. Looking at them, Dan realized how ancient men could come up with constellations that sometimes seemed to have nothing to do with the arrangement of the stars.

"A secret pleasure we can experience before killing," Uri said in a quiet voice.

"The stars seen in the desert are stunning, that's for sure."

"I've lost all personally from my career choice," Uri said. "But you. You're young enough to do something else.

Start a family, maybe live a normal life. Yet you're out here, with me, an old warrior with nothing to lose. Haven't you thought about leaving all of this? What the hell kind of life is this anyway?"

Dan kept staring at the diamond studded sky. "You mean beyond this moment? Cause right now, this is pretty special, if not all that comfortable."

"Like I said, a secret pleasure. But you know what comes next. Always the killing."

"I don't think about it too much. It's what I signed up for. And when I did, there were few options for me."

"But you have options now."

"Maybe. But it seems wrong to leave the field of battle. When I'm not out hunting the terrorists, I worry. They are always plotting the next attack and if I stop, I'm just giving them more room to succeed."

"But you're one against, what, thousands? Maybe more? Does Jane have more than you?"

"You know I can't answer that."

"Okay. But I wonder if you and Jane and her whole black op are not just pissing in the wind, trying to hold back the terrorist hoards."

"You have a better idea?"

Dan could hear the rustle as Uri shook his head. "I used to think we should just bomb them out of existence, but you can't bomb an ideology. It can survive and grow from just one twisted mind to many."

"So, we continue our futile battle because we don't know what else to do."

"That seems to be our fate. Or more accurately, your fate. I'm retired from the front lines."

"Some retirement."

"Screw you," Uri said.

"Maybe the solution is a reformation of Islam. The mainstream currents of the religion have to reform the radicals, purge them from their twisted view of orthodoxy. Right now, they can make a claim to being more pure, even if it's false."

"That will take generations, my altruistic friend. Meanwhile we carry on, sticking our finger in the dike, hoping to hold back the flood."

"You're full of metaphors. Maybe you have a poet's soul inside you."

"Don't mock me. I'm nothing more than a sanctioned killer."

There was a silence. It seemed as though the conversation crashed up against the recognition of the possible futility of it all. Dan's thoughts turned to how effective he had really been. *Must have been having some effect. They sent this monster after me. And when I kill him, the other terrorists will sleep uneasy, as will this wealthy Arab, Rashid.*

"You and Jane have a relationship?" Uri's question pulled Dan out of his thoughts.

"Where did you get that idea?"

"Intuition. I can read the signs. The way she spoke of you hinted at more than just a handler-operative relationship. Did she recruit you?"

"Yes, to the latter question. The other one, no comment. And it's none of your business anyway."

Uri chuckled. "Well, the two of you would share the same home life. That is, if you became a couple. You wouldn't end up like me, with wife and kids leaving."

Dan didn't say anything. It seemed to him that Uri still suffered from his family's abandonment, even if he denied it.

Chapter 32

The next morning, the men got up. Uri grunted as he forced his stiff body into action. Dan understood the effort as he gently limbered up his stiff body. The morning air was chill and moist. It brought the subtle smells of the desert flora, the faint order of sage and other spice smells which Dan could not identify. They all would soon disappear as the day heated up. After some water and an MRE, they packed up their night's cover and set off for the edge of the ridge overlooking the wadi where they hoped to find the monastery.

The ground did not drop off in a cliff, but gradually began to slope ever more steeply down. They crawled the last fifty yards to where they could observe up and down the valley. Neither needed to warn the other about sticking up above the skyline making it easy to be seen by anyone below looking in their direction.

They took their binoculars and searched the valley.

"There it is," Uri said. He had been looking farther up the wadi.

Dan turned in his direction. A couple of miles up the wadi, on the far side, they saw the outline of walls and roof on an outcropping of rock.

"I think you're right. It fits the old man's description."

"We can go back and hike to it along this ridge, it's broad and slopes away. We won't be seen."

Dan started to crawl back away from the edge of the slope. When they were safely out of sight, the two started hiking to the west, this time with increased vigor.

Two hours later, after slow going over the rough ground, they estimated they were parallel to the monastery and headed back to the edge of the slope. Now they could see the details and even the blue van in the courtyard.

"That confirms it," Dan said. "The blue van."

"Okay my assassin, what do you want to do now? Can you take him out from here?"

It was a mile across the wadi. They were higher, looking down. They were positioned in a perfect spot except for the distance.

"Not for sure. The .338 Lapua has a high probability, ninety percent up to about 1,600 yards. My range finder says the monastery is 1,800 yards out. Just over a mile. A .50 cal could do it."

"Why didn't you bring one?"

"You know why. Too heavy, too large. My Sako is a better all-around choice."

"Except that it can't make the shot."

"That means we just have to get closer."

"If we go down into the wadi, we lose the height advantage and you have no sight into the courtyard."

Dan thought about the problem as he scanned the far wall of the wadi. Farther to the west, probably eons ago, there had been an avalanche. The cliff face had broken off and collapsed down into the wadi, creating a steep slope of loose rocks and house-sized boulders. Along the course of the rock slope, were outcroppings of the existing hillside that resisted the slide and stood out like islands amid a sea of boulders.

Could they climb up the slope, probably a half mile from the walls of the monastery? The slope went to the rim, so they could get high enough to fire into the courtyard. It looked possible after some arduous and careful hiking so as not to be seen.

The adrenaline began to flow. Dan's operational habits kicked in. He was the hunter. He knew where the prey was. Now he had to find the way to set up his kill. He'd done this countless times, but the challenge never dulled. It was more than just a matter of life and death, it was the maneuvering, one mind against another. One killer against another. And now he had the advantage. Scorpion would not anticipate him finding his lair. He'd have his guard down.

"We go there, to the west. We can climb the scree left from that rock fall. It's close and most likely in the Sako's range."

Uri scanned the slope Dan mentioned. "We have to wait until nightfall. If anyone's keeping watch, there's no way we can descend this side without being seen."

They were carrying EOTech night vision goggles. They had infrared capabilities so they could spot heat signatures from bodies. This capability, however, would not be of much help in attacking the monastery as its range was just under 300 yards. The monastery was too far away.

The two men backed away from the slope and, again, hiked west, farther up the wadi. When they reached a point across from the rock slide, they sat down to wait for night.

"What's the plan when we get up the slope?"

"I find a shooting spot. Then we wait."

"You'll take him when he comes out into the courtyard?"

Dan nodded.

"What if he doesn't?"

"Highly unlikely. He thinks he's safe here. It's his hideout and he has no way of knowing we're out here."

"I'm just wondering if he maintains surveillance of the wadi. He could see us going across the flats. Anyone out here would be suspect."

"The odds of him monitoring his surroundings 24-7 are slim to none."

"We're banking a lot on that assumption."

"Got to risk something. The rockslide is the perfect place to set up a shot. We just have to be careful getting to it."

Uri didn't answer for a moment. He seemed to be thinking hard. "If I were hiding out here, I'd have some security watching both the eastern approach and this rockslide. It doesn't take a genius to see that this is a good ambush point."

"You think it's that obvious? Or does it seem so because I identified it as a good shooting spot?"

"It just seems safer to assume our foe will use maximum efforts to remain secure."

"I don't underestimate him, but it's human nature to let one's guard down, when one is in their lair. He's here because he thinks it's a safe place. A place where he can relax."

"As much as someone like him can relax. I don't want to think about his idea of relaxing."

"Neither do I. It's just important to understand that such a reaction is normal."

Uri was staring in the direction of the valley. "Not much cover down in the bottom. It's probably a kilometer across the wadi. That's a long way to crawl."

"Hopefully, we'll find parts where we can walk, even in a crouch."

The conversation drifted to an end as they settled down to wait for dark. Both men lost in thought.

"What do you do when we're back from this op?" Dan asked. His question sounded jarring, seeming to come from nowhere, interrupting the silence.

Uri looked at him. The sun was getting low in the sky and would soon drop below the horizon. They had about two hours before it would be dark enough to venture over the edge and descend into the wadi.

"What do you mean?"

"You going to go back to drinking yourself to death?"

"What business is it of yours? And who said I was doing that before? I don't ask about your private life, do I?"

"No, you don't. But everyone could see you were not leading the healthiest of lifestyles."

"*Lek tezdayen*," Go fuck yourself, Uri said.

Even in the dying light, Dan could see the anger in Uri's face that was evidenced in his voice.

"Sorry. It's just you're pretty impressive out here in the field. It makes me wonder why you don't put that to use back home."

"Not much call for ageing assassins. But don't worry about me, think about yourself. From what you said, you've got a problem maintaining close connections. They keep dying on you."

Dan tensed at the dig and started to get up.

"Sorry," Uri said. "That was a low blow."

Dan stopped. It would not be good to create a rift between them at this crucial moment.

"Apology accepted. I was probably out of line with my question. It came from a good place, though."

"Don't worry about me. Just worry about how we're going to get you your shot."

Chapter 33

After it got dark, the two men slipped over the ridge line and started down the slope. They used their NVGs to navigate down the steep slope, going around the places where it dropped off too precipitously for walking. An hour later they were on the floor of the wadi.

"We move in a meandering fashion," Uri said. "If we're seen, they won't be able to discern if the image is human or animal, so we don't want to move with purpose."

"We don't want to take too long, though. Safety is getting into the scree ahead. There we'll have plenty of rocks to hid in."

They walked in a slow, zig-zag manner, but always heading for the opposite wall of the canyon. When they got into a depression, they would crouch and move more quickly, but slow down when they emerged and could possibly be seen.

Two hours of maneuvering with Dan getting increasingly uncomfortable out in the open brought them to the base of the rock slide. Looking up, from the bottom, it was far more daunting than when scanning it from across the wadi.

"That's going to be some climb," Uri said, staring up at the jumble of broken rocks and boulders.

"Let's get going," Dan said.

He started up the treacherous slope. "Be careful to not dislodge any rocks." It would be easy to break an ankle, twist one's foot, or fall and break an arm. Even with the NVGs it was slow going. Neither man wanted to injure himself. Two hours later, the sky started to lighten in the east, presaging the coming of dawn.

Dan had begun to look for a deep cleft in which they could rest and hide. He was not sure they should climb during daylight. *Have to see how exposed we are on the slope.* He was willing to be patient, now that they had tracked Scorpion to his lair. When he found a suitable spot, he stepped into it and sat down.

"We stopping?" Uri asked.

Dan motioned for him to get into the chasm. "We wait. I want to assess how exposed we are. If we're seen and spook Scorpion, he'll be long gone before we can get to the monastery."

"If he runs, we trash the place. Deny him the benefits of this hideout."

"Maybe, but that doesn't catch him...or kill him. I don't want to keep looking for him. I want to end it here, so I'm taking it slow and careful."

Uri shrugged as he lumbered his thick frame into the tight cleft. It was not spacious, but deep enough to shield them from the monastery and its prying eyes.

"Let's not take so long, that this guy leaves on his own. He won't be staying put for months on end."

Uri sat back with a long sigh and shrugged his body, trying to find a comfortable place amid the jagged rocks.

"Not a great place to relax," he said.

They drank some of their precious water and both men ate a power bar. The sun finally burst over the horizon far to the east and down the wadi. Uri peaked over the edge of the depression.

"The sun is fierce, even this early."

He brought his binoculars up and started to study the building.

"Stop!" Dan said in a loud voice. He reached up and grabbed Uri's arm, pulling the binoculars from his face. "You'll reflect the sun and it will flash at the monastery. You'll give away our position."

Uri looked at him with an unbelieving expression, but lowered the binoculars and sat down.

"You think they can see that?"

"I'm sure of it. If someone is looking. Let's hope they weren't. We wait until this afternoon and then we'll have the sun over our backs and can study the grounds."

"So, we don't move out until the afternoon?"

"Maybe. Maybe not. If I can find a path with some cover, we can work ourselves higher. But there'll be no climbing out in the open."

Uri sighed. "Even slower going."

"You should know the value of patience," Dan said.

He got up and carefully peeked out, looking, not at the monastery, but upwards, for a path.

"Let's try to gain more height. Keep your head down."

The climb involved crawling over larger boulders, stepping carefully through smaller ones, and always keeping low, following any serpentine rift that ran down the jumble of stones. Sometimes Dan got stuck and had to quickly go over an exposed rock to get back to some form of cover. The backpack didn't help his maneuvering, but it was a necessary load. Uri followed with much grunting and panting but kept up. He was not as agile as Dan, so exposed himself more often and for more time. It worried

Dan, but he knew they should delay as little as possible to get into position.

Finally, the route demanded they get out on a large section of rock with no cover. Dan stopped.

"It's too exposed to go now. We'll have to wait here until this afternoon. The sun will be in their faces, if they're scanning the valley and it'll be harder to see us."

Uri said nothing and sat down with a grunt. He pulled a water bottle from his pack and took a long drink.

† † †

In the morning, with the sun from the east, the men in the monastery scanned the western reaches of the wadi. Scorpion had instilled in them a rigorous routine of daily monitoring of the wadi, east and west. The task produced no results except for the occasional wild animal. Knowing how easily lookout duties could become routine and ineffective, the men going through the motions, but not taking the point of the vigilance seriously, Scorpion had introduced severe punishment to anyone shirking the daily routine. That included, not doing their monitoring in a thorough manner. Any animal that didn't get noticed and reported resulted in being punished with confinement and reduced rations. In this respect, Scorpion ran a severe, medieval-style operation.

One man took his binoculars from his eyes and stared to the west.

"Did you see something?" his partner asked.

"A flash of light."

"Just the sun reflecting off of something shiny," the other replied.

"Probably, but I don't see it now. I can't seem to find it."

"It's nothing. It's never anything, yet we continue to go through this exercise."

"I will tell our Emir. I don't want to spend two days on just water."

His partner shrugged and the lookout descended the stairs from the walls and went to seek out Scorpion.

"Emir," he said when he found Scorpion in the kitchen area sipping coffee. "I saw a flash of light to the west. It may be nothing, just a piece of metal or glass, but I could not see it after the first time."

Scorpion looked up at the man, standing in the doorway of the kitchen. He was obviously nervous about disturbing his leader, but probably more nervous about leaving something odd unreported.

"So you question why you could not see it again when you re-scanned the area."

"Yes, Emir."

Scorpion took a sip of the coffee and got up. "Show me where you saw this glint."

Chapter 34

The guard pointed to the rockslide where he saw the flash of light. A search of the area showed no signs of anything reflective stuck in the rocks. Scorpion stared up the wadi. If someone were to try to climb to the ridge behind the monastery, that would be the place to do it. But why would someone go there? They could not get down from the ridge to attack the compound, it was a sheer cliff.

They could fire down into the compound, though. A sniper could have a clear sightline, at a reasonable distance to kill anyone showing themselves. The man chasing him was a sniper. He had come to that conclusion after listening to Rashid's recounting of the encounters he assumed were the work of this mysterious person working to defeat his plans.

Could he have evaded his spies? Could he be here? How could he have found his hideout? The questions came flooding into Scorpion's mind. All without answers. But the possibility that such a thing might have happened remained. Finding his lair was the hardest thing for Scorpion to assume had happened. Yet, what about the flash of light? A reflection from the glass of a scope or pair of binoculars? It was all possible, if improbable.

You must not underestimate the enemy. He's killed many who did. Scorpion turned to the lookouts.

"Keep careful watch along that rock fall. Even when the sun goes to the west. Shield your binoculars and keep watching. Look for any movement, something not natural, something other than a jumble of rocks. Report anything unusual to me."

The two guards looked at one another. Their emir, their leader, was taking this random light flash seriously. Without needing to say it, each one of them realized that they must also take the flash seriously and if it was something, they had better discover it before it threatened them.

Scorpion went back inside. He sat down in the kitchen and was handed a small cup of fresh, strong coffee, Turkish in style. His mind went over the possibilities, rejecting for the moment how impossible they seemed.

If someone had found his lair, and he couldn't imagine how that might have happened, they would not drive up the dirt road and knock on the front door. He knew that a few people, mostly merchants in the village a three-hour drive away, might know the whereabouts of the monastery, either from stories about its history, or from his staff who had to go there to purchase supplies. Not being self-sufficient, forced him maintain a connection to the outside world that kept his anonymity from being absolute.

Okay. If someone's found me. The assassin. He's out there. Now what do I do?

Scorpion put aside the incongruity of that idea. He should formulate a plan to deal with the possibility, which would, in the process, uncover whether or not it was real.

He called to his eunuch. "Assemble the men not on watch in the meeting room. Inside, not in the courtyard."

The Scorpion

Five minutes later his fifteen men were standing in front of him.

"Someone is hunting for us. A deadly assassin. He wants to thwart our plans. I want five of you to go up the cliff. Use the secret way up the wall."

Centuries ago monks had carved a torturous set of steps in the cracks of the cliff face that enabled one to climb to the ridge top. It was almost impossible to see and very difficult to use.

"You are to gain the top and hike to the rockslide and search for any intruders."

The men began to mumble among themselves. Scorpion held up his hand. We have seen some evidence of possible intrusion there. You are to find out if this is true or not."

His eunuch and chief of staff picked five men to go out.

† † †

The sun slowly worked its way overhead and towards the west. Uri kept fidgeting in a futile effort to find some comfort amid the jagged rocks. He cursed the heat as they had no way to shade themselves from the sun's onslaught.

"For a man of the desert, as you like to present yourself, you sure complain a lot."

Uri started to offer back a curse but stopped. "I'm uncomfortable. A man of the desert, as you call me, would not spend hours without shade sweating away his body fluids."

"We don't have much of a choice."

"You assassins seem to thrive on sitting quiet while being uncomfortable. Me, I like to get comfortable, or go into action."

"You need to learn patience...and stoicism. You complain too much."

"Go screw yourself," Uri said, now not concerned about the effects of his cursing.

Dan chuckled. "The man of the desert suggests an act that's physically impossible to accomplish, although many wished they could."

"Go…" Uri sighed. He didn't finish what Dan assumed was going to be another repeat of his curse.

"We can start in again," Dan announced. "First move is to crawl across this rock face. There's a low area above it where we can drop into."

Uri raised his head and looked up. "We got a long way to go."

Dan crawled out over the rock face. In a few seconds he dropped out of sight into another crevice. Uri followed more slowly. From there the two went slowly and painfully forward. Knees and hands were scuffed, scratched, and bruised as they alternately knelt among and crawled across the rocks, always being careful to not twist or jam their feet.

Three painful hours later, they had gained only about 400 feet. But it was enough to see into the courtyard. The van had been put away and was not visible any more. Anyone showing themselves, however, would be in danger of Dan's Sako cutting short their life. They were nestled as best they could behind an outcropping that had resisted the slide. It provided a slightly less uncomfortable place to sit and wait as well as give them cover from the monastery and the rim above.

"Now we watch and wait. He has to show eventually," Dan said. He busied himself with measuring the range and computing the trajectory of the shot.

The courtyard was 1,050 yards from their position and approximately fifty feet lower in height. The round would drop 250 inches or nearly twenty-one feet. Dan had computed the adjustments as exactly as he could taking into account he was starting with a fifty foot height advantage. He was ready. He began to settle into his routine, powering down his body to conserve energy, but keeping a watch on the compound. It helped to have Uri there to maintain a watch with him. It relieved his need to be constantly vigilant.

"This is the hard part for me," Uri said. "How long was your longest wait?"

Dan thought for a moment. "I waited for three days once in Iraq. Was sent out to intercept a known high-level officer of the Shia forces fighting us after the fall. Intel had him traveling to Mosul, and I was waiting along the way."

"You got him?"

Dan nodded.

"How'd you get back?"

"Got picked up by a chopper after I reported in the kill. Later we used jets and then drones, so I got reassigned back to troop oversight and support. Lying on rooftops, looking for shooters while the men cleared the streets below me, door to door."

Uri shook his head. "Not for me. Too much lying around, waiting."

"I hope you can stand it this once. We'll only have one chance. Once I take the shot, the game's afoot and he'll know we're on to him."

"I'm banking on you being a good shot. Jane says you are."

Dan smiled and lay back adjusting his body to the rocks. "If this works, we take Scorpion out. It'll sow confusion in his ranks, we carefully retrace our steps, and once we're over the next ridge and back to our old Toyota, we bug out."

Chapter 35

The five men worked their way up the narrow steps carved into the cleft of the cliff. They were not visible to anyone looking at the cliff which was what made them useful, for the monks during the days of the monastery, and now, for Scorpion. It was an escape route if all others were shut down.

The climb was long and stifling in the narrow defile. The men worked in silence; their labored breathing noisy in the narrow cleft. After an hour, they were on top of the ridge. With just a moment's pause, they set out toward the late afternoon sun in the west. A half hour later they came to the collapsed section which had formed the rock scree that flowed into the wadi below.

They approached the edge of the slide carefully, taking up positions behind the boulders left from the collapse. With binoculars, they began to study the slide. Scorpion had told them to watch for movement, and shapes not associated with the jumble of rocks.

After a half hour of searching, one of the men exclaimed, "*Ya lilmufaja'a!*" What a surprise! The men ran to him and he pointed down the scree and put his glasses back to his eyes.

"Where? What do you see?" the men asked.

"Movement, like a body, slipping between the rocks. It's softer than all the hard, jagged rocks. It comes and goes. I can't see it now, but I keep looking."

He pointed to a prominent boulder with a bright, pink color, unlike the gray and brown rocks around it. "Near the large boulder."

Now all the men watched. *"alhamdulilah,"* Praise be to God, one of the men said as he saw the movement. Another man, the leader, took out his phone and called back to the eunuch for instructions.

"We see some movement. At least one man. What do we do?"

"Capture or kill him and bring him back to the compound. Dead or alive."

He turned to the others and related the instructions. The men went back to their positions to watch. No more movement came from below. The figure was not moving. After some time, he thought he saw a head appear, only to vanish a moment later. If the figure did not continue to climb, they might have to descend to it. He didn't relish the thought, knowing he would be exposed. Waiting to kill the one below seemed like the best alternative. No one out here was an innocent. They were a threat. Scorpion had made that perfectly clear.

If a firefight ensued, the man below would be trapped. If he tried to retreat, he would be exposed and easily killed. They could kill him from above, or wait him out until his water ran out. No one could survive long in those rocks.

Suddenly a partial figure showed from behind the outcropping below. Before the leader could instruct his men, a shot rang out. He could see the rock chip from the bullet's impact and the figure disappeared.

"Mughfil!" Fool! he exclaimed. "You have given us away."

"Where can they go? You said we could capture them alive or dead."

"Holy shit!" Uri said as he ducked back behind the rocks. "There's someone above shooting at us."

"They know we're here. Fuck!"

Uri gathered himself for a moment. "This is a tight spot. They have the height advantage and we can't retreat. We move, up or down, we'll get picked off."

Dan crawled around to the other side of the rock protecting them from above. "I can see one, two heads, probably more. Looks like our prey has sent out a patrol to check out the slide."

"And they found us." Uri's face was screwed into a scowl. "There can't be too many of them. They're probably using Kalashnikovs with iron sights. So we won't be easy to hit. We have to lure them out to shoot and then pick them off. Can you get your Sako into action?"

"Not sure. It's a long gun, not like the bullpup. A bit awkward to use."

"Still, if you can get it to bear on them, you can do some damage."

"Agree, but they can send a lot of rounds down on us. That makes up for inaccuracies to some extent."

"Talking about it won't make it work." Uri repositioned himself and eased his Tavor around the boulder and let off a short round. He rolled back as gunfire erupted from the top of the ridge. "I can keep them focused on this side, if you can get your Sako around and pop off a few heads for me."

He put his rifle around the edge and, without looking squeezed off five more rounds.

"I'll keep them focused on me. They like to thunder away."

The return volley of shots confirmed Uri's statement. Dan slipped his rifle and body around the left side of the outcropping. It was the more dangerous side, requiring him to expose more of himself. Uri had them focused, however, and he quickly sighted in on one of the shooters. He did a quick mental adjustment for being half the distance away and squeezed off a round. It caught the man in the upper left chest and spun him backwards to the ground.

He's out of the action. Dan swung back as some of the firing now shifted to his side.

"One down, wonder how many to go?" Uri said. He started to slip down the slope staying under the protection of the tall outcropping. "Got to find another position."

Dan nodded. He watched Uri and waited. Uri, now lower and more to the right, pushed his Tavor through a crack and started firing. The return fire was random, they could not immediately tell where he was firing from. Dan, again slid around the side, only to be met with a burst from above. The rocks to his left exploded from the impacts, sending shards flying into his face. His sunglasses intercepted what would have otherwise been damaging pieces hitting his eyes. He swung himself back.

"Seems like they got one person watching my side, even while they return fire on you."

"Not good. I was hoping they weren't that disciplined."

Uri let off a few more rounds and then hunkered down as the return shooters had now found his location.

"We're pretty well pinned down here," Uri said. He was lying about fifty feet below Dan's position. "If they bring up more men, we're screwed. No way to advance, no way to retreat."

"The Sako is not much use in this environment," Dan said. He laid it down on its case and took up the Tavor 7. "I'm going to have to use the bullpup."

"I'm open to suggestions about our next course of action."

"We could wait for night and retreat. But that leaves Scorpion untouched. I don't like that."

Uri thought for a moment. "We just have to out shoot them. They must expose themselves when they shoot, just like we do. We have to be the ones waiting for them to peek around at us."

"Easier said than done."

"Crawl around, change positions. Each change gives us another 'free' shot before they come back at us. We keep up the exchange, we can gradually thin their ranks."

"How many do you think?"

"It's a patrol," Uri said. "Five to ten. Not sure how many this guy has at his command. We have a problem if he sends more, so we need to get at the job at hand. Time isn't on our side."

Uri turned to his left and started firing up the slope. No bodies were exposed, but he wanted to draw them out. Dan swung around to his left and did the same. The return fire came. Wild and unaimed, but hitting all around them, causing both men to duck. Then heads appeared and the shots drew closer.

Dan crawled across the opening to his left, drawing much of the fire. He grunted as he rolled into a crevice, landing on the rough, uneven rocks. Shots followed him. Uri now started in again when the attention had turned to Dan. The men at the top seemed to have also moved, as return fire came from another position and slammed into the rocks near him. Uri rolled back and made his thick body as small as he could.

Chapter 36

The leader of the patrol called the eunuch again.
"There's two of them. They're good shots."
"I'll call you back."
The eunuch went to report to Scorpion. He told him to send ten more men. When they arrived, they should work their way down the slope to surround the intruders. He'd make sure to overwhelm this assassin.

The men were quickly assembled, armed with AK47s and grenades. They set out for the hidden steps and the top of the wadi rim. It would be nearly an hour until they reached the first patrol.

During a lull in the shooting, Dan crawled over to Uri. "We're in a tough spot. We can't continue to exchange fire with these guys. We'll probably run out before they do."

"I'm worried about reinforcements. If Scorpion has enough men, he can sacrifice them to move down the slope and surround us. We'll have no way out."

Just then gunfire opened up from the rim above. Dan scooted downslope and looked out from a new position. The men were moving now. And their numbers had increased. It was Uri's concern coming to pass.

"They're on the move, and there're more of them." He said to Uri.

Dan began firing and in a short burst dropped one of the men, hitting him in the chest and arms. Others nearby, stopped and dropped for cover. Uri opened fire and pinned down some others. The men out on each side continued to move downward. Dan and Uri directed their fire to them. Uri hit one man in the chest and head with a long burst from the Tavor. Blood and brains sprayed out behind his skull and he dropped like a limp rage. The rest ducked for cover.

There was silence for a few long minutes. Dan figured they were coordinating with each other to move all at once. He and Uri would have targets, but more men could get closer to them.

Suddenly the rocks around them exploded with shards flying in all directions. The fire was coming thick and fast. Dan and Uri looked at one another and then each rolled to a different side and started to return fire. They were forced to send long volleys of shots at the targets to gain the upper hand. Men were dropped, but the price was an exorbitant expenditure of ammunition.

During the exchange, one round ripped through Uri's backpack and twisted him on his side. Another round tore through his right leg. He flopped back behind the rock.

"I'm hit in the leg. Fuck! I think the round broke my femur."

He pulled out his knife and cut open his pant leg. The entry was just above the knee on the inside and the exit was a large, jagged wound on the outside. Dan quickly crawled over to him. The wound was bleeding, but not pumping blood.

"It missed your femoral artery."

He opened his backpack and took out a clotting bandage and jammed it onto the entry and exit wounds, then wrapped a bandage around his leg. Next, he grabbed his belt and looped it around Uri's leg above the wound and pulled it tight. He handed the end to Uri.

"Hold this. Loosen it for a few moments and then re-tighten it. Don't know what other blood vessels are damaged, but this will help control the bleeding."

Then he swung back around the rock and started firing at the men moving down towards them. He hit two of them, killing one and probably just wounding the other one. Whether or not that was enough to take him out of the fight, Dan couldn't guess and didn't have time to wonder about. He ejected the empty clip and snapped in a full one, turning his fire to the other side.

"You should get the hell out," Uri said. "I can't move, and you'll be overwhelmed if you stay."

"Not going anywhere. I plan on getting Scorpion, and I don't leave partners behind."

"I appreciated the sentiment, but I'm a realist. They won't take me alive, and I can slow them down while you escape. Go, regroup, and come at this guy another way."

Dan didn't answer but checked Uri's magazines. He had two left, plus what was in his Tavor.

"Between us, we have just five mags left." At thirty rounds per magazine, that was 150 rounds. They could go through that in three or four exchanges, trying to slow down the advance.

Dan looked to the west. In an hour the sun would be setting. They had a chance if they could hold out that long. There was no fire coming from above. He heard some scrapping and rumbling of rocks and peered out. A few men were working their way down to the lower group. They had full backpacks, probably loaded with more ammunition. Dan trained his sights on one of the men and when he stepped into an opening, fired a short burst. The man's body swung violently sideways and he fell in a heap on the rocks. As Dan was drawing back, another attacker grabbed the man's pack and pulled it behind a rock just as Dan swung his rifle back to the target.

He glanced to his right and more men were now starting down. Dan fired, switching from target to target, hitting some with what were likely lethal shots, the others dropping to cover and stopped for the moment. His magazine ran dry, and he had to insert another one.

"How you doing?" Dan asked.

"Wonderful. This is just what I needed. Seriously wounded on a fucking rockslide in the middle of Yemen."

"I got an idea."

"I got one too," Uri said. "When the sun goes down, you get the fuck out of here and ambush Scorpion on his way down the wadi. He's not going to stick around after this attack. He'll think his cover's blown." Uri gave out a short, harsh laugh. "Little does he know, we're the only ones who know his secret."

"I got a better idea. When night comes, I climb up the rocks and take out the rest of the attackers. I'm guessing they had about ten men total, with both groups. We've killed, what, five or six? There can't be that many left. They won't come down after dark. They're probably asking their boss for more men. Not sure how many he's got, but I'm betting they'll all wait for daylight."

"That's a lot to bet on. Not only your estimate of how many are left, but that they won't move on us at night. How do you get the upper hand when you're outnumbered?"

"NVGs. They don't know we have them. It'll be like shooting fish in a barrel."

"Fish in a barrel?"

"Just a saying we have in the states."

"Chickens in a coop. I can relate to that." Uri was silent for a moment as he adjusted his tourniquet. He grunted with the pain. "I still think my plan is better."

Dan bent over his leg and studied the wound. He pulled off the clotting bandage and put another one on. Then he wrapped the leg back in a tight cloth bandage.

They both heard scrapping sounds from above and Dan rolled over, this time on Uri's side and opened fire. He went through the rest of his current magazine.

"I'm down to this one," he said as he clicked his last full mag in place. "Next I have to use yours."

"You're welcome to them."

Chapter 37

A loud explosion erupted just above and to the left of Dan and Uri. It sent rocks flying past them and raining down from above. Some of the rocks in the slide began to roll down around them. They were protected by the outcropping but if the slope gave way, they could be dislodged and crushed.

"What the hell?" Uri said. "Grenades?"

Dan nodded.

"We *are* fucked." Uri tied off his tourniquet and grabbed his Tavor. His magazine held twelve rounds. He handed the other one to Dan who had already taken one for his rifle. "Looks like a last stand. I don't know how we stop them now if they can lob grenades at us.

"Have to hit us. We've got pretty good cover here."

"Until one of them manages to drop one over the outcropping, right into our laps."

Dan didn't answer but crawled to the side of the cover. Up the slope, a man stood to throw a grenade, Dan shouldered his Tavor and hit him in the chest. The man and the grenade dropped backwards. Two other men jumped from where they were hiding nearby. Dan was able to drop one of them. The grenade went off. Dan hoped it had taken out the other man.

The sun had now gone below the horizon and the day was darkening quickly. Dan watched the light dimming. He could soon put his plan into action.

"When it gets darker, I'm going up."

Uri nodded. He lay back against the rocks, his face sunken and pained. His voice came more ragged and softer.

"This is a bad one. The femur is shattered and every time I move, I think I'm cutting soft tissue. You can't do anything for me. Even if you get them all. How do you get me off this rock slide and to some help?"

"Let's cross that bridge when we come to it. First, I want to take out those bastards above us."

Another explosion went off to their right. Both men ducked from the flying pieces of rock.

"Just a few more minutes and it'll be too dark for them to lob the grenades on us."

"Just go carefully. I expect to die here, but it would be dumb for you to do so as well," Uri said.

When the reinforcements joined the first party, the addition of grenades were well received. However, none of the men looked forward to moving farther down the slope to surround the two waiting for them. They had seen the effectiveness of their shooting and figured some of them would find the same fate as those already killed or badly wounded.

A few more grenades were lobbed down as the leader forced the men to descend the rock slope. None of the projectiles hit the outcropping that was shielding the two. As night fell, the leader called a halt. He wanted to make the best use of his advantage and wait until morning. Then he could start an intense grenade assault on the position and descend lower. His numbers had been reduced by the effective shooting. Even with the reinforcements, he was down to six men counting himself.

He also had two wounded men suffering who probably wouldn't last the night. When it became light, he'd have one man throwing grenades down the slope, two more shooting, and the remaining three, scrambling to surround the two intruders.

No more grenades came down. Dan got out two MREs and heated them. Uri shook his head.

"Just some water. I can't eat anything." His voice was strained and low. Dan could hardly hear him. Dan ate one of the meals and left the other one near Uri.

"If you get hungry."

Uri looked over at him. His eyes bloodshot, his face pale.

"Make sure you let the blood flow into the leg. You don't want to cut circulation off completely. It's to slow down hemorrhaging."

"I know how it works," Uri said in that pained voice.

"I'll be going out soon."

Uri nodded.

Dan busied himself, checking out his goggles and his Tavor 7. He'd use the tactical carbine. It was shorter. Better at close ranges. He figured he'd get in only two shots at best before the others started to return fire. Dan had no doubts he could be effective. He'd rely on his superior vision with the goggles to help him move and strike from new positions. That would keep the others off guard. The one wild card was that he didn't know how many men were left. And it would be lethal to not identify a last combatant who could ambush him when he thought the fight was over.

Two hours later, it was dark and Dan figured he had a little over an hour before the moon came up. One and a half clips. Forty-five rounds to finish the fight. Dan looked over at Uri. He took out one of the thermal blankets and spread it over the man.

"I'm heading out now."

Uri reached out his hand and Dan crawled over to him. Uri gripped his arm. "Don't get yourself killed." His voice while strained had strength in it. "One of us had to get out of here. You have your mission. You have Jane. I sense something more there than you admit to. I'm retired and now done. Let's both not die here."

"I won't die and neither will you."

Uri tried to smile and released Dan's arm. He slumped back against the rocks and looked off into the distant sky.

Dan rolled over and looked around the outcropping. He studied the slope above through his goggles. The scene was bathed in a diffuse green light. The stars, while not offering much light to one's naked eye, gave him enough background light allow the image enhancement to work.

Dan patiently scanned the rocks. He couldn't see anyone or any movement. He turned his gaze to the rocks in front of him and started out in a crouch. While he could see the rocks well, making out where to put his feet and seeing smaller rocks to avoid, so he would not dislodge them, he knew he was not invisible to anyone watching from above. There was enough starlight to see an object as large as a human moving, if he walked upright.

He had the Tavor slung over his back, the one spare mag tucked into his tactical jacket. He had left his backpack with Uri. He'd either come back to get it along with his wounded partner, or he wouldn't have any need for it.

He worked his way up the slope, keeping to the west of where he felt the attackers were hunkered down. He had to back up numerous times when his path gave out and left him with a large boulder to climb over, exposing himself to the skyline. He remained patient. He had limited time but rushing upward would destroy his chances of surprise. He needed that element in order to quickly reduce the number of men he had to engage.

Forty minutes later, Dan stopped and scanned the rocks at his level. He found two men lying separately behind two large boulders. They were relaxed, maybe sleeping. Dan couldn't tell. *Two of how many?* He kept scanning to try to find the others. He found a third man, behind and to the east of the first two. He could only see his legs, but noted his position. When the shooting started, he could direct his fire quickly to "legs" and, hopefully, take out a third attacker. Still the question, *how many?* loomed.

Another five minutes brought no new sightings. *They all seem to be on this level.* That was a good thing. It would not do to have men above him able to fire down on his position when he started shooting. His breathing came in slow, steady drafts. He felt the adrenalin flowing but controlled his reaction to it. Alertness, muscles charged and ready to move, but no shakes or unsteadiness. It was sniper-like in the sense he was striking unseen and unexpected, but un-sniper-like in that, after the initial strike, he'd be in a ferocious firefight with an unknown number of opponents. Still, he had the advantage of superior sight.

"Time to begin," he said to himself under his breath.

Chapter 38

Dan settled into a shallow cleft in the rocks that gave him a rest for his rifle. The bullpup design, with the magazine located behind the trigger, made for a small package, even with the suppressor attached, and the centered weight made handling the rifle easy.

He rechecked the location of the two men he could see as well as the legs of the third man. The others, if there were any, would have to show themselves after the shooting started. When he had his targets located, Dan went back to his first man. He was sitting with his back to a large boulder, his head slumped down, asleep. Dan squeezed the trigger, and the rifle made a sharp, flat pop sound. The man's head erupted, and he tipped over to his side, never to awake. Before he fell over, Dan moved to the next one who was looking up to see what the noise was. He never found out as Dan's shot hit him in the forehead, bursting his skull. He turned to "Legs", but the man had disappeared, but Dan watched the place where he had last seen him.

Suddenly, voices called out in Arabic. *Probably asking what was going on.* The suppressor wouldn't fool them but did create some initial confusion. Legs reappeared, peeking out from around a large rock. He was scanning for where the shots had come from but could see nothing. Dan, however, could see him. He squeezed off a third round and the man fell back and out from behind the rocks. Dan saw him drop limply to the ground.

Then gunfire erupted from three other locations. The shots were not well aimed as Dan's rifle didn't show much flash with the suppressor attached, so was not easily seen. Dan picked one of the shooters from his gun flashes. He could see the shooter popping out to deliver a short burst and then drop out of sight. The man was being careful. *Have to watch through a burst and hit him while he's exposed.*

Dangerous, but Dan felt the advantage was with him and his NVGs. He ignored the other shooters for the moment. They were also being careful to fire short bursts and then get back under cover.

The man reappeared and started firing. Dan returned a short burst from the Tavor just as the man dropped back down. *Damn!* He had just missed him. The other two shooters now had Dan's position located and they sent rounds too close for Dan to risk exposure. He crawled back to find more cover and began to work his way up the slope and then to his right, towards the shooters. They didn't know he had moved and continued to send short automatic rounds towards his last location. *Maybe wondering why they're not getting return fire. Do they think I'm hit?* If the men thought that, it would only help him in his attack.

Back at the monastery, Scorpion heard the firing. The AK47s were not suppressed and their sound carried in the night air. He knew his men wanted to wait until morning to attack using the grenades. Was this a counterattack? He turned back to loading the van. The eunuch had provisioned the vehicle with food and water and weapons. Standing nearby were the three men who remained at the monastery, awaiting Scorpion's orders.

The eunuch was busy gathering the two women, Scorpion kept at the monastery. He would get the women ready to come with them unless his master told him not to. It was always better to be overly prepared than to come up short. Although he had saved his life, Scorpion was a harsh taskmaster.

While Dan had been working his way through the rocks, he kept an eye out for the man he had missed as well as trying to pinpoint the two other shooters' positions. Once he had gained some elevation over his missed target, he found a place to sit down and rest the rifle. Through his NVGs, he watched as the nearest shooter, fifty yards away, stood up to fire another short burst. Dan was behind him now and put his sights on him. As the man started to rise again, Dan's shot hit him between the shoulder blades, near the base of his skull. His body was flung against the rock that he was hiding behind and then slid to the ground.

Shots rang out from a location Dan had not pinpointed. It was from the east, the direction of the monastery and even higher than Dan had climbed. The rounds hit the rocks next to Dan and fragments flew into his face and tore through his sleeve and pants, digging into his arms and legs. Without hesitation, he dropped to the ground and scrambled backwards. He had no protection from the shooter's position. As he crawled over the rough ground, tearing more of his clothes, more shots rang out. *Two more shooters. How many are there?*

Dan started to work his way up the rock scree again. He went slow and stayed under cover. He knew the shooters could not see him as he picked his way upward, crawling and crouching through the rocky jumble. He moved slowly, careful to not make noise and give away his movements. After gaining about 100 feet in height, Dan stopped to survey the rocks to his east, looking for the shooters.

At that moment, shots rang out from below. *Uri?* They came from the area where he and Uri had hidden. *He's trying to draw them out.* Uri must have watched the gun flashes as his shots seemed to be aimed at a specific area. Then Dan saw a man just east of him, at the same height stand up. He was probably the one who flushed Dan from his hiding place. The man aimed down below, looking for Uri's flashes. Dan quickly sited him and fired. The shot seemed to hit him in the right shoulder. He dropped his rifle and fell to one side with a cry of pain.

That'll keep him out of the fight. Possibly kill him before too long. One left? Dan hoped he had counted correctly.

Uri knew he was losing his battle to stay alert. The pain had increased and his wound seeped blood, even with the tourniquet and clotting bandages. He heard the shooting from above. Dan had engaged the enemy. Uri chafed at just sitting, injured, not able to help. He cursed his luck. A stray shot from someone who was probably a lousy shooter, had taken him out and maybe killed him.

Got to help, somehow. Contribute to the mission, before I give out. He grunted with the pain and shuffled his body to peer around the side of the rocks. He had a few shots left in his mag. *Might as well use them.* When he saw the flashes, above and to the east of him, definitely not coming from Dan, he squeezed off a round directed at each one. *If I can draw their fire, Dan should be able to take them out.*

Each precious round was well placed at the two separate shooters. They responded and began to send rounds back down to Uri's position.

With the shooters' attention drawn to Uri, Dan was able to shift his position and expose one of the shooter's locations. It was an easy shot and the man dropped as two rounds slammed into his side. The other shooter turned to fire in Dan's direction, but he hadn't pinpointed his position. With the dark, he was firing blind. Dan watched through his goggles and when the shooter exposed himself to fire off some rounds in his general direction, he sent a burst at his silhouette. The man cried out and collapsed.

Then it was all quiet. No more shots from the attackers, no shots from Uri. Dan didn't move, but scanned the area. He didn't want to get ambushed by one last shooter who had the good sense to hide and not give away his position when he couldn't see Dan. Nothing showed as Dan took time to carefully survey the area. Patience overruled his desire to get back to Uri.

Chapter 39

Dan called out to Uri as he approached the outcropping. He didn't want to get shot after they had won the battle. The moon was coming up and it looked like daylight through the NVGs.

"Uri, I'm coming in," Dan said in a loud voice.

"Come on." Uri's voice sounded weak and strained.

"You get them all?" he asked when Dan reached him.

"Yep. I watched for a while, but there's no one up there left alive or operational."

"Good. You get into position and take Scorpion out when the sun comes up, He may try to leave the compound when he figures out we've killed all his men."

Dan took off his NVG and picked up his binoculars. With the moonlight he could see into the compound. It was empty and nothing moved.

"Doesn't look like they're going anyway, at least for now."

"Good chance they will after dawn. You should be in position."

"Agreed. But I'm taking you up the slope with me."

Uri shook his head. "No, no. I'll just slow you down. How the hell are you going to get me up this rock slide?"

"With a lot of fucking effort."

"I'm not kidding. I'm not a light load. Just leave me here."

"I don't do that. I don't leave my partners behind. We go out together."

"Fuck that sentimentality. You got a mission to accomplish."

"I do. And that now includes getting you back. Don't worry. I can do both."

"You some kind of superman?"

"No. Just a hard-working assassin." Dan squatted down beside Uri. "Now let me look at that wound."

He took out his flashlight, not worried now about anyone shooting them. The wound looked raw but he could see no signs of infection…yet. *Got to get him some help soon. With the bone shattered, this isn't going to heal itself and he's gonna keep losing blood, even if I can slow it down.*

"Those guys got up on the rim from the monastery. There has to be a way down, a path, even though it looks like a cliff. We'll get up this slide and find where they came up. If we hustle, we can be there by dawn. I can set up on the rim and take out anyone in the compound."

"What then? That won't change my future. I'll just die on the rim instead of this rock slide. Might be a little more comfortable up there, though."

"We'll figure out what's next after we get to the rim. First things first."

Dan pulled on his backpack and reached down to Uri. "Got to get you on your feet for a moment. It'll hurt."

"Hurts now," Uri said.

He grunted through clenched jaws as Dan heaved him erect in one great heave. He held Uri as the man balanced on one leg.

"Leg's throbbing pretty bad now."

The Scorpion

Dan nodded. He picked up Uri's backpack. "Put this on. I'm going to carry you. I'll come back down for my backpack and the rifles after I get you to the top."

"You're a stubborn son of a bitch, you know that?"

"I've been told. And, for the record, so are you."

Dan leaned over and Uri reached up to his shoulders. He pulled as Dan reached back and grabbed Uri's good leg and hooked his arm around his bad leg, above the bullet wound. Uri gasped and groaned as Dan jerked him up onto his back. He staggered under the load. He guessed Uri weighed around 180 pounds. In spite of Dan's optimism, it would be a hard slog to get up the slope. Still there was the moonlight and the NVG amplified it, so he could at least see. He would just concentrate on his path right in front of him. Uphill was all that mattered, gaining the rim.

Dan moved in slow motion, every step a painful struggle. His back was bent to help Uri hold on. His head lowered to study the ground. A fall could be disastrous for both of them. As he slowly trudged upward, a rock slipped underneath him and he dropped in a controlled fall, his knee hitting hard on a rock.

"Damn!" he exclaimed.

Uri stepped off to relieve his weight from Dan as he recovered his feet. Then Uri climbed back on and they continued in their slow and painful pace upward. When they came to one of Scorpion's men. Uri called out. "Stop."

He slid off Dan's back and collapsed to the ground. There he squirmed around until his leg was above the rest of his body. "Got to slow down the bleeding." His voice was hoarse from the pain. "Hanging off you seems to open things up. I feel like I'm pouring blood out of my leg."

Uri looked over at the dead terrorist. "Grab his AK and bring it to me. Also grab any full mags. We can use the ammunition."

"Roger on the mags, but we don't need the rifle. We'll just load the rounds into our mags."

"I want the rifle for a crutch. If you help, maybe I can walk by using this to take weight off my leg. If we stop every few minutes, for me to elevate the leg, maybe I can make it up. At the pace we're going, we'll be late to the rim. And if you fall again, we may never make the rim with me along."

Dan retrieved the rifle and four magazines from the dead man and came back to where Uri was lying.

"This ain't much of a crutch."

"It'll do. I don't care if I fuck it up. I'm not going to shoot it later. Go back down and get your pack and rifles. I don't mind lying here for a few more minutes."

When Dan returned, he helped Uri to his feet and the two of them began to hobble slowly up the slope. Dan was on Uri's injured side; Uri had his arm over Dan's shoulder. He held the AK47, muzzle down, with his other arm and used it to take weight off his injured leg.

"Not less painful, but we're going better and there's less chance of falling."

Two hours later, they made it to the rim and relatively flat ground. Uri lay back on the dirt, happy to be off the rocks. "This feels great. Almost as good as a feather bed."

Dan could hear the pain and fatigue in his voice even as Uri tried to joke about his situation. The rim had some of the scrubby, thorny trees that they had found on the south rim of the wadi. The ground was a mix of sand, dirt, and smaller rocks, with occasional bedrock projecting out of the thin soil.

"Help me get under one of those trees. I'll wait there. You go ahead. We're running out of nighttime and you need to be in position."

"Those are the thorn trees."

"I'm not going to climb the fuckers, just use their shade if you'll kindly sweep the ground."

After settling Uri in, getting him water and an MRE, propping up his leg, Dan set out to find the way down the cliff. He used his goggles and was able to follow the footprints of the two groups. *That's going to make it easier to see where they came up the cliff.*

Chapter 40

"What do you think, *majistir*? Of all the shooting?" Faquir, the eunuch, thought the worst, but wanted his master to weigh in on the situation.

"My men may have attacked at night." He paused for a moment. "But I doubt it."

"Did the intruders attack?"

"Maybe. There were only two, but if they had night vision goggles..." He let the thought trail off. If they had NVGs, they would have an advantage. But could they overcome all the men he had sent? Scorpion doubted it, but his instincts again cautioned him to not underestimate his opponent. Those men had found him, against all odds. What else could they accomplish? He had to be ready to leave and regroup to fight again.

He could not call in a helicopter. Rashid would not respond. He only sent one to bring Scorpion to him. There would be no copter to evacuate him. Nothing to link Rashid to Scorpion. His black eyes darkened even more in anger. That was his position and such was his fate. He had to rely on no one but himself, as he had done for most of his life.

Reputable people did not want to associate with him. It didn't bother Scorpion. He knew who he was. He was not capable of polite company. He was a killer, one with a twisted mind. There was no remorse about it. He indulged his sick urges. They satisfied the dragon inside of him, for a while at least. In between assignments, the dragon grew restless and that was when innocents were in danger. When he was on a mission, the dragon was focused on business. Now it was time for business, the business of retreat. At least for a while.

"Is the van ready?"

"Yes, *majistir*."

"Let's see what the morning brings."

On the rim, Dan scoped the compound yard with his range finder. Then he pulled out his ballistic notes. It was just over 500 yards out and below the rim. He'd be shooting downward, so any drop correction had to be increased as the round would drop more when aimed downward. After going over the numbers again and again, he finally was satisfied that he had a good computation of the correction and dialed in his scope. There was little wind and it would be calm in the morning as well. When his calculations were done, he settled down with the thermal blanket over him and waited.

There had been no sleep that night and maybe little in the coming day, but that was how it went sometimes. One had to act when the time required action. Rest had to be put aside. An MRE helped bring fuel to his body. He decided against the instant coffee. He wanted calm nerves. The coffee could come later. Now he had to remain prepared to take the shot and end this cat and mouse chase over half of Europe and most of the Middle-East.

The sun broke over the horizon. It produced a sharp glare but with Dan's downward aim, it didn't interfere with his vision. The courtyard below was shrouded in shade from the high walls and would remain that way for another hour.

As the day grew light, Scorpion listened for the sound of renewed battle. Nothing. He pulled out his phone and called the team leader. There was no answer. He tried another number. It rang and rang with no answer. His face remained implacable, but his mind raced. *Are they all dead? Could this assassin have done that?*

He would not sit around waiting for his enemy to find a way into his fortress. If he had done the impossible, Scorpion figured he'd get inside the monastery. He would not wait for him, but go and disappear. The man would not find him twice. He'd become a nomad. There would be no redoubt, no sanctuary where he could be found. He'd lived that way before and would again.

"Faquir, call the men."

There were only three fighters left in the compound along with Faquir, the cook, two maids, and the two girls he kept for pleasure. When the men were assembled, Scorpion told them to gear up and report back to him at the van in ten minutes.

"I am leaving with the three soldiers," he told Faquir. "You stay with the staff and girls, as always. Keep things ready. I may be gone for a while, but I will be back, as always. The two men out there, on the rim of the wadi, may come. They will not harm you or the others. They are searching for me. But they won't find me. And I will repay them for the loss of my men."

"Yes *majistir*."

Scorpion could see the eunuch's disappointment, but he was too loyal to protest. There were very few in the world he could trust and Faquir was one of the few.

When the men came back, Scorpion got into the van. One of his soldiers got into the driver's seat. Scorpion had his own weapons, an AK47 and a Sig Sauer P320 in a hip holster. All the men had grenades attached to their tactical vests with multiple magazines in the pockets. Scorpion nodded to Faquir who pushed the door open.

Dan forced himself to keep a steady watch, allowing his eyes to roam over the monastery, but always sweep back to the courtyard where he expected to find his target. Scorpion had to know by now something was wrong. Dan couldn't guess his reaction; anything from fleeing and going into hiding, to sending out more fighters. He had to be ready for any response. His Sako was equipped with a five-round magazine. The bolt action had a 60-degree opening angle for a rapid cycling of shots. He had four magazines laid out on a cloth near him and more in his pack.

As he looked over the monastery, a set of double doors swung open. Dan immediately centered his eye behind the scope and watched. His whole body now alert, almost tingling in anticipation. Despite the surge of adrenalin, he lay still, allowing it to course through his body. It would be just a moment, and then he could sink back into that zone, but with more focus and intensity. His breathing became calm again. His heart rate slowed as if on command. The invisible thread that connected him and his rifle to the target now stretched out. He could envision the looping path the round would take on its flight. The world around him disappeared and there was only what he saw in his scope. That was his world.

Instead of bodies coming out of the building, the blue van appeared, headed for the main gate. A man ran ahead of it, perhaps to open the gate. Dan's brain registered the thought in a moment, *he's fleeing*. Then he sighted through the windshield and stroked the trigger. The Sako let out a sharp, crack, even with the suppressor, as it bucked against Dan's shoulder. The sound was not loud enough to be heard below. The supersonic crack of the round would alert them, just after the round struck.

The windshield shattered and the van swung to one side and stopped. Dan immediately loosed two more rounds into the front seats. Two men jumped from the van, on the protected side. Dan's next shots were through the radiator. He quickly ejected the spent mag and snapped in a fresh one. Automatic fire came from behind the van. Not well aimed. *Don't know where I'm at, yet.*

The figure that had been in front of the van, heading to the main gate, now ran back to the cover of the van. Then the van started to back up. *Someone's still alive in there.* They must have crawled forward and now were moving the van while lying below the windshield, out of sight. He sent more rounds into the front of the van and the engine to little effect. The Toyota backed towards the garage and bumped against the wall. The side door opened and someone jumped out. It looked like three men made it back into the garage.

Chapter 41

Dan pulled back from the Sako and took out his binoculars. He studied the compound. The van had stalled against the garage door, partially blocking it. How many were in there dead? Dan didn't know. It didn't make any difference. They were out of the equation at this point. What mattered was three men made it back inside; one of them was the Scorpion.

Dan watched for a few more minutes and then got up. He hurried back to where he'd left Uri.

Uri had sagged down some from where Dan had left him propped against a tree. He looked up with a haggard face, full of pain.

"Heard the shooting. You get him?"

Dan shook his head. "He's not leaving by vehicle, but he got back under cover before I could take him out."

"What do you do now?" Uri's voice was strained and thin sounding.

"We're going to the monastery. He's either in there and I'll find him, or he's got another secret way out. If he left, he'll be on foot and I'll catch him."

"Leave me in the monastery? Why not leave me here?"

"You'll be more comfortable. If you can make it up that rock slide, you can make it to the monastery." He bent over Uri. "Let's go."

"Ahhh!" Uri groaned as Dan yanked him to his feet.

He put Uri's pack back on him and they set out as before, only the going was much easier on the relatively flat ground. Soon they came to Dan's shooting spot. Near it, there was a crack in the surface of the ground. Looking in, one could see steps carved in the side of the stone. They led into a deeper cleft that worked its way down the cliff face.

"That'll be hard going. I'll stay in front of you. If you lose your balance, you'll fall into me."

"And we'll both fall to our deaths."

"No. I'm going to catch you. I'll make sure I'm always braced."

Dan started down. Uri dropped the AK47 and gingerly started down the crevasse. The steps were not much more than footholds cut into the rocks. Near the top it was narrow. Uri's back was against the opposite wall, which helped protect him from losing his balance. As they descended, the opening widened some and soon, they were able to step down the stairs rather than climb down them as if on a ladder.

Part of the way, Uri called out for a stop. He was panting from the exertion.

"This is tough. My leg is throbbing like it's going to burst from blood."

"I feel for you, but we have to keep going. There's no place to relieve the pressure until we get to the bottom."

Uri grunted. "Better get moving then. I only have so much left before I collapse. And a collapse on these stairs would not be good."

They continued; Dan going patiently, carefully, while Uri grunted and heaved behind him, trying to not load his injured leg. A long hour later, they were at the bottom. Uri collapsed to the ground. They were just outside the walls of the monastery.

"You go on from here. I'm tapped out."

"I'll get something to use to drag you in after I check things out."

† † †

Scorpion stood inside the stable which he had transformed into a garage. The van and its supplies were pushed up against the door, blocking the exit for the additional vehicle in the garage. The driver was dead. Faquir and two soldiers stood with him.

One of the soldiers slipped out of the door, using the van as cover, and crawled inside. A moment later, the bags they had packed were dropped outside. The other soldier crawled out to help pull them back into the garage. Scorpion stood in deep thought. He was not sentimental, nor was he one to panic. Two intruders had decimated his men. His numbers advantage had disappeared. Now he was clearly the hunted. He had no illusion that the assassin would not be coming. Why was he not down the stairs by now?

Scorpion thought it through. Only one shooter. Only one figure up on the rim. He had seen a fleeting glimpse of that figure headed back towards the rock slide. And two men had clearly been reported by his men. Then it came to him. The other one was injured, probably shot. The assassin went back to get him. He was not going to leave him.

A humorless smile cracked Scorpion's face. His enemy had saddled himself with a liability. One that gave some advantage back to Scorpion. It would slow his pursuit or even keep him from pursuing. In any case, his odds of escaping had just improved. If he pulled the man off the rock slide, he wouldn't then leave him up there, or even at the monastery in order to pursue him. That was not what Scorpion would do. He didn't admire the effort. To him it was a distraction from the mission. But he was glad his opponent felt the way he did. It compromised his mission and helped Scorpion.

"Do we wait for them to come?" the man asked.

Scorpion shook his head. "No, we will leave. Disappear. We'll come back another day to kill this attacker. But for now, his search will come up empty."

He turned to repack the gear into four backpacks: ammunition, water, food. His soldier caught on and quickly stepped forward to help. In a few minutes, they had finished the task.

"Do we use the car?"

Scorpion shook his head. We can't get it out. And the attackers will be watching."

Scorpion shouldered one pack and motioned to his men to do the same.

They tramped down the stairs to the kitchen. There he told the cook and two serving girls they were leaving. He told them to stay. The man who would come would not harm them. In fact, he had a partner who needed help. They would be safe. The group looked at Scorpion with eyes full of dread. The two pleasure girls came down to the kitchen to hear the last of what Scorpion said. They started crying but stifled their sobs after he gave them an angry look.

"I'm going with you, *majistir*," Faquir said.

Scorpion looked at him intently.

"My place is with you. These," he swept his arm in the direction of the servants, "don't need my protection."

Scorpion nodded. Without another word, he and the three men, started down the hall to the basement stairs where the wine and supplies were kept. Down there was also a small door to a tunnel that came out near the road about 500 feet below the monastery. From there the men could work their way down the many ravines that carried water to the wadi floor in the wet season and, from there, continue east. It was a two day hike out of the wadi and then another two days to the nearest town, but they were on familiar ground. Scorpion had kin, not too many days hike away. Relatives who would shelter him and deliver him farther into the wilds of the desert, out of reach of any western assassin.

Chapter 42

Dan studied the compound through a crack in the gate doors. Nothing moved. He could see only a sliver of the inside of the garage, but nothing showed there either. It was well into the day, but still a long way from night. *If I wait until dark to slip in, if he's leaving, he'll be long gone.* That fact, plus Uri's condition, which was not improving, meant he had to take some chances; ones he normally wouldn't take.

He tested the latch. It lifted. The door was solid wood and would stop most rifle rounds. Still, he didn't want to bet his life on it. He gave the large panel a pull and stepped back behind the mud, brick wall. The door slowly swung open. No gunfire came from the compound. *Either not there or well-disciplined.* Again, he had to roll the dice and choose. He looked through the joint between the door and the wall but saw only the same empty, still compound.

If he went through the entrance, there was no place to hide before getting to the wall of the building. He would be exposed as he traversed the thirty yards. Dan looked over at Uri who lay against the outer wall, panting. He had a bottle of water and his leg on the backpack.

"I'm going in," Dan said in a quiet voice.

Uri looked over at him and gave him a feeble thumbs up. Dan took off his backpack, put down his Sako, now back in its cover and readied his Tavor. He had loaded two magazines from ammunition scavenged from the attackers. He inserted one and kept another full one and his partially emptied mag in his vest pocket. With a deep breath and one last look, he stepped around the edge of the massive door and sprinted for the building in a low crouch.

It took only a few seconds to cover the distance. Dan stared hard at the opening until he reached the shelter of the wall, to one side of the van. After catching his breath, he worked his way around the Toyota and now could see more clearly inside. The garage was empty.

He stepped in and crouched down, waiting a moment for his eyes to adjust to the darker interior. The contrast with the intense brightness outside was severe. In a few seconds, he could clearly see the interior in detail. There were some items scattered on the floor along with two duffel bags. To one side was a door leading into the rest of the building. Dan moved carefully through it, carbine at ready. He stalked down the corridor, checking each room as he went. It was slow going, but he couldn't allow an ambush from behind. He moved along the corridor keeping note of places he could dive to if someone ahead started shooting. He'd have only the briefest of moments to gain cover and return fire.

When he got to a central hallway, he stopped. *Too many choices and I don't know the layout.* There was the muffled sound of voices coming from another hallway. Dan turned towards the sound. *Find out who this is. Scorpion would not be so careless.*

As he went down another corridor, the sound grew in volume. People talking in Arabic, quietly, yet it carried through the silent halls. Dan crept down the corridor without a sound until he came to an open doorway. It was a kitchen. He could smell the rich mixture of seasonings and cooking.

He stepped through the doorway, the Tavor up and ready to fire. There was a scream as Dan swept the room with his carbine, searching for a threat. The people put up their hands in surrender.

"'*Ajlis,*" sit down. Dan used one of the few Arabic words he knew. The group lowered themselves to the floor. There was one man and four women. Two of the women were dressed plainly and looked to be servants or maids. The other two were more glamorous and younger.

"Scorpion? Where did he go?"

They looked at him, not understanding, shaking their heads.

"Scorpion." he said again. "Boss. Leader."

Still the uncomprehending looks. Finally, the cook said something in rapid Arabic and pointed his finger in the direction down the hallway beyond where Dan had come.

"Gone," he said.

Can't leave them here without securing them. Dan cast around the room for something to tie up the captives. He grabbed some towels and cut them into strips with his knife. One of the younger women started whimpering when she saw the knife.

After shouldering his Tavor, Dan took each person and tied them in separate parts of the kitchen.

Not too secure, but that'll have to do for the moment. He needed to confirm Scorpion had left before getting Uri inside and making arrangements for him. Uri could speak Arabic and that would help.

After tying them up, Dan went back to the hallway and started down it again. One of the doors he tried opened to some stairs leading down. *Basement. An escape route?* Dan started down. He made no noise on the stone steps, worn into a shallow dish shape from centuries of use. The Tavor was held up and ready to spit out a lethal round of fire if anyone showed.

At the bottom was a large room with wine racks and shelving holding food supplies. Dan crouched and listened while scanning the room for any signs of ambush. Nothing stirred. Nothing showed. At one end was another door, lower and smaller. It looked like it had seen little use. It now stood slightly ajar, not closing properly after having been forced open.

Dan crept over to the small exit. Inside was a dark tunnel lit by only a single bulb about thirty feet inside. The tunnel slanted downward and the light gave just enough illumination to show a bend farther down. *An escape route. They've gone.* He listened, but no sound came from the dark path cut through sand and rock.

Dan pulled back. He worked the door closed and latched it. No one from the tunnel could get back into the basement. *Got to make sure he left no one behind.* Dan crept back up the stone steps and returned to the kitchen. No one had moved. He untied the cook and motioned for him to go in front of him, back to the garage.

Once in the garage Dan sat the cook down in front of Uri.

"Looks like Scorpion's gone. With three men as I counted. This is the cook. There are also four women tied up in the kitchen. I want you to stay in character as a Middle-Easterner, an Iraqi as you established. They're going to have to take care of you while I go after Scorpion."

Uri nodded. His face was still ashen and drawn, but his eyes now flashed some intensity.

"Tell them we're after a bad criminal, their boss. He tried to kill someone. You pick the person they would be sympathetic to. Play on that. We're the good guys. They need to help you."

"How do I explain you?"

Dan shook his head. "I don't know. You'll have to figure that out and wing it. But make sure they know I'll be coming back. I've killed Scorpion's soldiers and I'll kill them if you're not alive. So they must make sure you stay alive."

Uri cracked a thin smile and began to speak in Arabic to the cook.

When he was done, the man got up. Dan raised his carbine.

"He's going to get a chair. He'll get me to the kitchen where he can clean the wound."

The man went over to a corner of the garage and came back with an old wooden chair. Dan and the cook helped Uri into the chair.

"Make sure he tells the rest of them they have to keep you alive, or they all die."

"Pretty harsh…killing everyone."

Dan stooped over Uri. "I mean it. They must not doubt me on this. Everyone will die if I don't find you alive when I get back. Everyone."

Uri nodded and spoke to the cook whose face grew pale as Uri explained how dangerous Dan was and how committed to Uri he was. When Uri was done, the cook spoke rapidly with a pleading tone in his voice.

"He wants you to know he'll do his best, but Allah only knows if I will live or not. He's not a doctor."

Dan looked at the cook with cold, dangerous eyes. "Tell him I will be as merciless as his boss if you die. If Allah chooses you to die, I'll choose him and the others. They go with you." He turned back to Uri. "But if you're alive, I'll reward them with lots of money. They are not to worry about their boss, he is not coming back for them. They should only worry about me."

Chapter 43

Scorpion and his three men hurried through the descending tunnel. It emerged, five hundred feet below the monastery in a ravine, halfway down to the floor of the wadi. The men stood for a moment in the harsh, bright sun, squinting as their eyes had to adjust from the dark tunnel.

"We go down the ravine where we have cover. If those pursuing us use one of the vehicles, they will catch us quickly. We must not be seen from the road."

The men worked their way downward, moving in a quick, sure-footed manner, having lived their lives in the rocks and sand of the desert. Scorpion kept a watch over his shoulder, looking for the inevitable pursuit. If he were in the right position, he could set up an ambush, as he originally wanted to do. The irony flooded over him. His pursuer didn't show at the last ambush, but now, after discovering his lair, might find himself the victim of another one. Scorpion would have his prize in the end.

† † †

When Uri was more comfortably situated in a bed, his wound cleaned and bandaged, his leg partially splinted with two wood planks bound to it, Dan sat down on the edge of the bed.

"There's a Land Cruiser in the garage. I'm going to take it and go after Scorpion."

Dan had explained to Uri how Scorpion had left through a tunnel but was now somewhere down on the wadi floor, on foot.

"I can catch him out in the open."

"He's got men with him."

"I've been outnumbered before. I have to strike while he's close. Then I'll get you out of here."

"He'll see you coming. He'll set up his own ambush."

"I'll take that chance. If I can survive the first shot, we'll be on even ground and I'm better than his men, better than he is."

"He's a successful killer."

"Of untrained men and women."

Dan made sure Uri had a sidearm with him. "Don't let that cook and the others forget. Anything happens to you, I take it out on them."

Uri nodded.

Dan went down to the garage and, as he hoped, the Toyota Land Cruiser had the keys in the ignition. The Land Cruiser wasn't a surprise. It was ubiquitous in many rugged areas such as Africa and the Middle-East. The U.S. Army and the U.N. made it their vehicle of choice for its reliability and off-road capabilities.

Dan went to the van and got it started. He moved it from the garage door and jumped into the Toyota and headed out. He had his Tavor 7 with him and his Sako in its carry case. He drove fast down the rough dirt two-track that descended from the monastery to the wadi floor. When he was about half of the way down, he slowed and started watching the sides of the path. From this point on, he knew he could be ambushed at any moment.

Slouching behind the steering wheel, he kept his head just above the windshield, balancing his need to watch with his desire to not present too large a target. His body tingled, knowing his enemy was out there, probably waiting.

They were down on the floor of the wadi. Scorpion heard the engine and, looking back, could see the Land Cruiser descending the hill. It was a mile away at this point. He motioned to the men to get down in the shallow ravine. There was not as much cover on the flatter terrain, but there were bushes, fed from the monsoon rains, they could hide behind. The bushes were dry and dormant, waiting to come alive when the life-giving rains came. Their effectiveness at hiding the men was limited, but they would have to do. With the men all dressed in brown and tan clothing, they could easily blend into the desert.

"Separate and wait for my shot. When I shoot, you open fire. Nothing inside the cab lives. Understand?"

The men nodded and quickly scattered among the brush. They all trained their carbines on the road. Scorpion watched as the Toyota slowed when it reached the floor of the wadi. The driver was probably aware of the danger of ambush and wanted to scan the terrain ahead of him. *Patience.* Scorpion readied his carbine.

Scorpion and his men were on the passenger side of the road. He'd rather be on the driver's side, where there was a better chance of killing his pursuer, but he had decided to not risk crossing the road. Their path from the exit of the tunnel had all been on the south side of the dirt road which had more cover.

Dan's sense of danger grew. Scorpion could not be too far ahead. He had some sense of when the man left the monastery. He saw nothing, looking farther ahead. No figures on the horizon. They had to be hiding, waiting for him, knowing they could not outrun the Toyota. He was driving himself into an ambush, a hasty, but potentially deadly trap. Still, there was no other way.

His eyes zeroed in on any increase in cover, brush, rocks, anything where shooters could hide. The flat, open spaces of the desert floor didn't interest him. The threat was not there. It was within one of those places near the road that he could not see into or through. As each possible spot was passed, his heart rate, which had accelerated, would go back down and he'd take a deep breath. Dan had his Tavor 7 in his lap and his Sako lying next to him on the front seat.

Ahead the cover thickened. Dan's level of alert increased. The road was barely elevated above the floor of the desert; maybe two feet at most, no feet in some areas. There would be no berm to go down to get out of the line of fire. He had to be ready to jump from either side of the vehicle. The thicker cover was on his right, so Dan concentrated on that spot. He looked for any movement but everything was still in the late morning sun. No breeze stirred the ground.

Then he saw it. A straight line. There were no straight lines in nature. Dan had learned this long ago in sniper school. The line had something popping up at the end of it. It could be a rifle barrel. Dan tensed and slouched down even more. He could not see the road ahead, but he knew it went straight.

Then a shot. The windshield burst and the round screeched over his head and through the cab of the Toyota.

Multiple rounds followed, each ripping through the windshield. Dan veered off to the left before more rounds could come through the doors and hit him, even hunkered down as he was. The shots continued as the Toyota lurched off the road and came to a halt.

Dan grabbed his Tavor and Sako and dove out of the door. He hit the ground and immediately went forward to hide behind the engine, which would stop any rounds from coming through the sheet metal to reach him. Taking a glance around the front of the Land Cruiser, Dan could not see where the shooters were hiding. The rounds that came at him were hitting the roof of the Toyota. *They can't see me.* The two feet of elevation change, coupled with prone shooting positions, meant the ambushers were as blind as he was.

Dan looked around. Behind him, farther from the road, was the main channel of the stream that had carved the wadi eons ago. It was about seventy yards away, lined with scrub brush along its banks. The bed was wide with a two-foot or more drop into it.

He immediately got up and ran in a crouch towards the stream bed. When he reached the bed, he threw himself down into it without hesitation as shots now flew over him with their deadly whistles. Once in the bed, Dan crawled to his right about twenty feet and then cautiously peered up behind a thick piece of brush. He could see some men lying just on the south side of the road, with their rifles pointed towards the stream bed. They occasionally fired at where he had dropped in, but it was clear to Dan that they hadn't seen him. Then the barrels pulled back down from the road.

They're going to spread out, come at me from both sides. He analyzed his situation. No fear, only adrenalin coursed through him. This was a tactical game. One of hide and seek, cat and mouse. Only the stakes were death to the loser. There was no retreat farther back. To climb out of the stream bed, even away from the road, was to invite death. He'd be in range of iron sites and the 7.62mm round could easily kill him at this distance. The shooters might miss on their first shot, but with multiple shooters they'd nail him after a few shots.

Dan started crawling forward towards where he had been heading. His best chance lay in outflanking one side of the attack. He had only three or four men to deal with. If he could take out one prong, it could cut his attacker's numbers in half. *Be where they don't expect you to be.*

On the other side of the road, Scorpion divided his men. He sent two forward a hundred yards and told them to find a place to cross. He went with Faquir, back towards the monastery. The assassin might try to work his way back west, to the rougher ground that would provide him more cover. If so, Scorpion planned to be there.

When the men who headed east stopped, they began to look for some cover on the far side of the road. Neither of them wanted to crawl over the road only to drop down exposed. This enemy had proved himself to be an extraordinary shooter. If there were no solid hiding places, they at least wanted the limited cover provided by the harsh brush that grew in the wadi. They slowed their progress as they spent more time studying what lay on the other side of the road.

Dan crawled as fast as he could. If Scorpion had split up his men, then one group was going to drop down into this stream bed behind him and he'd have no protection. His only play was to take out the ones to his east and get out of the depression. This open wadi provided much less cover than the rocks on the hillside behind him. But those rocks were too far away. And if he could get to them, Scorpion might just go back to the Toyota and take it. No, the fight had to be here, out in the open.

Chapter 44

Dan risked a crouched run for a moment, then dropped to the ground to scan the space between the stream bed and the road. Nothing...yet. He pressed on, scrambling over the sandy soil in a half crawl, half run on all fours. When he reached a large group of bushes, he stopped and watched. The two men came over the road and down behind some bushes similar to the ones shielding Dan from view. The difference was that Dan had the embankment to protect him. The other men did not.

Dan wasted no time in sliding his Sako out of its case. He adjusted the scope back to its zeroed settings; one hundred yards on flat terrain. He could use the mil dots to adjust his aim on the fly. In a short moment he had the rifle resting on the embankment with its barrel poking through the brush. He got the bushes in the scope and waited.

Hope they don't take too long. Dan's back tingled with the danger that could come from behind. He'd never know when the other men would drop into the stream bed and see him. A good shot, and he expected Scorpion to be one, could take him out, or cripple him with one round. In the scope, Dan saw the brush part as a barrel poked through the tangle of branches.

He could sight along it and guess he'd hit the shooter at the butt end of the barrel. He slowed his breathing down, forced his mind from the threat behind him, and concentrated on his target, looking for that connecting thread that would send his round unerringly to its destination. The trajectory would be flat. In between slowed heart beats, Dan's finger caressed the trigger as his hand gently squeezed closed.

The rifle kicked against his shoulder. The shot hit almost instantaneously from his trigger pull. In the bushes he could see the barrel fly up and disappear. Shots came from nearby. The puffs of dust from the muzzle gave away the other shooter's position. Dan shifted his aim and fired off two more rounds. After the first volley from the bushes, there was nothing.

He got up and ran as fast as he could, his Sako held at ready and his Tavor over his shoulder. From behind him, to the west, shots were fired, and the rounds splashed in the sand and dust in front and behind him. Dan didn't stop but dove across the road into the depression on the south side of it with rounds zinging overhead in their deadly, high-pitched whistle.

He landed hard, his elbows and knees taking the impact, trying to protect his weapon. He grunted with the pain and took a moment to rub his limbs, trying to diffuse the pain of the landing. Then he crawled to the edge of the road to peer over the surface and locate the shooters.

A quick scan located them. Two men hurrying towards the rocky hillside of the north rim. *Running away!* Dan sighted the retreating figures in his scope. He focused on the one in front.; that would most likely be Scorpion. He squeezed off a round. The puff of dirt was short and just behind the first figure. They were two hundred plus yards away now and moving fast. He worked the bolt in a rapid movement. His next shot caught the figure high, in the left shoulder and spun him to the ground. The following figure grabbed the downed man and dragged him forward. They were now among the rocks and disappeared from sight.

"Damn!" Dan said out loud. He had come so close and now Scorpion was getting away. He ran back to the Toyota and jumped in. The engine wouldn't start. One of the rounds fired at it must have hit something in the engine. He pounded the wheel in frustration. He wanted to start after them. He only needed to keep them in sight with the Sako to get a shot. He grabbed his binoculars and studied the rocks on the hillside where the two had disappeared. He caught a glimpse of a head farther up the slope, and then it was gone. The slope provided good cover. Scorpion, if he had hit him, was still able to move as they were making good progress up the incline. They would soon be over the rim, which was lower here, and be gone.

A part of his brain shouted to get going. The other part counseled that he could track them. He should take care of Uri and then he could set out for as long as it took. No one walked this part of the desert, so tracks would show. Plus, Scorpion was hit. He would slow eventually; maybe stop. Dan could follow them, catch them, finish it. He grabbed his gear and headed back to the monastery.

"You get him?" Uri asked. He looked up from the bed he was in, his face drawn and pale, his voice weak.

Dan shook his head. "There was an ambush, like I expected. There were four of them, I killed two, but Scorpion and one other got away. I wounded him with a long shot, but they got over the rim."

"Why didn't you follow?"

"I need to get you to some help. I can track them. They're a long way from any help and Scorpion's wounded, so I can catch him."

"And kill him."

Dan nodded.

"How are you going to get me help? We're in the middle of nowhere."

"Not sure. I have to think on it." He paused for a moment. "There's a helipad out in front of the monastery. Maybe we can call in a chopper?"

Uri looked back at Dan. His eyes were sad, almost resigned. "I doubt they'll risk that for me."

"There must be a phone around here somewhere. Scorpion had to be able to contact people, or be contacted by them. Ask the help. Talk to them."

Uri gave him a weak nod.

Dan left and rounded up the four women and the cook. They had not left because of two things. First was the arduous journey on foot over the desert. Second was the admonishment from Uri, that such a move would be considered traitorous to the powers in charge who would hunt them down and kill them and their families.

With Uri's coercion, and the threat of dire consequences if they did not assist them, one of the servant's said she thought there was a special phone in a safe. One of the pleasure girls confirmed the fact. The young girl that had seen the safe opened by Scorpion, had memorized the combination, watching him use the number pad.

Dan followed the girl to the room and she showed him the safe. He nodded for her to open it. She put in the numbers with a shaky hand and the door pulled open. Inside was a satellite phone and other documents. Dan grabbed everything, threw it into a pillow case and they went back down to where Uri was lying in bed.

"Got it," Dan said, holding the phone up high like a trophy.

"What are you going to do?"

Dan looked at the help. "Tell them to prepare some food for all of us to eat. Tell them they will all taste it before we eat it."

After receiving the instructions, the staff left. Dan powered up the phone and dialed Jane's number.

"Who's this?" Jane said.

"It's me. Your not-so-secret agent," Dan replied.

"Who's phone is this? I don't recognize it."

"Scorpion's."

"Is he dead? Did you get him?"

"Not quite. We've had a few encounters and he's just escaped the last one. He's pretty much on his own, though. Just one man left in his personal little army."

"Are you in Yemen?"

"Yeah. And I need your help."

"What is it? You know I can't do much for you there."

"I know." Dan stepped out of the room and closed the door. "It's Uri. He took a bullet in the leg. It shattered his femur. He's going downhill and he needs an exfil ASAP."

"We can't send any choppers in, you know that."

"I got that the first time you said it, back in Tel Aviv. What I need is for you to drop someone in like Uri and I did. I can get you the coordinates of where we are."

Dan went on to describe the monastery and his plan.

"Who could I get to do that? I don't think I can get Eitan to send anyone. He really wants to stay at arms-length from this op."

"I figured. I've got another idea. A bit more complicated, but it will work."

He went on to outline his plan to Jane.

"It's crazy. If I can bring this off, it would take a couple of days to arrange things. And there would be no time to train."

"It'll take a day to arrange the flight, there's no training needed. Trust me it will come together. This gets Uri out and I can pick up Scorpion's trail and end him."

"You think you can find him after two day's head start?"

"He's wounded, losing blood. There're no villages nearby. No one within two days or more of hiking. No tracks in the desert, except for his and the man with him. I'll be able to follow him and move faster. I'll catch him."

Jane was silent on the other end.

"We do the impossible, right?" Dan asked.

Finally, she spoke. "Yes…we do." Her voice grew business-like, a decision made. "I'll get on it right away. Turn this phone on in six hours and I'll update you."

"Thanks, Jane." He paused for a moment. "We make a good team, you and me. Let's spend some time together when I get back."

"Are you flirting with your supervisor?"

"Always. Go get me those assets, dear. I'll get Scorpion for you."

"For all of us."

The phone went dead.

Chapter 45

The two men sat in the Pilatus PC-12 on side benches. It was the same plane Dan and Uri had used for their insertion; considered to be the best single engine turbo prop plane in the world. It was powered by a Pratt & Whitney turbo engine giving it a cruising speed of 280 knots. This one had the stripped-down interior for cargo use. They could easily converse, but both men said little. They were geared up for a HALO insertion. The word had come from Jane the day before. She had hunted them down, both men in different places. One had been in bed with a buxom lady in Fayetteville, North Carolina, the other had been out camping in the Cherokee National Forest. He was harder to find, but with the help of his check-in record at park headquarters, Jane's men had located him after only four hours of searching.

They both had been brought to Charlotte and flown by private jet to Dulles Airport, just outside of Washington, DC. There Jane had briefed them on their task and without much banter, sent them on their way. They were allowed to bring only their favorite sidearm and knife with them. They'd be issued Tavor 7 carbines when they arrived in Djibouti. Both men complained bitterly about the substitution, and after facing almost a rebellion, Jane relented and allowed the men to bring their familiar M4 carbines and ammunition.

Marcus Johns and Roland Hammond were two ex-Delta Force soldiers who had worked with Dan on other missions. They were ex-military men, who looked the part. They couldn't hide it, nor did they try. Marcus stood about six feet, two and weight in at two hundred pounds. Roland was a full six feet, four inches tall and scaled at two hundred and twenty-five. He could have made a good tight end in the NFL, except that his interests and career choices took him in another direction.

Roland was more the jokester, if a two hundred-twenty plus pound fighter could be labeled a "joke". He had an irrepressible funny streak that always looked for the humor in situations, even ones involving the potential of death. Marcus, on the other hand, was quieter, more cerebral, even if no less deadly in combat. Neither man would blend in when walking through a city. Neither had the stealthy capacity that Dan possessed, which enabled him to follow targets without detection. They often kidded him about always wanting to hide, kill from afar, as if afraid of close combat. Dan took their jibes good naturedly, knowing that each of them had different roles to play. The two men had been battle tested and trusted one another with their lives.

"Got to pull Dan's ass out of the fire again," Roland said.

"Ain't that the case,' Marcus replied.

"We should get a medal for the times we've had to do this."

"All in a day's work, my friend," Marcus said.

"But you were only playing Boy Scout, camping. Me, I was almost in heaven when I was so rudely interrupted." He shook his head. "I don't think she'll go out with me again, after having to leave her in a hurry...and so unfulfilled. It offended my sense of a man's duty to a woman."

Marcus only smiled. Roland often bragged or joked about his female conquests, but Marcus knew the one that got away, the one he had met in the Congo, would remain a spark he couldn't extinguish. She was an ember that would not go out, but smoldered deep inside of him, keeping the faint hope of something more alive.

"Thirty minutes out," the jumpmaster said.

He went to both men and had them put on their oxygen masks and checked the flow of pure oxygen. He'd check them again for hypoxia minutes before they jumped. As before, the Pilatus was bumping along at its ceiling height of 30,000 feet. The two men went over their gear in a methodical fashion, checking straps, pack, weapons, altimeter strapped to their wrists, adjusting their goggles and oxygen masks.

"Got to hit the mark, or we'll never hear the end of it from Dan," Roland said, his voice muffled behind the mask, as the two men waddled to the cargo door. When the light flashed green, the men dove out into the sky and dropped out of sight of the plane which continued its flight to Abu Dhabi.

Dan watched the sky at the appointed hour, looking for the two figures. He spotted them, small dots, dropping at an astonishing speed, just before their chutes opened at around 1,000 feet. A third chute opened as well. The two men maneuvered their chutes, banking to aim at the helipad landing area, while the unguided chute drifted off down the slope.

After gathering their chutes, the men trudged down the dirt path to retrieve the third chute and the gear it carried, all banded to a wooden frame. Then they made the hike back up to the monastery where Dan awaited them.

He strode up to the two men and hugged each one in turn. He couldn't suppress a smile and surge of relief to have the two warriors join him. Whatever the next few days held, they could be approached more confidently with these two along.

"So glad you could drop in," Dan said, his face fairly beaming.

Despite his welcoming smile, he was dirty, his sleeves torn, and he had multiple knicks, cuts, and scratches all over his face and neck in various stages of scabbing.

"Funny man," Marcus said.

"You look terrible," Roland said. "Like you got caught in the middle of a cat fight."

"It's been a difficult few days. Let's go inside. I'll introduce you to Uri and bring you up to speed."

He turned and entered the monastery. After meeting Uri and getting caught up on the story, the mood of the two men grew somber. Marcus indicated that he wanted to talk to Dan outside Uri's room. The three men went to another room and sat down.

"He doesn't look good," Marcus said. "You sure this will work?"

"You brought the gear. We can assemble the trace. It'll work."

"Yeah, but he'll be bouncing along on it for two or three days until we get to the coast. That's not only going to be painful, but it'll open more bleeding."

"We give him a transfusion from the blood you brought before you start. You've got clotting bandages and morphine. It's the best we can do."

"All this? For a retired Mossad agent? You must really like the guy," Roland said.

Dan gave him a harsh look. "We don't leave comrades behind, you know that."

Roland stared back at Dan whose eyes were alight with anger. After a moment, he looked away.

"Yeah, I get that. Didn't mean to sound callous, but it is quite an expenditure of assets, you have to admit."

"We do what we have to do." Dan kept looking at Roland. "Roland, you in? If not, let me know now."

"He's in," Marcus said.

"Yeah. I'm in." He stretched and sighed. "Just sometimes have to question the wisdom of some decisions."

"I don't want to pick at this, but would you leave me on the field if it would take extraordinary measures to get me home?"

Now Roland glared back at Dan. "You know I wouldn't. Don't talk stupid."

"Maybe it's just that we don't know Uri," Marcus said. He wanted to cut off any tension between the other two men. "We haven't had time to bond with him, like you have. Don't worry, though. We'll get the job done."

Dan relaxed. "Okay. I'm good. After all, it was you two that I thought of to help me in this situation."

"So you're the reason my sexual encounter was interrupted. You owe me one." Roland smiled. "And you know we've got your back," Roland said. "If that means taking care of Uri, then that's what we do."

"You boys gonna kiss now?" Marcus asked. "That would seem to be the appropriate way to close out this little spat."

"Go fuck yourself," Roland said with a smile. "You know the sacrifice I made to be here. Broken hearts all over North Carolina."

"Going to be a busy man when you get back, mending all of them," Dan said as he smiled as well.

They immediately set out to assemble the trace that would carry Uri to the coast. The plan was to get him to the coast where they could either load him onto an Israeli sub or a helicopter to exfil out of Yemen.

In an hour they had the equipment assembled. It consisted of two aluminum frame rails with wheels at the end. There were cross tubes in an "X" shape to stiffen the structure which was then laced with webbing. The person pulling the trace wore a harness that let the trace be attached near the waist. It could not be considered comfortable, but it was the best possible way to transport someone who could not walk.

Roland spoke up when the men had finished their preparations. "Dan, it doesn't take two strong guys to transport Uri. I know it's going to be hard, but one person can do it. You, on the other hand could use an extra man going after the guy. You don't know what you'll run into. He may have other support he can reach. You might be up against more than just him and his sidekick."

Dan looked thoughtful.

"The thought also occurred to me,' Marcus said.

"Marcus could take Uri to the coast," Roland said. "He knows a few words of Arabic. I can go with you."

"Why do you get to have all the fun?" Marcus asked.

"Because I'm more handsome than you." He paused. "Seriously, neither of us wants to not be in the action, but I do think Marcus would be more useful with Uri, than I would."

"Uri is fluent in Arabic, if he's conscious. So, no one needs to worry about speaking it," Dan said.

"Fair enough. But it only helps if the other person can at least grunt a few words if they have to try to pass themselves off."

"Neither of you would ever pass for an Arab," Dan said,

"Right, but we could pass for Chechens," Roland said. "And Marcus knows a few words of Russian. No one here would know the difference."

Dan thought about the suggestion. Roland was right. His desire to save Uri didn't demand the two men, both formidable fighting assets, to be used to exfil an injured combatant. He nodded in agreement. Better to split them up.

"Marcus, since you're the linguist of the two, I think Roland's right. You should take Uri to the coast. That won't be without its danger and I'm sure it will challenge you. Roland and I will go after Scorpion." He looked at both men. "Are you both good with that idea?"

They nodded.

"Then it's settled. Let's get moving."

Chapter 46

"You going to clean up?" Roland asked Dan as they packed and checked their gear.

Dan shook his head. "No time. We have to go now."

"You do know it's the afternoon. Gets dark after that."

"We have NVGs. We'll follow and hunt at night. He's wounded and can't go all day or night. We have some catching up to do. He's got a two-day head start."

"You're the boss."

They had water, MRE's, power bars, ammunition, and the thermal, foil blankets that Dan and Uri had used. Dan packed his Sako and its .338 Lapua Magnum rounds, along with his 9mm side arm. Roland took his pistol and his M4 carbine along with its 5.56mm ammunition.

When they were ready, Dan spoke to the group in the bedroom where Uri lay. He went over the cover story for himself and Marcus. They were on the trial of an assassin who they had information on. He wanted to kill so and so; and here they would insert the name of whoever their listeners would be sympathetic to. In chasing said assassin, Uri was wounded and his partner, a Chechen, was helping him get to their pickup point. It was a flimsy story at best. Probably capable of only fooling the most gullible of listeners. Their best bet was to avoid detection by and contact with the locals.

Uri got his pint of blood and a fresh bandaging of his wounds. Dan assembled the staff in the bedroom and Uri spoke to them. He told them that their boss was not coming back and they were free to leave. Of course, they had no transportation and didn't like the prospect of walking out. Dan made sure he collected any phones and computers. They were isolated here in the monastery. It would be days, more likely weeks before they got help and could report on the incidents. The men would be long gone by then. There were enough supplies in the compound so they could stay for months, if they chose to do so. Dan didn't care since they couldn't affect their operations within any reasonable amount of time.

Finally, they were all ready.

"You have your satellite phone?" Dan asked.

Marcus nodded. "Got yours?"

"Yeah. I don't anticipate using it much. There's not much Jane and Eitan can do while we're so far in the interior. But when you get to the coast, you know what to do."

"Call Jane and get a helo or sub to exfil us."

"Right. If it's a helo, they penetrate near the coast. They'll fly you and Uri out to Djibouti where he'll be put on a plane to Israel. He'll have good triage from the moment you get on the chopper."

"And a sub?"

"You'll have to get on the actual coast. Commandos will come ashore and transport you both. You'll wind up in Eilat and fly from there to Tel Aviv."

"Longer trip."

"Probably, but Uri will have good medical support along the way."

Uri was helped outside and loaded onto the trace. Dan reached down to grab his shoulder.

"You hang in there. You got lots more years of trouble making ahead."

Uri gave him a weak smile. "Going to be a rough ride. I feel like useless baggage."

"Not useless, my friend. I'll see you back in Tel Aviv."

Marcus strapped himself to the frame and, with some claps on the back, started down the hillside. Dan and Roland watched them go and they shouldered their own packs and headed down the hillside, towards the north rim of the wadi. They would intersect Scorpion's trail where he climbed out of the valley and follow him.

† † †

Scorpion and Faquir made it to the rim of the wadi and kept moving north. Night would soon fall and with it, the temperatures. Scorpion held his left arm, trying to cushion it against the jarring of walking. He knew he would not be able to keep up a rapid pace in his injured state. His pursuer, the assassin, however, would be able to close on him. He gritted his teeth. He had to continue as long as he could. They had water and some food. Once he had gotten far enough away to risk stopping, he would have Faquir look at his wound and try to close it with some bandaging.

They continued in silence punctuated by Scorpion's heavy breathing. The eunuch was silent, helping Scorpion over some of the rougher places to keep him from falling. He was faithful and, even in his condition, half a man, he was a fearsome fighter and accurate shooter. Scorpion let a harsh smile cross his face. *Faquir might be able to take down this assassin. He doesn't know how deadly my eunuch is...and how loyal.*

As the sun was setting, they stopped in a rocky outcropping that provided cover and a good view to the south, from where their pursuer would come. Faquir immediately set about removing Scorpion's jacket and shirt to look at his wound. The bullet, a large one from the looks of the damage, had hit Scorpion's shoulder blade and exited below the shoulder joint. The joint had not been shattered, but the shoulder blade had been. It looked like no arteries had been hit. The wound was seeping, not pumping blood. He took some bandaging from his pack and began to wrap it around the shoulder, pinning his upper arm to his body in an attempt to immobilize it. Scorpion grunted with the pain, but did not cry out. He was used to pain; giving it as well as living with it.

When he was done, Faquir gave Scorpion some water. They both rested with Faquir taking a long look to the south with his binoculars.

"You do not see him?" Scorpion asked.

"No *majistir*. Nothing moves behind us."

"He will be coming. But I wonder why he is taking his time?"

"Perhaps going back to the monastery to help his partner. You thought he might be wounded."

Scorpion thought about that for a moment. "He will help him. But he will not give up pursuit. He has come too far. We will encounter him again."

"*Majister*? May I suggest that if we can make it to Shabwah, we will be safe. It's at the edge of the great sand emptiness. We have friends, supporters there. They will help."

"He will still come."

"Yes, but when he does, we'll have others to help us eliminate him, as you planned. He will be alone now, without any help."

"It is as good a plan as any. Allah willing, we'll get there, and, Allah willing, we'll kill the infidel and end his interference."

"Indeed."

The two men sat in silence. Scorpion steeling himself for the long, three-day trek and Faquir keeping watch to the south. After some minutes, Scorpion grunted and lurched to his feet. Faquir was quick to get up and help him.

"We go now. Walk as far as I can. Then we stop to rest. We take turns keeping watch and then we walk again. We start before it is light and stop in the full heat of the day. Then we walk again, deep into the night."

"Yes *majistir*."

The two got up and started north, across the rough ground. They would find another wadi heading west and follow it before traversing two more ridges. Then another wadi would empty to the west, out into a sea of sand. Shabwah was a small desolate village of one and two-story mud houses located on a rock outcropping at the edge of a great sandy waste with dunes stretching to the horizon. It had long been abandoned but more recently, re-inhabited with fighters. There was water below the sand, dug and drilled into many centuries ago, which gave the village life. From the water, they could grow wheat and, when the rains came, vegetables. Goats were kept and used as a source of milk and protein in this harsh land.

The town was at the edge of the ancient Hadhramout region. It had been recently retaken by government forces from the Houthis and now was in more friendly hands from Scorpion's perspective. The village had been settled in the thirteenth century BC and continued to support inhabitants. There were only about fifty in the village, most of them fighters loyal to Sunni/Arab interests and, hence, the government, not the Houthi rebels.

Chapter 47

As the sun was getting low, Dan and Roland came across Scorpion's trail. They found the disturbed dirt of shuffling feet, not moving carefully or slowly, but with a rushed scrapping, shoving of sand and rocks aside in the haste to get to cover. Then there were a few drops of blood. Not much, but enough to confirm they were on the right trail.

The men looked up towards the rim and could see nothing. They felt the two men fleeing would not have waited to re-engage but would have kept moving.

"With a two-day start, they're long gone from this position," Dan said.

Roland studied the disturbed dirt and sand. Little rocks were pushed and disturbed, and the sand was pushed in small lumps along the path of the feet. "It shouldn't be hard to track them. If one of them is wounded, it'll be hard for them to walk carefully enough to conceal any signs from us."

"Agreed. We just have to close down the head start."

"So, we go all night. It's cold then, and I'd rather walk than shiver under that thermal sheet."

The two started to climb towards the ridge. Once over it, they descended into the next wadi and kept going. The sun set, and after stopping for some water and a few bites from a power bar, they started again. As the sky grew dark, they put on their NVGs and were relieved to find that they could still make out the impressions in the sand. If Scorpion and his companion set out over hard, rocky ground, Dan knew it would be harder to follow and they would have to wait for daylight to continue.

"Where do you think they're headed?" Roland asked as they trudged along, heads down.

Dan looked up to scan the way forward. His mind could come up with no towns or villages on the map he had studied.

"No idea," he said.

"I'll bet they have an idea. This is their country, they're the locals here. They'll be going for help somewhere."

"That's why we have to close the distance sooner rather than later."

"We'll do our best, boss."

Roland used that word often when they worked together. It seemed humorous to him and was accurate to the most part. Dan ran the missions, even if Roland or Marcus could weigh in on parts of it.

† † †

By the third day, Scorpion was starting to falter. Faquir knew they had to reach Shabwah soon or he would have to carry his benefactor. They had crossed two ridges and were now on a wadi floor, where the going was easier. They had turned more westerly. Later in the day, they could see the open expanse of the sea of sand. It had no special name, but it was an unhabitable and forbidding place. It was as if they were coming to the end of the world. A desolate corner where no one went. Scorpion smiled grimly. That was what he wanted; seclusion so deep it could not be penetrated.

The afternoon brought the sun to the front of them, glimmering in the haze coming off the sand, stirred by a soft, hot breeze. The two men wrapped their faces in their scarves to filter out the growing haze of dust floating in the air. Two hours later, they could see rocky ground rising out of the sand ahead like an island in the sea. It was the last piece of land before the sandy expanse which went for two hundred miles until reaching the "shore" on the other side. Here, no rain would fall, even in the monsoon. The rocky island ahead was the last outpost and where the village of Shabwah sat.

"It will be late tonight, but we can reach the village before the night is done," Faquir said.

Scorpion nodded but didn't answer. His breathing was hard, but he would carry on. He would persevere in his striving. Allah honored such perseverance. Allah would overlook Scorpion's twisted desires because he was useful to Allah. Scorpion knew that his usefulness kept him safe. It allowed others to use him and therefore protect him, at least to a certain degree. And that was enough. Scorpion had nothing in his life but his desires and his ability to kill for Allah and advance jihad upon the infidel.

The two men trudged on. Faquir now was holding Scorpion to keep him from stumbling. Their shuffling feet slowly and steadily took them forward towards the distant island of hills and help.

The moon, now waxing, came up and lit their progress. The night grew colder, but the men kept going. Faquir hoped there would be medical support there. Usually there was one man among the fighters who could help the wounded. His master would heal, but he needed help and rest.

† † †

Dan and Roland hiked through the night as fast as they could go while still keeping sight of the footprints. The tracks led the two up into some rocks.

"They stop here?" Roland asked.

"Probably spent the hottest part of the day. They understand the desert. I'm thinking, like us, they'll do most of their walking during the night."

"Navigate by the stars?"

"Something like that. Just like sailors. There's a lot of seafaring metaphors in describing the desert."

They could see blood on the rocks.

"He may have bandaged Scorpion's wound here. Made him more comfortable," Dan said. "In any case, we go on. Let's find their exit trail."

The men cast about to find the set of tracks going off to the north again. They continued their relentless pace; each man absorbed in his own thoughts. All Dan's thoughts centered on closing on and killing Scorpion.

"You ever wonder about our lives? We don't live like normal people," Roland said. His voice almost startled Dan, breaking the still of the night. The only sound they had heard for hours was the crunch of their feet on the sandy ground and their steady breathing.

"We don't. But I don't think about it much."

"You've been in this fight, if you want to call it that, longer than Marcus and me. You get used to it?"

Both men kept their heads down as they walked, making sure not to lose the trail.

"In a way." Dan thought for a moment. "But this experience with this assassin has shown me I can't have relationships with regular people. Civilians. Too many innocent people can get hurt."

"Yeah. Jane told us what happened. I'm sorry about that."

"You might have run into similar issues with Yvette if that had worked out."

"You heard?"

"Yeah. No secrets among us black op guys."

"Marcus. That dog."

"He was worried about you. I think he mentioned it to Jane—"

"And, of course, she mentioned it to you."

"It's good to know what everyone on the team is going through."

"Some things should be left unshared. They're embarrassing."

Dan looked over at Roland as they walked through the night. The moon was coming up and it made the desert brighter, almost too bright for their NVGs.

"You're not the first to run into the summer romance-thrill of adventure experience with a young woman. You get serious, but she isn't ready to leave her comfortable life behind. She's not to blame. She is just young and looking for adventure. And she found that in you."

"I'm just one of her 'conquests', that it?"

"Maybe. But I'm sure you left a lasting impression on her. Getting kidnapped and then rescued by your thrill lover is something she'll never forget."

"I guess that's my fate. To be a memorable experience to the fairer sex."

"You could do worse."

"But seriously," Roland said. "Are we doomed to not have regular private lives?"

"Hell, Roland, I don't know. For me that seems to be the case, but I chose this after my wife was murdered."

"And now you have Jane."

Dan looked over at Roland.

"Hey, don't deny it. There's something between the two of you. I can sense it. Marcus agrees. It's fine you have someone, especially someone who lives the same kind of life, who understands."

Dan sighed. "So, it's obvious to everyone? My connection to her?"

"To anyone who looks closely."

"I'm not sure myself what it really is. She's someone who understands what I'm doing. She has made the same sacrifices, no family, no children, no normal life. All to fight back against the jihadists. For Jane the outrage of nine-eleven has not faded."

"She recruited you, didn't she?"

"Yep. Just as she recruited you and Marcus. She's good at spotting the right ones to fight this battle." Dan thought for a moment. "And we're in a battle. We fight back against the darkness. Against those who want to end western civilization as we know it."

"A war that will never end."

"Maybe. But we carry on."

They lapsed into silence, each man with his own thoughts.

Chapter 48

Marcus worked his way down the snaking two-track that led from the floor of the wadi up to the monastery. He had to brace himself against the trace which wanted to accelerate faster down the slope. Uri's weight, close to two hundred pounds, was not going to be an easy load to drag the hundred miles they had to go to the coast. He thought of commandeering a car along the way to speed the process. *We'll see what opportunities come up,* he promised himself.

When they reached the floor, the going was easier. Marcus quickly realized he had to avoid soft spots in the dirt road. Along the harder surface, the trace rolled along with little resistance. Except for the chaffing of the harness, he could easily pull Uri and the gear they brought. Marcus's M4 carbine was looped over his shoulder while the Tavor 7 lay next to Uri on the trace.

"How you doing back there?" Marcus said looking back over his shoulder.

"Feel like a damn fool, bouncing along behind you. Sorry to put you through this. Dan should have left me at the monastery." His voice shook with the vibration of the trace along the stony ground.

"Couldn't do that. You wouldn't get the help you need and there was no way of knowing if the staff would have killed you, or just left you there by yourself. And who knows when we would…or could have gotten back? If the shit hits the fan from this operation, no one knows where Dan and Roland wind up."

"Still don't like you having to haul me along on this makeshift stretcher."

"It is what it is, old man. Roland and I seem to be always pulling Dan's fat out of the fire, as we say in the states."

"And I'm the fat in the fire, right?"

"You said it, not me." Marcus smiled to himself.

There was silence behind him. Marcus figured Uri was too weak to continue long conversations. It would be a quiet trek.

He would continue east to the mouth of the wadi where it joined a larger plain. He wanted to avoid the ridges. Climbing over them would be difficult in the extreme. This trek would test his strength and reserves.

As the day sank into evening, Marcus stopped at an outcropping that partially blocked being seen from the broader valley. They had been on the move for seven hours with only two rest stops.

He unhitched himself from the trace and set it down slowly. Then he took off his backpack and, gently lifting Uri's leg, he put the pack underneath to lift the leg. Uri grunted with pain while Marcus moved his leg. When he was finished, Uri sighed.

"That's better now. It throbs less when elevated. Hurts like hell to lift it, though."

Marcus got out two MREs and began to heat them. When done, he offered one to Uri who took it and tried to eat. Marcus wolfed down his meal. Uri gulped down the water offered, but only picked at the food.

"Don't like the U.S. government's fare? It was created by professional cooks to be good tasting and nutritious."

"Maybe nutritious, but not so good tasting."

"That's just because you're injured. You're off your feed as they say."

"What the hell does that mean?"

"A farm saying that's gotten into our English language. If an animal doesn't eat, it's off its feed. Meaning it's probably sick."

"I'm not sick, but I'm definitely off my feed. Hurts too much to eat."

"As my mother would say. You can't get better if you don't eat, so chow down. We got a few hard days ahead of us and you shouldn't fast along the way."

When he had finished, he ate the rest of Uri's meal and stood up. Marcus stretched and turned back to Uri, lying on the ground.

"We better get going. I'm thinking we should carry on through the night. It'll be cold, but we'll keep warm by moving."

"You will. I'm just lying here getting bounced around. Maybe later, you can break out that foil blanket and put it over me."

"You got it."

Marcus lifted Uri's leg and retrieved his pack. He noticed the dampness on the leg. *Still bleeding. Hope he can hold on.*

After wrapping Uri in the foil blanket, he lifted the arms of the trace and hooked them onto his harness and set out. The trace jolted along on the rugged ground as Marcus headed back to the dirt road. Once on the road things smoothed out again and they made good time. As the night deepened, Marcus broke out his NVG to continue. Uri alternately slept and groaned as he rattled along behind Marcus.

† † †

It was quite late into the night when Scorpion and Faquir reached the village. They had trudged over the featureless sand for hours with the faint line of rocks before them, shadows in the moonlight, seeming to be out of reach, like a mid-day mirage. But inexorably they had closed on the shadows and they became more solid. Finally, the ground firmed up under their feet and they gently climbed upward onto rocky ground, more solid than the sand over which they had been walking for hours.

As they approached the village, a sentry challenged them. Scorpion, in a voice made weak from pain, declared who he was, his tribal connection to the men, the sentry called them in. Other men were awakened; Scorpion and Faquir were led into a dust covered room. They helped Scorpion onto a bed.

Another man entered with a case. As Faquir had hoped, it contained first aid equipment. He helped Scorpion out of his jacket and shirt and unwrapped his shoulder. The bullet had clipped the back edge of his scapula and exited the upper arm, just missing the shoulder joint. It had left a large, ugly exit wound which is where most of the bleeding had occurred.

The medic tried to give Scorpion a shot of morphine, but he stopped him.

"No drugs," he said. He lay back, weak with pain and fatigue but didn't want to go under the influence of drugs that would cloud his already compromised thinking.

The medic began to work on stitching Scorpion's wound. The other men began to mutter among themselves. Someone had guessed who Scorpion was and the information had a profound effect on the men. This was the famed and dangerous killer of infidels. He was protected by his rich but unknown Saudi benefactor who also supported these men and their civil war in Yemen.

It was said that Scorpion had knives inserted into his fingers. Some of the men looked over at him, hoping to see evidence of such a lethal modification to his body. Faquir stood between them, imposing in his own right. His posture indicated that he was not to be trifled with and that he would protect Scorpion at all costs.

Finally, the medic shuffled the men out. Just after they left, the leader of the fighters came into the room. He looked over at Scorpion. The medic finished up and scurried out of the room.

"Why are you here?" The chief asked.

Scorpion looked at him with his black eyes. His arm was now in a sling with the wound sewn shut. A local anesthetic had been applied which lowered his pain level considerably. He studied the commander. *Was he jihadi? Would he help?* Scorpion wasn't sure, but he knew the decision would soon have to be made.

"I escaped an attempt on my life. Men searching for me, because of my work for others, in the service of Allah, somehow found my retreat, my hideaway. They penetrated it and I was wounded in my escape. Faquir," Scorpion gestured to his eunuch, "helped me get away. I will live, as you can see, to fight another day. But those pursuing me will be coming."

"How do you know? We are at the edge of nowhere."

"They are thorough. They are persistent. They have the ability to follow tracks, even through the desert."

"Where is your sanctuary? How far is it away?"

"Three day's walking. You would not find it. No one would. Somehow, they did. And they will follow our tracks through the desert.

The commander studied Scorpion. "I have heard of your exploits. I am shocked that outsiders could find you and send you fleeing. They must be formidable fighters."

"Indeed. If you know of my reputation, you also know that I am in the service of powerful men. Men who will embrace and help those who help me."

The commander didn't say anything. Scorpion knew that he understood Scorpion's comment. He and his fighters would be rewarded for helping Scorpion. Conversely, if anyone found out they had refused, deadly consequences would follow.

"How many pursue you?"

"One man."

The commander looked at Scorpion trying to hide his surprise. Scorpion knew it was shocking. The man probably expected a squad of twenty or more men on their way to his remote village.

"One man? He must be exceptional."

"He is all that is left. But he will be coming."

Scorpion did not let on that the raid started with only two men, who took out all of his men, leaving him only with his trusted Faquir.

"You are sure he will follow, even alone? After his other fighters were killed?"

"He is as committed as I am."

Chapter 49

Dawn found Dan and Roland hiking northwest along a broad wadi, heads bent, following the tracks. They could walk into the mid-day but had decided they would seek shelter during the hottest part of the afternoon. They trudged along, not talking. Both men had fashioned a turban of sorts around their heads with the lower part covering their mouths to keep out the ever-present dust that floated in the air over the floor of the wadi. Dan longed for the clearer air on the ridge tops. The hiking would be more strenuous with the rocky ground, but the air much cleaner and the heat less. The need to follow the trail, however, kept them on the valley floor, heads down, watching the faint tracks until their eyes swam.

After a water break, they continued their trek. By noon both men were bleary-eyed from continued intense focus on the ground. Dan called a halt.

"Nowhere to get out of the sun," Roland said.

"We use our thermal blanket in reverse. Prop them up over us with our rifles and sit in our own shade. It'll help."

"If you say so. I just need to rest my eyes. Not sleepy, but tired." Roland looked ahead. "There doesn't seem to be an end in sight."

Dan took out a folded paper map and spread it out on his lap. "From what I see on the map, this wadi opens to a large sand basin. Just sand. No villages, no people, no shelter, for hundreds of miles."

"They can't cross that, can they?"

Dan shook his head. "No. They've got to head off before entering that emptiness. We'll see the tracks, though. We'll follow."

After a short rest, they continued for another two hours and then stopped for the hottest part of the day. Again, taking shelter beneath their own thermal blankets.

† † †

Marcus trudged through the dawn until Uri told him he had to stop. The bleeding was getting more severe, and Uri needed to elevate his leg. Marcus set the trace down, propped Uri's leg up causing much grunting and grinding of teeth, and then collapsed against a rock. The sun beat down, but neither man showed any strength to erect a shelter.

After ten minutes of dead-like stillness, Marcus stirred himself and stretched out the two thermal blankets to provide some reflective shelter from the sun which was getting high in the sky sending the temperatures soaring.

"Maybe we should wait out the worst of the heat of the day," Marcus suggested.

Uri nodded. He seemed too spent to say much.

"I'm thinking we should continue east until we intersect a road. I can flag down a vehicle going south and get their help.

Uri glanced over at Marcus, his eyes were red and bleary. His voice was hoarse and croaked.

"Not a good idea."

"They'll report us?"

Uri nodded.

Marcus sat to consider his options. Getting a ride would take two or more days off the trip. Was that worth having to fight off some sort of police action later?

"Almost rather duke it out with the police than keep walking."

"I told you before. Leave me."

Marcus shook his head. "Nah. You know I said I'd do this. For Dan, for you. Sometimes we don't get to have our way, but have to carry out the task that's given us.

"I'm your task?"

Marcus nodded. "Better try to get some rest. We'll start again this afternoon and go late into the night."

† † †

Scorpion ignored his pain, which was now lessened after the medic's administrations while the commander of the village talked with him.

Finally, the commander said, "I am at your service, as are my men. You came here purposefully, injured, what is it you want of me?"

"Help me kill this man who follows."

"That should not be hard. A single man against my experienced fighters. I am happy to accommodate your wishes."

"Do not underestimate this man," Scorpion said. "He is a deadly foe and should be given respect."

"He may be deadly, but so are my men. And there are thirty of us. We are rested and ready for action. He must cross the open expanse of the sand to get to us. There is little to hide him. We let him come to us and then kill him when he is in range."

"He will not walk openly up to you, like a sacrifice. He will come at night. He is a sniper, an assassin. Such men are accomplished in stealth, in not being seen or heard."

Stealthiness was well understood by Scorpion. He was a master of such behavior and had seen it in this enemy.

"We will keep a watch, twenty-four hours a day. There is no way we will not see him as he approaches. At its closest, there is over a kilometer of distance between us and the rocks where the wadi empties into the sand desert. He cannot cross unseen. We will be ready."

Scorpion didn't say anything. This island in the sea of sand certainly helped. For all the remoteness of the monastery, once discovered, there were numerous places from which to approach it unseen. This village was different. But for one of the few times in his life, he felt doubt creep in. The assassin had already exceeded his expectations. Would this be different?

The commander left to instruct his men to watch for the man following. Scorpion knew he would doubt the warning, but he hoped the man would take the appropriate steps. Scorpion was not in condition to go any farther. And on this rocky island with an ocean of sand facing him on one side and the rocks and hills leading back to his pursuer on the other side, there was no place to go. He had to finally kill this man and then he could arrange some help with the commander to get him back to civilization and proper medical care. From there, he would go into hiding to heal and then receive his reward from his benefactor.

A grim smile almost spread across his dark face. It had been hard, but he would finally take this assassin down. The man followed him, now to the end of the earth. One of them would not come out alive and Scorpion held the advantage. His pursuer was out-manned, out-gunned, and Scorpion knew he was coming. No more surprises.

Chapter 50

Jane strolled down the Tel Aviv street, ever watchful for any tails or other surveillance. She had received a note from Eitan asking for her to meet. He gave the address and told her to sit down outside and order a coffee. She followed the directions and after ordering, sat looking casually around. Eitan was probably watching, making sure she had not been followed; something she was already sure of. He had become increasingly worried about leaks getting back to the Mossad headquarters. They might have put a tail on Jane, knowing who she was and wondering why she was in Israel. Eitan could not be seen meeting with her. It would result in too many questions which he could not outright lie about. And once the truth was out, his masters would pull the plug, order Jane out of the country, and leave Dan and Uri on their own. Neither of them wanted that result.

After nursing her coffee for ten minutes, Eitan stepped up to her table and sat down.

"Checking for a tail?"

Eitan nodded. "Can't be too careful. People are sniffing around. They know you're here and that we've met. I told them it was personal. You had some time off and came to see me. I apologize, but I set it up for them to indulge in their own fantasies and draw some innocent, if salacious conclusions."

Jane smiled. "As long as we don't have to prove the rumors."

"I think we're past that. Besides, I sense you and Dan are more than agent and handler. Am I correct?" Eitan smiled at her.

"Everyone wants to weigh in on our relationship. I'm beginning to think it's becoming a form of entertainment."

"We who live quiet lives, enjoy stories about those of us leading more exciting ones."

"I may have to talk to Dan. To quote the line of a song, 'Let's give them something to talk about'. It seems like we're getting to that point."

"As long as you can handle the professional side of things, why not?"

"The why not is that I won't do anything to interfere with taking the fight to the terrorists. Every one of them that we take out…that Dan takes out, is one less to threaten America." She leaned forward to look Eitan in the eye. "You've heard the reports. Terrorists have been dropping all over the world, but especially in Europe. They are all nervous, they all feel threatened. That interferes with their ability to function, to plan and carry out missions."

"But they don't mind dying. They look forward to the martyr's death."

"True enough. But they don't want to die in bed, or while enroute somewhere and not on a mission. They fear that. That won't get them their ticket to paradise and all the virgins. They want to die in action." She leaned back. "There's a difference."

"And Dan is the reason for this?"

"You draw your own conclusions. I won't admit to anything."

She smiled at Eitan. "Now why did you want to meet?"

"I haven't heard from Uri since Dan asked you for the additional men. He's badly wounded and I wanted to know what you've heard."

Jane looked thoughtful. "I told Dan to update me on the mission. However, he often goes dark until it's over. He immerses himself so far, he doesn't think to communicate until it's over. His asking for help was unusual for him. I think you're right to worry about Uri. But as far as the overall mission is concerned, I'm not worried but, shall we say, concerned."

"You think he's still chasing Scorpion?

"I don't know what's going on. He would use the two men to exfiltrate Uri. Whether or not he got Scorpion or is still chasing him, I can't tell. We should hear when they're ready to exfil from the coast. That was the arrangement."

"They can't be too far from an exit position."

"Once they've completed the mission. But it will be slow going. They can't just hike along the road or catch a bus. That would raise too many questions and they'd find themselves in a police station, waiting for the government authorities."

† † †

That night, under a diamond-studded sky, Dan and Roland trudged along. The moon had come up and they were able to take off their NVGs, only having to put them on occasionally when the tracks grew faint. The two men walked in silence. The darkness, only relieved by the star and moonlight, created a fantasy land of soft shadows and distant hills showing themselves as ghost images. Distance was impossible to guess in this land of soft, pale light. The silence was utter. Their boots crunched rudely in the sand as they walked. The stillness suppressed their desire to talk. What little they said, was spoken in a whisper as if trying to not disturb the immense quiet that spread to the horizon.

The hours passed and the sky began to grow lighter behind them as the sun neared the rim of the earth. Gradually, almost unnoticed, the light increased, damping the brilliance of the stars and moon. The NVGs were taken off and pocketed for the coming day.

Finally, Roland stopped and pointed ahead. Dan followed his arm to gaze at what faced them. The wadi spread out like a broad river delta. Ahead lay an expanse of sand that went, unbroken, to the horizon. To their left and right, they could see the solid ground of rocks and sand, the wadi ridges, sloping downward to disappear into the sand, like the shore disappearing under the sea along the coast.

The men looked at each other. The tracks didn't falter or veer. As far as they could see them, they pushed ahead, seeming to go into the sand.

"These fuckers just walk out into that?" Roland asked to no one in particular.

Dan just kept squinting, shading his eyes as the light grew. To the right of the vista ahead of them, he could make out a rise of rocks, with scrub bushes. His eyes locked into the outcropping and, as the light grew, he could make out shapes that didn't look natural. They had not yet reached the end of the wadi, so the rocks were still far off. He took out his binoculars and scanned the area.

"There's an outcropping ahead. They might have headed out to it. It looks like there are some small mud-brick buildings."

"That makes more sense. I have to believe they didn't just walk out into that sand sea."

"I agree."

Dan looked to his right. "Let's head to the north side of the valley. I don't want to walk straight out of the wadi into the open. If those are buildings and they're in them, they'll see us. They know we're following, but don't know where we are."

"Scorpion also won't know that there's two of us. That's an advantage."

Dan nodded and the two men turned to the north and the rocky ground that sloped down to the sand sea.

When they reached the rocks, they began to move forward, now being careful to use all the cover available to them and take care to avoid showing their silhouettes against any horizon. Near where the rocks gave out, they were crawling. The two settled into a depression about three feet deep. There were cuts and gaps in the rock at the edge where they could spy on the island that stood out before them without exposing themselves.

Both men lay silent, patient, studying the landscape. With their closer position, the improved light, and binoculars, they could see there was a small village. It looked long abandoned except for the fact that occasionally they could see some movement.

Dan took out his spotting scope, a Vortex Viper 20 x 60 power. With it he could make out clear details that were missed by the binoculars. The village was inhabited. There were some goats and chickens penned in at one end. There was a small garden which Dan assumed grew vegetables. It was covered by a netting to cut back some of the fearsome sun. After watching for another ten minutes, a patrol and lookout routine started to emerge.

"He's there," Dan said.

"You see him?"

"No. But this is the only place where he has shelter. There're other men there as well. Men who will defend him. There's nowhere else to go."

"We're at the end of the world," Roland said. "How far are those buildings?"

"I'm measuring 1,365 yards.

"That in your range?"

"Yep. And he's trapped in there."

"Yeah. But he's got shelter, food, and water. Kind of necessary things that we don't have. So, we can't wait him out. He has only to wait us out. Force us to come to him."

Dan took his eye away from the scope. "You're right. We'll have to go in, but we need to know more. I'd like to get an idea of how many we have to deal with. And I'd like to thin the herd a bit first."

Roland looked over at Dan. "That's that sniper stuff. Strike from far away. I'm used to close-up fighting. We get the layout in our minds, where everyone is, we go in and take them out. Superior shooting, superior tactics will win out."

"These may be pretty experienced fighters. We shouldn't underestimate them. They're well-armed from what I've seen through the scope."

He handed the instrument to Roland and lay back to take a drink of water.

Chapter 51

After the worst of the day's heat began to dissipate, Marcus picked up the arms of the trace and clipped them to his harness.

"Here we go old man," he called out as he started forward.

"Old man, my ass." Uri's voice came back weak but with an edge.

Marcus smiled. Uri needed to find an edge, something to piss him off, something for him to hold on to, so he didn't sink into his injury and let it overcome him. Marcus understood, one's mental toughness often was the key to whether or not one survived. Uri, he figured, was a tough guy. He needed to regain that attitude. That mindset that said, "Fuck it. I'm going to make it, no matter what happens." Marcus expected that much was going to happen.

Marcus kept them going eastward. He wanted to get out of the wadi before turning south, to the coast. He had no desire to work his way up the slope of the southern ridge, over the rocks, with Uri trailing behind him. Brutal work. He'd take his chances on flagging a ride and worry about whatever came of that. They could hide the guns under the aluminum blankets and Uri could come up with a passable cover story. Maybe after they were dropped off, the driver would report them, but Marcus was determined that they would not be in the area. He'd move fast and, hopefully, stay ahead of anyone searching for them.

As the southern ridge sloped down to the valley floor, Marcus started angling south. The walking was easy interspersed with hard pulls through softer ground. To the east, over his left shoulder he could see what looked like a road. A rise in the ground near the horizon that seemed too flat, too level, to be natural. Finally, he saw a faint object go past. *Definitely a road*. Now he had a choice to make. He could just continue, paralleling the road. There was little chance of being seen. Or he could head to the road and catch a ride.

No sense in just walking south, he thought. *If I'm going to risk the road, better to risk it now, than later. Nothing to be gained by waiting.*

Marcus stopped and unhooked the trace.

"Why are you stopping?"

The day was fading.

"I thought you wanted to walk at night," Uri said.

"I do. But there's a road over to the west. We're going to go there and flag a ride. Preferably a truck. We'll save days off our trek."

Uri shook his head. "Damn it. I told you that's not a good idea. You'll alert the authorities. The government will have men. There's more of them as we get closer to the coast. They'll come after us. You can't get away if you're dragging me along."

"Look," Marcus said. He squatted down to look Uri in the eye. "You're not getting better. Who knows how bad you'll be after two or three more days of walking? You've already told me to leave you behind. What the hell's the difference if I leave you here or further south?"

Uri stared back at Marcus. "You said you wouldn't leave me. So, the difference is we don't get caught if we keep walking."

"Well, old man, maybe I *will* leave you if things get too hot."

Uri didn't look away. "No, you won't. You're saying that so I'll go along with this crazy idea to hitch-hike on the road. We're not normal foot traffic. A man being carried on a stretcher, bullet wound, guns strapped to the frame. You think no one is going to report that?"

"Probably. But I'm going to hide the guns and you'll come up with a good cover story. Just enough to put some doubt in the driver's head. When, or *if*, he calls the soldiers, I'll make sure we're long gone."

"You're crazy. This won't work."

"It won't work to drag your ass around for the next three days, watching you slowly die on me. I'm going to exfil a live body, not a corpse. And, since you're strapped to the trace, and I'm in charge, I get to make the decision."

He sat back and took out two MREs from his pack. "We'll spend the night here and tomorrow walk to the highway."

Uri just lay on the trace which had grown more uncomfortable over the past two days.

"Roll me off this contraption and let me rest on the ground. I'll be more comfortable on the ground."

† † †

Scorpion lay in a bed through the next day. His shoulder was going to take a long time to heal. The medic had done what he could, but the .338 round had done significant damage even though it had not fully penetrated him. If that had happened, his shoulder would have been destroyed from the round's energy. As it was, he expected he'd have limited mobility. The current danger was infection and the soft tissue damage that would hinder motion. Bone chips from his scapula had to be considered as well; something well beyond the medic's capabilities or equipment.

Faquir was his connection, his eyes and ears to the commander, and what was going on in the compound, as well as his voice.

"No one has seen him?" Scorpion asked when Faquir came in to check up on him.

"No *majistir*. I have checked and the men are keeping watch, just as the commander promised. He understands your importance and I believe he is dedicated to protecting you.

"Maybe he expects to find a reward at the end of this. When we kill the assassin."

"It would not be inappropriate."

"I can arrange that with my benefactor. He will be pleased with the outcome, and therefore, generous."

Scorpion paused for a moment. "But I am surprised and concerned. I did not expect him to be so far behind us. We could not move as fast as he could. I know we left a trail in the sand and I expect him to be able to follow it. Yet he doesn't appear. Our tracks would lead him out into the open sand. Easy to see."

"I do not have an answer. It is you who can understand the tactics of such an enemy."

† † †

Dan and Roland watched throughout the day. All they accomplished was to learn that someone had set a schedule of sentries with their focus aimed back towards the rocky ground at the mouth of the wadi. Making a rough estimate from the guard rotation, they guessed there were more than twenty men in the otherwise abandoned village. They spotted some women tending the livestock and gardens as well. Dan guessed there would also be women kept for pleasure as well. It was less a village, scrapping out an existence on the edge of the inhabitable, than an armed camp acting as an R&R retreat.

Very fortuitous for Scorpion. Still, he was here and Dan had another opportunity to avenge Carrie and rid the world of this dark and deadly man.

"How long do we wait?" Roland asked. "We have the element of surprise right now. And the longer we wait, the more lax they'll be about keeping watch."

"That'll end when I start thinning their ranks."

"You sure that's the best option?"

"I can create terror. They'll be afraid to stick their heads out of those mud huts."

"They'll know we're here."

"But not exactly where. And they won't know what we'll do next."

"So, we'll go in at some point."

Dan nodded. "At some point. We'll have to get across that open sand. Then it'll be close quarters fighting."

"My kind of action."

The two men watched for the rest of the day. The afternoon sun was in their faces making it harder to shoot. Dan decided to wait until the next morning. Then he would let loose the terror only a sniper could unleash.

The next morning, Dan took his Sako out of its case and went over the rifle carefully. He took his time cleaning it, making sure there was no dust or grit in the barrel or action. The scope was covered and the lenses clean and clear. He loaded five, five-round magazines and laid them on the gun case. He took his pack and, using some rocks, made a shooting rest with it. He could sit down and establish a solid shooting platform with his arms braced against his knees. The barrel would point through a cleft in the rocks that protected him from being seen. The suppressor and lack of dirt meant there would be no dust signature with each round fired. Also, with the suppressor, no one would know the exact direction of his shot. There would be a sonic boom as it arrived, with no directionality.

Dan knew those in the camp would understand the general direction, but have no clear indication. Their rifles would not reach out this far unless they had a sniper of their own. A larger weapon, like a mortar could reach them and take them out, but those firing the weapon would have to expose themselves to Dan's firing, which would be lethal for them. His plan hinged on not allowing the men in the camp to mount a successful defense or counterassault. The helplessness of being on the receiving end of a sniper and not being able to neutralize that threat would cause terror in the ranks.

The cleaning done, Dan set up for shooting. The sun was behind him, no worries about any reflecting of light on his lenses. Roland, with some instructions, was acting as his spotter. Dan went through his shooter's notes and dialed in the corrections for distance. The round would drop just over twenty-five feet in its journey to the target 1,365 yards away and smash into it with over 1,200 foot-pounds of energy. Enough to destroy the chest cavity and the organs inside.

"My first shots may be off target, so you'll have to give me an estimate of how far left, right, up, or down so I can adjust the scope."

"They'll have run for cover by then."

"Maybe, maybe not. They may not know what has happened, especially if they don't see the round's impact. In any case, I'll have the adjustment for the next time someone shows up in my area of fire."

"Not quite shooting fish in a barrel."

"It can get pretty complicated, but once dialed in, the kill zone becomes a shooting gallery." Dan looked over the ground towards the village. "Not much wind this morning, so that helps."

He settled himself down and started his small movements to scrunch himself into a solid platform.

"We're going for the courtyard. Most of the men come out of the building on the right. A few of them have entered the left building, so someone or something important is in there. The two buildings behind those also house people. The women usually come and go from the back, right building to tend to their chores. Some of them go into the back left, I think to join the men."

"The fun room."

"Could be. In any case, the open space between the two front buildings is a clear shot and has traffic. Importantly, the sentries have to go through that area to get to the wall facing us. I can see them when they're going to and from sentry duty. I can also see them at the wall, although when I start shooting, they'll be keeping their heads down. Fewer opportunities then."

"I'm ready when you are," Roland said. He had the spotting scope propped against the rocks to steady it.

Dan laid his rifle on the pack and began the minute motions to settle himself into a comfortable and solid position. He needed to be locked in to the rifle, so they were acting as one, a unit. Roland watched with interest at the small adjustments Dan made. When he was done, his body grew still. He settled his eye behind the scope and placed the reticle on the open ground that would become his killing field.

"They're a little slow to come out this morning," Roland said. He was looking through the spotting scope at the same scene Dan saw through the rifle.

"No talking," Dan said.

He stilled himself again. His breathing slowed. His heart rate slowed. When someone came into his field of fire, he had to be ready.

A man stepped out into the morning sun, stepped away from the door, stopped, and stretched. After lowering his arms, he dug into his pocket for a cigarette and began to put one in his mouth and light it. Dan's finger tightened in a smooth motion on the trigger and without any effort his grip closed on the light pull. The rifle barked and jumped back against Dan's shoulder with a satisfying kick. Its flat sound could not be heard in the compound; only a hundred yards out from where he shot.

Two seconds later, there was a dust spurt behind and to the right of the figure.

"Three feet high and two to the right," Roland said.

Roland made the calls in feet, but Dan was able to translate them into clicks on the scope. He reached up and quickly dialed the adjustment. The man seemed startled by the sonic boom. At first, he didn't recognize it. However, the accompanying spurt of dust told him he was in danger. He turned to go back inside, when the next round slammed into his back, shoving him against the door with his spine severed and his heart burst open.

The door opened and someone stepped out to look at his dead comrade. The next round hit him in his lower left rib cage, spinning him around and to the ground in the doorway. Someone from inside dragged his body back into the darkness and the door slammed shut. The men at the wall were shouting back to the huts. Others seemed to be shouting orders. The sentries put binoculars to their faces started scanning the desert.

Dan changed his aim to one of the sentries. His next shot disappeared.

"Couldn't see where that hit. Assume it's high," Roland said.

Dan didn't answer. He adjusted his aim rather than disturb the scope's zero on the killing area and squeezed off another round. This time the sentry's head exploded and he dropped behind the wall. All the other sentries ducked behind the edge of the wall. Five shots, three kills and no more targets presenting themselves.

Dan took a few breaths but kept settled on his rifle, watching the kill zone. *Patience. They have to come out. You'll get your shot.* He ejected the magazine and clipped a fresh one in the Sako.

Roland kept quiet, following Dan's admonishment.

Chapter 52

With the first shot, Scorpion knew what had happened. The assassin had successfully tracked him and had veered off before being seen by sentries in the compound. He was using his sniper skills. There was a second shot in close succession. Faquir and one of the men in the room with him started for the door.

"Don't go out there," Scorpion said.

Faquir stopped at his master's order. The soldier didn't heed him and stepped out into the morning sun.

"Ali's been shot," he said.

Just then another shot rang out and the man's body slammed back into the door closing it. Another in the room opened the door and dragged the dead man back inside. He looked at Scorpion with his eyes wide.

Scorpion worked his way to a sitting position on the bed. His left arm was in a sling to immobilize his injured shoulder. Movement caused pain and he winced with its onslaught. He looked down at the body. The bullet strike was low and to one side. The massive tissue damage indicated a large caliber rifle. He looked at the remaining two soldiers in the room with himself and Faquir.

"To go out that door is to die. This man is a very good shooter," he said.

"Where is he? There is no place to hide except the rocks and they are over a kilometer away."

"He is in those rocks. You must find a back way out of this room and get the commander. I need to talk to him."

The man nodded and walked to the rear of the room. He climbed out of a window.

"Do not expose yourself to the courtyard," Scorpion called after him.

Another shot rang out, followed by a fifth. Men outside, the sentries cried out. Scorpion guessed one of them had been killed. *A head shot from such a distance?* Everything went quiet. No one moved outside and no shots rang out. *He's waiting*, Scorpion thought. *Let him wait. We have water and shelter. He has nothing.*

A few minutes later the commander climbed through the window. The action seemed to offend his sense of dignity, but a good sense of caution prevailed over vanity.

"This man who follows you. He is here. How is it that he can shoot from so far away and hit my men? I have snipers, but they are not so accurate over eight hundred meters. We are over a kilometer from the nearest rocks, yet he kills three men so easily. And we didn't see him as he approached.

"Like all snipers, he is stealthy. He would have seen the buildings and veered off before we saw him. He is carefully positioned. He has to be close to the edge to minimize the distance. It is a long shot, but he has shown he is capable. Right now, Commander, the courtyard is a killing zone. As is probably the wall facing the shooter. We can wait him out. We have water, food, and shelter. He had nothing except what he brought on his back."

"The well is in the courtyard. How do we reach it?"

Scorpion thought for a moment. "Have your women pump the water. I am thinking he is one of those westerners with principles, with morals. He won't shoot unarmed women."

"We need water. We didn't store up jugs in anticipation of such an assault."

"Send them out. You will see. We just have to find ways to move around without exposing ourselves."

"The men are spooked. They are fearless before an enemy, but this," he waved his hand towards the door, "is death they can't see coming."

"Tell them to stay calm...and stay out of sight. Send your women out to test my theory. If it goes well, we only have to wait."

The commander left, as he came, with an awkward climb through the back wall window.

† † †

All had gone quiet. Dan and Roland watched.

"Nothing stirring. They've got their heads down. You may not get any more shots."

"They have to move around." Dan kept his eye behind his scope while talking. "See the pump in the courtyard? They have to go there to get water."

"That puts pressure on them if they don't have reserves stored up, or another well."

"Most small villages don't. I'm betting with this remote location, no one felt the need to store water. Just pump it when needed. If that's so, they will be under pressure soon enough."

"You know we've got limited time here," Roland said. "We need to keep enough water in reserve in order to get out of here when we're done."

"We can use their well, when they're all dead."

Roland took his eye off the spotting scope and looked at Dan hunched over his rifle, still in his shooting position. "That's placing a big bet on the outcome."

Dan didn't answer.

Roland turned back to his scope. "Someone's coming," he said.

"Copy that. Two women."

"They got buckets. Heading for the well?"

The well was a pump system with a metal handle. It pulled up water from a drilled well that had replaced the shallower hand-dug well years ago when the military had taken over the village. The result was a cleaner, more reliable source of water for the compound. It consisted of a steel tube housing the pipe going into the ground, linkage for the pump, and a long handle to pull the water up from a great depth. The spout stuck out of the housing opposite the handle.

Dan fired off a round that hit in front of the women, stopping them in their tracks. His next shot was at the pump housing. The .338 round tore through the metal casing. His next shots were aimed at the handle where it joined the pump housing, finally tearing it loose as the rounds ripped into the steel.

"Good shooting!" Roland said. "I'd give you a medal. You killed the pump!"

"Only took five shots," Dan said. "Not my best performance."

"Now they got problems. We both have limited supplies if this turns into a waiting game."

The women, after being stopped by the first round, dropped their buckets, and turned to run for cover as Dan's rounds slammed into the pump. The commander watched, peeking from a corner window that gave a slim view of the courtyard and the pump installation.

"La'an," Damn, the commander said. "He has destroyed the pump."

Scorpion was still sitting on the bed. It was painful to move and there was no need for that now. Better to sit quiet and assess the situation. Faquir had brought him some tea. The room he was in had a ten-liter water jar which was half full. Scorpion noted the supply in his quarters. He hoped the kitchen had more water stored, although he doubted there would be much extra. Water had been pumped each day. The compound had slipped into only holding a daily supply. Why, after all, would you need to store water since it was just a few pumps away?

His stomach churned. They would not have the luxury of waiting out the sniper. Food was available, but the water was the critical supply. Without it, they would have days, no more than a week. Could the assassin hold out that long?

"You may have to send men out to find and kill this man," Scorpion said.

The commander turned to him. "That would be suicide. We have to cover the kilometer of sand between us and he can just shoot at will behind whatever rocks he is hiding."

"You have vehicles, the pickups, you have machine guns mounted on them, do you not? You have mortars and RPGs. You must assemble all those assets and charge him. With enough firepower and speed, one man cannot stop you."

"I will lose many men in the attempt."

Scorpion didn't answer. Was the commander reevaluating his commitment to Scorpion? Would he sacrifice so many men to save one wounded warrior?

"You will be well compensated for the loss. My benefactor can supply many more weapons for you. You can recruit new men, train them, and become an even more deadly fighting group. Thus, elevating your status among your tribe."

The commander looked back out the window. Scorpion could sense he was weighing his options. One of which would include killing him along with his eunuch and dumping their bodies outside of the village wall for the assassin to see.

"My benefactor, the Saudi who will remain unknown to you, knows about this village compound. I let him know it was one of my retreat positions if my headquarters ever came under attack. He will know I have departed my sanctuary and will, in time, look into my retreat options to find me. It would not benefit you to have him find I received no help."

"But you did receive help. My medic attended to your wounds. We are letting you rest, heal here. But it seems you have unleashed on us a formidable foe by coming here."

"He is formidable, but he is one man. Are your men not able to overcome one man?"

"You said yourself to not underestimate him. Now you want me to send my men out to charge him? Send them to their death? When we don't even know exactly where he is?"

"Every time you send them out, you send some to their death. This is no different." Scorpion glared at the commander with his dark eyes showing the full force of his energy. "I would deal with him myself, except that I am wounded."

"I will think on it," the commander finally said. He walked to the back window. "I must speak with my men."

"I suggest you assemble your weapons. Mortars can reach him, even if your RPGs can't. Use them from the safety of your walls, then you can charge with a greater chance of success. Send your men out in the pickups with their machine guns. You can lay down overwhelming fire and he won't be able to shoot back."

The commander climbed out of the window without answering.

Chapter 53

The next morning Marcus rose before the sun broke over the rim of the desert. He nudged Uri awake and gave him some water. He ate an MRE while Uri only could munch on a power bar.

"You had a bad night?" Marcus asked.

Uri nodded. He looked down at his wounded leg. The bandage was moist with blood. Marcus followed his gaze. The man was losing blood, not rapidly, but steadily. He foresaw the inevitable outcome without medical intervention; death by blood loss or infection.

"We go to the road today. Got a good story for us?"

"Let me think on it," Uri said. He gave Marcus a weak smirk.

Marcus helped Uri back on the trace, really a stretcher with a set of wheels on one end. There was, again, much grunting with the pain before he got the man settled and strapped in. Marcus tucked the Tavor 7 and M4 under the thermal blanket. Both carbines had thirty-round magazines fully loaded, with two more nearby. Marcus wore his 9mm Sig Sauer on his belt, under his shirt. He attached the poles to his harness and started for the road to the east.

"I'm going to change the story," Uri said. His voice evidenced the effort to speak, but he continued. "We're the friendly archeologists who were attacked by bandits and robbed, with me nearly killed. You, being such an inventive guy, cobbled together this contraption and you're trying to get me back to medical help in Al Mukalla."

"That sounds good unless they want to take us to a local clinic. When you're handled, the rifles will be uncovered. Or someone could drive us all the way to Al Mukalla and its hospital with no jumping off point before that. It'd be a dead end for us."

A sigh came from behind Marcus as he leaned forward to pull Uri along.

"You're the one who wants to get a ride."

"Yep. To save your life. And you're the one who's supposed to come up with a cover story."

There was silence from behind.

Then Uri spoke, again in a strained voice. "We could add that we have a medical team waiting to meet us to take us to Jordan where my special doctors are waiting. Therefore, we can't stop at a local clinic or the hospital in Al Mukalla."

Marcus turned that over in his mind. "Might work," he said.

Both men lapsed into silence except for some grunting from Uri when the trace jolted especially hard over the uneven ground.

Two hours later they were at the edge of the pavement.

"We'll start south. I can flag any vehicle when they approach," Marcus said. He started down the road, pulling Uri behind him. It was much easier going on the pavement and he began to settle into a rhythm. "Even if no one comes along, this is much easier going."

Uri didn't answer. After another hour, he called out in a weak voice for Marcus to stop. "I need to elevate my leg again. The angle increases the bleeding."

"I can't pull you along with your head at the bottom."

"No. Just stop at regular intervals."

Marcus silently cursed. He needed a ride to come along before Uri lost consciousness. He needed his language skills if they hoped to get any help that wouldn't involve government authorities.

While they were stopped, Marcus sitting on the pavement, Uri laying on the trace with his leg elevated, both men heard the sound of an engine to the north—coming in their direction.

"Showtime," Marcus said as he stood up.

Uri nodded. He seemed to try to gather his strength.

The speck at the horizon grew larger until Marcus could see it was a small straight-body truck. the kind one used to move smaller goods around. Marcus stood on the road's edge, waiting, as the truck grew in size. He raised his hand to wave it down as it approached. The brakes squealed and the truck slowed to a stop in front of them. The driver got out and seemed to ask something unintelligible to Marcus. Uri waved his hand from the trace on which he was lying. The driver walked over to him.

Marcus could tell Uri had forced himself to speak with a stronger voice. He waited as Uri told the tale they had concocted. The driver listened intently; his eyes fixed firmly on Uri. When Uri was done, the man spoke rapidly and with much animation. When he was done Uri turned his head to Marcus.

"I think he believes me. He is much angered that someone in his country would harm scientists such as us and leave us for dead and he'll be happy to take us to Al

Mukalla. He had one question. Why such a large, strong man such as you could not stop them and avoided injury. I think he suspects you are a coward and ran away, but who knows? I told him you were knocked out at the start of the attack and when I tried to help, they shot me. They were bad shots, so I got hit in the leg.

"I told him it was a serious injury, given my medical condition and that I needed to get to the coast so I could be picked up by the wealthy man that sponsored our trip. I would be taken to a hospital in Jordan where my doctor could treat me. I could not wait to stop at the hospital in Al Mukalla. A helicopter would meet me at the airport and transport me to Jordan."

"He bought our story."

Uri gave Marcus a wan smile. "Maybe…most of it. It's a lot to believe, but he is just a simple truck driver and knows little of foreign archeologists, or even his own country's ancient history. He knows where ruins are but knows little about their story. I told him we were uncovering the important past that every Yemeni could be proud of." Uri paused for a moment to gather his strength. "He liked that."

"Good. Don't let the guns rattle, keep them covered. We'll load you into the truck."

Marcus wheeled Uri around to the back of the truck. The driver pulled open the roll door. Inside were boxes of vegetables and sacks of grain piled high.

"We can wedge the trace with those sacks and keep you from rolling around."

He motioned for the driver to grab the arms of the trace while he grabbed the wheeled end. Together they lifted Uri inside. Marcus jumped up to stuff some sacks around the trace.

"This should hold you."

Uri motioned for him to come close. "*Tawaquf*" he said in a whisper. "It means stop. *Mahata*. It means stopping place, or terminal. Use those two to get the driver to stop. He can't take us into the airport."

"Got it. You hang tight." He gave Uri a bottle of water and jumped out of the box.

Marcus got into the cab as the driver moved his personal items from the passenger seat. They started off for Al Mukalla. Marcus had his backpack between his legs. He got out the satellite phone and put in a call to Jane.

"Jane here. What's happening. Were you successful?"

"Still working on it," Marcus said. "We split up. Uri got shot in the leg. He's not in good shape. I'm taking Uri to the coast, near Al Mukalla."

At the mention of the city, the driver looked over at Marcus who nodded back to him.

"We'll get dropped off somewhere near the city. I'll hike us out into the countryside. Can you get a chopper in there to pick us up...with a medic aboard? It'll be faster than a sub."

"How long?"

Marcus looked over at the driver and tried to ask how long the drive would be to no avail. Pidgin English and hand gestured did not work.

"Maybe as soon as tonight. For sure tomorrow. Have them ready to go. I've gotten us a ride but it will be reported to the authorities. I have to assume they'll be on our trail, so we won't have much time."

"Chopper time will be about three hours from your call."

"Got it."

"Now what's going on with Dan and Roland?"

"Don't know. The target got away and headed farther into the interior. They're going after him."

"I haven't heard a thing from him."

"You know how that is. He goes radio-silent until the objective's achieved."

"Yeah. But I keep telling him to update me."

"He'll be okay. He and Roland make a formidable team."

He heard Jane sigh.

"I'll be standing by. Be careful."

"Roger that."

Marcus hung up. The driver sneaked a peek at him at the use of what he knew to be a military phrase. Marcus stared out of the windshield. He hoped he wouldn't have to shoot the driver at the end since he was trying to be a good Samaritan.

They rolled on with neither man trying to speak. Not only was there the language gulf, but the cab was a noisy place. The truck engine whined as it labored up the hills. The tires made a loud hum over the pavement. The springs jolted and bounced over the bumps and ripples in the pavement.

Marcus tried to recall the map of the area around Al Mukalla in his head. Once dropped off, he had to assume the driver would report the strange duo and the authorities would head out to the drop-off point to start a search. He had to be beyond any perimeter they established.

Chapter 54

A half-hour later the commander came back through the window. He glared at Scorpion, the man who brought this danger to his retreat compound. Scorpion understood his anger. The commander had to deal with the danger. Scorpion understood he was someone for whom tribal loyalties and connections demanded protection.

"My men will try to get mortars on the wall. We will start sending the rockets towards the hills and, hopefully, take out this sniper."

"Good." Scorpion said. "It is the right thing to do. I suggest you make your pickups ready to launch once the mortars are hitting the rocks."

"I cannot send all my men out. I will not risk them all."

"It is your choice, but the more you send, the greater chance of success."

The commander turned without comment and left the room.

Outside, he worked his way around to the barracks area and assembled his men. He instructed them to take four mortars to the wall facing the rocks and set them up. They were to fire one at a time, so each mortar team could adjust their inclination from the previous hits. With that, they would more quickly zero in on the rocks at the desert's edge. Where he hoped the sniper lay.

† † †

"Got some movement," Roland said. He had kept watch through the spotting scope while Dan had stretched his muscles. He could lay in the prone position for hours waiting for a shot, but the sitting position created more tension on his body, even though he worked to settle into a locked position. It helped to stretch after a half hour for a brief moment and then get back on target. Dan quickly settled down with the Sako and searched the compound with his scope.

"On the far right. There's some movement."

Dan brought his reticle over to where Roland had indicated. Heads were popping out from behind the building. There was thirty yards of open space between the building and the wall. Dan settled in on that space, waiting.

A man jumped out from behind the building and started across the open area. He was carrying a mortar. Dan fired. The man ran into the bullet heading his way and his body was jolted from a forward crouch to an upright posture, arms flung open, dropping the mortar, and twisting to the ground. Blood spurted in the air from the center-mas shot.

Without hesitation, two more men ran out, each taking different angles towards the wall; both carrying what looked like mortars. Dan switched to the first one and fired. His shot hit the man but not before he had covered most of the ground. The mortar he was carrying was flung forward in the man's last dying move. The other man disappeared behind the protection of the wall before Dan could get off a shot.

"Bringing mortars to the wall. They can make life difficult for us," Roland said.

Dan only grunted, keeping his eye on the open ground. There seemed to be a pause in the action. *They must have more. They'll try again.* He stayed in his shooting position, locked onto his rifle.

A man burst into sight, then another. One carried a third mortar, the other ran to the abandoned mortar in the open ground. As he stooped to pick up the weapon, his chest exploded with a .338 round and he was flung backwards to the ground. Now two bodies lay close to the abandoned mortar. The other man reached the wall.

The commander watched as his men were cut down. He could hear the astonished sounds of his other fighters in the protection of the building where the weapons were kept. This sniper could hit his men even when they were on a full run. Now he had two mortars at the wall, with only two operators. That would slow the rate of fire. He needed a loader and gunner for each weapon. One man to adjust the angle, the other with a rocket ready to drop and fire.

He ordered a pickup, one without a machine gun mounted, to drive around. He would use it to protect his men. It would pull in front of the abandoned mortar, the driver would jump out, along with another hiding in the bed. They would be shielded from the sniper and could load the mortar. Then the driver would climb in and without sitting up and exposing himself, move the truck out of the line of fire while the other man walked behind its cover. It was not a great plan, but he couldn't send more men out to get shot. He could sense the fear being generated by this shooter. Shortly, no one would want to risk that deadly distance between the shelter of the building and the village wall.

"Truck coming around the building," Roland said.
"Got it."
Dan moved his sights over to the vehicle as it emerged from the protection of the building. He squeezed off two rounds in rapid succession. They hit the windshield, but the driver must have been crouched low. The truck continued. It was heading towards the downed man with the mortar. Dan watched through the scope as the truck stopped and the driver's door opened. A figure tumbled out without offering Dan a target. Then another figure flung itself out of the bed to the ground.

After a moment, both men could see the mortar being shoved over the edge of the pickup bed. Still there was no shot. Then came a case of rockets, this time more slowly as they were heavier.

"Disable the truck?" Roland asked.
"Yep."
Dan put two more rounds into the cab, aiming at the dashboard, hoping to take out something electrical that would disable the truck. His next rounds went through the engine hood, again, hoping to hit something vital. A fifty-caliber round would have penetrated the engine block, but with the .338 Lapua Magnum, the best Dan could hope for was to take out some appendage, such as a carburetor or fuel injection. His next two rounds went through part of the front grill, hoping to pierce the radiator.

They waited. There was something going on. Dan could see the driver's door move. *Trying to work the truck while staying on the floor. Can't hit him there. Hope it doesn't start*. The two men waited. They couldn't hear what was going on, but the truck didn't move.

"Looks like you've stopped it."

"Yeah It's stuck there and the mortar tube with it," Dan said.

He walked some rounds along the edge of the pickup bed from the rear to the front, working the fast-acting bolt of the Sako with a smooth, rapid motion.

"That's enough," Dan said. "Don't want to waste rounds."

"You think you got the man hiding behind the truck?"

"Maybe. The driver is behind the engine. He's safe. The other guy might not have realized that I can send rounds through the side panels of the truck. Good chance I hit him. Even if he's only wounded, it's another out of the fight."

"You know we're going to have to go in there at some point. They could take the other trucks and just leave. Out the back door so to speak. We can't follow."

Dan kept to his shooting posture.

"I know. I don't think they're ready to quit. They still have numbers and firepower. They'll try to get the rest of the mortars to the wall, or just launch them from the back of the building. The aiming feedback will be slower but they won't lose any more men."

"So, we got two at the wall. They'll be most active. One in the courtyard, out of the equation for now. Wonder how many they have?"

"Don't know. But you should look around for a second, fallback position if they get too close. They can reach us if they've got eighty or even sixty-millimeter tubes."

The commander watched as his plan unfolded and then went awry. The pickup was disabled, out in the middle of the killing zone, with the mortar and rockets hostage in the bed. If that were not bad enough, he had a wounded man lying behind the truck. The driver was safe, but could not move and no one could come to aid the wounded man. He could bleed out there in front of all his men and they were powerless to help him.

He ground his teeth in anger. Scorpion had brought this whirlwind of death to his remote compound. The solitude and relaxation it offered was now shattered with this sniper picking his men off, one by one. He could always depart and leave Scorpion behind to meet his fate. That, however, would show defeat in front of his men. Men who looked up to him. The commander realized that he could not run from one man. He had to defeat him.

He turned and ordered the men to set up the remaining three mortar tubes to set up behind the building. He could see relief in their eyes that they wouldn't be picked to try to make the run across that deadly space. The rear tubes would take longer to adjust their aim and cycle through their rockets, but they would still close in on the target. His problem was that he was still not sure where the target was.

He thought about that. He didn't have unlimited rockets to throw at the rocks. If he couldn't be sure of taking out the sniper, he was loath to use one of his men, exposed in the courtyard to check on his results. He would not sacrifice men just for that.

Suppression. That was the key. That was how he would use the mortars. Since he couldn't be sure, once the rounds were hitting in the rocky areas, he'd send out a dozen men in six pickups with machine guns. They could race over the open ground and gain the rocks while the sniper was pinned down by the mortars, if not killed or wounded.

Once his men had reached the rocks, they could find the sniper. If they didn't kill him, they could keep him from firing as he sent the rest of his men across to complete his victory. He started shouting orders and the men began to move.

Scorpion watched the exchange of shooting from the corner of a window, careful to keep out of any line of fire. He was unsteady, but able to walk. Faquir had brought him a tactical jacket which he put on with the left sleeve cut off. He brought Scorpion an AK47 carbine and four extra thirty-round magazines. Scorpion felt better with the carbine in his right hand. He would be able to manage it by placing his left hand over the rifle, keeping it from walking up as he fired. The kick would be painful, but Scorpion was not unfamiliar with pain. He had delivered it both in battle and sexual recreation. And he had felt it for much of his life, starting at an early age with abuse from older men.

Would the commander leave? Abandon him? Scorpion caught his anger at having led this deadly man to his door. Would his loyalties hold in the face of his men getting killed? He watched the fight as the commander tried to counter the shooter. Getting the mortars to the wall seemed to have failed. What else was the commander going to do? Then he heard the *whomp* of a mortar rocket firing. The first round came from the wall. There was a pause. *Waiting to see where it landed.* Voices called out and Scorpion could see the second mortar team at the wall adjust the elevation downward. *Landed short.*

Whomp. The second rocket fired off. Again, the wait and then more shouting. Adjustments were made and a third round fired from the back of the building. *Good thinking*. His face cracked into what passed for a smile across his grim features.

Roland and Dan watched the first round splash into the sand well short of the rocks and to their left.

"They don't know where we are. They'll walk the rounds towards the rocks and hope to hit us or flush us out," Roland said. His voice was flat. The danger was obvious and closing in. But it was just a factor in the deadly game of warfare. They just had to have a counter. Staying put would not be the best. Nor would panicking and exposing themselves.

Chapter 55

Marcus stared down the road. The driver gave him furtive glances now and again. *Probably thinks I'm oddly cut for being a scientist, whatever his idea of one is.* He knew they would be reported after they dropped off. The day grew old and the sun began to sink in the west. *Good. Darkness helps.*

Then, far ahead he could see a glow of lights as the sky darkened.

"Airport?" Marcus asked.

The driver looked at him. Marcus spread his arms like wings in flight and repeated the word. Understanding lit up in the driver's eyes and he nodded. The airport was west of the city. He expected the driver would divert in that direction before entering the city. That would allow the two men to get off and head further away, but still close enough for helicopters to reach them.

Sure enough, as they closed on Al Mukalla, the driver swung to the right and started down another road, curving around the northern edge of the city. It was still dark on the road, but to his left, south, Marcus could now see the full glow of the town. It was a major port on the Gulf of Aden and, with a population of 300,000, the fifth largest city in Yemen.

After ten minutes, Marcus could see more lights ahead. *Time to leave.* He spoke the words Uri had given him.

"Tawaquf, mahata."

The driver looked at him with a question on his face. Marcus repeated the words more forcefully and pointed to the side of the road. The driver said something in Arabic and pointed ahead. He took his hand off the steering wheel and mimicked the bird-like gesture Marcus had used earlier.

Marcus shook his head and repeated, *"Tawaquf,"* and *"mahata."* He jabbed his finger towards the driver and then outside to towards the side of the road. His tone and face projected a warning of danger if he was not obeyed.

The driver's eyes widened. He shook his head in disbelief, but slowed the truck and pulled over on the sand.

"Out," said Marcus, pointing to the door. The driver shut off his engine and opened his door. When he was out of the cab, Marcus grabbed his pack and exited. He stepped around the front to walk back with the driver. If the man had any foolish idea of taking off, Marcus prevented him from executing what would have been a bad idea.

The driver pulled up the roll door. Uri blinked and looked out. "Time to go?"

Marcus nodded. "Keep the weapons hid. He's going to unpack you."

He motioned to the driver to climb up and move the bags of grain away from the trace. When that was done, Marcus joined him in the truck and they slid Uri to the edge. Marcus jumped down and caught the wheels as they cleared the lip of the truck. The handles bumped over the edge as the driver had to let them go and Marcus let the wheels touch down. He then took the handles and moved Uri away from the truck.

When the driver jumped down, Marcus handed him three one-hundred-dollar bills and said, "Thank you."

From behind him Uri, said, *"Shukran,"* thank you.

The man looked past Marcus and said, *"Afwan"* you are welcome. And with a slight bow he headed back to his cab. The truck rumbled to life and pulled back out on the road.

"You think he's okay?" Uri asked.

"Not on your life. Even with my large tip." He picked up the trace arms and hooked them onto his harness. "We got to move. This won't be comfortable."

"Neither was the back of that truck. I'll survive, I think."

"Be a shame to lose you after all this work. Before the night's out, we'll be on a chopper and you'll be full of feel-good drugs."

"Looking forward to it," came the weak reply.

Marcus looked around. To the south there was the glow of Al Mukalla. Beyond it, the dark expanse of the Gulf of Aden. To the right and left the glow faded as the city gave out. West were the lights of the airport. To the north, away from Al Mukalla, was the dark of the desert. He turned to the north and started out, pulling hard, running when he could. He'd have only an hour or two before the authorities would stop where they were let off. They would follow, slower, so as to not lose his trail.

As the dark closed in, Marcus put on his NVGs and continued as fast as he could. The ground was stone-laden sand with flat sections thirty to one hundred yards in length. They were broken up by ravines running from a shallow three feet to over eight feet deep. Some were narrow with steeper sides, making it hard to get in and out. Others had gently sloping sides which required effort but didn't risk the trace tumbling over and dragging both men to the ground.

The scrub bush smacked at Marcus' legs and Uri's face. He could hear Uri grunting from behind, but no call came out to go more slowly or carefully. Both men knew speed was required.

After one hard climb from a ravine that Marcus had to attempt three times, before gaining the top, he sat down and pulled out two water bottles.

"Still got the rifles?"

"Tight and snug" came Uri's weak response.

Marcus pulled out the satellite phone.

"Jane," he said when she answered.

"You ready for pick up?"

"Not yet, but get the chopper on its way. We'll be north of Al Mukalla. Probably not more than ten miles inland. I'm going to find a pickup point and I'll send you the coordinates in time for the helo to adjust his route."

"Why not wait?"

"We'll have men on our trail. I couldn't get here without a lift. The driver will report us. They'll be searching the area in a couple of hours. We'll be farther into the desert but we won't be able to wait anywhere for long."

"They'll hear the chopper?"

"Probably. But they'll be too far away to do anything and we'll be out of there like a scalded cat."

"Sketchy, but we can do it."

"Everything about this mission is sketchy."

"No word from Dan?"

"You'll be the first to hear, I'm sure. Don't worry. Roland will keep him safe. That's what we're here for, isn't it? To babysit your boy?"

There was a humorous tone in Marcus' voice.

"You are getting to be a smartass, just like Roland."

"But *smarter*. I'll be in touch. Got to go now."

Chapter 56

"If they're going to adjust their aim, they have to spot," Roland said.

"I'm thinking the same," Dan said without taking his eye off the scope. "May provide an opportunity."

He scanned the wall with his scope. A second and then a third round came from the compound.

"Got a spotter about five yards to the left of the wall junction," Roland called out.

Dan moved his aim to the point Roland referenced and waited. The spotter would be back.

After the next round, he saw the head as the man watched to see where it would land. Dan sent a round downrange with a gentle squeeze on the lightened trigger. The bullet spattered against the wall just to the right of the spotter.

"Dial in something for windage. It's getting stronger," Roland said. "The other spotter is about twenty yards to right. This one won't show his head for a while."

Dan swung the barrel in a smooth arc to the spot Roland called out and waited. He'd have to acquire the target quickly when it appeared.

The top of a man's head appeared over the wall with the next round. His eyes were just above the rim of the wall. Dan's world again closed down to just him and the target.

He was locked to his rifle, without motion, his aching limbs forgotten. No sound intruded on his consciousness. His breathing, which remained slow, now almost stopped. Then, in between heartbeats, he closed his hand and the Sako snapped back against his shoulders. When the scope resettled, there was no head showing.

"You got him. Took the top of his head off."

Dan didn't answer but swung back to the left. Nothing. That spotter must have seen what happened and was keeping his head down. There was a pause in the incoming rounds.

"Must be trying to recruit new spotters," Roland said. "Dangerous job, I hear."

Dan kept his focus on the target area. The next rounds hit the edge of the rocks where they dove under the desert sand, to the right of their position.

"They'll aim them farther up into the rocks and sweep towards us. They have a good idea of the arc from where you're shooting."

"Got a fallback?"

"Yep. Thirty yards behind us and to the right. I'm betting they'll aim across in front of us. You'll have to recalibrate. I'll scope the distance for you when we move."

"Let's go," Dan said. "It's getting late and the sun is not in my favor, even with a large sun shade. And there's the danger of a glare from the lens letting them pinpoint us."

"They may try to move out tonight, under cover of dark."

"I thought about that."

"And?"

"Let's relocate. First things first."

Dan zipped his Sako in its case and the two men started crawling over the rough ground, going uphill and away from the sand. In a few minutes they could see the lip of rock that formed a good shield for them to their right as they crawled. They turned and headed to it. The rocks scrapped at their knees and elbows. The mortar rounds were now coming faster, and, as Roland predicted, moving across behind them, opposite of the direction they were crawling.

When they got into the depression, Roland took out the scope and got the range to the wall for Dan. He dialed in the adjustments for the extra thirty yards of distance and the windage adjustment for the wind which was now blowing steadily across the range at around 8 miles an hour.

With the changes made, he found a new position. This time he could lie prone and slot the barrel through a crack in the rocks. It was cushioned by his backpack as before. The prone position allowed him to hold his aim for much longer periods.

The mortar rounds peppered the rocky area, crossing close to where the two men had been lying. The sun was now low in the sky, almost blinding Dan when he swung the rifle in a certain direction.

From the glare of the sun, they both saw the pickups charging across the sand. The mortars had started up again. The trucks had large tires that could ride over the sand and were moving at a high rate of speed, bouncing over the crests of the dunes, or slamming through their tops.

"Here they come," Roland said. He grabbed his M4, pulled the charging handle, and flipped on the safety. "Locked and loaded."

Dan swung the Sako in the direction of the trucks and started firing. With Roland spotting, he met them head on, the .338 rounds slamming through the windshields into the cabs. One truck veered to the side and went over, throwing the machine gunner out of the back. The others kept going.

The commander readied six trucks with a driver and machine gunner. The trucks carried the Type 85, a Chinese heavy machine gun. It was belt fed from an attached cannister and fired a 12.7 by 108mm round at 600 to 700 rounds per minute. The large caliber round hit hard and did a lot of damage. He instructed the men to fire when able, even though they couldn't aim in what was going to be a mad dash over the sand. The idea was to suppress the deadly return fire by the sniper if the mortars hadn't taken him out already. There had been no return fire after the mortar rounds had started sweeping over the rocks.

With shouts of *Allahu Akbar*, the men drove off, eager to fight. The commander went to the rear of the building and climbed to the roof. He was taking a great risk, but felt the sniper, if alive, would be focused on the trucks. He wanted to watch his men in action.

The pickups roared over the desert. The machine gunners held off. *Fire, damn it!* the commander thought to himself. It seemed as though the men wanted to wait until they were closer.

He heard the report of the sniper's rifle and saw the first truck veer off to one side and flip. The other trucks kept going. Now they started firing. The commander hoped their rounds would be effective.

Dan hit another truck.

"Got him in the grill," Roland called out.

Dan kept firing at the wounded truck. The windshield shattered, but the driver was staying low and didn't get hit.

Steam started to come from the engine hood and the vehicle began to slow. A couple of hundred yards from the rocks, it stopped. Dan had already turned his attention to the other four trucks.

They were closing fast on the rocks. The machine gun fire was growing more intense although still wildly erratic.

"Sounds like a heavy caliber. Big bore, lots of rounds per minute," Roland said. "Don't want them to get on to us."

He stopped spotting and unslung his M4. Firing only a 5.56mm, it was badly outmatched by the Type 85 at 12.7mm. But as they got closer, he could make some kills with more accurate shooting.

Dan was in the zone. Roland's spotting was no longer needed. He adjusted on the fly as the trucks closed. Another truck was stopped when the driver died with a .338 round to his chest. Another round found the machine gunner who was flung backwards and dumped out in the rear. The driver kept going.

The driverless truck rolled to a stop fifty yards from the rocks. The fifth and sixth trucks made it to the rocks. Now they had to slow and, without the others for support, were in danger. The mortars also stopped. They didn't want to take out their own men.

Dan turned to the two remaining trucks and started firing. The drivers were now being careful as were the machine gunners. Roland opened fire as well. One of the machine gunners identified where the shots were coming from and swept the area with his Type 85.

Dan and Roland had to flatten themselves to the hard ground to avoid the spray of rounds that swept over them with their deadly shrieks. This allowed the two pickups to move forward. The machine gun mounted in the truck near the rocks opened up as well. A withering level of fire poured over and around where the two men lay flat on the rocks.

"We're in a pretty hot spot, boss," Roland said.

"Let's split up." Dan began to crawl away in the depression, heading for a slight drop off that would offer more cover and a chance to return fire.

Roland, after firing some rounds at the pickups, crawled up the slope to get more separation.

Dan crawled along as machine gun fire swept the area he and Roland had abandoned. The rounds either screamed overhead or smashed into the rocks spraying large, jagged pieces in dangerous bursts through the air. He had to find a new position to set up with the Sako. His advantage was not rounds per minute, but deadly accuracy. A few well-placed shots would give pause to this onslaught.

Chapter 57

Marcus pushed hard into the desert, away from the lights of Al Mukalla. The ground slowly rose before him as he traversed the ravines. Another hour of hard slogging and he'd be ready to call in the chopper. Uri bumped along behind him; silent, except for an occasional grunt of pain from a hard jolt.

Finally, Uri called out for Marcus to stop. "Have to elevate for a few minutes. The bleeding's getting worse."

Marcus set the trace down and pushed his pack under Uri's leg. He could see the wetness across his pants. He looked back, now about two hundred feet higher than from where they started. He could see the road where they had left the truck. To his right, from the direction the truck went, came a string of three headlights, moving together.

"They're coming. Three vehicles. Probably not more than a dozen men. I'm surprised the driver was able to call out that many."

"He had a good story."

Uri coughed and grunted at the effort to speak.

"We got to go," Marcus said.

Uri sighed. "Let's do it."

Marcus picked up his backpack and hooked the trace to his waist. He started forward with a lunge and broke into a short, choppy trot. Behind him Uri moaned and grunted but didn't say a word. Marcus put his head down and drove forward, now less careful about finding a smooth path. His arms pumped and his lungs burned as he pulled his load like a horse pulling a loaded cart.

"Another half hour," Marcus said in between his heavy breathing. "Give me that and we'll have you out of here."

There was no answer from behind him.

In a half-hour, as promised, Marcus started looking for some flat ground for the helicopter. Behind he could see the lights of the three cars at the side of the road and what looked like flashlights. The lights were fanning out along the roadside and into the desert. *Looking for the trail.*

In a few minutes, they began to move forward in a column, the lights splaying out in different directions. *No NVGs, that's a help.* Marcus checked his GPS coordinates and got on the sat phone.

When Jane picked up, he gave her the coordinates and she ended the call to transfer them to the chopper. Then she called Marcus back.

"They're twenty to a half-hour out," she said.

"That's cutting it close. Some men have arrived and are following our trail."

"How far ahead are you?"

"Maybe an hour, maybe a bit less. They can move faster than me, but they have to follow our trail. Depends on how clear it is. They don't seem to have night vision, so that's a plus."

"Can you hold them off?"

"Of course…for a while, but that would put the chopper under fire and that's a problem."

"I'll warn them the LZ might be hot and to come in fast. Can you light the zone?"

Marcus started rummaging through his backpack. "I got a few glow sticks. The chopper can see them easily with night vision goggles. If I put them on the ground, they may not be seen by the ones following. We're a bit higher in elevation."

"Better than nothing. Hang in there."

"Yes, ma'am."

"They going to make it?" Uri's weak voice came from behind him.

"Be close. When they come in, I'm going to manhandle you into the chopper. It might be a bit brutal."

"Do what you have to do. You got me further than I expected. Figured this was my last mission. Hell of a thing to die in the Yemeni desert."

"We're not doing that tonight."

He got up and walked off a square space apart from where they were sitting. He'd deploy the glow sticks when he guessed the chopper was ten minutes out. They'd glow for an hour.

"We don't have any goggles," Marcus said. "If you want to see, close your eyes when the bird comes in. He'll be powered up for a quick exit."

After a ten-minute wait, Marcus placed the glow sticks at four corners, demarcating a place for the chopper to drop down. He kept his night vision goggles on. They wouldn't offer much protection from the dust but make it easier to see when it landed.

The men pursuing had advanced more quickly than Marcus had hoped. It didn't seem as though they could see the glow sticks, but they were getting uncomfortably close. Now probably a half-mile away. It was hard to judge the distance, in the desert and at night.

Marcus sat still and watched the uncomfortable advance of the search party. He fingered his M4. Fighting against a dozen men didn't cause him fear. He knew he was better at that game than those coming after him. But the chopper could be a casualty of such a battle and he wouldn't get Uri out.

While going over options in his mind, he heard beat of the chopper coming from the south. The men pursuing heard it as well. Flashlights were aimed at the sky to the south. The group started running forward, faster now. Marcus checked his M4 again, locked and loaded. If he had to use it, he knew they were too close and the chopper would be vulnerable.

The sound grew louder. It was coming in fast. Low and fast. A shot was fired from the group chasing, then a couple of more. Then no more. Someone must have given an order to stop wasting ammunition. Instead, the group started forward at a more rapid pace.

Marcus did a quick check on the straps holding Uri, and turned back to the advancing pursuit. Then the helicopter was on them. It came in fast. The pilot pulled the nose up and it jerked to a stop, like a horse reined in from a full gallop. He flattened the helo out and let it drop to the ground, between the glow sticks. It slammed down hard with the door opened and bounced on the ground. *Don't break* it, Marcus thought.

Shots now rang out from the pursuit. Three men jumped out. The LZ was a maelstrom of rotor wash with desert dust and sand flying all around. A machine gunner swung his M60 into the doorway and opened fire. Marcus squinted to keep the grit from blinding him. The men, all with goggles, ran and without a word, grabbed the trace and yanked Uri towards the door. Marcus ran after them, glancing over his shoulder at the advancing authorities.

The machine gunner kept firing, but shots rang out from the pursuers. They were in range now. Marcus started to turn and fire, but the third man grabbed his shoulder and jerked him towards the chopper. He shouted, "Mount up." Marcus ran to the open door and, without hesitation, he dove through the opening and rolled away.

It was a Bell "Huey" Iroquois, a machine in use since Vietnam and now all over the world. The machine gunner at the side of the door was spraying rounds at the pursuit group. He couldn't see much through the swirling sand, but his fire suppressed most of the incoming rounds. Someone yelled "clear!" and the Iroquois lifted off with a lunge pressing Marcus down for a moment. The gunner's knees sagged from the force, but he kept firing. At only fifty feet, the pilot banked the machine and roared off to the southwest, away from the pursuit, looking for speed, not altitude. In a few moments they were out of range of the ground fire and he started climbing and heading more west to clear the airport, before turning to the south.

Once out over the Gulf of Aden, the pilot throttled back, even as he kept climbing. Marcus looked over at Uri. There were two medics attending him, inserting an IV and cutting off his pant leg to get at the wound. He was now in good hands. The man who grabbed Marcus grinned at him as did the gunner.

"Got your ass out just in time," the gunner yelled over the noise

"Got that right." Marcus gave him a thumbs up.

"Special forces?"

"Kind of. Can't say, but I'm grateful to you sons-of-bitches. That's some flying. Your pilot, he's quite a guy."

The grin on the face of the soldier who pulled Marcus grew larger. "Want to meet him?" he yelled.

Marcus nodded and yelled back, "Yeah, if he's not too busy."

The guy started forward. Marcus slipped off his pack and followed. He let Marcus step in front and gave him a head set. Then he grabbed one for himself.

"Captain, our exfil wants to thank you."

The pilot, busy settling the chopper into an efficient, steady climb kept at the task for a minute, then turned the controls over to the co-pilot before turning to Marcus.

"Glad to help out," she said.

Marcus stared at a good-looking woman. For one of the few times in his life, he was at a loss for words.

"I think he expected a guy, Captain."

"They all do."

She smiled at Marcus, then looked back at her instruments.

Finally, Marcus found his voice, even if a little uncertain. "I've been in a lot of hot situations, exfilled by some good chopper pilots. That was an amazing piece of flying."

"Name's Johnson, Captain Robin Johnson."

"Glad to meet you. I'm Marcus Johns, no special rank, just special ops."

"How about that. We might be related with our last names so close."

"Maybe, but I hope not."

"Why is that, Marcus Johns?"

Marcus could only smile.

"Anyway, don't thank me yet. We put extra tanks on the side pods instead of rockets. It'll still be touch and go to get back to Djibouti. Let's hope none of that incoming fire nicked a tank or we'll all be getting wet."

She turned back to her controls and Marcus went back to the belly of the chopper.

"You set me up," Marcus said as they sat down.

"Set yourself up," the man replied. "Got to not assume too much in today's military."

Chapter 58

Once he had found a suitable position, Dan went back to his scope. The sun was getting near the horizon, but he wasn't shooting directly into it. He took aim at one of the machine gunners that had become complacent about keeping his head down. He was reloading a new cannister into the Type 85 which consumed rounds at a rapid rate. When he stood up to start firing, Dan gently stroked his finger on the trigger and the rifle gave its satisfying kick in his shoulder. The man's head erupted as the round entered his jaw area and tore through his face and brain.

Dan quickly chambered another round and turned to one of the other gunners who had now swung their machine guns to his new position. The incoming rounds caused him to flatten against the ground.

Then he heard Roland's M4 start in from farther up the rock slope. He only got off a few rounds before he stopped. The other machine gunner had pinned him down as well. Their divide and split up strategy was not working. The machine guns still in action kept them pinned down and allowed the other men to advance.

The driver of the pickup replaced the machine gunner and started firing. The third truck that lost its gunner in the sand had now made it to the rocks and the driver also stopped to man the Type 85. There were now three machine guns and a fourth shooter with an AK47 arrayed against Dan and Roland. Both the men had been roughly located and as long as the gunners had ammunition cannisters, Dan and Roland were in a difficult position.

"Let's retreat!" Dan yelled. "We can regroup farther up the slope. There's more cover and they higher ground will help."

"Roger that," came the reply.

Dan began to crawl and slid himself over the rocks, keep to the depressions, however slight. If he raised his head or tried to crouch and run, he'd be cut down for sure. Accuracy wasn't so necessary if one could throw enough rounds at him.

It was slow and painful. Occasionally some rounds would come close, chipping off rocks that barely protected him from being seen, sending sharp shards flying through the air. The shooters had a sense of their retreat, but couldn't pin them down. They were also loath to abandon their machine guns and the advantage they gave.

The sun was now at the rim of the hills that defined the edge of the sand sea, miles to the west. It would soon get dark. *Would they continue?* Dan could only hope so. The night gave him and Roland an advantage.

Both men gained a deeper gully behind a bulwark of jagged, sharp rocks.

"You look like hell," Roland said.

Both men were lying in the gully. Dan's sleeve was torn, as was the knee of one of his pant legs. His face and arms were bleeding from cuts caused by the flying rock chips. Dirt clung to his face, moistened by his sweat.

"You don't look so good yourself," Dan said.

From their new position it was going to be much easier to dominate the shooting. As long as the gunners didn't abandon their machine guns, the one solo ground shooter was not going to advance on his own. If they all started pursuit, Dan and Roland could pick them off. They could not sneak up on them with their night vision advantage.

The firing slowed and then stopped. Dan and Roland could hear the voices calling to each other, talking.

"Deciding if they want to come at us?" Roland asked.

"Maybe. Or maybe discussing retreating back to the village now that it's getting dark."

"We let them go?"

"Right now, they only know we're somewhere up higher. We haven't shown ourselves by firing at them. Let's keep it that way."

"If they go back, they'll probably say we've been killed to save face."

Dan thought about that for a moment. "Maybe not. If the commander decides to pull out, they don't want to be left behind. They could say they've run out of ammo. Those machine guns go through a lot of rounds."

"May be right. They weren't stingy with them, that's for sure."

While they were talking the trucks started up and turned back into the sand. They moved fast, as if worried about getting shot from behind.

"You're not shooting?"

Dan shook his head. "Hard to hit them in the cab, going away from me. And I'm getting short on rounds for the Sako."

"We go in then."

"Yep. Wait until full dark."

The three trucks pulled into the village and drove up to the garage area. The commander was waiting for them.

"You kill him?" he asked as the four men got out.

"There are two of them," one of the soldiers said. "We cannot be sure. They retreated from our machine guns. To higher ground. They may be wounded, dying. We ran out of ammunition and could not advance. They would have been able to pick us off from a superior position."

"Could not or would not?" The commander gave the men a dangerous look indicating his displeasure.

The four men didn't answer, but stood still. They knew, even if their commander did not, that to have gone forward would have meant death. The main shooter was fearsome with his ability to kill at a distance. And he had another fighter with him.

"Never mind," the commander said. "Re-stock the pickups with ammunition." He turned on his heel and walked out.

It was dark and the commander didn't order more mortar rounds to be fired. He'd be just wasting them. They were at a standoff. Both groups had limited water, which was the key item. He might have more ammunition, but another attack across the open sand would probably not produce better results. It might be time to go. But he had this burden. The Scorpion.

He headed out into the dark and made his way under cover to the building Scorpion was in. As before, he climbed through the window.

Scorpion was sitting in a chair, an AK47 in his lap. His companion was standing next to him, also armed with the same carbine. They both looked at the commander.

"My men were unsuccessful in killing your pursuer. We discovered that there are two men out there. They may be wounded from this last attack of ours, but we do not know. It was expensive, both in men and materiel. This is a formidable foe you have brought to us."

Scorpion didn't answer but stared at the commander with his black eyes. They gave no hint of his thoughts except to show no glint of remorse or compassion at the commander's tale of woe.

"We cannot out wait these two, now without water."

There was a silence in the room. Still Scorpion didn't say a word. His eyes never left the commander who now was beginning to look uncomfortable.

"We have to leave," the commander finally said. "By dawn at the latest. We can leave this place to your pursuer. There will be nothing here for him except for a few goats and chickens. But without the well, they will all die, as will he and his companion. They will be on foot and have no ability to find help before the desert claims them."

"You run from two men?" Scorpion spoke. "With your squad?"

The commander now starred back at Scorpion with anger. "You ran from one man, who now turned into two. I think we can agree that this is a deadly foe. Let the desert take him."

Scorpion looked at the commander but didn't respond.

"Neither you nor I could take him," the commander said. "Leave him to the desert."

After a long, uncomfortable pause, Scorpion spoke up. "How long will it take to get ready?"

"We must re-fuel the trucks, load the ammunitions and supplies, as well as the livestock and women. We will be heavily loaded, but must bring along as much as we can. I do not want to leave anything of value to this enemy."

"If you wait too long, he will be upon us," Scorpion said.

"You think he will attack?"

"He already has."

Chapter 59

Once it grew dark enough Dan and Roland set out. They could walk upright initially with no fear of their silhouettes showing above the horizon. The rock slope behind them hid their figures. Only later, when closer, would they have to crawl.

"They'll probably still post lookouts," Dan said. "We'll veer off to the right to get out of their direct line of observation. They'll be fixated on the rocks where we were shooting."

"We go in stealth mode."

"Yeah. For as long as we can. Who knows how long they'll stick around? I'm betting they'll want to head out before it gets light."

"You think they're expecting us?"

"Scorpion is. He'll try to convince the leader of this group."

The two walked on, heading to the side of the village. The wind had pushed the sand into low dunes, waves in regular intervals about three to five feet high. As they got closer, they stopped in one of the troughs.

"We should be careful from here to the wall."

Roland nodded. They set out crawling over the top of each dune and sliding down the backside as quickly as they could. Before going over each crest the men scanned the wall, looking for sentries. With their NVGs they could easily spot them.

"Tempting to take them out?" Roland whispered as they got closer.

"It might be, but we're after bigger fish. We don't want to alert them. At least not yet."

When they reached the wall, they sat back against it, unseen by anyone above.

"We go to the right some more. Get around to what is the backside. All the attention will be focused on this side."

"We see a break or opening, let's go in. We can work our way around from there." Roland put his hand on Dan's arm as he was starting to get up. "You got a plan, boss?"

Dan looked over at him. There was no fear on his face. Just a cold, hard look. He knew how this would work. A plan to start would be better than nothing, even though both men understood most plans don't survive first contact.

"We get in, find where the troops are. Take out as many as we can quietly, without alerting others. Then find Scorpion."

"Then kill him."

"Yeah. I'd like to be the one. It's personal. But either of us has the chance, take the shot."

"How do we get out?"

"That's the part I haven't figured out yet."

"It's always like that. Just once, I'd like to have the exit plan worked out."

"You ask a lot."

"I know. Gettin' fussy in my old age."

The two men started towards the back in a low crouch, keeping in the depression of the sand waves. Farther around, there were no sentries as Dan expected. They came to a broken part of the wall and made their way to it.

The break provided hand and footholds for them to climb over. Dan went first, stopping at the top to scan the interior. It was quiet in this back area, but closer to where the action had been. Towards the front of the village there were lights on and people moving around.

"Clear," he whispered and dropped to the ground, putting his M4 to his shoulder, ready to fire.

In a moment, Roland dropped beside him without a sound. It always impressed Dan how such a large man could move so quietly. Both he and Marcus were masters at being stealthy, even if they could not blend in with a crowd, especially in the third world.

"Sentries first?" Roland asked.

Dan nodded. The sentries could be taken down without alerting the others. Their superior position for shooting also meant that they needed to be eliminated before the firefight started. The two men crept forward with their M4 carbines at the ready. They kept close to one of the dark buildings, giving wide berth to the ones where people were busy gathering equipment and loading the trucks. The animal pens, thankfully, were on the other side of the compound. The women were busy rounding up the livestock to load.

"Pulling out as fast as they can," Roland said under his breath.

Dan nodded without speaking.

When they got the first of three sentries in sight, Roland whispered to Dan. "I'll take it from here. He slid his pack off without a sound, laid his M4 on the ground and unsheathed his tactical knife. He crept forward. The raised section where the sentry stood was four feet off the ground. Standing, the sentry could see over the eight-foot wall. The next sentry was about fifty yards farther around the wall. Without an NVG one couldn't see much of the other sentry. When the moon came up later that would not be the case. But for now, Roland had the advantage of darkness.

When he got within twenty feet, Roland crouched and flattened himself against the wall. He was just a bulge in the darkness near the base of the wall. He picked up a small rock and tossed it on the ground of the compound, just beyond and behind the sentry. The man turned to stare down in the darkness, but his gaze didn't wander in Roland's direction. Seeing nothing, he turned back to look out over the desert.

Roland tossed another small rock in the same direction. Again, the sentry looked back for a moment and, not seeing anything, turned back. Roland moved forward without making a sound, closing the distance between him and the sentry to ten feet. He tossed a third rock. This time the sentry looked and stepped down from his platform.

As he bent low to see what was causing the sound, Roland closed the ten feet in two large, silent strides. He put his large left hand over the man's mouth and slashed his throat with his knife. There was a quiet, gurgling sound as the man inhaled his own blood from his throat. The carotid artery was sliced open and additional blood spurted out from his neck. Roland caught his rifle with his knife hand, keeping his left over the man's mouth. The man struggled but was no match for Roland's strength. After only a few moments, his struggles faded and Roland let him slowly sink to the ground.

He wiped his blade on the man's jacket and started for the next sentry. Dan watched through his goggles as Roland dealt death to the next sentry. Roland started for the third man. As he moved along the base of the wall, the sentry turned his way and called out to his fellow lookout. No one answered. Roland froze against the wall. After calling again, louder and getting no answer, the sentry shouldered his rifle and started forward. Roland didn't move. He was just a lump in the shadow of the wall.

When the man reached him, Roland rose and yanked him down from the wall. The AK fell from his hands and clattered to the ground as the man yelled out in surprise and fright. Roland clamped his hand over the man's mouth and quickly dispatched him with a stab to the base of his skull.

A call came from the closest building; someone calling out to the sentries and getting no answer. Dan moved to the wreck of the well pump and crouched. He took out his own knife and waited. Soon a soldier came walking towards the wall, calling to the men. As he passed the well, Dan leapt upon him and thrust his knife into his neck, cutting his carotid artery. The man cried out before he was stifled by Dan's hand on his mouth as the two fell to the ground. He struggled against Dan's grip but soon his efforts faded as death took him.

Roland came up and the two dragged the dead body behind the pump and ran to the wall of one of the buildings. Another man called out. Roland looked at Dan and indicated he'd go forward to the building's corner. Both men understood that the more fighters that could be taken down before an open gun fight erupted, the better it was for them.

The second man came out into the courtyard, apparently calling out his comrade's name. As he walked past the corner, Roland was on him in two quick steps. The man turned with a startled cry. In the next instance, before the man could raise his rifle, Roland crashed into him with both men going to the ground. Roland covered his mouth with one hand and thrust his knife into the man's neck with the other. There were muffled cries as he struggled but his fate was sealed and he quickly sank into death as he bled out, while choking on his own blood.

Roland retreated to the wall. "How many you think are left?"

"Didn't keep count. Probably less than ten."

Roland nodded. "Good odds for us."

Suddenly the voices from the building stopped. The men inside must have sensed something wrong.

"Time to go in?"

Dan nodded. You take the door that last man came out of. I'll take the window around the corner. We'll have them in a crossfire. Wait for my shot."

Chapter 60

Roland nodded and moved out. Dan turned and crept around to the back window. Inside the room, which was the garage, the men were loading the trucks and checking to make sure they were filled with gas. Radiators were topped up, tire pressures checked, spare gas cans filled and stacked in the truck beds. The women were standing in one corner with blankets, mattresses, food, and the chickens, all in cages. Just outside, they had some goats hobbled and bunched together nearly panicked by the unusual activity. They would not go willingly into the pickups.

Dan surveyed the scene. The men now stopped their loading and were grabbing their rifles. Two of their men had gone out to check on the sentries and hadn't returned. Their calls to them got no response. Something was up. As the men turned to go out the back door to investigate, Dan opened fire with his M4. Immediately two went down. Then Roland started firing from another angle. The men dove for cover and started shooting. The garage burst into a cacophony of gunfire as they sprayed rounds at the walls, windows, and the door on full auto.

A pickup started and, before Dan or Roland could disable it, lurched forward, and drove through the garage door and into the night. Roland and Dan continued to pick away at the fighters inside the garage until there was no return fire. Dan saw Roland slip through the door and crouch down, looking for combatants still alive. With him covering, Dan jumped through the window and rolled on the ground, coming up with his M4 to his shoulder, looking for any movement.

The two men circled the room, careful to not get into the other's line of fire. There were two of the eight men in the room wounded. One would not make it; the other might with some medical help.

"Dispatch them?" Roland asked.

Dan shook his head.

"Going to let him die a slow death." Roland turned away from the wounded man who was pleading for help with his eyes.

From the front of the garage, behind some bales of hay came a voice. "I surrender."

Both Dan and Roland dropped to one knee and pointed their carbines in the direction of the voice.

"Throw out your weapon," Dan shouted.

An AK47 came flying through the air to clatter on the stone floor.

"Hands up. Raise your hands."

Two hands appeared from behind the bales.

"Now stand up. Slow."

The commander stood up; half his body still shielded by the hay bales.

Dan stood up and motioned for him to come forward. Roland stayed on one knee, his M4 aimed squarely at the man's chest. When the man was twenty paces away, Dan motioned him to his knees and then gestured for him to turn around. While Roland kept guard, Dan removed a belt from one of the dead fighters and took it over to the kneeling man. He pulled his arms around his back and tied his wrists together. Once done, Roland lowered his rifle. Dan squatted in front of the man.

"You speak English."

The man nodded.

"You're the leader of this group?"

The man looked around at his dead warriors, then turned back to Dan with sad eyes and nodded. "No more it seems."

"We're looking for a man called Scorpion. Is he here?" Dan waved his hand around the room.

The commander followed his hand, looking around the garage. The women had fled outside and were now trying to round up the animals which had fled when the shooting started. Two of them peeked through the broken door. Roland noted them, but they didn't seem to pose a threat.

"He is not here. He left with the pickup along with his eunuch, Faquir."

Dan grunted in frustration, not wanting to verbally vent his anger. "Do you know where he went?"

"No. He has his own resources. Sadly, this ancient village was one of them. He brought you here and you brought death." The commander paused and then looked Dan in the eyes. "There are only two of you?"

Dan nodded.

"Two of you did all this." The commander shook his head. Looking back at Dan, "What will you do with me? Are you also going to kill me?"

Dan gazed back at him. "You are aligned with the government or with the Houthi rebels?"

"With the government."

"And al Qaeda?"

"Only when we have to. This territory changes control. I try to take a middle path."

"You have tribal connections to support you?"

The commander nodded.

"Does Scorpion have tribal connections?"

Again, the commander nodded.

Dan stood up and stretched his body out. "You help us. We'll spare you. Scorpion is our target. You, unfortunately, got in the way."

"I am sorry he came."

"I bet you are."

Dan walked over to Roland who was keeping watch on the door, making sure no women would try some martyr move and shoot at them.

"See what truck is still serviceable. We need to go after Scorpion. He was in that truck."

"That's a pretty good head start."

"Yeah, I know. He keeps a step ahead."

"But we're whittling his defenses down."

"Not soon enough, I fear."

Dan turned and walked back to the commander. He took a cigarette out of the man's pocket, lit it, and offered it to him. The commander gratefully started puffing on it. After a few puffs, Dan took it out and laid it on the ground.

"Where would Scorpion go? I need to know. If you send me in the wrong direction, if I don't find tire tracks when the sun comes up, I will come back and kill you and the women."

"I will not lie to you. Don't kill the women."

"Scorpion killed women. Someone close to me. In a terrible way. He is not a warrior for Allah. He is of the devil, so I don't have any sympathy for anyone who helps him." Dan stabbed his finger in the man's chest. "That means you, and the women."

The commander sighed. "He is Hadramawt. They are to the east. He will head there. There he will find support, protection, and help for his wounds. His left shoulder is damaged. My medic fixed it as much as he could, but he needs more medical attention."

"How far?"

"A full day's drive. Twenty-four hours."

Just then Roland came back. "One of the trucks is not too damaged, but we have to swap out a tire."

"I'll get on it." Dan stood up. "You round up two AKs and as much ammo as you can. We're going to have to swap weapons, I'm almost out."

"Me too, boss. I'd like to take some cannisters for the machine gun. It might be fun to use on Scorpion's truck."

Dan nodded and Roland went to work.

Chapter 61

Scorpion sensed something was wrong. He watched the preparations for departure, which seemed to him to be going too slow and casual. His instincts told him they had no time to lose before this assassin would be in their midst. He'd told the commander that in no uncertain terms.

"This man has killed many of your fighters. Your attack with half your trucks didn't work. He's not going to sit out in the desert and let you depart, along with me. We must leave immediately."

The commander glared back at Scorpion. He was the reason his fighters had been killed, with only a small number left to flee. He'd be damned if he was going to leave behind precious supplies.

"I'm not going to panic and run away like a scared dog," he said. The implication of his response was clear to Scorpion, as he meant it to be.

"I will take our supplies with us. When we're gone, I must rebuild my force, since they have died protecting you. You would do well to remember what I have sacrificed to protect you. You are alive today because I gave you help."

He turned and left the room to go to the garage and oversee the departure efforts.

"He is coming. I sense him," Scorpion said to Faquir. "He is very near and with a companion to help. The commander still doesn't realize what this man can do."

Scorpion had developed a new attitude towards this assassin who had taken out his personal defenders, forced him to flee his compound, wounded him, and now had taken out most of the commander's forces. He was not to be stopped.

"We must prepare to depart. Alone, if necessary," Scorpion told Faquir. "Go pick out a truck and put our gear in it. If the commander asks, tell him we want to be ready to leave when he goes. We don't want to hold him up. Act respectful."

Faquir bowed and left the building with their packs. Scorpion struggled to strap a sidearm to his pants. Then he picked up his AK47, stuffed extra magazines in his jacket and walked out after Faquir. It was a slow and painful walk. He forced himself to not think about the pain. Death was too close.

The hair on the back of his neck bristled as he made his way to the garage. The assassin was close, maybe inside the compound. He repressed the urge to run forward. If the man had already seen him, he'd be dead by now. He and Faquir just needed to be ready to flee. There was no doubt in Scorpion's mind that the assassin would strike. And he would be lethal.

When he got to the garage, he saw that Faquir had claimed a pickup farthest in the corner. It faced a roll door. The eunuch was making sure it was full of gas and putting some extra twenty-liter cans in the back. This pickup did not have a machine gun, so the commander didn't object to Faquir's claiming it. Scorpion didn't need a machine gun. He needed a fast truck to flee and get away before the carnage started. Faquir had loaded some food and water and stood ready.

"We are ready?"

Faquir nodded. "You expect him soon, *majistir*?"

"He is close, inside. I can sense his presence. It won't be long."

"Should I tell the commander? Perhaps he should send out some men to find him?"

Scorpion shook his head. "He doesn't believe me. He will carry on to show his bravery and pride. It will kill him."

Scorpion struggled into the passenger seat. Faquir stepped up into the driver's seat.

"We go now?" he asked.

Scorpion shook his head. "We would be targeted. We wait until this assassin strikes. He has to take out the commander's men before he deals with me. Once he attacks, we leave. He will be too busy to stop us and it will give us a head start."

"We go back east? To your people?"

Scorpion nodded. "With the truck, we can reach the village and hide there to regroup. This is the beginning. There will be more rounds in our battle against each other. I may not claim victory, but he will have failed as well. And I have killed one close to him." A grim smile traced across Scorpion's face, replacing the pained look. "And I will strike the other woman. I will kill everyone close to him."

Faquir was about to add a comment, when Scorpion put up his hand.

"Shhh. Did you hear that?"

Faquir gave his master a questioning look and shook his head.

"In between the noise in here, I heard the sound of a man dying. He's begun. Put the keys in the ignition. We must be ready."

A few minutes later shots rang out behind them, from a window. A second round of shots came from one of the doors on the other side.

"Go!" Scorpion shouted. The room erupted into a cacophony of shooting as the soldiers recovered from their shock and grabbed their weapons. They returned fire, using full auto to sweep both sides of the room trying to hit shooters they didn't see.

Scorpion's truck lurched forward and smashed through the garage door. It spun to the right, scattering livestock and women as it headed out the back of the village, into the desert. The truck turned east, following the tracks of the previous trucks used in the failed assault on the assassin's position.

"Drive as fast as you can," Scorpion said. "We must make use of this head start."

"He will come?" Faquir asked as he fought the wheel to keep the truck going half-way straight.

"He will come after killing all the commander's men. If we are blessed, he will not have a truck that can run after the shooting." He paused and gasped as he was flung into the air when the truck careened over a sand ridge. He took hold of the grab bar with his right hand to stabilize himself. "But he is a resourceful foe."

The sound of the shooting faded as they bounced through the sand. Once in the wadi, the going would be easier. Scorpion grimaced and held on tight.

Chapter 62

The Huey leveled out at two thousand feet and throttled back as much as possible while still maintaining altitude and air speed. After some hours, they could see the lights of the harbor and town. The chopper began to sputter. Captain Johnson got on the radio and alerted the base they would have to land without delay. A plane readying for takeoff was told to wait and the control tower brought the chopper in as the engine began to misfire and stumble.

They smacked down hard on the tarmac and the engine was shut down.

"Sorry about the hard landing," Captain Johnson said as she got out of the seat. "We didn't have any fuel left to make it nice and pretty."

"I'm happy you could nurse this bird here and get us on the ground in one piece," Marcus said.

"We aim to please. Especially when someone so important is aboard."

"Me? I'm not important." He jerked his thumb over his shoulder towards Uri who was being gently unloaded from the helo and heading to the waiting ambulance. "But maybe he is."

"Just the same, glad to help," Captain Johnson said with a smile.

"So, what happens next?" Marcus asked.

Johnson shrugged her shoulders. "I go back to the barracks for some rest. I don't have any idea where you go."

Marcus stood up and climbed out of the Huey with her.

"I think I'm going to Israel with my partner there. Once he's able to be moved." He paused to think. "That might be awhile. Would you show me the canteen? I'll buy you something to eat and drink. To celebrate our safe delivery."

Captain Johnson looked over at Marcus and smiled. He could tell she was sizing him up, now able to give him her full attention. Marcus gave her his best, innocent smile.

"You trying to go on a date with me? Just after we got you out of what was soon going to be a killing zone?"

"Nothing like an encounter with death to whet one's appetite." His smile broadened. "And to increase one's appreciation of skill and beauty." He nodded to her with that last comment.

Johnson laughed and thrust her hand into Marcus' arm and led him off towards a side building.

"I have to file a report, but there's not going to be a record of you, or your partner. The report will say we flew over to evac a tourist for a medical issue. I think it will be buried in a ton of daily reports. It can wait."

She turned towards a building back from the tarmac. "We can go here. They have good beer and burgers. The people calling the shots may come looking for you, but you won't be hard to find. There's really no place else to go."

"You have made my day, my night, my week," Marcus said as the two walked up to the canteen. He'd get some crap from Jane, but didn't care. Robin Johnson was the reward for hauling Uri's ass around in the desert for so long.

† † †

Dan untied the commander as Roland went off to gather ammunition. Dan shouldered his rifle and took out his sidearm.

"You're going to change the tire. If you try anything, I'll shoot you. No warning."

The commander bent to his task.

"What are you going to do with me? With the women?"

"That depends on how helpful you are. I need to know where Scorpion has gone."

"Will you leave us with water? We have none since you shot up our pump."

"If you're clever you can fix the pump. That is what I would do. We'll leave you some, but get the well pump repaired and then you are safe and can leave when you want. I have no interest in the women or your alliances. I'm only after Scorpion. You should not feel a duty to hide him from me. He is why I took out all your men. He brought this on. Then he ran out on you."

The commander didn't answer. When he finished changing the tire, he stood up. Roland had loaded some cannisters for the machine gun along with the water supplies. He flung their packs into the bed and strapped them down.

"Ready to go, boss."

Dan looked at the commander. "Which way?"

He looked back at Dan. "He will go east towards the wadi from where he came. He has tribal connections with the Hadramawt and will go there to hide and recover. If you want him, you must catch up before he gets to Saww or A'Kudud. These are villages friendly to him. They will hide him, move him to keep him away from capture.

Dan thought about what the commander said. The man could tell him anything to get him to leave. What leverage did he have?

"We will go east. There are many truck tracks going east from your assault. We will find the one not stopping at the rocks, but continuing into the wadi. That will be Scorpion. If we do not find those tracks, we will come back and kill you. If you leave, we can track you and catch you. You will feel my anger if you have led me astray."

"You have defeated me. Yet let me live. I do not mislead you. I have no love for Scorpion, even though he is allied to my people. He has done nothing for them. He is always about his benefactor, a rich Saudi who sends him abroad to kill. He doesn't kill our enemies here. We are left to deal with them. The Saudis offer some help, but that is only from the sky. The bombs rain down, but that doesn't stop the Houthis. We must fight them on our own."

"A rich Saudi. Do you know who it is?"

The commander shook his head. "He never has spoken more than I just said. No one but him knows."

"Boss. Let's get. We have a lot of catching up to do," Roland said from the passenger door.

Dan looked at the commander. It would be easy to kill him and not have to worry about him, but the man had lost all his men and looked only like he wanted to survive this last encounter. His command had been shattered along with his reputation.

He turned and stepped into the cab. The truck roared to life and he drove out of the garage with Roland keeping an eye on the commander.

"He's going to have a lot of explaining to do to someone about his whole team getting wiped out," Roland said.

"He'll probably make up a story about a pitched battle with some Houthis with him as the sole survivor, and hero."

They drove out of the back gate and slowed. The many tire tracks swung to the east. They turned to follow. Dan pressed hard. When they got to the rocks, he slowed. They had to cast about to find a separate set of tracks, not aiming for the rocky outcropping, but heading into the mouth of the wadi.

"Looks like the trail," Roland declared.

Dan accelerated forward. The ground flattened out as they left the sand sea. While the floor of the wadi was not flat, it didn't have the wavelike undulations of the sand, so they could move faster.

"Look!" Roland called out. "Way up ahead."

Dan scanned the dark horizon. He saw nothing. Then there it was. The blink of two red lights.

"He's driving without lights, but when he brakes, the lights go on," Roland said. "That's our quarry."

Dan didn't worry about his headlights. He used them to press on, hopefully faster than Scorpion could go.

Chapter 63

Scorpion could see the headlights in the distance. They were miles behind but could easily be seen in the dry desert air as bright spots, bobbing up and down. It didn't matter. The assassin was on his tail. He would not make it to safety before the pursuing truck with its two men caught up with them.

"Turn on the headlights. We are being followed. Somehow, they know the path we're on. We need to go as fast as possible."

Faquir nodded. The beams illuminated the floor of the wadi and allowed him to increase his speed.

"If I go too fast, it might damage your shoulder."

"Do not mind my shoulder. We need to stay ahead of those behind us. If we can get as far as Saww, we will get help to fight them off. They cannot defeat a whole village."

Faquir nodded and pressed the accelerator more, sending the truck bouncing through the soft spots in the trackless floor of the wadi.

"Watch for the rocks. They will break the truck," Scorpion said to warn Faquir.

He alternated between watching Faquir steer the truck over the trackless desert and watching the headlights behind them. *Were they getting closer?* Scorpion could not tell. He understood that a point might be reached where he had to turn off and stop at rocks along the sides of the wadi to set up a defensive position. He and Faquir had weapons; AK 47s as well as a Dragunov SVD sniper rifle. It fired a 7.62 cartridge from a five-round magazine and was good out to 800 meters. Scorpion was a very accurate shooter, although most of his killing had been done up close, unlike the assassin who was pursuing him. Still, he felt ever-hopeful if he had to make a last stand along the wall of the wadi. The assassin would have no way to flank him, and he had similar weapons. Unlike the other encounters, Scorpion felt he could be successful when all others had proven to be disastrous.

Hours later, Faquir was struggling at the wheel of the pickup. The night wore on, with dawn not yet in sight to the east. His observations finally convinced Scorpion that the pursuing pickup was gaining; slowly, but steadily. The village of Saww could not be reached until the next afternoon and the truck would be on him before then.

"We must head south to the wall of the wadi and find a place among the rocks. From there we will defend ourselves and take out this assassin once and for all."

Faquir looked at his master with concern in his face. "We cannot make Saww?"

"No, he is closing. Concentrate on the driving, I will look for a place to turn to."

Faquir turned back to the road ahead. Scorpion turned his gaze to the slopes of the wadi's south ridge. The sky was still dark, but the moon, now beginning to set in the west, still lit enough of the south slope of the wadi that he could see the rocks and cliffs.

And there it was, a rocky outcropping a hundred feet up on the slope from the base of the wadi. They could drive the truck up to it, hopefully park it behind some rocks and climb up to the outcrop. It looked from the distance to be a rock fortress capable of hiding them while giving them protected positions from which to fire down at his pursuers.

"Turn off your headlights and slow down. Don't use the brakes, Scorpion said. "Do you see the rocks jutting out from the slope near the floor of the wadi?"

Faquir nodded.

"We go there. You must not put the brakes on. They light up the rear and will guide our pursuers. Drive as fast as you can. We need to park the truck near the rocks. Hide it if possible, and then climb into them. We will set up our shooting positions from there."

Faquir turned the truck to the south. There was no change in the ride, as there was no road in the wadi. But the closer, they came to the slope, the rougher the ground became. It heaved up and down more and Faquir had to go more slowly, even though that frustrated Scorpion. They needed to be hidden in the rocks before the pursuit reached them. There was just a chance that they would go past and not realize it until it got lighter.

Now the ground rose, gently at first, but growing steeper as they approached the jutting rocks. Faquir did his best. The truck lurched right and left as he sought to find a path forward. The wheels alternately spun and grabbed traction. Finally, as he lost momentum, he turned the truck towards the rocks and it ground to a stop, the wheels spinning in the loose sand.

"It can do no more, *majistir*," he said.

Scorpion heard the apology in his voice. "It is fine." He grabbed his door. "We must get into the rocks. "Bring the extra weapons and ammunition. I will climb by myself."

Scorpion had a Kalashnikov slung over his good shoulder and the Dragunov in his right hand. He picked his way up through the rocks until he got to the top of the outcrop. As he had hoped, there was space to nestle in. It provided protection against incoming rounds and offered niches that they could shoot out of. Scorpion could place the Dragunov in one of the niches, place the stock against his right shoulder, and shoot with his good right hand. It would suffice.

A few minutes later, Faquir came in out of breath. He had a backpack with water bottles and ammunition, an AK47, and a grenade launcher. He set the items down and disappeared back down the hill. When he returned, he had a pack and an armful of ammunition.

Scorpion looked at the grenade launcher. It was a Russian GP-25, first used in the late seventies and designed to mount under an AK47. His black eyes seemed to light up in anticipation. The weapon could be aimed out to 400 meters. It would give them an advantage and his enemy a surprise.

"You did good to bring this." Scorpion pointed to the launcher.

Faquir nodded. Without a word, he began to attach the launcher to one of the AK47s they had brought with them.

In the quiet of the desert, they could hear the oncoming pickup. The sky was also getting brighter as the day approached. Scorpion looked down at the wadi floor. He didn't hold out much hope of fooling the assassin. The final act would be here, among the rocks.

When Faquir finished his task, the two men watched the approaching truck. It could be now seen as a shadowy object moving across the floor of the desert, leaving a plume of dust behind it.

"Soon. Soon we will have our revenge," Scorpion said under his breath, more to himself than Faquir.

Chapter 64

Dan could see they were closing on the pickup. They had turned on their headlights, indicating to him that they knew they were being followed and there was no need for stealth. It was a race now. Would Scorpion get to a friendly village? Or would they catch him out in the desert? Roland, he knew, would love to have a go at the truck with the W85 machine gun in the back.

With their goggles, they could still see the truck. Dan could tell they were closing. They bounced onward, always close to disaster, but the pace meant they might catch the truck before it reached any help.

"Don't tip us over, boss," Roland said as he held to the grab bar. The man was so large that bounces caused him to slam his head against the roof of the cab. "Almost feel like I'd to better hanging on in the back."

"Sorry. Can't stop and I don't want to lose you over the side trying to climb back there while we're moving."

"You take all the fun out of this. I might break my neck in here."

"Slouch down and duck your head. We can't stop. We're closing."

"Just let me get to that W85 before we do. I can do a lot of damage with it."

"I'll try to make that happen."

Dan eyes alternated between the desert floor just in front of them with quick glances at the truck ahead. The sky was beginning to lighten, signaling the coming day.

"Where the hell did he go?" Dan asked. He had just looked up after some time looking at the ground in front of them as they went through a place with multiple rocks that could disable the truck.

Roland looked ahead. He had been watching the road, like Dan, worried about crashing the pickup and letting their quarry get away.

"The truck?" Roland asked.

"Yeah. I don't see it."

Dan turned back to the ground in front of the truck. He could afford only short glances ahead.

"You drive, I'll look for them," Roland said.

After a minute of searching, Roland shouted. "They've turned off to the right. I can see a plume of dust. Hard to see the truck. The ground gets lumpier close to the side of the valley."

"They know we're catching them. He's turning off to make a stand."

"Last stand for him."

"Don't get cocky. He may have a surprise up his sleeve."

"We going to follow?"

"Not exactly," Dan said. "We'll get close, but I think it's better if we stop while we have some ability to maneuver."

"But no plan."

"What is it with you and plans? How the hell do I get a plan for all of this?"

"Just pulling your chain, boss. You sniper guys are a sensitive bunch."

"Fuck you and the donkey you rode up on."

The Scorpion

Roland let out a laugh. Dan could tell he was energized by the upcoming fight. Finally cornering their foe. No quarter asked or given from either side. Killing Scorpion would not bring back Carrie. It would not even adequately avenge the horror of what she endured before she died. But it would have to suffice. And it would strike a blow to the Saudi's plans. *Bring it on.* Dan leaned forward over the steering wheel.

"Let me know when we're getting close to where he turned. See if you can spot where he's placed himself. He can't get up the slope with the truck and I doubt he's going on foot. He's injured and if he's hoofing it, we'd just catch him sooner."

Scorpion and Faquir watched. Scorpion with the Dragunov and Faquir with the AK and launcher.

"Can you reach the floor of the wadi where they'll come up?"

"Maybe. The weapon can be aimed out to 400 meters. It may shoot farther, but only by improvisation. I have set the sights for maximum distance."

"We will wait to surprise them. Between your weapon and mine, we have the advantage."

"Also, our position, *majistir*. It was well chosen."

"See that pile of rocks near the valley floor?"

Dan slowed and looked over. "Yeah."

"He's up in there somewhere. Must have parked the truck to the far side. I don't see it, but that's where it was headed. I'm betting he's climbed up there. It's a good position to defend."

"Definitely puts us at a disadvantage."

"Seems to be our lot in life on this mission."

Dan didn't answer but now slowed down, scanning the ground to the right, looking for a more protected way to approach the outcropping.

"We're going to be exposed as we move towards the rocks. I'll try to keep the truck in ravines as much as possible, but they're pretty shallow."

"Every little bit helps. Now that we're going slower, I'm getting in the back."

Without waiting for Dan to respond, Roland opened the door, and, with his AK slung over his shoulder, he stepped onto the running board and swung himself around, into the bed of the truck.

"I'm manning the W85," he called out. "If I see them, I'll send a round their way. Keep their heads down."

Dan lowered his window to better hear what Roland was saying. He turned the truck to the south and ran it up a shallow depression. He could see it narrowing ahead. *Got to climb out at the right moment so I don't get stuck.* He wanted to spend as little time as necessary fully exposed. Now, going slower he could hear Roland getting the W85 charged and ready to fire.

"Keeping an eye on the rocks, boss."

"You see anything, fire a short round. I'll head for the nearest cover."

"Ain't much of that until we get closer to the slope."

Dan didn't answer. He was busy sawing the wheel, steering the truck over and around the rougher ground while trying to use the ravines to give them some cover.

"You see them coming?" Scorpion asked.

"Yes, *majistir*. They are not yet in range."

"As soon as they are, don't wait. Try to cripple the truck so it can't go forward. It will stop them while they're most exposed."

"*Na'am, sayidi,*" Yes, master.

Scorpion adjusted his position to better brace his damaged left shoulder. His Dragunov rested steady on the rock cleft. He had his right hand on the pistol grip, pulling the rifle back into his right shoulder. It was not ideal, but would do. He could shoot at a greater distance than the AK47s he expected his pursuers were carrying. The only weapon that worried him was the Chinese W85. It could send its large caliber 12.7 by 108mm round farther than the grenade launcher and the rate of fire was overwhelming. If they weren't hit, they would be pinned down.

"*Soon, majistir,*" Faquir said while scanning through his sight.

Chapter 65

Dan kept the truck moving. They would get stuck soon. The gradient was getting steeper. He began to search for a route forward on foot. They needed to gain some height and then find a way to work towards the rocky area while staying under cover. If Scorpion left in his pickup, they'd have to get theirs back down to the floor to continue the chase.

Just then there was a flash from the rocks.

"Grenade launcher!" Roland shouted. The sound and flash were different from a bullet being fired.

Dan stopped and both men jumped out of the truck and dove for any cover they could find. Roland scrambled away using the truck and flattened himself to the ground next to a rock barely a foot high. Dan ran to his left, towards the rocks and dove into a shallow depression that he had been aiming for with the truck. It took only moment until the grenade slammed into the ground behind the truck and exploded. It had a blast radius of about twenty feet.

Roland jumped back into the bed and grabbed the W85. He swung the barrel up toward the rocks and let loose a burst. Both men could see the rocks exploding in shatters near where he saw the flash. He paused. A hollow sound came from the rocks indicating another grenade on its way. The shooter did not take aim this time, not wanting to expose himself to the machine gun. Roland fired another burst into the rocks and dove off the truck, this time staying close to it. The round exploded short of the truck.

"You okay, boss?" Roland shouted.

"Yeah. Ears are ringing." He took the Sako out of its case and slammed a five-round magazine in it. "Got my Sako. I'll try to take out the shooter next time he appears."

"We got to get the truck into the ravine," Roland yelled.

Just then Dan saw the AK barrel with the launcher under it poke out from behind the rocks. He settled his sights on it, took a guess, and fired. There was no time for working out the range and doing the math. This was a firefight, and he had a rifle that could shoot the distance with accuracy. He needed to adjust on the fly. The first shot was low and to the right. He worked the bolt in a rapid movement and loosed another round. This one, close to the opening. Dan's right hand flew through the motion to expel the spent round and insert a fresh one in the chamber.

As he was shooting, Roland jumped back into the bed and loosed another burst of rounds from the W85. He kept them short, knowing how fast the gun went through ammo. The rocks shattered from the impact. The rifle retreated from view.

Roland paused and the AK barrel appeared as Dan closed the bolt on his Sako. There was a flash from the rocks and the barrel disappeared as Dan's shot hit the opening.

"Incoming!" Dan shouted.

Roland jumped off the truck and flattened himself partially under the engine of the truck. He had no idea where the round would land, but the engine at least provided vertical cover. The round hit behind the truck, but closer. Roland could hear the shrapnel whistling past. He felt the searing pain as a piece skimmed across the back of his legs. The screech of pierced and shredded metal indicated that the truck had absorbed much of the explosion. After the round exploded, he slithered back out from the truck and ran to the depression Dan was in.

"Too hot at the truck," he said as he rolled down and out of sight. Better chance of survival down here."

"Not much, but a little."

"I'll take all the help I can get."

"You're wounded." Dan looked over at Roland's pants, growing wet with his blood.

"As Monty Python would say, 'it's only a flesh wound'."

Dan smiled and turned back to the rocks. I know where he's shooting from now. I'll try to catch him when he takes his next shot."

"I'd like to help with the W85, but I'm not sure I can do much but burn up ammo."

"If I can pin him down, maybe you can get it into the ravine. It's not much, but then you'd be more protected, especially when you jump off. Now, you're just out there like the truck, exposed to all the shrapnel."

Just as Dan finished, another grenade round came out of the sky, hitting the front of the truck. The two men flattened themselves in the sand as shrapnel flew over their heads. When they raised their heads, they could see the engine hood and part of the front fender blown off, the windshield shredded, and an unknown amount of damage to the interior of the cab.

"Damn!" Roland exclaimed. "We're fucked. That ain't gonna run now and they can just drive off and leave us."

"Can't let that happen."

"Fuck."

Dan didn't answer. He was already crawling down the ravine to get a better angle to the far side of the rocks. Roland followed. Dan crawled for about fifty yards and then started running in a crouch. A shot was fired from the rocks above. The round smacked the dirt short and behind Dan. He kept going. Another shot followed. This one hit ahead, just on the far side of the ravine. Dan hit the ground but kept crawling. The third shot flew just over his body. Had he been standing; it would have hit him.

Then another grenade was fired. Both men flattened themselves in the depression. It had deepened to about three feet. Only a direct hit could impact them if they kept low. The grenade hit in front of the depression and the shrapnel flew over them with a whistling sound that meant tearing flesh or death if they were in its path.

Dan didn't stop. He kept crawling forward. When he reached a point where there were a few rocks littered on the rim of the depression, he stopped and slipped his Sako out through a narrow gap. He got his sights on the target in quick order and waited. The distance had changed by a hundred yards, so he made a mental adjustment on where to place his reticle.

Roland caught up to him. His larger frame was not to his advantage in trying to stay low and out of sight. He had learned over the years, as an act of self-preservation, to go at a pace that kept him low, even if it was slower than others.

"Keep going down-slope," Dan said without taking his eye from the sight. "If you can, move to the east to get closer to their exit path if they take off. I'll cover from here."

"Copy that."

Roland crawled farther downhill and then scanned to the east to see where he could advance.

"On my way," he said as he leapt over the edge of the depression and ran forward in a crouch.

Dan fired at the gap in the rocks, working the Sako's bolt action to keep sending rounds on target. A shot rang out from the rocks in Roland's direction, but it was not close. Roland reached his objective and dove for cover as a second round hit closer.

"All good here," Roland called out.

"Whoever is working the rifle, he's not very fast." Dan shouted in Roland's direction. They had no comms so shouting was the only way to coordinate. At least they now presented two separate targets which made things more difficult for the enemy.

"Probably Scorpion," Roland yelled back. "He's got an injured shoulder or arm, so he's firing one-handed."

"Better for us."

"Except for that other guy with the launcher."

There was no sound from the rocks. Dan thought about advancing but his current location provided adequate cover and a good sightline to the gaps in the rocks above. He felt sure he could suppress their fire and maybe take one of them out if they lingered too long aiming down at him.

Then both men heard an engine starting up. Dan ran forward towards Roland's position. He dropped in close to him. He took out a fresh mag and inserted it into the Sako and settled the rifle on the rim of the depression.

"Got to stop the truck. When it comes out from behind the rocks. They'll try to go downslope in a ravine."

"Let's hope there isn't a nice deep one to hide them."

"We've disabled their truck," Faquir said.

Scorpion could see the damage to the front of the truck. The engine most likely would not start. He caught a glimpse of the two men heading down the ravine. They knew their truck was useless. They were probably trying to get into position to keep him from leaving.

He took aim and fired off a shot at the lead man. It was off target. Scorpion struggled to work the bolt and load another round. When he closed the bolt, he fired again.

"Use the launcher," he said to Faquir. "We have to keep them from cutting us off."

Faquir sent more grenades down towards the men as Scorpion fired more shots.

"I think they're stopped," Scorpion said. "Let's go. We can leave them behind here. They can't pursue on foot."

"Then we are free of them," Faquir said. "You don't want to kill them?"

Scorpion shook his head. "I'm wounded. We must get to Saww and then men can be sent back to find them and kill them."

They picked up their gear and started down from the rocks. Their truck was sheltered from the shooting and had incurred no damage.

"Keep your AK ready in your lap," Scorpion said. His damaged left shoulder would not let him drive. He switched from the Dragunov to his own AK47. If he had to shoot, he could only do so one-handed. Still, it would be better than not shooting. Faquir started the truck and then spent some time maneuvering it back and forth to free it and turn it around. Once pointed down the hill, he started off. The going was still slow. The ground rough with large rocks that threatened the truck. They could break the suspension or high-center the pickup, leaving it stranded.

Dan and Roland watched with their rifles aimed. The truck emerged from the rocks, gaining speed as it left the rougher ground above. Dan sighted it and fired a round.

Roland opened up in full auto spraying rounds ahead of, and then hitting the truck. Dan's shots quickly zeroed in on the pickup and one shattered the driver's window. The truck veered and then recovered just in time to avoid crashing into a large boulder. The driver looked to be turning towards a depression that could hide them from the incoming fire. Roland kept up a stream of fire until his magazine emptied. The bolt flew back and stayed open indicating the weapon was empty.

He ejected the magazine, grabbed a fresh one from his vest, and slammed it in. Dan worked the Sako's bolt and put more rounds through the cab. Roland's next volley went low, taking out the tires on the left side of the truck. Now it slewed to the left, was yanked back to the right, and rolled into the ravine, disappearing from sight.

Dan jumped up. "Let's go!" he shouted and started forward in a run.

Roland was right behind him, ejecting the spent mag from the AK as he ran. The two men raced over the three hundred yards that separated them from where the truck had disappeared.

The shots came as soon as the truck appeared in sight. Faquir went as fast as he could, but near the rocks, the ground was too rough. They heard the automatic fire from an AK47 and the dirt sprayed up in front of them. Single shots hit the bed of the truck. One shattered the driver's window and Faquir lurched to one side, slamming into Scorpion's injured shoulder.

Scorpion grunted with the pain and grabbed the wheel to get the truck back on course. Faquir looked at him and took the wheel with his right hand. He pulled himself upright and stepped on the throttle. Scorpion swung his carbine behind Faquir who was hunched over the steering wheel. He needed to return fire. Just then another round slammed into Faquir and he flopped over into Scorpion's lap. His eyes stared up at him for a moment and then went sightless as death took him.

Scorpion dropped his weapon and reached over to the steering wheel. He yanked the truck back to the right, towards the ravine. It was deep but it was his only hope to get out of the gunfire. Another round of automatic fire came from the attackers. The truck shuddered as both tires on the left were punctured. The truck slewed to the left and Scorpion pulled it hard to the right again.

He drove it off the edge and into the ravine. As it went down, it twisted back to the left and started to go over. It stopped six feet down, digging into the ground on its right side, but not quite falling over.

Scorpion climbed over Faquir and shoved the door up and open. He crawled through the opening, holding it with his right shoulder to keep it from slamming closed on him. Once outside, he let himself drop the three feet to the ground, bringing his carbine with him. They would be coming. He had to be ready. There were no thoughts of surrender. There was no surrender in this deadly game that had played out for the last weeks. No quarter asked, no quarter given.

Chapter 66

Dan and Roland slowed as they approached the ravine. It wouldn't do to get shot by charging in without caution.

"Better split up," Dan said. The two men angled away from each other.

When they got closer, a rifle barrel appeared over the edge of the ravine.

"Down!" shouted Dan as he hit the dirt. A burst of automatic fire flew over his head. It was followed by another, probably aimed at Roland. Dan couldn't see with his face buried in the sand. He clamored to sparse cover behind a rock and swung his AK around the side just as Scorpion was turning his weapon back in Dan's direction.

Dan fired and the rounds slammed into the ground in front of Scorpion, spraying sand all around. He dropped back down over the edge. Roland meanwhile jumped up and ran forward to another rock, closer to the ravine. There was no way Scorpion could hold off both men as they advanced alternately from different directions. When Scorpion's barrel appeared again, Roland loosed a short burst, driving him back out of sight. This time, Dan ran ahead to better cover. Both men were now thirty to fifty yards from the edge of the ravine. Dan decided to move to his right to create more separation. If he could make it to the edge, without a direct, frontal assault, he could get off a kill shot on Scorpion's flank.

The next burst came from Scorpion who raised his AK without showing himself and sprayed the positions that Dan and Roland had last taken. The problem was they weren't there anymore.

Dan crawled forward. At the edge of the ravine, he lay on the ground and slid his body, rifle first over, partly over the edge. He saw Scorpion lying up against the rim. He was breathing hard and working to insert a full magazine with only one hand.

Dan took careful aim and fired. The round hit Scorpion in his damaged left shoulder, spinning him around. Dan's second shot hit his right side and the AK went clattering away. Scorpion tried to reach for it, but it fell away from his grasp.

Dan stood up.

"All clear," he called out.

A moment later Roland appeared at the top of the ravine. His carbine trained on Scorpion who lay panting in the dirt, alternately looking at Dan and then up at Roland. Dan walked forward; his rifle held at ready. But Scorpion seemed to have no more cards to play. His right hand went into his jacket pocket.

"Stop!" Dan shouted.

When Scorpion didn't, Dan raised his rifle and shot his hand inside his pocket. Scorpion cried out as his body twitched. Then Roland was on him. He pulled his shattered hand out of his pocket and then reached in again. When he drew it back out, he had some capsules in his hand. Dan walked up and looked.

"Looks like suicide capsules. He didn't want to give us the satisfaction of killing him."

Roland nodded. "Total defeat." He stepped on Scorpion's broken hand. The man cried out and squirmed on the ground.

Dan put out his arm to let Roland know to stop.

"Search him for anything else he might want to surprise us with."

"Can't do much with two torn up arms and hands."

"You can't be too careful with this man," Dan said.

He squatted down while Roland went through Scorpion's pockets.

"Nothing, boss."

Dan laid his AK down, out of reach of his foe. Roland sat down just above the man and held his rifle pointed at him. Scorpion's black eyes burned with hatred as he stared at his nemesis. Dan took in the look, his face implacable. Now, at the end, he felt no elation, only fatigue. He was tired. He hadn't slept in two days and had fought for his life most of the time he was awake.

He had the man who had pursued him across Europe; the man who had murdered someone close to one who Dan cared for. He had been an effective part of Rashid's terror activities. Now he was sitting in the dust and dirt of the Yemeni desert, defeated with no options, at Dan's mercy.

The man looked dark and evil. Dan's mind tried to picture how Carrie would have seen this image. It was too repulsive and he rejected it. She was staring into pure evil when she died. This was the last thing she saw. Dan's lips thinned with a grimace he knew was spreading on his face.

Scorpion didn't say a word, but kept staring at Dan.

"This is the end...for you." Dan finally said. "You've caused much destruction and destroyed a young life that shouldn't have been destroyed. You should have just come after me and left the civilians alone."

Scorpion stared back at Dan. Dan knew his face gave no hint of mercy. He didn't expect to offer any. Some people just needed to die so the planet could be rid of their evil acts.

"There are no civilians in this battle."

"That's where we differ, among many things."

"How about we skin him alive and leave him for the buzzards to feast on?" Roland spoke up.

Scorpion looked over at the huge man. Roland's face showed the full intent of his words.

"We could do that," Dan said. "Let me think a moment. It's been a long, hard pursuit."

Scorpion now looked back at Dan. He guessed the man was wondering what fate he would decide for him.

"Your Rashid will find out about his loss."

Scorpion could not hide the shock on his face to hear his mentor's name. *They knew!*

"He'll have to work without you," Dan said. "Of course, you know you were only a tool of his. One he would discard when it became too awkward to keep. You were always expendable. Not quite the master assassin you thought you were."

Dan stretched. The fatigue now had him firmly in its grip as his adrenalin wore off.

"I guess I'm doing Rashid a favor."

Scorpion's face reflected a mixture of pain and anger. His eyes shone with their dark energy, even through his agony. His left shoulder was damaged and unmovable. His right shoulder shattered from Dan's round and his right hand now shattered as well. He squirmed on the ground in what looked like an attempt to find a more comfortable position; all to no avail.

"Hurts, doesn't it?" Roland said, more as a statement than a question. "Maybe we should just leave him to die out here? He doesn't look to be able to travel much."

While they talked, Dan never took his eyes off the man. He kept reminding himself of the horror Carrie went through before Scorpion finally killed her.

"You had no mercy on that young girl you killed. She told you all she knew. You could have left her. She didn't know who you were. She would have been no help to any authorities. But you didn't. There seems to be no mercy in you." He stood up. "I'm surprised Rashid would use such a warped tool as you. It must mean he's getting desperate."

Dan kicked some dirt at Scorpion and turned away. Roland watched him walk over to the pickup to check on the driver.

"Whatcha thinking, boss?"

Dan didn't answer. His mind raced with dark thoughts of revenge. Torture such as he saw Carrie had experienced. Part of him wanted Scorpion to feel what she felt; what others he had killed over the years must have felt. Another part of him said that would corrupt him in ways he couldn't now imagine. It would implant some of Scorpion's depravity and evil into himself. In effect, letting the man live on in some way inside of Dan.

The revenge was a white-hot surge of emotion; almost with a sense of cleansing. The cautionary thought was colder, more calculating, calmly trying to withstand the rush of other's heat.

Dan sighed and turned back to his enemy and now his captive.

"He deserves to feel what Carrie felt. He deserves to experience what he's inflicted on others throughout his twisted life."

"Got that right."

"But to administer that, brings us down to his level. It taints us with his stain, maybe forever."

"Don't worry about that. I'll be happy to administer the punishment."

Dan shook his head. "No. If I went that way, I could not leave it to others. That would be a burden only I could rightfully take on."

"You saw the girl, I didn't. But from what you told me, I'm ready to deliver what's due him."

Again, Dan shook his head. "If I could have killed him with a long-range shot, quick and almost painless, I would have done that. God knows I tried. He'd have died with even less pain than now."

"But that didn't happen and now we have the opportunity to give him some of his own medicine."

"That's just it. It's his 'medicine' as you say. His evil. Not ours."

Dan stepped closer to Scorpion who watched him carefully with his black eyes. Dan's anger rose. He had made a decision and now directed his anger to a purpose.

"Stand him up," he said.

Roland seemed to be caught off guard by the anger and command in Dan's voice. He walked to Scorpion and yanked him to his feet. The man cried out even as he seemed to try to suppress any sound.

He stood before Dan. His body was shaking and unsteady. He was held by Roland's meaty hand on the back of his collar, like holding a rag doll erect.

"Look at you. You are not worthy of spending more time on your fate. For killing Carrie, an innocent, I have pursued you through two continents and many countries. All your plans for luring me to my death were only met by me killing your people and now capturing you."

Scorpion let what passed for a smile spread across his face. "The ones who enjoyed the girl...before I took my pleasure. They are alive and well. You will not find them and they will remember the fun they had. They also know where she came from and that there is another, even more beautiful, waiting there."

Roland cuffed the man in the head. He would have fallen if not held up by the scruff of his neck.

Scorpion lifted his face and looked at Dan. "You cannot protect your women. We will overcome you because we take care of our women and they breed well. You let your women out, to dress like harlots. They are put in danger, they don't produce offspring."

Dan stood straighter, looking Scorpion in his dark eyes. His tone was formal, like a judge.

"Scorpion, or whatever is your real name, I sentence you to death for the murder of Carrie Rohner. Your execution will be carried out immediately and you will be left in the desert to feed the vultures."

Dan pulled out his sidearm from its holster.

"May your soul live in hell forever."

Roland took his hand off Scorpion's neck and stepped back.

Scorpion opened his mouth to speak, *"Sanafuz fi alnihaya."*

Dan's hand closed on the trigger and a 9mm round pierced his forehead snapping his head back. The body collapsed like empty cloth and lay in a heap at Roland's feet.

Both men looked at the body. That it was once the formidable Scorpion seemed hard to imagine now.

"Done and done," Roland said. There was a forced finality to his voice. He turned to Dan and pulled him away from the corpse. "What now, boss? Got an exfil plan?"

Dan turned to his companion. "You know I never have one of those." A faint smile spread across his face.

Chapter 67

Dan sat in the same room in the same modest office building where the trek to Yemen had begun. His face was drawn with fatigue. He felt as though he could sleep for a month. At the table were Eitan, Jane, Uri, along with the two ex-Delta Force fighters, Marcus and Roland.

Uri had his leg encased in a large splint and was using crutches but he seemed to be rested and in good spirits.

It had been seventy-two hours since Dan and Roland had killed Scorpion. They had wrestled the truck upright, mostly through Roland's great strength, changed two shot-out tires from their damaged truck and drove to the outskirts of Al Mukalla where a helicopter piloted by a striking female pilot picked them up and took them to Djibouti. From there they flew to Tel Aviv and were immediately escorted to the present location. Dan noted that the female who piloted the Huey helicopter was American along with her crew. She remembered Marcus and the injured Uri from her previous flight. The rest of the trip involved Israelis.

"I know you're tired," Eitan said. "But we'd like to hear from you before you stand down. A short meeting and then we'll take you to your rooms to clean up and get some rest."

Dan and Roland just stared at him with almost vacant eyes.

"You got Marcus and Uri's report?"

Eitan nodded.

"Ours is, we chased Scorpion, killed a lot of men, almost got killed ourselves. Roland here was wounded in the mission. In the end we caught and killed Scorpion."

Eitan looked frustrated and turned to Jane.

"Maybe," Jane said, leaning forward towards Dan, "you can give us a bit more than the Cliff Notes version." Her voice was soothing and gentle. "I know you're pretty-well spent but help Eitan. He needs to write up a report, starting tonight. We can fill in more detail later, after you two have rested."

Dan sighed. The bureaucracy would not be denied. It took precedent over all other needs. He hunched himself over the table and proceeded to give a run-down of events. Roland sat still. He didn't care what Dan said. He wasn't going to bother to interrupt or contradict.

When he was done, the room was silent. Finally, Eitan spoke.

"From my informal count is seems as though between the four of you, you killed all fifteen of Scorpion's men, twenty or more of the soldiers he sought refuge with, and then Scorpion himself and his close companion."

"Not a close companion," Dan said. "I don't think Scorpion has any close companions. From the servants at the monastery, I got the impression the guy was like a slave and certainly would die for his master. We managed to do that for him."

"The count," Eitan said. "It's incredible. Four men. They all come back and thirty-five or more left dead on the other side."

"Is that going to piss someone at Mossad off?" Roland finally spoke up.

"On the contrary, it's going to reinforce the value of our ops...of METSADA. You've given us not only something to brag about, but something to use for increasing our funding and support within Mossad."

"Glad we could help," Dan said. "Now I have a request of you, since we've done so much to advance your department."

Eitan gave Dan a questioning look.

"You should reinstate Uri. He's strong. He's good in the field. He kept up and did more than his part. We couldn't have done this without him. I made sure he got back, even against his wishes, because I didn't want METSADA to lose such an asset."

Eitan smiled as if Dan were making a joke.

"I'm serious. What the hell good is he to you, his country, or himself if he keeps spending his time drinking and womanizing? It's an unhealthy lifestyle."

Now Eitan broke into a grin. "And being a special operative in a foreign country with death ever-present is healthier?"

"Yes."

"Really?"

"Look. If you've never been in the field, you wouldn't understand."

"But I have been in the field—"

"But you didn't relish it, did you?"

Eitan stared at Dan and slowly shook his head. "If I'm honest, no."

"Uri does. End of story." Dan stood up. "Now do me, do us, this favor."

Uri wrestled his thick body upright. "It's all right my friend. You saved me. Even if METSADA doesn't want me, I'm back and can take up where I left off."

"And where is that?" Dan asked. "You need a mission, a purpose."

"All right." Eitan spoke up from the other side of the table. "I'll consider it. Get some rest. I'd like to continue in more detail tomorrow after you've had a good sleep. Marcus and Uri should also be here." He turned to Uri. "So don't go out and get drunk with Marcus. I want you back here by eight."

"Sounds like you're my boss. And we haven't signed a contract," Uri said with a grin on his face. "Besides, Marcus has other plans. They involve a certain helicopter pilot, if I'm not mistaken." And the doctors say I must stay away from alcohol and not be on my feet for too long. He winked at Marcus and headed for the door.

Jane showed Roland and Dan their rooms. After Roland left them, the two stopped at Dan's room. He unlocked the door. The interior was furnished in mid-price motel style. Enough spent to be comfortable, but nothing spent for style.

Dan turned to Jane. "How is Evangeline?"

"She'll be okay. It was hard for her, especially not getting Carrie's body back for a proper burial. She thinks of the poor girl's remains just left there."

"She blames me."

Jane stepped close to Dan and stared up at him. His face was aged from the stress and fatigue. He looked ten or more years older than when he had left. Still handsome, still the face and person who attracted her, but older, now spent.

"She did at first. That's natural. She needed someone to blame. But that's fading. She can't stop being in love with you. I think that also frustrates her."

"I've not led her on."

"I know that." Jane moved closer to him. He smelled of dirt, sweat, guns, and the desert. None of which repelled her. It was him. It was how he smelled now. "It is something she'll learn to live with. But I don't think she'll find a man to replace you."

She placed a hand on his chest. "I don't know if there is anyone out there who could."

She started to reach up to Dan, when Eitan walked up the corridor. Jane, hearing the footsteps, pulled back.

"After you put him to bed, can you join me downstairs? I'd like to talk about how we wrap up this operation."

"Sure," Jane said. "He's a big boy. I think he can do that by himself." She turned back to Dan and winked. "I'll come now."

Dan entered the room and Jane walked off down the hallway with her old partner, Eitan.

Chapter 68

Before they were flown out of Djibouti, Marcus had convinced Robin Johnson to meet him in Tel Aviv. She agreed, but indicated she had to remain in place to exfil his two friends, if, and when they called.

"Don't go getting yourself shot down. I don't want to have to rescue you from a Yemeni prison."

"You envision being my knight in shining armor?"

"It's what Delta Force guys do. Except without the shining armor. We're a bit more stealthy than that."

He looked at her with a serious face.

"You're not kidding, are you?"

Marcus shook his head. His eyes never wavered from hers. "Serious as a heart attack ma'am. It's what I do. And now knowing you, I'd do it with a vengeance that would shock those foolish enough to capture you."

Robin met his gaze and then began to smile. "I've never had someone use that line on me before. It's quite unique...and effective, I must say."

"More than a line, although if that helps our relationship, I'll take it."

Robin took out a slip of paper and wrote her number on it. She handed it to Marcus.

"Call me when you get free. I must write my report now. They'll start looking for me soon. I should be able to get some time off after my next flight. I can meet you in Tel Aviv."

Marcus gave her a broad smile. "I'll look forward to it."

Marcus had disappeared. The debriefings were over and Jane wanted to gather up her team and fly home. Staying around longer in Israel would only increase chances for rumors to start flying. Thankfully, only a few reports came out of Yemen about some attacks. One outside of Al Mukalla involving a helicopter that seemed to have penetrated Yemen airspace in an unauthorized manner. There was speculation that it involved Iranians or possibly other middle-east players interfering in the civil war that was ongoing. The other attack was attributed to Houthi rebels. They had wiped out a crack squad of fighters supporting the current president. It fit the facts except that the attack took place far outside Houthi territory and if it was true, led many to worry about the increased strike capabilities of the rebels. Jane didn't need anyone to start associating those sparse reports with her presence along with some curious, hard-bitten men surrounding her.

"Leave him," Dan said. "Marcus is smart. He's with the pilot who exfilled both teams. She seems to have captured his heart. Let him have this time together with her. God knows what will become of that relationship, but let him pursue it. He can fly home commercial if necessary."

Jane reluctantly agreed.

"And I want to be dropped off in Venice, if that's not too inconvenient."

Jane looked at Dan with a question on her face.

"It's my home. I need time there."

Jane looked down at the floor. They were sitting in a café, enjoying their espressos and the warm sunshine on what would otherwise be a chilly day. The wind had not yet come up from the Mediterranean. When it did, the day would get cooler.

"Do you want to be alone?" Jane asked.

"Would you like to join me?"

Jane looked up at him. "A girl likes to be invited, not invite herself."

Dan hesitated, feeling suddenly awkward. He reached a hand across the small table and covered Jane's.

"I'd like that…if you would join me. I've never spent time with you there. It's a bit large for one person." Dan began to warm to the idea. "We won't go sailing, like we did before. I've had enough travel for a while. We can cocoon in my place. You can offer adjustments to my choice of décor. We'll sleep late, eat brunches, laze around, and get bored."

Jane looked over at him. An odd feeling of shyness crept over her. She couldn't remember the last time she felt that way—vulnerable and coy.

"I'd like that. It sounds marvelous."

"Henry won't be pissed?"

"I'll take care of Henry. I'll tell him that you are experiencing severe withdrawal and I need to stay close, to protect my asset."

"That wouldn't be far from the truth."

Dan squeezed her hand and then pulled back.

"Roland gets to fly home alone, then."

"Yep. He'll probably drink up all the booze on the flight."

"How will you get back? I mean later?"

"We'll figure that out, like you said, later."

Chapter 69

Jane woke up in the king-sized bed. The sun was shining through the six-foot tall windows. She stretched under the light, fluffy comforter. Her naked body relished the smooth feel of the high-quality sheets. Dan had certainly known how to pick quality materials. Her loins rubbed against the sheets and mattress, still seeking stimulus from last night. She felt luxurious, like a well-fed cat; properly stroked and loved.

Their night had been filled with passion, now unleashed after all the killing; an affirmation of life expressed through their bodies, satisfying some deep, inarticulable need. She reveled in the memory of his hardened body, scars and all; how she yielded to him, enveloped him as he entered her, how her whole body shook and tingled with electric shock waves as she climaxed in tandem with him; both riding that wave of physical exhilaration over its crest to crash, spent, in the aftermath.

She got up and walked to the large bath. It was tiled in Venetian style with large mirrors and special lighting. There was a substantial walk-in shower with multiple shower heads. Her hands stimulated her as she washed, arousing her sexual excitement that had been indulged in last night. Every stroke awakened her desire to find Dan and feel his touch again.

After showering, she wrapped herself in a thick Turkish towel bathrobe and walked to the stairs. She could hear Dan in the kitchen.

There was classical cello music playing somewhere. The rich sounds of the instrument floated through the house into the hallway and kitchen. She entered without a sound and slid her arms around him as she pressed her body to him. He had on sweatpants and a light T-shirt. Her hands slid under it to feel his hard stomach and chest.

"I could have been an assassin. I just snuck up on you without you knowing."

"*Au contraire*, dear. I heard you on the stairs and recognized friendly footfalls, not foreign ones."

He put down the mixing bowl and turned to her. The bathrobe opened revealing her firm breasts, now evidencing her sudden arousal. He pulled her close and kissed her long and deep. Her body crushed against his, her hands roamed over his back, scarred from past battles, but well-muscled. She could feel his own arousal pushing against her abdomen. She wanted that, inside of her. It was unabashed lust for the man she had grown to appreciate and love over the years.

"We should eat first," Dan said. "We have all day and all night."

"Hmmm. Food is not what comes to my mind right away."

"You are a lusty lady. I didn't expect that."

"Yes, you did. You knew that those of us who keep our passions deep inside are more intense when we let them loose."

Dan smiled at her. "And I get to be the beneficiary of that."

"Indeed, you do."

Jane released her hold and Dan went back to mixing the batter for mid-morning crepes with strawberries.

"What is that music? It's very nice."

"Bach's Cello Suite in D minor."

"You are quite knowledgeable about classical music now. Is that from your time with Christina?"

"Yes." Dan kept at his preparation of their food. "She taught me much and I discovered I had a good ear for the music."

Jane thought about the young woman, a renown pianist, who had saved Dan's life in Provence, France. They had fallen in love with one another, but Dan's world of terrorists and assassins crashed in on them. Dan had realized that he lived in a different world than did Christina and no amount of affection for one another could bridge that deep, violent chasm. He left her to live her life without him. He could only bring danger and heartbreak to her world. The same danger and heartbreak had come to find Carrie. Dan had avenged the girl, but there would always be Carries out there, innocent victims of terrorists who she and Dan fought.

"Do you miss her?"

It was a dangerous question; one Jane would never have thought to ask before they had consummated their affection for one another during the previous nights in the villa. Now she felt she had a right to ask, even if she might dread the answer.

"Now and again. It is part of what's lost in my life. Almost like Rita was lost."

He turned to her.

"So much is lost in our fight, don't you think?" Without waiting for an answer, he continued, "But we have something we can share, you and I. We are both part of this world. We've both experienced loss from this fight. But now we have each other."

Jane relaxed at his answer. They were the product of the same, violent, often deadly world. As such, it seemed inevitable that they could only find happiness, companionship with one another. She resolved at that moment, that she would do all in her power to make their relationship a bulwark of strength against the evil they fought. For her and for the man she loved.

She reached up and kissed him long and deep.

† † †

Eitan met with Uri after the Americans had left. They agreed that Uri would work for him again. This time not just in the field, but more supervising, teaching those younger how to survive and operate in the field, undercover. For Eitan it was a time of exercising the leverage he had while it was still fresh. He had been given more assets and the ability to direct and shape new approaches to the dark operations in which they operated.

"You know, Eitan, this battle may go on forever," Uri said one day. "We can't kill an ideology."

"No, but we have to maintain our defense against it until some sort of reformation may come about."

"Don't hold your breath."

"You are not hopeful? Why do you still want to be in the fight if you think it's futile?"

Uri shrugged. "What else can we do? We must survive."

"Yet you are not optimistic."

Uri shook his head. "Dan asked me to translate something Scorpion said. His last words. Dan repeated the Arabic as best he could."

Uri paused and Eitan looked at him with interest.

"Sanafuz fi alnihaya. We will win in the end."

† † †

Word finally came to him. A month after sending inquiries to all his sources in Yemen. He knew the tribal connections. He knew of the safe redoubt and retreat deep in the desert. He'd never visited, of course. He could not involve himself so directly. Now he learned that the retreat had been emptied. Men killed and left in the desert nearby; men missing. No sign of his assassin. The next investigation discovered the village, Shabwah, long thought abandoned, near the edge of the great sandy wasteland. There his investigator found signs of much fighting and many dead. Then the trail went cold. No sign of Scorpion. No word of him from his tribe and the friendly villages where he could be expected to hide.

He sat in his chair in his oasis retreat. Built in the Bedouin style, but with the improvements one could add if one were a billionaire. He watched the sun sinking in the west, looking up into the long wadi populated by the wind-carved monoliths of stone, eroded by centuries of blowing sand.

His assassin was dead. There was no other conclusion he could reach. The enemy had killed him which meant the enemy was still on the loose, hunting down terrorists across Europe, interrupting any plans he might enact.

Rashid sighed. He'd been blocked many times on his road to riches. It was his perseverance and willingness to change course, that enabled him to overcome the obstacles that inevitably came up. Now would not be different. He was not a man used to losing. If one path forward closed, he would take another.

He had learned something from the loss of Scorpion. Communications with him during his fight, led Rashid to conclude that it was one man, someone named "Dan". He worked for the U.S., probably the CIA and he had been responsible for so much disruption. It was an expensive, but valuable piece of information.

Maybe it was time to take the fight back to America, he thought. Years ago, he'd been thwarted in such an attempt, but now, with the southern border so open, and the U.S. at war with itself over how to behave rather than how to lead the world, there was an opportunity. *Forget the assassin in Europe. I will strike them at home.*

He clapped his hands and a servant appeared with sweetened tea. Rashid took it and the man retired. He sat and sipped on his drink while he watched the sun sink in the west. He would sink the west's own sun before another year had passed. His mind began to sift through the opportunities he could exploit and the turmoil he could inflict.

The End
† † †

Afterword

The Scorpion is the sixth book in the Dan Stone series.

If you enjoyed this tale, please consider writing a review on Amazon. Reviews do not have to be lengthy and are extremely helpful for two reasons: first, they provide "social proof" of a book's value to a reader unfamiliar with the author, and second, they help readers filter through thousands of books in the same category to find choices worthy of their time investment. You provide an essential service to other Amazon readers with a solid review. I very much value your support.

You can get access to behind-the-scenes activities and special features by joining my Reader List. Go to *davidnees.com* and scroll down the landing page to follow the adventure. No spam; I never sell my list and you can opt out at any time. You can also follow me on Facebook at *facebook.com/neesauthor*

Other novels published by David Nees:

Jason's Tale	book 1 in the *After the Fall* series
Uprising	book 2 in the *After the Fall* series
Rescue	book 3 in the *After the Fall* series
Undercover	book 4 in the *After the Fall* series
Escape	book 5 in the *After the Fall* series
Payback	book 1 in the Dan Stone series
The Shaman	book 2 in the Dan Stone series
The Captive Girl	book 3 in the Dan Stone series

The Assassin and the Pianist   book 4 in the Dan Stone Series

Death in the Congo; book 5 in the Dan Stone Series

Thank you for reading this book. Your reading pleasure is why I write my stories.

Printed in Great Britain
by Amazon